To Charles Fort,
with Love

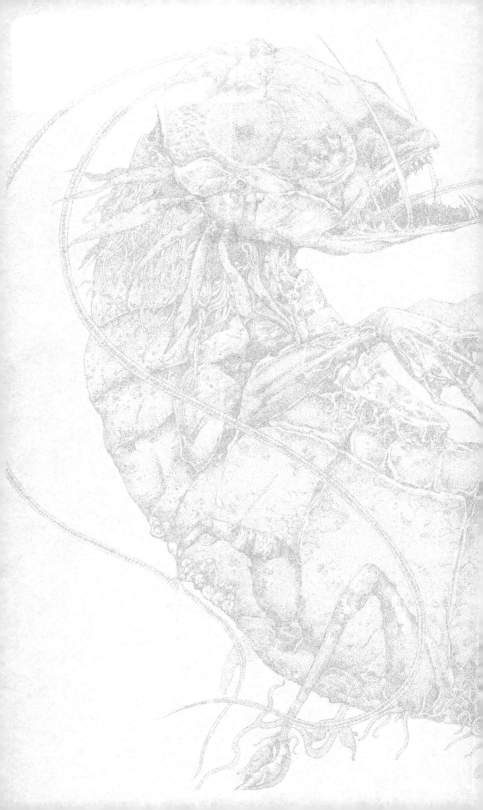

To Charles Fort,
with Love

Caitlín R. Kiernan

AFTERWORD
Ramsey Campbell

Design & Layout by Michael Smith
Printed and bound in England by T. J. International

PS PUBLISHING LTD
Grosvenor House, 1 New Road, Hornsea,
HU18 1PG, England

e-mail: editor@pspublishing.co.uk
website: www.pspublishing.co.uk

Publication History

"Valentia," first published in *Dark Terrors 5*, Stephen Jones and David Sutton eds.; Victor Gollancz, 2000.

"Spindleshanks (New Orleans, 1956)," first published in *Queer Fear*, Michael Rowe ed.; Arsenal Pulp Press, 2000.

"So Runs the World Away," first published in *The Mammoth Book of Vampire Stories* by Women, Stephen Jones ed.; Carroll and Graf, 2001.

"Standing Water," first published in *Darker Side: Generations of Horror*, John Pelan ed.; Roc, 2002.

"La Mer des Rêves," first published in *A Walk on the Darkside: Visions of Horror*, John Pelan ed.; Roc, 2004.

"The Road of Pins," first published in *Dark Terrors 6*, Stephen Jones ed.; Victor Gollancz, 2002.

"Onion," first published in *Wrong Things* by Poppy Z. Brite and Caitlín R. Kiernan; Subterranean Press, 2001.

"Apokatastasis," first appearance in *The Spook* (webzine), Anthony Sapienza ed.; 2002.

"La Peau Verte," previously unpublished.

"The Dead and the Moonstruck," first published in *Gothic! Ten Original Dark Tales*, Deborah Noyes ed.; Candlewick Press, 2004.

"A Redress for Andromeda," first published in *October Dreams: A Celebration of Halloween*, Richard Chizmar and Robert Morrish eds.; Cemetery Dance Publications, 2000.

"Nor the Demons Down Under the Sea," first published in *The Children of Cthulhu*, John Pelan and Benjamin Adams eds.; Del Rey, 2002.

"Andromeda Among the Stones," first published in *Embrace the Mutation* (limited-edition chapbook), Bill Schafer ed.; Subterranean Press, 2003.

In Memory of Charles Hoy Fort
(1874-1932)

I go on with my yarns. I no more believe them than I believe that twice two are four.

If there is continuity, only fictitiously can anything be picked out of the nexus of all phenomena; or, if there is only oneness, we cannot, except arbitrarily, find any two units with which even to start the sequence that twice two are four. And, if there is also discontinuity, all things are so individualized that, except arbitrarily and fictitiously, nothing can be classed with, or added to, anything else.

CHF, *The Book of the Damned* (1919)

TABLE OF CONTENTS

LOOKING FOR INNSMOUTH

1

I'VE BEEN WALKING about in increasingly smaller circles for days now, trying to find a preface for this book. Yesterday, I wrote 1,488 words on a preface, what I *thought* would be the preface, then tossed it all out this morning. So, I'm walking in circles again. Smaller and smaller circles to describe my own decaying orbit, which could easily lead inward in an infinite spiral, were I to allow it to do so. Give me enough words, enough attendant gravity, and I might fall into myself forever, crushed infinitely flat by my own hubris. It'd be a neat trick, I admit. I'd pay to see it—but from a safe distance, of course.

It's time to make an end to this.

So.

Charles Hoy Fort wrote, "By the damned, I mean the excluded." I would mark that as one of the single most powerful sentences in 20th-Century literature. Most will disagree. But most are probably *un*damned people. Fort, like the unruly phenomena he so obsessively cataloged and from which he spun his inflammatory and absurdist theses, was himself a damned thing.

"But damnation is nothing new to me," he wrote. "I offer the data. Suit yourself."

I could not say it better and shall not try.

My best effort is the thirteen stories collected in this book. I *call* them stories, haphazardly, conventionally, but I know they are actually something else. They are love letters. They are tokens of my affection. They are damned.

Fish fall from the sky.

And frogs.

And lumps of anthracite coal.

Red rains, black rains, yellow rains.

People vanish. And appear.

There are lights in the sky.

I have my own accounts, my own damned experiences, surely more of them than I deserve. More than my fair share, I'd say. Sometimes I keep them secret, or only tell one or two people, and sometimes I parade them like carnival freaks. See, for example, entries to my online journal for the following dates: 10 July, 2002; 31 October, 2003; 3 March, 2004; 30 March, 2004; 2 January, 2005. Also, what I wrote in "On the Road to Jefferson" (Subterranean Press, 2002). And there are other things—damned, indecent things—which have never been written down.

The afternoon I watched from my bedroom window as something which resembled a large, flattened cardboard box floated about not far above Red Mountain in Birmingham. The sky was clear. The day wasn't windy. The object was brown.

Or an old house where I grew up, where books were heard to fall, and glass was clearly heard to break, but, upon inspection, neither fallen books nor broken glass were ever found. A house where one often felt watched. Where one night something sat down heavily on my parents' bed, pressing itself into the mattress, invisibly.

Or a peculiar cry I once heard deep in the woods.

I could go on.

I could.

I have a stack of red paper hearts. The paper was red, as well.

I clipped them out myself. I suppose that they were there all along, the hearts, embedded in a matrix of potential, only waiting to be drawn out. I just counted them again. There are thirteen. I find comfort in these small certainties, things which may be demonstrated again and again, like a trained tiger leaping through burning hoops. The fish don't fall when you ask them. Go ahead and try. The frogs are just as stubborn. They do as the damned well please.

Paper hearts. A black crayon. A bit of ribbon.

Glitter.

Call it a Valentine.

And this bit here, which I haven't told before:

2

I included the following in my online journal entry for Monday, 26 November, 2001:

Today I did not make any notes for *Low Red Moon*, but I did spend hours and hours searching for Innsmouth Harbour. That ought to count for something. This all ties into that story ["From Cabinet 34, Drawer 6"] I'm trying to find the ending for. I'd hoped that it would be no more than about 6,000 words, but now it's looking like nine or ten instead. At any rate, proceeding from the belief that HPL did have an actual locale in mind when he conceived of Innsmouth, and following his description in "The Shadow Over Innsmouth," as well as the speculations of S.T. Joshi and others, I have narrowed it down to a short stretch of Massachusetts coastline south of Plum Island and west of Cape Ann.

Lovecraft indicates that the narrator's bus, after leaving Newburyport, is traveling southeast, following the coast.

HPL writes: "Out the window I could see the blue water and the sandy line of Plum Island, and we presently drew very near the beach as our narrow road veered off from the main highway to Rowley and Ipswich." This definitely indicates that the direction of travel is, in fact, southeast. A little father along, "At last we lost sight of Plum Island and saw the vast expanse of the open Atlantic on our left." At this point the road on which the bus is traveling begins to climb to higher ground; at the crest of the rise, the passengers "... beheld the outspread valley beyond, where the Manuxet joins the sea just north of the long line of cliffs that culminate in Kingsport Head [another HPL invention] and veer off towards Cape Ann. . . . but for a moment all my attention was captured by the nearer panorama just below me. I had, I realised, come face to face with rumour-shadowed Innsmouth." The narrator must, at this point, be looking to the east or southeast.

For me, the key is finding the Manuxet River. Of course, there really is no Manuxet River, per se—it's yet another of HPL's geographical fictions, but there are many rivers between Plum Island and Cape Ann, winding, swampy things that eventually empty into Plum Island Sound or Ipswich Bay. The river closest to Plum Island (and the bus doesn't *seem* to travel very far from the point where the narrator loses sight of the island before reaching the crest of the hill from which Innsmouth is visible) is the Ipswich River. A little farther on, there's the Castle Neck River. It's the mouth of this river that I'm favoring at the moment as the location of Innsmouth, based on HPL's statement that the Manuxet "... turned southward to join the ocean at the breakwater's end." Now, as the sea lies to the north, most of the rivers along this part of the coast do not make southerly turns, but flow north and east to the Atlantic. Notably, the Castle Neck River does have a distinct southeast kink just as it enters the estuary at the northwest end of Ipswich Bay.

Of course, HPL obviously took considerable liberties with the local geography, and I suspect that he may have also shortened the distance between Cape Ann and Plum Island in his head, recalling some excursion or another and compressing or expanding distance as we all tend to do. So, blah, blah, blah, and in my story at least, Innsmouth Harbor is at the mouth of the Castle Neck River (i.e., the Manuxet). And that should give you some idea how my day went.

So, that's the first of it. Armchair cryptogeography. Nothing the least bit damned there, unless perhaps you're one of those people who doggedly persists in the belief that Lovecraft meant Innsmouth to be located at Gloucester or Marblehead or some such place.

But we never leave well enough alone.

Well, hardly ever.

The following is taken from my journal entry for Tuesday, 6 July, 2004:

Yesterday, which I believe was Monday [July 5th], we were up early and, despite the rain, headed for Massachusetts. One of my main objectives on this trip was to reach Ipswich and follow the Argilla Road northeast to the place where I believe Lovecraft meant the doomed seaport of Innsmouth to lie, at the mouth of the Castle Neck River (Manuxet to Lovecraft). The constant reader will recall that this was also the location I chose for the house where Narcissa Snow was raised by her grandfather (*Low Red Moon*), that long spit of sand known as Crane Beach. This obsession began back in October 2001, when I was working on an Innsmouth-related short story, "From Cabinet 34, Drawer 6," and began trying to locate Innsmouth using Lovecraft's narrative and various reference sources. Go back to my entry of November 16, 2001 ... for details and an account of my thoughts on the subject. My conclusions—that Innsmouth was fashioned from bits of Newburyport and Gloucester, then placed at the mouth of the Castle Neck—agree with those of certain other writers, such as Jack Morgan (*The Biology of Horror*, 2002) and, as I learned a few days ago, researching at the Athenaeum, the author of *The H. P. Lovecraft Companion* (1977). And though I was fairly certain of my reckoning, I've always wanted a degree of visual confirmation.

We took I-95 around Boston and into New Hampshire, driving out to Hampton Beach before turning south on 1A through Salisbury, Newburyport, and Rowley to Ipswich. We paused in Ipswich, to walk through the Old Burying Ground, which includes the oldest surviving headstone in America (1634). It was still raining, light rain and heavy mist, but we walked up steep, uneven, tiled stone steps to the top of the cemetery. From that vantage point, we could look back down on the cemetery and High Street, and west to the wooded, fog-shrouded hills beyond. After a wrong turn that led us through a salt marsh to the town dump, we asked directions at a gas station. We crossed the Ipswich River and followed Argilla Road to the spot where it ends at the sea.

To the south of us, the marshes and islands at the mouth of the Castle Neck River (i.e., Manuxet) spread out flat and green, seeming almost impenetrable. In the near distance, Choate Island rose from the marshes, studded with old trees and shadows. We left the car and, walking east, crossed the dunes on foot, then followed Crane Beach south and east for a mile or so.

The sky was still spitting rain, there was a strong, chilly wind (from the northwest, I think), and a heavy mist covered everything. The beach was littered with several species of seaweed (Southern Kelp, Sea Lettuce, Irish Moss, and a number of other forms), washed up in clumps across the sand. There were mermaid's purses and the dismembered arms and legs of crabs, the shells of razor clams and many other mollusks. There were gulls, of course, as well as Piping Plovers and terns. We took off our shoes, rolled up our pants, and waded in the freezing surf. We passed two fisherman, standing maybe thirty yards out in the shallows, casting lines. I found broken bits of sand-dollar tests, which made it impossible not to think of Narcissa as a child, picking the beach with Aldous. I found the place in the dunes where the Snow house would have been. Off to the north and east, across Ipswich Bay, the southern tip of Plum Island was a distant blue ghost.

It was all perfect and the best end for this long trip that I could have asked for.

The day left us exhausted and wet, but determined to return to Ipswich and Crane Beach for further explorations. I have been to Innsmouth.

And if it actually ended here, if *that* were really, truly *that,* if I'd been entirely truthful in my first account, then I'd have nothing more than a perfectly undamned travelogue to show you. But that is not that. And I'm a little sad to say so, because I rather like the whitewashed version. It's clean. I can look directly at it and feel not the least bit of unease. But there's just a *little* more, if you'll bear with me, if completeness counts for anything. Given what I'd already admitted in the journal and elsewhere regarding my *affaire d'amour* with the damned, I'm still not sure why I chose to omit this from the original account of mine and Kathryn's visit to Crane Beach.

You'd think I'd be used to these things by now.

Fort wrote, "The little harlots will caper, and freaks will distract attention, and the clowns will break the rhythm of the whole with their buffooneries—but the solidity of the procession as a whole: the impressiveness of things that pass and pass and pass, and keep on and keep on and keep on coming."

One should not be surprised at each new damnation. Novelty, shock, consternation—these things are only achieved by denying what has come before.

On the long walk back up the beach, as the rainy day neared an early twilight, exhaustion began to set in. It was getting very cold. We were both wet. The digital camera was acting up from all the moisture and salt, and Kathryn feared we'd ruined it. My feet hurt, and I'd begun to tire of shells and mermaid's purses and sand dunes. The parking lot where we'd left the car would be closing soon. Even the two fisherman in their hip waders had finally called it a day, and we were entirely alone on the windy beach. About halfway back, Kathryn, who was a little ways ahead of me, stopped and stared out to sea.

"Do you see that?" she asked, sounding a little anxious; she pointed east, and my eyes followed her finger. It took me a moment to see what she was pointing at. The water was almost the same steely grey-blue as the sky, blurring the horizon, misleading the eye. But then I saw it.

She might well have kept it to herself.

There was something standing in the shallow water not far from shore. It was farther out than the two fisherman had been, but not very much farther. It was close enough that I could see it clearly. It looked like a man, a *very* tall man standing waist-deep in the water, only its skin was a greenish black and gave the impression of being iridescent (we agreed on these details later). The skin seemed very smooth, and I could make out no sign of

clothing. It's head was bald, and it's hands seemed dispropor-
tionately large; indeed, I had the impression of someone wearing
a catcher's mitt on each hand. The shoulders seemed hunched
to me, though Kathryn doesn't agree on this point. It was too far
away to make out much about a face, but I could see its mouth,
which seemed to be constantly opening and closing. The interior
of the mouth appeared to be whitish. Its jaw was square and
broad, and there may have been something like a short beard or
goatee on its chin. I might also have seen dark eyes, but I'm
uncertain on that point. We stood there and watched it, the
water lapping at our feet, the gulls screeching overhead, the
wind whistling through the dunes at our backs. After five minutes or so, it turned around, turning its back to us, and appeared
to stare up at the sky for perhaps another minute or two.

"Should I try to get a picture?" I asked (I was carrying the
bag holding the possibly ruined digital camera).

"No," Kathryn replied. "I don't think so."

And then the dark figure slipped beneath the water and was
gone. We waited another five minutes, maybe, but it never reap-
peared. Finally, Kathryn mentioned the time, and that the lot
would be closing soon, and we might have difficulty getting the
car out if we didn't hurry.

By the time we got back to the car it was raining fairly hard,
and we were both drenched and shivering. The camera was fine,
as it turned out, and we even stopped on the Argilla Road to
get some photos of the marshes off Choate Island. We didn't
discuss what we'd seen standing in the sea off Crane Beach
until sometime the next day, back at her parents' house in
Rhode Island, and then we only talked about it briefly. We both
seemed unaccountably ill at ease discussing it, despite our
usual grim enthusiasm for odd events and sightings. Until now,
neither of us has told anyone else this story.

Harlots. Freaks. Clowns. Take your pick. The impressiveness
of things that pass and pass and pass.

And caper.

I have considered the possibility that what we saw that afternoon might only have been a scuba diver in a wet suit. But there was no sign of a mask or air tanks, or even a snorkel, for that matter. And the hour and conditions were certainly poor for diving. Earlier on the trip, we'd encountered a few divers farther south, near the Beavertail Lighthouse and around Mackerel Cove and Jamestown Harbor, all on Conanicut Island (RI). I'd seen them up close on land and at a distance in the water, and they did not look like what we saw at Crane Beach.

So.

Did we share an hallucination, Kathryn and I? Were our imaginations so whetted with thoughts of Lovecraft's amphibious hybrids and my own ghoulish half-breeds, Narcissa and Aldous Snow, that we saw nothing more than what some part of our minds *expected* to see?

Hallucinations, especially *shared* hallucinations, are convenient things, as are mistaken impressions and tricks of light and shadow. They're good to keep on hand, should a damned and unsightly nuisance arise.

Or was it only a man in the water? Certainly, the world is filled to overflowing with men, often in places they should not be, and they are always likely to be seen. Could it have been a seal? Zoologists have cataloged five species of seal, from three genera, along the coast of Massachusetts. But I've seen seals, and if, for convenience sake, I call this thing a seal, I might well as call it a rhinoceros or a mermaid or a taxi cab. We often make one thing into another, that the damned might find proper salvation.

Fort wrote, "The interpretations will be mine, but the data will be for anybody to form his own opinions on."

Paper hearts. Black figures standing in the surf. Rains of blood and beef and salt. Shadows on the moon.

Love notes, one and all.

The stories that make up this collection were written over a five-year period between 1999 and 2004. However, this is not a complete accounting of my short fiction for these years. My recent sf tales haven't been included here, nor have a couple of "shared world" pieces and my stories involving Dancy Flammarion, because I felt they would have seemed out of place. There are a few stories I would have liked to have included, but, for one reason or another, they were not available for reprint. The most glaring omission is "From Cabinet 34, Drawer 6," the story that led to my first speculations on the location of Innsmouth. However, it will shortly appear in Stephen Jones' *Weird Shadows Over Innsmouth* (Fedogan and Bremer, Stephen Jones, ed.). I'd have also liked to have included "The Daughter of the Four of Pentacles" and "Houses Under the Sea," both slated to appear in *Thrillers II* (Cemetery Dance Publications), as well as "Mercury" (which has just been released as a chapbook from Subterranean Press). I hope that you will seek out these four stories and consider them as an extension of this collection.

But I've held up the show long enough.

We need to proceed.

The harlots are growing impatient. The freaks may forget their lines. The clowns are getting rude.

Open your umbrellas.

Watch your heads . . .

—Caitlín R. Kiernan
Atlanta, Georgia
2 February 2005

To Charles Fort,
with Love

VALENTIA

*A*LL *NIGHT TOSSING* and turning on the flight from JFK to Shannon, interminable jet drone and the whole autumn-long night spent sailing through ice-crystal clouds far above the black roil and churn of the Atlantic. Finally, the ragged west coast of Ireland appearing outside her window like a greygreen gem, uncut, unpolished, and then the plane was on the ground. Routinely suspicious glances at her passport from the customs agent—her short hair still blonde in the photograph and now it's red, auburn—and Anne was grateful when she spotted one of Morris' grad students waiting for her with a cardboard sign, DR. CAMPBELL printed neatly in blue marker on brown cardboard. She dozed on the long drive down to Kerry, nodding off while the student talked and the crooked patchwork of villages and farms rolled by outside.

"It's so terrible," the student says, has said that more than once, apologized more than once, like any of this might have been her fault somehow. Máire, pale, coal-haired girl from Dublin with her tourist-brochure eyes, green eyes that never leave the road, never glance at Anne as the car rolls on south and west, the slatedark waters of Dingle Bay stretching away to the north and all the way down to the sea. Past Killorglin and there's a tall signpost, black letters on whitewashed wood, paintwhite arrow pointing the way on to Cahirciveen, still forty kilometers ahead of them, and so Anne closes her eyes again.

"Do you have any idea how it happened?" she asks, and "Ah, Christ. I'm so sorry, Dr. Campbell," the girl says, her voice like she might be close to tears, and Anne doesn't ask again.

Two hours later, and the blue and white car ferry from Renard Point is pulling away from the dock, plowing across the harbor towards the big island of Valentia. Only a five-minute crossing, but the water just rough enough that Anne wishes there were a bottle of Dramamine tablets packed somewhere in the Army surplus duffel in the rental car's trunk. She stands at the railing because she figures it's more polite to puke over the side than on the decks, stands with nervous, green-eyed Máire on her left, emerald eyes and wringing hands, and *None of this feels real,* Anne thinks. *None of this feels the least bit real.* The girl is clutching a rosary now, something shiny from a sweater pocket, silver crucifix and black beads, and Anne turns away, watches the horizon, the indefinite confluence of the grey island and greyer sea. The air smells like saltwater and fish and coming rain, and she concentrates on the questions she's carried with her all the way from New York, unpleasant thoughts to drown her old dread of seasickness. The questions that began two days earlier with the first news of Morris Whitney's death, with Dr. Randall's Sunday afternoon phone call, and "Can you come in this evening, Anne?" he said, sounding tired, sleepless, sounding like all his sixty years had finally, suddenly, caught up with him.

"It's Morris. Something's happened. There's been an accident," but she didn't want to hear the rest, said so, made him stop there, no more until she took the subway from her TriBeCa apartment uptown to the museum. No more until she was sitting in her tiny, fifth-floor office, listening to Arthur Randall talk. Everything he knew, scant and ugly details, and at first none of it seeming to add up—the phone call from the police in Cahirciveen, Morris' body hauled from the sea by a fishing boat out of Knightstown, the vandalized excavation. But Anne listened silently, the old man's shaky voice and her eyes lingering safely on the cover of a back issue of the *Journal of Vertebrate Paleontology* lying on her desk—glossy orange and white paper, black print, the precise line drawing of an Eocene percopsid, all safe and sensible things so she wouldn't have to see the look on Arthur's face.

"Do you have any idea what he was doing out there after dark?" she asks, almost a whisper, and Máire turns her head slightly, her eyes still on the rosary in her hands, and "No," the girl says. "None of us do."

Anne glances back at the mainland, growing smaller as the little ferry chugs diligently across the harbor, and she knows now that she shouldn't have come, that Arthur was right, and there are probably no more answers here than would have found her in Manhattan. Not if this skittish girl at her side is any indication, and something else, besides, a quiet anxiety beneath the leadweight ache of her loss, beneath the disorientation. A vague unease as the shores of Valentia grow nearer; but *He would have come for you*, she thinks, and then Máire is talking again.

"Dr. Whitney had us back in Knightstown, you know. Me and Billy both. He said he was worried about whether or not the grants would be renewed. Said he needed the solitude to write at night, to work on the progress report for the *National Geographic* people, but we knew he was havin' bad dreams."

"So you weren't at the field house Friday night?" and Máire shakes her head, no, "This last week, we've been riding out on our bicycles every mornin', an' ridin' back again in the evenings. It's only half an hour, maybe . . . "

And then the ferry whistle blows, shrill and steamthroat

bellow to smother whatever Máire might have said next, and the girl slips the rosary back into the pocket of her sweater.

Valentia Island, seven miles by three, rocky exile cut off from the Irish mainland long ago by the restless Atlantic and the thin, encircling finger of the Portmagee Channel. Sheep and cattle, and a century ago strong men mined slate from a huge quarry near the island's northeast corner, mined stone for roofing tiles in London and railroad pavement in Nottingham and Leicester. A small but sturdy white lighthouse where Valentia Harbor meets the ocean proper, once upon a time a fortress for Cromwell's men, its beacon automated years ago. Farther west, the land rises abruptly to Reenadrolaun Point more than a hundred feet above the sea, rocky precipice where the rollers have carved away the world, and from there, the raw charcoal and ash periphery of the island stretches from Fogher Cliff to Beennakryraka Head. And on these weathered ledges Morris Whitney found the "Culloo trackway" in 1992; two months in Ireland on an NSF grant to study a poorly-curated, but valuable collection of Devonian lobe-finned and placoderm fishes at the Cork Geology Museum and led astray to Valentia by persistent rumors of footprints in stone. First, a local farmer's stories of "dinosaur tracks" and then a letter to the curator of the museum from a birders club, and so he finally took a day off and made the drive from Cork. And not believing his eyes when the old man led him across a pasture to the ledges, the famer's gap-toothed pride at the expression on the paleontologist's astonished face when he saw the perfect, single trail, winding across the slate towards the sea.

"Didn't I tell you? Are they not dinosaurs, then?" the old man asked, and Morris could only shake his head, his own grin grown almost as wide as the old man's, clambering down to get a better look as the waves slammed loud against the rocks.

"No, Mr. O'Shea, these are definitely *not* dinosaur tracks. Whatever made these tracks lived . . . " and he paused, doing the math in his head, calculating the age of rocks and the duration of geological periods. "Whatever made them was walking around a hundred and fifty million years before the first dinosaurs. These are something much, much *better* than dinosaur tracks." The old man's eyes went wide and doubtful, then, and he sat down on the grass and dangled his short legs over the edge of the little cliff.

"Ah," he said, "Well, now that *is* a bloody wonder, wouldn't ye say?"

And Morris on his knees, a cheap, black plastic Instamatic camera from his backpack, and he was staring at the fossils though the viewfinder. "Yes sir, it is. It certainly is that," and he snapped away a whole roll of film before following the old man back across the field.

Two hours after dawn and Anne Campbell, jetlagged and shivering in the October gales, stands beside the tracks, a single bedding plane exposed along the thirty-foot ledge, narrow, almost horizontal rind of bare stone to mark this place where the island is slowly being reclaimed by the Atlantic. Overhead, gulls and kittiwakes wheel and cry like lost and hungry children. Behind her, Máire is still talking to the constable, the red-cheeked, pot-bellied man who escorted them from Kingstown; they speak in hushed voices, as if they're saying things they don't want Anne to hear.

There are still traces of Morris' chalk marks, despite the tides and salt spray, despite everything his killers did to the site. White chalk lines to measure the width of manual and pedal strides, faint reference numbers for his photographs; another day or two, and the sea will have swept the ledge clean again. Tears in her eyes and she isn't sure how much of that's for Morris, how much for the ruined treasures, and how much is merely the stinging, icy fingers of the wind.

Over a hundred tracks to begin with, according to Morris' notes, a hundred already exposed when he first saw the ledge and another fifty or sixty uncovered as he and Máire and Billy followed the prints back into the cliff's face, sledges and pry bars to clear away the heavy blocks of Valentia Slate. And now, only five or six that haven't been damaged or obliterated altogether. *Desecrated,* Anne thinks, *This place has been desecrated.* As surely as any church that was ever burned or any shrine that was ever looted, and she sits down beside one of the few tracks that hasn't been chipped or scraped or smashed beyond recognition. The gently rippled surface of the rock shimmers faintly, glitterdull interplay of mica crystals and the sun, and she puts her fingers into the shallow depression on the ledge, touches the clear imprint left by something that passed this way three hundred and eighty-five million years ago. She looks up, past the trackway, at the rest of the ledge; patches of algal scum the unhealthy color of an infection and small accumulations of brown sand, bright against the slate, a few stingy pools of water stranded in the low places, waiting for the next high tide.

"He got everythin' on film," Máire says behind her, trying to sound reassuring, trying to sound responsible. "And we have the casts. Dr. Whitney sent a set of them off to Cork just last week, and another to the Survey in Dublin."

"I want to see the photographs, Máire. Everything that's been developed. As soon as possible, okay?"

"Aye," the girl says. "They're all back in town. It didn't seem safe to leave anythin' in the field house." And "No," Anne says, as much to herself as Máire, "No, I guess not." And then Máire's talking with the constable again, and Anne stares past the ledge at the wide, cold ocean.

— ◇ —

Her room in Knightstown, dingy plaster walls and faded Catholic icons, the oilyfaint smell of fish, but some place warm and dry against the rain that started falling an hour after sunset. Cold drops that pepper the windowpane and she sat there for awhile, waiting for Dr. Randall to return her call, stared down at the drenched and narrow streets, a pub across from the hotel and its windows glowing yelloworange through the downpour, soft and welcoming glow, and she wished she'd asked Máire to stay. She could have thought of an excuse if she'd tried—help with Morris' records, questions about the sediment samples sent to Dublin for radiometric tests, anything against the sound of the storm and her loneliness. But the girl made her uncomfortable, nothing she could quite put her finger on, and on the way back from the site, Máire leaned close and asked if it was true, that Anne and Morris were lovers, whispered question so Constable Bryce wouldn't overhear. Anne blushed, confused, embarrassed, and "That was a long time ago," she replied, nothing else, though, her surprise turning quick to anger and unasked questions about what this girl might know about her, what she might *think* she knew.

So relief when the phone rang, the voice at the other end sounding far away, distance-strained, cablefiltered, but relief anyway. The familiarity something to push away her homesickness for a few minutes, at least, and Arthur Randall asked if she was okay, if she was holding up, and "Yeah," she said, "Sure," an unconvincing lie, and he sighed loudly; she could hear him lighting a cigarette, exhaling, before he asked her about the trackway, if there was anything at all that might be salvaged.

"Only if it's still buried. You absolutely would not *believe* this shit, Arthur. I've never seen a site so completely...so..." and that word from the ledge coming back to her again, ... *so completely desecrated*, but it was nothing she wanted to say aloud, so "They trashed everything," she said instead, and then added "It just doesn't make sense."

"Then you *don't* think it was someone after the tracks?"

"No. If this was someone trying to steal fossils, it's the most fucked-up attempt I could imagine. And there's no sign they actually tried to remove anything. Nothing at all. Whoever it was, they wanted to *erase* the tracks, Arthur, not steal them."

And now she sits on her bed listening to the rain on the roof, the rain at the window, and all Morris' photographs are spread out in front of her, glossy 8"x10" documents of his month on Valentia, every inch of the trackway painstakingly recorded, these photos to back up Máire's maps and diagrams of the ledge, carefully-gridded sketches recording the relative position and size of every footprint. And so at least the data has been saved, the fossils themselves gone but not the information. Enough that she can finish what he began, a description of the oldest known tetrapod ichnofossils, the earliest evidence of the ancestors of all terrestrial vertebrates. Something a little more than a meter in length, no longer fish, but not quiet yet amphibian, either.

Anne puts down one of the photographs and picks up another, no tracks in this shot, the fossilized ripple marks from the bed of an ancient stream, and for a moment she thinks that's all. Silt and sand shaped by the currents of warm Paleozoic waters and then that pattern frozen there for almost four hundred thousand millennia and she's about to put this picture down, too, when she notices something small in the lower left-hand corner. Something embedded in the slate, glinting in the sun like metal, and she holds it under the lamp beside her bed for a better look.

And her first impression is that Morris has placed an unfamiliar coin in the shot for scale, one of the seven-sided Irish fifty-pence pieces, maybe. She leans closer to the photograph, squints, her nose almost touching the paper now, and she can see that the surface of the thing is smooth, so it's no coin, and there's no doubt that it's actually embedded in the stone, not merely lying on the surface. She chews at her bottom lip, turns the print upside down, and at this angle she can see that it isn't perfectly smooth after all, that there's the faintest suggestion of a raised pattern on its surface, ridges and dimples worn almost away by years of exposure to the wind and sea. A single crinoid plate perhaps, broken away from the calyx, or some other echinoderm fossil, only a heptagonal bit of silica and a trick of light and shadow to make it *look* metallic.

No, not a crinoid, she thinks. *Not a crinoid or a cystoid, not a plate from a primitive sea urchin, because these beds were laid down in fresh water.* And so maybe it's a bit of bony armor, then, from one of the placoderm fishes. And didn't she see a note somewhere in Morris' papers, or something Máire mentioned in passing, that they'd found remains of the placoderm *Bothriolepis* in nearby strata? But under the dim lamp light the thing certainly *looks* metallic, and her first impression, that she was seeing a coin, lingers stubbornly in her mind; Anne rubs at her tired and burning eyes.

"Jesus," she whispers, still too exhausted from the flight and then the long day out at Culloo, and it's no wonder she can't think straight. The reality of Morris' death hasn't even sunk in yet, and Anne Campbell gathers up the photographs and slips them all back into the big manila envelope, the mystery shot lying on top. In the morning, she'll ask Máire about the odd fossil, or Billy, if he's at breakfast. But it can wait until then. The clock on her nightstand reads ten twenty-five, and Anne switches off the lamp and sits for a moment in the darkness, thinking of home as the wind buffets and rattles at the window.

— ✧ —

In the dream, she's standing on the marblesmooth steps of the American Museum, and there are pigeons on the bronze statue of Theodore Roosevelt; bronze gone to verdigris, and Roosevelt proud atop his horse, noble tarnished savages on his left and right as he leads them away, and where the street ought to be there's a shallow brook with sandy, sidewalk banks, restless water sparkling bright in the New York sun. Anne looks past the stream, expecting the autumnfire of Central Park, all the uncountable shades of orange and gold and ruddy browns, but instead—a green so dense, so primeval, the inviolable green of the world's first forests. Eden past Central Park West, and as she descends the steps, bare feet silent on stone and discarded hot-dog wrappers, she cannot take her eyes off the strange plants rooted on the far side of the stream, the mad bloom of foliage sprouting from the cracked and weathered cement; towering canopy of club mosses and *Archaeopteris* and the sun slanting in cathedral shafts between the impossible branches, falling across scalebark and the impenetrable underbrush of ferns and scouring rushes. Only a dozen yards in and that forest's already so dense the green has faded black, and *Anything might live in there*, she thinks, *anything at all.*

Past Roosevelt and the Indians and a man selling Snapple and hot pretzels, she stands at the shore, the concrete and sand and there's no rude blat of taxi horns here, no ceaseless background drone of human voices; an always-summer wind through the trees, the cool murmur and purl of the water between avenuestraight banks and the buzz of dragonflies the size of ravens. Earth turned back, past man and ice ages, past the time of terrible lizards and screeching, kitewinged pterodactyls; continents torn apart and reconfigured for these long, last days before all the world will be squeezed together into the supercontinent Pangea.

This is not a new dream, her entire adult life spent chasing these ghosts, her unconscious always resurrecting and refining this wilderness. But never half this real. These sounds and smells never half so alive, the quality of sunlight never this brilliant, and she kneels beside the stream, stares down at the logs jammed together just below the surface, the water plants she knows no names for and tiny, alien fish dart away into the submerged jumble of shattered limbs and trunks. The water not deep here, and there are tracks on the muddy bottom, prints left by fins that will be toes someday, toes that haven't yet forgotten fins, and her eyes follow the tracks upstream to the place where there's something big slipping off this shoal into deeper water. Frogwide head breaking the surface, wary black eyes watching her, and then it's gone, one flick of its tail and the sinuous thing glides away in an obscuring cloud of silt.

And Anne Campbell knows *where* she is this time, not just *when*, this wilderness that will be a rocky Irish coast someday, and she glances back at the forest. The forest darker and deeper than all the tangled dreams of humanity, and she closes her eyes, can hear the cold rain falling on the hotel's roof eons and eons away. "Not yet, Anne," someone says close behind her, someone speaking with Morris' voice, and so she opens her eyes again, but there's no one there, only the pretzel vendor, and he hasn't even seemed to notice her. She stands up and brushes the sand from the knees of jeans.

And spots the silver thing shining up at her from the water's edge, a seven-sided disc that isn't a coin. She knows that now, knows that it isn't part of anything that ever lived, either. Something shaped from metal, fashioned, and she bends down, picks it up, ice cold to the touch, and it burns the palm of her hand. But she has to see the markings worked into the thing, the symbols she doesn't recognize and cannot read, runes or an unknown cuneiform set around the image at the disc's center—the tentacled face, its parrot beak—and then there's a deafening clap of thunder from the clear sky, and Anne drops the thing. It falls into the water with a small but definite splash, sinks between the dead branches where the little fish disappeared. She almost reaches for it, but thinks of the jointed, razor jaws of arthrodires, the serrate claws of scuttling, scorpion-legged eurypterids and looks up at the infinite blue vault of Heaven overhead.

"What was I supposed to see?" she dreams herself asking the unclouded sky, no clouds but there is thunder anyway, just as there was Morris Whitney's voice without his body. And she's scared for the first time, wants to wake up now, because there's something moving about in the ferns on the other side of the stream, something huge, and the sound that isn't really thunder from the sky again, the sound like a tear in the sky, and it's raining, but it isn't water that falls. Anne shuts her eyes tight, no ruby-slipper heels to click, so she repeats Morris' name, again and again and again, while the scalding filth drips down to blister her face and pool red and steaming at her feet.

Morning and the storms have passed, blown away south to Bantry and Skibbereen, the Celtic Sea beyond, and the sky is perfect blue as Anne makes her way back to the cliffs alone. A rusty purple bicycle borrowed from the hotel's cook, and she follows the winding road north through the Glanleam woods, on past the lighthouse and then takes a narrower road west, little more than a footpath for sheep, really, past the steep rise of Reenadrolaun and down to Culloo. The sea air chilly on her face, on her hands, and her legs aching by the time she reaches the site.

She sees the girl standing by the cliffs long before she's close enough to recognize it's Máire, tousled black hair and one of her heavy wool cardigans, and she's staring out at the foam-white rollers, something dark held in her right hand, and Anne stops, lowers the bike's kickstand and walks the last ten or twenty yards. But if Máire hears her, she makes no sign that she's heard, standing very still, watching the uneasy, storm-scarred sea.

"Máire?" Anne calls out. "Hello? I didn't expect to find you out here," and the girl turns slowly, moves stiff and slow like someone half asleep, and Anne thinks that maybe she's been crying, the red around her eyes, wet green eyes and bruisedark circles underneath like she hasn't slept in awhile. "I want to ask you a question, about one of the photographs. I have it with..."

And then Anne can see exactly what she's holding, the small, black handgun, and Máire smiles for her.

"Good morning, Dr. Campbell."

A moment before she can reply, two heartbeats before she can even look away from the revolver, the sun dull off its stubby chrome barrel, and "Good morning, Máire," she finally says. Her mouth is dry, and the words come out small and flat.

"Did ye sleep well, then?" the girl asks, and Anne nods her head, and Máire turns back towards the ledge, back towards the sea. "I was afraid you might have bad dreams," she says. "You know, after lookin' at those pictures."

"What is it, Máire, the disc in the photograph? You *know* what it is, don't you?" and Anne takes one step closer to the girl, one step closer to the point where the sod ends and the grey stone begins.

"I didn't kill him," the girl says. "I want ye to *know* that. I didn't do it, and neither did Billy." Her finger tight and trembling around the trigger now, and Anne is only a few feet away, only two or three more steps left between them, and "It's bad enough, what we've done," Máire says. "But it wasn't murder."

"You're going to have to explain to me what you're talking about," Anne tells her, afraid to move, afraid to stand still, and the girl turns towards her again.

15

"You weren't meant to see the pictures, Dr. Campbell. I was supposed to burn them. After we'd done with the tracks, we were supposed to burn everything."

Fresh tears from the girl's bright eyes, and Anne can see where she's chewed her lower lip raw, fresh blood on her pale chin and Anne takes another step towards her.

"Why were you supposed to burn the pictures? Did Morris tell you to burn the pictures, Máire?"

A blank, puzzled expression on the girl's face then, her ragged smile gone for a moment before she shakes her head, rubs the barrel of the gun rough against her corduroy pants.

And then she says something that Anne doesn't understand, something that sounds like "Theena dow'an," and "I don't know Irish," Anne says, pleading now, wanting to understand, and she can see the hurt and anger in Máire's eyes, the bottomless guilt growing there like a cancer. The girl raises the revolver and sets the barrel against her right temple.

"Oh god, please Máire," and then the girl says it again, "Theena dow'an," and she turns back towards the sea at the same instant she squeezes the trigger, and the sound the gun makes is the sound from Anne Campbell's nightmare, the sound of the sky ripping itself apart, the sound of the waves breaking against the shore.

In the west there is still a tradition of the Fomorii who dwelt in Ireland before the arrival of the Gael. They are perhaps the most feared of all the water fairies and are sometimes known as the Daoine Domhain, *the Deep Ones, though they are rarely spoken of aloud.*
—Lady Wilde, *Ancient Legends of Ireland* (1888)

Afterword

"Valentia" was written in July 1999, shortly after a visit to Manhattan and the American Museum of Natural History, where I spent a couple of days examining mosasaur material in the museum's collection. So, when I returned to Birmingham and to my writing, my head was still very much in New York and the paleontological work that I'd been doing there. "Valentia" was also inspired, in part, by a recent article in *National Geographic* (May 1999) regarding the discovery of an early tetrapod trackway in the southwest of Ireland. As with "In the Waterworks (Birmingham, Alabama 1889)," much of this story would soon be reworked for *Threshold*, most notably the mysterious septagonal object in the stone and the "dream" scene where Anne Campbell finds herself standing in a Devonian landscape (though in *Threshold*, Chance Matthews would find herself in the Carboniferous). Discovered by Ivan Stössel in 1994, the trackway described in "Valentia" is real and dates from the late Middle Devonian (Givetian) or early Late Devonian Period (Frasnian).

SPINDLESHANKS

(New Orleans, 1956)

THE END OF JULY, indolent, dog-day swelter inside the big white house on Prytania Street; Greek Revival columns painted as cool and white as a vanilla ice-cream cone, and from the second-floor verandah Reese can see right over the wall into Lafayette Cemetery, if she wants—Lafayette No 1, and the black iron letters above the black iron gate to remind anyone who forgets. She doesn't dislike the house, not the way that she began to dislike her apartment in Boston before she finally left, but it's much too big, even with Emma, and so far she hasn't even bothered to take the sheets off most of the furniture downstairs. This one bedroom almost more than she needs, anyway, her typewriter and the electric fan from Woolworth's on the table by the wide French doors to the verandah, so she can sit there all day, sip her gin and tonic and stare out at the whitewashed brick walls and the crypts whenever the words aren't coming.

And these days the words are hardly ever coming, hardly ever there when she goes looking for them, and her editor wanted the novel finished two months ago. Running from that woman and her shiny black patent pumps, her fashionable hats, as surely as she ran from Boston, the people there she was tired of listening to, and so Reese Callicott leased this big white house for the summer and didn't tell anyone where she was going or why. But she might have looked for a house in Vermont or Connecticut, instead, if she'd stopped to take the heat seriously, but the whole summer paid for in advance, all the way through September, and there's no turning back now. Nothing now but cracked ice and Gilbey's and her view of the cemetery; her mornings and afternoons sitting at the typewriter and the mocking white paper, sweat and the candy smell of magnolias all day long, then jasmine at night.

Emma's noisy little parties at night, too, all night sometimes, the motley handful of people she drags in like lost puppies and scatters throughout the big house on Prytania Street; this man a philosophy or religion student at Tulane and that woman a poet from somewhere lamentable in Mississippi, that fellow a friend of a friend of Faulkner or Capote. Their accents and pretenses and the last of them hanging around until almost dawn unless Reese finds the energy to run them off sooner. But energy is in shorter supply than the words these days, and mostly she just leaves them alone, lets them play their jazz and Fats Domino records too loud and have the run of the place because it makes Emma happy. No point in denying that she feels guilty for dragging poor Emma all the way to New Orleans, making her suffer the heat and mosquitoes because Chapter Eight of *The Ecstatic River* might as well be a cinderblock wall.

Reese lights a cigarette and blows the smoke towards the verandah, towards the cemetery, and a hot breeze catches it and quickly drags her smoke ghost to pieces.

"There's a party in the Quarter tonight," Emma says. She's lying on the bed, four o'clock Friday afternoon and she's still wearing her butteryellow house coat, lying in bed with one of her odd books and a glass of bourbon and lemonade.

"Isn't there always a party in the Quarter?" Reese asks, and now she's watching two old women in the cemetery, one with a bouquet of white flowers. She thinks they're chrysanthemums, but the women are too far away for her to be sure.

"Well, yes. Of course. But this one's going to be something different. I think a real voodoo woman will be there." A pause and she adds, "You should come."

"You know I have too much work."

Reese doesn't have to turn around in her chair to know the pout on Emma's face, the familiar, exaggerated disappointment, and she suspects that it doesn't actually matter to Emma whether or not she comes to the party. But this ritual is something that has to be observed, the way old women have to bring flowers to the graves of relatives who died a hundred years ago, the way she has to spend her days staring at blank pages.

"It might help—with your writing, I mean—if you got out once in a while. Really, sometimes I think you've forgotten how to talk to people."

"I talk to people, Emma. I talked to that Mr...." and she has to stop, searching for his name, and there it is, "That Mr. Leonard, just the other night. You know, the fat one with the antique shop."

"He's almost *sixty* years old," Emma says; Reese takes another drag off her cigarette, exhales, and "Well, it's not like you want me out looking for a husband," she replies.

"Have it your way," Emma says, the way she always says "Have it your way," and she goes back to her book, and Reese goes back to staring at the obstinate typewriter and watching the dutiful old women on the other side of the high cemetery wall.

Reese awakens from a nightmare a couple of hours before dawn, awake and sweating and breathless, chilled by a breeze through the open verandah doors. Emma's fast asleep beside her, lying naked on top of the sheets, though Reese didn't hear her come in. If she cried out or made any other noises in her sleep at least it doesn't seem to have disturbed Emma. Reese stares at the verandah a moment, the night beyond, and then she sits up, both feet on the floor, and she reaches for the lamp cord. But that might wake Emma, and it *was* only a nightmare after all, a bad dream, and in a minute or two it will all seem at least as absurd as her last novel.

Instead she lights a cigarette and sits smoking in the dark, listening to the restless sounds the big house makes when everyone is still and quiet and it's left to its own devices, its random creaks and thumps, solitary-house thoughts and memories filtered through plaster and lathe and burnished oak. The mumbling house and the exotic, piping song of a night bird somewhere outside, mundane birdsong made exotic because she hasn't spent her whole life hearing it, some bird that doesn't fly as far north as Boston. Reese listens to the bird and the settling house, and to Emma's soft snores, while she smokes the cigarette almost down to the filter, and then she gets up, walks across the wide room to the verandah doors, only meaning to close them. Only meaning to shut out a little of the night, and then maybe she can get back to sleep.

But she pauses halfway, distracted by the book on Emma's nightstand, a very old book, by the look of it, something else borrowed from one or another of her Royal Street acquaintances, no doubt. More bayou superstition, Negro tales of voodoo and swamp magic, zombies and grave-robbing, the bogeyman passed off as folklore, and Reese squints to read the cover, fine leather worn by ages of fingers and the title stamped in flaking crimson—*Cultes des Goules* by François Honore—Balfour, Comte d'Erlette. The whole volume in French, and the few grim illustrations do nothing for Reese's nerves, so she sets it back down on the table, making a mental note to ask Emma what she sees in such morbid things, and, by the way, why hasn't she ever mentioned that she can read French?

The verandah doors half shut, and she pauses, looks out at the little city of the dead across the street, the marble and cement roofs dull white by the light of the setting half moon, and a small shred of the dream comes back to her then. Emma, the day they met, a snowy December afternoon in Harvard Square, Reese walking fast past the Old Burying Ground and First Church, waiting in the cold for her train, and Emma standing off in the distance. Dark silhouette against the drifts and the white flakes swirling around her, and Reese tries to think what could possibly have been so frightening about any of that. Some minute detail already fading when she opened her eyes, something about the sound of the wind in the trees, maybe, or a line of footprints in the snow between her and Emma. Reese Callicott stares at Lafayette for a few more minutes, and then she closes the verandah doors, locks them, and goes back to bed.

"Oh, that's horrible," Emma says and frowns as she pours a shot of whiskey into her glass of lemonade. "Jesus Christ, I can't believe they found her right down there on the sidewalk, and we slept straight through the whole thing."

"Well, there might not have been that much noise," Carlton says helpfully and sips at his own drink, bourbon on the rocks, and he takes off his hat and sets it on the imported wicker table at the center of the verandah. Carlton the only person in New Orleans that Reese would think to call her friend, dapper, middle-aged man with a greying mustache and his Big Easy accent. Someone that she met at a writer's conference in Providence years ago, before Harper finally bought *The Light Beyond Center* and her short stories started selling to *The New Yorker* and *The Atlantic*. Carlton the reason she's spending the summer in exile in the house on Prytania Street, because it belongs to a painter friend of his who's away in Spain or Portugal or some place like that.

"They say her throat, her larynx, was torn out. So she might not have made much of a racket at all."

Reese sets her own drink down on the white verandah rail in front of her, nothing much left of it but melting ice and faintly gin-flavored water, but she didn't bring the bottle of Gilbey's out with her, and the morning heat's made her too lazy to go back inside and fix another. She stares down at the wet spot at the corner of Prytania and Sixth Street, the wet pavement very near the cemetery wall drying quickly in the scalding ten o'clock sun.

"Still," Emma says, "I think we would have heard *something*, don't you Reese?"

"Emmie, I think you sleep like the dead," Reese says, the grisly pun unintended, but now it's out, and no one's seemed to notice, anyway.

"Well, the *Picayune*'s claiming it was a rabid mongrel stray—" Emma begins, but then Carlton clears his throat, interrupting her.

"I have a good friend on the force," he says. "He doesn't think it was an animal at all. He thinks it's more likely someone was trying to make it *look* like the killer was an animal."

"Who was she?" Reese asks, and now there are two young boys, nine or ten years old, standing near the cemetery wall, pointing at the wet spot and whispering excitedly to one another.

"A colored woman. Mrs. Duquette's new cook," Carlton says. "I don't remember her name offhand. Does it matter?"

The two boys have stooped down to get a better look, maybe hoping for a splotch of blood that the police missed when they hosed off the sidewalk a few hours earlier.

"What was she doing out at that hour, anyway?" Emma asks, then finishes stirring her drink with an index finger and tests it with the tip of her tongue.

Carlton sighs and leans back in his wicker chair. "No one seems to know precisely."

"Well, I think I've had about enough of this gruesome business for one day," Reese says. "Just look at those boys down there," and she stands up and shouts at them, Hey, you boys, get away from there this very minute, and they stand up and stare at her like she's a crazy woman.

"I said get *away* from there. Go home!"

"They're only *boys*, Reese," Carlton says, and just then one of them flips Reese his middle finger, and they both laugh before squatting back down on the sidewalk to resume their examination of the murder scene.

"They're horrid little *monsters*," Reese says, and she sits slowly back down again.

"They're *all* monsters, dear," and Emma smiles and reaches across the table to massage the place between Reese's shoulder blades that's always knotted, always tense.

Carlton rubs at his mustache. "I assume all is *not* well with the book," he says, and Reese scowls, still staring down at the two boys on the sidewalk.

"You know better than to ask a question like that."

"Yes, well, dear, I had hoped the change of climate would be good for you."

"I don't think this climate is good for anything but heat rash and mildew," Reese grumbles and swirls the ice in her glass. "I need another drink. And then I need to get back to work."

"Maybe you're trying *too* hard," Carlton says and stops fumbling with his mustache. "Maybe you need to get away from this house for just a little while."

"That's what I keep telling her," Emma says. "But you know she won't listen to anyone."

The pout's in her voice again and it's more than Reese can take, those horrible boys and the murder, Carlton's good intentions, and now Emma's pout, and she gets up and leaves them, goes inside, trading the bright sunshine for the gentler bedroom shadows, and leaves her lover and her friend alone on the verandah.

Saturday and Emma's usual sort of ragtag entourage, but tonight she's spending most of her time with a dark-skinned woman named Danielle Thibodaux, someone she met the night before at the party on Esplanade, the party with the fabled voodoo priestess. Reese is getting quietly, sullenly drunk in one corner of the immense dining room, the dining room instead of the bedroom because Emma insisted. "It's such a shame we're letting this place go to waste," she said, and Reese was in the middle of a paragraph and didn't have time to argue. Not worth losing her train of thought over, and so here they all are, smoking and drinking around the long mahogany table, candlelight twinkling like starfire in the crystal chandelier, and Reese alone in a Chippendale in the corner. As apart from the others as she can get without offending Emma, and she's pretending that she isn't jealous of the dark-skinned woman with the faint Jamaican accent.

There's a ouija board in the center of the table, empty and unopened wine bottles, brandy and bourbon, Waterford crystal and sterling-silver candlesticks, and the cheap dime-store ouija board there in the middle of it all. One of the entourage brought it along, because he heard there was a ghost in the big white house on Prytania Street, a girl who hung herself from the top of the stairs when she got the news her young fiancé had died at Appomattox, or some other such worn-out Civil War tragedy, and for an hour they've been drinking and trying to summon the ghost of the suicide or anyone else who might have nothing better to do in the afterlife than talk to a bunch of drunks.

"I'm bored," Emma says finally, and she pushes the ouija board away, sends the tin planchette skittering towards a bottle of pear brandy. "No one wants to talk to us." The petulance in her voice does nothing at all to improve Reese's mood, and she thinks about taking her gin and going upstairs.

And then someone brings up the murdered woman, not even dead a whole day yet and here's some asshole who wants to try and drag her sprit back to earth. Reese rolls her eyes, thinking that even the typewriter would be less torture than these inane, morbid parlour games, and then she notices the uneasy look on the dark woman's face. The woman whispers something to Emma, just a whisper but intimate enough that it draws a fresh pang of jealousy from Reese. Emma looks at her, a long moment of silence exchanged between them, and then she laughs and shakes her head, as if perhaps the woman's just made the most ridiculous sort of suggestion imaginable.

"I hear it was a wild dog," someone at the table says.

"There's always a lot of rabies this time a year," someone else says, and Emma leans forward, eyes narrowed and a look of drunken confidence on her face, her I-know-something-*you*-don't smirk, and they all listen as she tells about Carlton's policeman friend and what he said that morning about the murdered woman's throat being cut, about her larynx being severed so she couldn't scream for help. That the cops are looking for a killer who wants everyone to *think* it was only an animal.

"Then let's ask her," the man who brought the ouija board says to Emma, and the blonde woman sitting next to him sniggers, an ugly, shameless sort of a laugh that makes Reese think of the two boys outside the walls of Lafayette, searching the sidewalk for traces of the dead woman's blood. There's another disapproving glance from Danielle Thibodaux, then, but Emma only shrugs and reaches for the discarded planchette.

"Hell, why not," she says, her words beginning to slur together just a little. "Maybe *she's* still lurking about," but the dark-skinned woman pushes her chair away from the table and stands a few feet behind Emma, watches nervously as four or five of the entourage place their fingers on the edges of the planchette.

"We need to talk to the woman who was murdered outside the cemetery this morning," Emma says, affecting a low, spooky whisper, phony creepshow awe, and fixing her eyes at the dead center of the planchette. "Mrs. Duplett's dead cook," Emma whispers, and someone corrects her, "No, honey. It's *Duquette*. Mrs. Duquette," and several people laugh.

"Yeah, right. Mrs. Duquette."

"Jesus," Reese whispers, and the dark-skinned woman stares across the room at her, her brown eyes that seem to say, *Can't you see things are bad enough already?* The woman frowns, and Reese sighs and pours herself another drink.

"We want to talk to Mrs. Duquette's murdered cook," Emma says again. "Are you there?"

A sudden titter of feigned surprise or fright when the tin planchette finally begins to move, haltingly at first, then circling the wooden board aimlessly for a moment before it swings suddenly to no and is still again.

"Then who *are* we talking to?" Emma says impatiently, and the planchette starts to move again. It wanders the board for a moment, and members of the entourage begin to call out letters as the heart-shaped thing drifts from character to character.

"S . . . P . . . I . . . N," and then the dark-skinned woman takes a step forward and rests her almond hands on Emma's shoulders. Reese thinks that the woman actually looks scared now and sits up straight in her chair so that she has a better view of the board.

"D . . . L," someone says, and "Stop this now, Emma," the dark woman demands. She *sounds* afraid, and maybe there's a hint of anger, too, but Emma only shakes her head and doesn't take her eyes off the restless planchette.

"It's okay, Danielle. We're just having a little fun, that's all."

"F... no, *E*..." and now someone whispers the word, "Spindle, it said its name is Spindle," but the planchette is still moving, and *"Please,"* the dark woman says to Emma.

"S... H," and now the woman has taken her hands off Emma's shoulders, has stepped back into the shadows at the edge of the candlelight again. Emma calls out the letters with the others, voices joined in drunken expectation, and Reese has to restrain an urge to join them herself.

"A... N... K... S," and then the planchette is still, and everyone's looking at Emma like she knows what they should do next. "Spindleshanks," she says, and Reese catches the breathless hitch   in her voice, as if she's been running or has climbed the stairs too quickly. Fat beads of sweat stand out on her forehead and glimmer in the flickering orangewhite glow of the candles. "Spindleshanks," Emma says again, and then, "That's *not* your name," she whispers.

"Ask it something else," one of the women says eagerly. "Ask Spindleshanks something else, Emmie," but Emma shakes her head, frowns and takes her hands from the planchette, breaking the mystic circle of fingers pressed against the tin. When the others follow suit, she pushes the ouija board away from her again.

"I'm tired of this shit," she says, and Reese can tell that this time the petulance is there to hide something else, something she isn't used to hearing in Emma's voice. "Somebody turn on the lights."

Reese stands up and presses the switch on the dining room wall next to a gaudy, gold-framed reproduction of John Singer Sargent's *The Daughters of Edward Darley Boit*—the pale, secretive faces of five girls and the solid darkness framed between two urns—and in the flood of electric light, the first thing that Reese notices is that the almond-skinned woman has gone, that she no longer stands there behind Emma's chair. And she doesn't see the second thing until one of the women cries out and points frantically at the wall above the window, the white plaster above the drapes. Emma sees it, too, but neither of them says a word, both sit still and silent for a minute, two minutes, while the tall letters written in blood above the brocade valance begin to dry and turn from crimson to a dingy reddish brown.

When everyone has left, and Emma has taken a couple of sleeping pills and gone upstairs, Reese sits at one end of the table and stares at the writing on the dining-room wall. SPINDLE-SHANKS in sloppy letters that began to drip and run before they began to dry, and she sips at her gin and wonders if they were already there before the reckless séance even started. Wonders, too, if Danielle Thibodaux has some hand in this, playing a clever, nasty trick on Emma's urbane boozers, if maybe they offended her or someone else at the Friday night party, and this was their comeuppance, tit for tat, and next time perhaps they'll stick to their own gaudy thrills and leave the natives alone.

The writing is at least twelve feet off the floor, and Reese can't imagine how the woman might have pulled it off, unless perhaps Emma was in on the prank as well. Maybe some collusion between the two of them to keep people talking about Emma Goldfarb's parties long after the lease is up and they've gone back to Boston. "Remember the night Emma called up Spindle-shanks?" they'll say, or "Remember that dreadful stuff on the dining-room wall? It *was* blood, wasn't it?" And yes, Reese thinks, it's a sensible explanation for Emma's insistence that they use the downstairs for the party that night, and that there be no light burning but the candles.

It almost makes Reese smile, the thought that Emma might be half so resourceful, and then she wonders how they're ever going to get the wall clean again. She's seen a ladder in the gardener's shed behind the house and Carlton will probably know someone who'll take care of it, paint over the mess if it can't be washed away.

In the morning, Emma will most likely admit her part in the ghostly deceit, and then she'll lie in bed laughing at her gullible friends. She'll probably even laugh at Reese. "I got you, too, didn't I?" she'll smirk. "Oh no, don't you try to lie to *me*, Miss Callicott. *I* saw the look on your face." And in a minute Reese blows out the candles, turns off the lights, and follows Emma upstairs to bed.

A few hours later, almost a quarter of four by the black hands of the alarm clock ticking loud on her bedside table, and Reese awakens from the nightmare of Harvard Square again. The snow storm become a blizzard, and this time she didn't even make it past the church, no farther than the little graveyard huddled in the lee of the steeple, and the storm was like icicle daggers. She walked against the wind and kept her eyes directly in front of her, because there was something on the other side of the wrought-iron fence, something past the sharp pickets that wanted her to turn and see it. Something that mumbled, and the sound of its feet in the snow was so soft, like footsteps in powdered sugar.

And then Reese was awake and sweating, shivering because the verandah doors were standing open again. The heat and humidity so bad at night, worse at night than in the day, she suspects, and they can't get to sleep without the cranky electric fan and the doors left open. But now even this stingy breeze is making her shiver, and she gets up, moving catslow and catsilent so she doesn't wake Emma, and walks across the room to close the doors and switch off the fan.

31

She's reaching for the brass door handles when Emma stirs behind her, her voice groggy from the Valium and alcohol, groggy and confused, and "Reese? Is something wrong?" she asks. "Has something happened?"

"No, dear," Reese answers her. "I had a bad dream, that's all. Go back to sleep," and she's already pulling the tall French doors shut when something down on the sidewalk catches her attention. Some quick movement there in the darkness gathered beneath the ancient magnolias and oaks along Sixth Street; hardly any moon for shadows tonight, but what shadows there are enough to cast a deeper gloom below those shaggy boughs. And Reese stands very still and keeps her eyes on the street, waiting, though she couldn't say for what.

Emma shifts in bed, and the mattress creaks, and then there's only the noise from the old fan and Reese's heart, the night birds that she doesn't know the names for calling to one another from the trees. Reese squints into the blacker shades of night along the leafy edge of Sixth, directly across from the place where the police found the body of the murdered cook, searches for any hint of the movement she might or might not have seen only a moment before. But there's only the faint moonlight winking dull off the chrome fender of someone's Chrysler, the whole thing nothing more than a trick of her sleep-clouded eyes, the lingering nightmare, and Reese closes the verandah doors and goes back to bed and Emma.

Afterword

"Spindleshanks (New Orleans, 1956)" was written in the spring of 2000, and is the last story that I wrote about New Orleans. For a long time, a couple of years, at least, I considered it my most accomplished short story, in part because I'd managed to achieve an economy of language which I had not enjoyed before. When I started work on the piece, I had in mind a story about a ghoul cult living in a vast necropolis beneath Lafayette Cemetery, with dashes of lycanthropy thrown in, and "Spindleshanks" is what came out, instead. Looking back, I realize that it's actually a story about the difficulties I was having finishing my second novel, *Threshold* (née *Trilobite*), with Reese Callicott's *The Ecstatic River* standing in for my own unfinished manuscript. Upon completing the story, the editors of *Queer Fear,* the anthology for which it had been commissioned, were alarmed that it was about women, as they'd wanted all the stories in the book to revolve around gay *men*, a fact they had neglected to ever tell me. The suggestion was made that I might change the sex of my protagonists merely by changing the gender of their pronouns, I said no, and the story appeared in the anthology as I'd written it. To date, that is almost certainly the most bizarre and laughable request any editor has ever made of me (which is saying something). "Spindleshanks" is no longer my favorite, but I still like it a lot.

So Runs the World Away

"**A** FALLING STAR for your thoughts," she says, and Gable, the girl with foilsilver eyes and teeth like the last day of winter, points at the night sky draped high above Providence and the wide Seekonk River. Nightsecret New England sky, and a few miles farther north you have to call it the Pawtucket River, but down here, where it laps fishy against Swan Point and the steep cemetery slopes, down here it's still the Seekonk, and way over there are the orange, industrial lights of Phillipsdale. Dead Girl blinks once or twice to get the taste out of her mouth, and then she follows Gable's grimy finger all the way up to Heaven, and there's the briefest streak of white light drawn quick across the eastern sky.

"That's very nice, but they aren't really, you know," she says, and Gable makes a face, pale face squinched up like a very old woman, dried-apple face to say she doesn't understand, and "Aren't really *what?*" she asks.

"Stars," says Dead Girl. "They're only meteorites. Just chunks of rock and metal flying around through space and burning up if they get too close. But they aren't stars. Not if they fall like that."

"Or angels," Bobby whispers and then goes right back to eating from the handful of blackberries he's picked from the brambles growing along the water's edge.

"I never said anything about angels," Gable growls at the boy, and he throws a blackberry at her. "There are *lots* of different words for angels."

"And for falling stars," Dead Girl says with a stony finality so they'll know that's all she wants to hear about it; meteorites that stop being meteors, Seekonk changing into Pawtucket, and in the end, it's nothing but the distance between this point and that. As arbitrary as any change, and so she presses her lips against the jogging lady's left wrist again. Not even the sheet-thin ghost of a pulse left in there, cooling meat against her teeth, flesh that might as well be clay except there are still a few red mouthfuls, and the sound of her busy lips isn't all that different from the sound of the waves against the shore.

"I know seven words for grey," Bobby says, talking through a mouthful of seeds and pulp and the dark juice dribbling down his bloodstained chin. "I got them out of a dictionary."

"You're a little faggot," Gable snarls at the boy, those narrow mercury eyes and her lower lip stuck way out like maybe someone's been beating her again, and Dead Girl knows she shouldn't have argued with Gable about falling stars and angels. *Next time,* she thinks, *I'll remember that. Next time, I'll smile and say whatever she wants me to say.* And when she's finally finished with the jogging lady, Dead Girl's the first one to slip quiet as a mousey in silk bedroom slippers across the mud and pebbles, and the river is as cold as the unfalling stars speckling the August night.

An hour and four minutes past midnight in the big yellow house on Benefit Street, and the ghouls are still picking at the corpses in the basement. Dead Girl sits with Bobby on the stairs that lead back up to the music and conversation overhead, the electric lights and acridsweet clouds of opium smoke;

down here there are only candles, and the air smells like bare dirt walls and mildew, like the embalmed meat spread out on the ghouls' long carving table. When they work like this, the ghouls stand up on their crooked hind legs and press their canine faces close together. The very thin one named Barnaby (his nervous ears alert to every footfall overhead, every creaking door, as if anyone Up There even cares what they're up to Down Here) picks up a rusty boning knife and uses it to lift a strip of dry flesh the colour of old chewing gum.

"That's the gastrocnemius," he says, and the yelloworange iris of his left eye drifts nervously towards the others, towards Madam Terpsichore, especially, who shakes her head and laughs the way that all ghouls laugh. *The way starving dogs would laugh,* Dead Girl thinks, *if they ever dared,* and she's starting to wish she and Bobby had gone down to Warwick with Gable and the Bailiff after all.

"No, that's the soleus, dear," Madam Terpsichore says and sneers at Barnaby, that practised curl of black lips to flash her jaundiced teeth like sharpened piano keys, a pinkred flick of her long tongue along the edge of her muzzle. "*That's* the gastrocnemius, there," she says. "You haven't been paying attention."

Barnaby frowns and scratches at his head. "Well, if we ever got anything fresh, maybe I could keep them straight," he grumbles, making excuses again, and Dead Girl knows the dissection is beginning to bore Bobby. He's staring over his shoulder at the basement door and the warm sliver of light getting in around the edges.

"Now, show me the lower terminus of the long peroneal," Madam Terpsichore says, her professorial litany and the impatient clatter of Barnaby digging about in his kit for a pair of poultry shears or an oyster fork, one or the other or something else entirely.

"You want to go back upstairs for a while?" Dead Girl asks

the boy, and he shrugs, but doesn't take his eyes off the basement door, doesn't turn back around to watch the ghouls.

"Well, come on then," and she stands up, takes his hand, and that's when Madam Terpsichore finally notices them.

"Please don't go, dear," she says. "It's always better with an audience, and if Master Barnaby ever finds the proper instrument, there may be a flensing yet," and the other ghouls snicker and laugh.

"I don't think I like them very much," Bobby whispers very quietly, and Dead Girl only nods and leads him back up the stairs to the party.

Bobby says he wants something to drink, so they go to the kitchen first, to the noisy antique refrigerator, and he has a Coke, and Dead Girl takes out a Heineken for herself. One chilly applegreen bottle and she twists the cap off and sips the bitter German beer; she never liked the taste of beer, before, but sometimes it seems like there were an awful lot of things she didn't like before. The beer is very, very cold and washes away the last rags of the basement air lingering stale in her mouth like a dusty patch of mushrooms, basementdry earth and a billion microscopic spores looking for a place to grow.

"I don't think I like them at all," Bobby says, still whispering even though they're upstairs. Dead Girl starts to tell him that he doesn't have to whisper anymore, but then she remembers Barnaby, his inquisitive, dogcocked ears, and she doesn't say anything at all.

Almost everyone else is sitting together in the front parlour, the spacious, booklined room with its stained-glass lamp shades in all the sweet and sour colours of hard candy, sugarfiltered light that hurts her eyes. The first time she was allowed into the house on Benefit Street, Gable showed her all the lamps, all the books, all the rooms, like they were hers. Like she belonged here, instead of the muddy bottom of the Seekonk River, another pretty, broken thing in a house filled up with things that are pretty or broken or both. Filled up with antiques, and some of them breathe and some of them don't. Some, like Miss Josephine, have forgotten how or why to breathe, except to talk.

They sit around her in their black funeral clothes and the chairs carved in 1754 or 1773, rough circle of men and women that always makes Dead Girl think of ravens gathered around carrion, blackbirds about a raccoon's corpse, jostling each other for all the best bits; sharp beaks for her bright and sapphire eyes, for the porcelain tips of her fingers, or that silent, unbeating heart. *The empress as summer roadkill,* Dead Girl thinks, and doesn't laugh out loud, even though she *wants* to, wants to laugh at these stiff and obsolescent beings, these tragic waxwork shades sipping absinthe and hanging on Miss Josephine's every word like gospel, like salvation. Better to slip in quiet, unnoticed, and find some place for her and Bobby to sit where they won't be in the way.

"Have you ever *seen* a firestorm, Signior Garzarek?" Miss Josephine asks, and she looks down at a book lying open in her lap, a green book like Dead Girl's green beer bottle.

"No, I never have," one of the waxworks says, tall man with slippery hair and ears that are too big for his head and almost come to points. "I dislike such things."

"But it was *beautiful,*" Miss Josephine assures him, and then she pauses, still looking at the green book in her lap, and Dead Girl can tell from the way her eyes move back and forth, back and forth, that she's reading whatever's on the pages. "No, that's not the right word," she says, "That's not the right word at all."

"I was at Dresden," one of the women volunteers, and Miss Josephine looks up, blinks at the woman as if she can't quite remember what this particular waxwork is called.

"No, no, Addie, it wasn't like that. Oh, I'm sure Dresden was exquisite, too, yes. But this wasn't something man did. This was something that was *done* to men. And that's the thing that makes it truly transcendent, the thing that makes it..." and she trails off and glances back down at the book as if the word she's missing is in there somewhere.

"Well, then, read some of it to us," Signior Garzarek says and points a gloved hand at the green book, and Miss Josephine looks up at him with eyes, eyes that seem somehow grateful and malicious at the same time.

"Are you sure?" she asks them all. "I wouldn't want to bore any of you."

"Please," says the man who hasn't taken off his bowler, and Dead Girl thinks his name is Nathaniel. "We always like to hear you read."

"Well, only if you're sure," Miss Josephine says, and she sits up a little straighter on her divan, clears her throat, and fusses with the shiny folds of her black satin skirt, the dress that only looks as old as the chairs, before she begins to read.

"'*That* was what came next—the fire,'" she says, and this is her reading voice now, and Dead Girl closes her eyes and listens. "'It shot up everywhere. The fierce wave of destruction had carried a flaming torch with it—agony, death and a flaming torch. It was just as if some fire demon was rushing from place to place with such a torch. Flames streamed out of half-shattered buildings all along Market Street.

"'I sat down on the sidewalk and picked the broken glass out of the soles of my feet and put on my clothes.

"'All wires down, all wires down!'"

And that's the way it goes for the next twenty minutes or so, the kindly half dark behind Dead Girl's eyes and Miss Josephine reading from her green book while Bobby slurps at his Coke and the waxwork ravens make no sound at all. She loves the rhythm of Miss Josephine's reading voice, the cadence like rain on a hot day or ice cream, that sort of a voice. But it would be better if she were reading something else, 'The Rime of the Ancient Mariner,' maybe, or Keats or Tennyson. But this is better than nothing at all, so Dead Girl listens, content enough, and never mind that it's only earthquakes and conflagration, smoke and the screams of dying men and horses. It's the *sound* of the voice that matters, not the words or anything they mean, and if that's true for her, it's just as true for the silent waxworks in their stiff colonial chairs.

When she's finished, Miss Josephine closes the book and smiles, showing them all the stingiest glimpse of her sharp white teeth.

"Superb," says Nathaniel, and "Oh yes, superb," says Addie Goodwine.

"You are indeed a wicked creature, Josephine," says the Signior, and he lights a fat cigar and exhales a billowing phantom from his mouth. "Such delicious perversity wrapped up in such a comely package."

"I was writing as James Russell Williams, then," Miss Josephine says proudly. "They even paid me."

Dead Girl opens her eyes, and Bobby's finished his Coke, is rolling the empty bottle back and forth across the rug like a wooden rolling pin on cookie dough. "Did you like it?" she asks him, and he shrugs.

"Not at all?"

"Well, it wasn't as bad as the ghouls," he says, but he doesn't look at her, hardly ever looks directly at her or anyone else these days.

A few more minutes and then Miss Josephine suddenly remembers something in another room that she wants the waxworks to see, something they *must* see, an urn or a brass sundial, the latest knick-knack hidden somewhere in the bowels of the great cluttered house. They follow her out of the parlour, into the hallway, chattering and trailing cigarette smoke, and if anyone even notices Bobby and Dead Girl sitting on the floor, they pretend that they haven't. Which is fine by Dead Girl; she dislikes them, the lifeless smell of them, the guarded desperation in their eyes.

Miss Josephine has left her book on the cranberry divan, and when the last of the vampires has gone, Dead Girl gets up and steps inside the circle of chairs, stands staring down at the cover.

"What does it say?" Bobby asks, and so she reads the title to him.

"*San Francisco's Horror of Earthquake, Fire, and Famine,*" she reads, and then Dead Girl picks the book up and shows him the cover, the letters stamped into the green cloth in faded gold ink. And underneath, a woman in dark-coloured robes, her feet in fire and water, chaos wrapped about her ankles, and she seems to be bowing to a shattered row of marble columns and a cornerstone with the words "In Memoriam of California's Dead—April 18th, 1906".

"That was a long time ago, wasn't it?" Bobby asks, and Dead Girl sets the book down again. "Not if you're Miss Josephine, it isn't," she says. *If you're Miss Josephine, that was only yesterday, the day before yesterday. If you're her*—but that's the sort of thought it's best not to finish, better if she'd never thought it at all.

"We don't have to go back to the basement, do we?" Bobby asks, and Dead Girl shakes her head. "Not if you don't want to," she says. And then she goes to the window and stares out at Benefit Street, at the passing cars and the living people with their smaller, petty reasons for hating time. In a moment, Bobby comes and stands beside her, and he holds her hand.

Dead Girl keeps her secrets in an old Hav-A-Tampa cigar box, the few she can't just keep inside her head, and she keeps the old cigar box on a shelf inside a mausoleum at Swan Point. This manicured hillside that rises up so sharp from the river's edge, steep and dead-adorned hill, green grass in the summer and the windrustling branches of the trees, and only Bobby knows about the box, and she thinks he'll keep it to himself. He rarely says anything to anyone, especially Gable; Dead Girl knows what Gable would do if she found out about the box, *thinks* she knows, and that's good enough, bad enough, that she keeps it hidden in the mausoleum.

The caretakers bricked up the front of the vault years and years ago, but they left a small cast-iron grate set into the masonry just below the marble keystone and the verdigris-streaked plaque with the name "Stanton" on it, though Dead Girl can't imagine why. Maybe it's there so the bugs can come in and out, or so all those dead Stantons can get a breath of fresh air now and then, though there's not even enough room for bats to squeeze through, or the swifts or rats. But still plenty of space between the bars of the grate for her and Bobby to slip inside whenever she wants to look at the things she keeps inside the old cigar box.

Nights like tonight, after the long parties, after Miss Josephine finally loses interest in her waxwork ravens and chases them all away (everyone except the ghouls, of course, who come and go as they please through the tunnels in the basement); still a coalgrey hour left until dawn, and she knows that Gable is probably already waiting for them in the river, but she can wait a few minutes more.

"She might come looking for us," Bobby says when they're inside the mausoleum and he's standing on tip toes to see out but the grate is still a foot above his head.

"No, she won't," Dead Girl tells him, tells herself that it's true, that Gable's too glad to be back down there in the dark to be bothered. "She's probably already asleep by now."

"Maybe so," Bobby says, not sounding even the least bit

convinced, and then he sits down on the concrete floor and watches Dead Girl with his quicksilver eyes, mirror eyes so full of light they'll still see when the last star in the whole goddamned universe has burned itself down to a spinning cinder.

"You let me worry about Gable," she says and opens the box to find that everything's still inside, just the way she left it. The newspaper clippings and a handful of coins, a pewter St. Christopher's medal and a doll's plastic right arm. Three keys and a ragged swatch of indigo velvet stained maroon around the edges. Things that mean nothing to anyone but Dead Girl; her puzzle, and no one else knows the way that all these pieces fit together. Or even *if* they all fit together; sometimes even she can't remember, but it makes her feel better to see them, anyway, to lay her white hands on these trinkets and scraps, to hold them.

Bobby is tapping his fingers restlessly against the floor, and when she looks at him he frowns and stares up at the ceiling. "Read me the one about Mercy," he says, and she looks back down at the Hav-A-Tampa box.

"It's getting late, Bobby. Someone might hear me."

And he doesn't ask her again, just keeps his eyes on the ceiling directly above her head and taps his fingers on the floor.

"It's not even a story," she says and fishes one of the newspaper clippings from the box. Nutbrown paper gone almost as brittle as she feels inside and the words printed there more than a century ago, and "It's almost like a story, when you read it," Bobby replies.

For a moment, Dead Girl stands very still, listening to the last of the night sounds fading slowly away and the stranger sounds that come just before sunrise; birds and the blind, burrowing progress of earthworms, insects and a ship's bell somewhere down in Providence Harbour, and Bobby's fingers drumming on the concrete. She thinks about Miss Josephine and the comfort in her voice, her ice-cream voice against every vacant moment of eternity. And, in a moment, she begins to read.

— ✧ —

Letter from the *Pawtuxet Valley Gleaner,* dated March 1892:

"Exeter Hill"

Mr Editor,
As considerable notoriety has resulted from the exhuming of three bodies in Exeter cemetery on the 17th inst., I will give the main facts as I have received them for the benefit of such of your readers as "have not taken the papers" containing the same. To begin, we will say that our neighbor, a good and respectable citizen, George T. Brown, has been bereft of his wife and two grown-up daughters by consumption, the wife and mother about eight years ago, and the eldest daughter, Olive, two years or no later, while the other daughter, Mercy Lena, died about two months since, after nearly one year's illness from the same dread disease. About two years ago Mr. Brown's only son Edwin A., a young married man of good habits, began to give evidence of lung trouble, which increased, until in hopes of checking and curing the same, he was induced to visit the famous Colorado Springs, where his wife followed him later on and though for a time he seemed to improve, it soon became evident that there was no real benefit derived, and this coupled with a strong desire on the part of both husband and wife to see their Rhode Island friends, decided them to return east after an absence of about 18 months and are staying with Mrs. Brown's parents, Willet Himes. We are sorry to say that Eddie's health is not encouraging at this time. And now comes in the

queer part, viz: The revival of a pagan or other superstition regarding the feeding of the dead upon a living relative where consumption was the cause of death and now bringing the living person soon into a similar condition, etc. and to avoid this result, according to the same high authority, the "vampire" in question which is said to inhabit the heart of a dead consumptive while any blood remains in that organ, must be cremated and the ashes carefully preserved and administered in some form to the living victim, when a speedy cure may (un) reasonably be expected. I will here say that the husband and father of the deceased ones, from the first, disclaimed any faith at all in the vampire theory but being urged, he allowed other, if not wiser, counsel to prevail, and on the 17th inst., as before stated the three bodies alluded to were exhumed and then examined by Doctor Metcalt of Wickford (under protest, as it were, being an unbeliever). The two bodies longest buried were found decayed and bloodless, while the last one who has been only about two months buried showed some blood in the heart as a matter of course, and as the doctor expected but to carry out what was a forgone conclusion, the heart and lungs of the last named (M. Lena) were then and there duly cremated, but deponent saith not how the ashes were disposed of. Not many persons were present, Mr. Brown being among the absent ones. While we do not blame any one for these proceedings as they were intended without doubt to relieve the anxiety of the living, still, it seems incredible that any one can attach the least importance to the subject, being so entirely incompatible with reason and conflicts also with scripture, which requires us "to give a reason for the hope that is in us," or the why and wherefore which certainly cannot be done as applied to the foregoing.

With the silt and fish shit settling gentle on her eyelids and her lungs filled up with cold river water, Dead Girl sleeps, the soot-black ooze for her blanket, her cocoon, and Bobby safe in her arms. Gable is there, too, lying somewhere nearby, coiled like an eel in the roots of a drowned willow.

And in her dreams, Dead Girl counts the boats passing over-head, their prows to split the daydrenched sky, their wakes the roil and swirl of thunderstorm clouds. Crabs and tiny snails nest in her hair, and her wet thoughts slip by as smooth and capricious as the Seekonk, one instant or memory flowing seamlessly into the next. And *this* moment, this one here, is the last night that she was still a living girl. Last frosty night before Halloween, and she's stoned and sneaking into Swan Point Cemetery with a boy named Adrian that she only met a few hours ago in the loud and smoky confusion of a Throwing Muses show, Adrian Mobley and his long yellow hair like strands of the sun or purest spun gold.

Adrian won't or can't stop giggling, a joke or just all the pot they've been smoking, and she leads him straight down Holly Avenue, the long paved drive to carry them across The Old Road and into the vast maze of the cemetery's slate and gran-ite intestines. Headstones and more ambitious monuments lined up neat or scattered wild among the trees, reflecting pools to catch and hold the high white moon, and she's only having a little trouble finding her way in the dark.

"Shut up," she hisses, casts anxious serpent sounds from her chapped lips, across her chattering teeth, and "Someone's going to fucking hear us," she says. She can see her breath, her soul escaping mouthful by steaming mouthful.

Then Adrian puts his arm around her, sweater wool and warm flesh around warm flesh, and he whispers something in her ear, something she should have always remembered but doesn't.

Something forgotten, the way she's forgotten the smell of a late summer afternoon and sunlight on sand, and he kisses her.

And for a kiss she shows him the place where Lovecraft is buried, the quiet place she comes when she only wants to be alone, no company but her thoughts and the considerate, sleeping bodies underground. The Phillips family obelisk and then his own little headstone; she takes a plastic cigarette lighter from the front pocket of her jeans and holds the flame close to the ground so that Adrian can read the marker: August 20, 1890—March 15, 1937, "I am Providence," and she shows him all the offerings that odd pilgrims leave behind. A handful of pencils and one rusty screw, two nickels, a small rubber octopus, and a handwritten letter folded neat and weighted with a rock so the wind won't blow it away. The letter begins "Dear Howard," but she doesn't read any farther, nothing there written for her, and then Adrian tries to kiss her again.

"No, wait. You haven't seen the tree," she says, wriggling free of Adrian Mobley's skinny arms, dragging him roughly away from the obelisk; two steps, three, and they're both swallowed by the shadow of an enormous, ancient birch, this tree that must have been old when her great grandfather was a boy. Its sprawling branches are still shaggy with autumnpainted leaves, its roots like the scabby knuckles of some skybound giant, clutching at the earth for fear that he will fall and tumble forever towards the stars.

"Yeah, so it's a tree," Adrian mumbles, not understanding, not even trying to understand, and now she knows that it was a mistake to bring him here.

"People have carved things," she says and strikes the lighter again, holds the flickering blueorange flame so that Adrian can see all the pocket-knife graffiti worked into the smooth, pale bark of the tree. The unpronounceable names of dark, fictitious gods and entire passages from Lovecraft, razor steel for ink to tattoo these occult wounds and lonely messages to a dead man, and she runs an index finger across a scar in the shape of a tentacle-headed fish.

"Isn't it beautiful?" she whispers, and that's when Dead Girl sees the eyes watching them from the lowest limbs of the tree, *their* shimmering silver eyes like spiteful coins hanging in the night, like strange fruit, and "This shit isn't the way it happened at all," Gable says. "These aren't even *your* memories. This is just some bitch we killed."

"Oh, I think she knows that," the Bailiff laughs, and it's worse than the ghouls snickering for Madam Terpsichore.

"I only wanted him to see the tree," Dead Girl says. "I wanted to show him something carved into the Lovecraft tree."

"Liar," Gable sneers, and that makes the Bailiff laugh again. He squats in the dust and fallen leaves and begins to pick something stringy from his teeth.

And she would run, but the river has almost washed the world away, nothing left now but the tree and the moon and the thing that clambers down its trunk on spiderlong legs and arms the colour of chalk dust.

Is that a Death? and are there two?

"We know you would forget us," Gable says, "If we ever let you. You would pretend you were an innocent, a *victim*." Her dry tongue feels as rough as sandpaper against Dead Girl's wrist, dead cat's tongue, and above them the constellations swirl in a mad kaleidoscope dance about the moon; the tree moans and raises its swaying branches to Heaven, praying for dawn, for light and mercy from everything it's seen and will ever see again.

Is Death that woman's mate?

And at the muddy bottom of the Seekonk River, in the lee of the Henderson Bridge, Dead Girl's eyelids flutter as she stirs uneasily, frightening fish, fighting sleep and her dreams. But the night is still hours away, waiting on the far side of the scalding day, and so she holds Bobby tighter, and he sighs and makes a small, lost sound that the river snatches and drags away towards the sea.

— ✧ —

Dead Girl sits alone on the floor in the parlour of the house on Benefit Street, alone because Gable has Bobby with her tonight; Dead Girl drinks her Heineken and watches the yellow and aubergine circles that their voices trace in the stagnant, smoky air, and she tries to recall what it was like before she knew the colours of sound.

Miss Josephine raises the carafe and carefully pours tap water over the sugar cube on her slotted spoon; the water and dissolved sugar sink to the bottom of her glass and at once the liqueur begins to louche, the clear and emerald-bright mix of alcohol and herbs clouding quickly to a milky, opaque green.

"Oh, of course," she says to the attentive circle of waxwork ravens. "I remember Mercy Brown, and Nellie Vaughn, too, and that man in Connecticut. What was his name?"

"William Rose," Signior Garzarek suggests, but Miss Josephine frowns and shakes her head. "No, no. Not Rose. He was that peculiar fellow in Peace Dale, remember? No, the man in Connecticut had a different name."

"They were maniacs, every one of them," Addie Goodwine says nervously and sips from her own glass of absinthe. "Cutting the hearts and livers out of corpses and burning them, eating the ashes. It's ridiculous. It's even worse than what *they* do," and she points confidentially at the floor.

"Of course it is, dear," Miss Josephine says.

"But the little Vaughn girl, Nellie, I understand she's still something of a sensation among the local high-school crowd," Signior Garzarek says and smiles, dabs at his wet red lips with a lace handkerchief. "They do love their ghost stories, don't you know. They must find the epitaph on her tombstone an endless source of delight."

"What does it say?" Addie asks, and when Miss Josephine turns and stares at her, Addie Goodwine flinches and almost drops her glass.

"You really should get out more often, dear," Miss Josephine says, and "Yes," Addie stammers. "Yes, I know. I should."

The waxwork named Nathaniel fumbles with the brim of his black bowler and, "I remember," he says. "'I am watching and waiting for you.' That's what it says, isn't it?"

"Delightful, I tell you," Signior Garzarek chuckles, and then he drains his glass and reaches for the absinthe bottle on its silver serving tray.

"What do you see out there?"

The boy that Dead Girl calls Bobby is standing at the window in Miss Josephine's parlour, standing there with the sash up and snow blowing in, a small drift of snow at his bare feet, and he turns around when she says his name.

"There was a bear on the street," he says and puts the glass paperweight in her hands, the glass dome filled with water, and when she shakes it, all the tiny white flakes inside swirl around and around. A miniature blizzard trapped in her palm, plastic snow to settle slow across the frozen field, the barn, the dark and winterbare line of trees in the distance.

"I saw a bear," he says again, more insistent than before, and points at the open window.

"You did *not* see a bear," Dead Girl says, but she doesn't look to see for herself, doesn't take her silver eyes off the paperweight; she'd almost forgotten about the barn, that day and the storm, January or February or March, more years ago than she'd have ever guessed, and the wind howling like hungry wolves.

"I *did*," Bobby says indignantly. "I saw a big black bear dancing in the street. I know a bear when I see one."

And Dead Girl closes her eyes and lets the globe fall from her fingers, lets it roll from her hand, and she knows that when it hits the floor it will shatter into a thousand pieces. World shatter, watersky shatter to bleed Heaven away across the floor, and so there isn't much time if she's going to make it all the way to the barn.

"I think it knew our names," the boy says, and he sounds afraid, but when she looks back, she can't see him anymore. Nothing behind her now but the little stone wall to divide this field from the next, the slate and granite boulders already half buried by the storm, and the wind pricks her skin with icing needle teeth. The snow spirals down from the leaden clouds, and the wind sends it spinning and dancing in dervish crystal curtains.

"We forget for a reason, child" the Bailiff says, his rustcrimson voice woven tight between the air and every snowflake. "Time is too heavy to carry so much of it strung about our necks."

"I don't hear you," she lies, and it doesn't matter anyway, whatever he says, because Dead Girl is already at the barn door; both the doors left standing open, and her father will be angry, will be furious if he finds out. The horses could catch cold, he will say to her. The cows, he will say, the cows are already giving sour milk, as it is.

Shut the doors and don't look inside. Shut the doors and run all the way home.

"It fell from the sky," he said, the night before. "It fell screaming from a clear blue sky. No one's gone looking for it. I don't reckon they will."

"It was only a bird," her mother said.

"No," her father said. "It wasn't a bird."

Shut the doors and run...

But she doesn't do either, because that isn't the way this happened, the way it *happens*, and the naked thing crouched there in the straw and the blood looks up at her with Gable's pretty face. Takes its mouth away from the mare's mangled throat, and blood spills out between clenched teeth and runs down its chin.

"The bear was singing our names."

And then the paperweight hits the floor and bursts in a sudden, merciful spray of glass and water that tears the winter day apart around her. "Wake up," Miss Josephine says, spits out impatient words that smell like anise and dust, and she shakes Dead Girl again.

"I expect Madam Terpsichore is finishing up downstairs. And the Bailiff will be back soon. You can't sleep here."

Dead Girl blinks and squints past Miss Josephine and all the colorful, candyshaded lamps. And the summer night outside the parlour window, the night that carries her rotten soul beneath its tongue, stares back with eyes as black and secret as the bottom of a river.

In the basement, Madam Terpsichore, lady of rib spreaders and carving knives, has already gone, has crept away down one of the damp and brickthroated tunnels with her snuffling entourage in tow. Their bellies full and all their entrail curiosities sated for another night, and only Barnaby is left behind to tidy up; part of his modest punishment for slicing too deeply through a sclera and ruining a violet eye meant for some graveyard potentate or another, the precious vitreous humour spilled by his hand, and there's a fresh notch in his left ear where Madam Terpsichore bit him for ruining such a delicacy. Dead Girl is sitting on an old produce crate, watching while he scrubs bile from the stainless steel tabletop.

"I'm not very good with dreams, I'm afraid," he says to her and wrinkles his wet black nose.

"Or eyes," Dead Girl says, and Barnaby nods his head.

"Or eyes," he agrees.

"I just thought you might listen, that's all. It's not the sort of thing I can tell Gable, and Bobby, well—"

"He's a sweet child, though," Barnaby says, and then he frowns and scrubs harder at a stubborn smear the colour of scorched chestnuts.

"But I can't tell anyone else," Dead Girl says; she sighs, and Barnaby dips his pig-bristle brush into a pail of soapy water and goes back to work on the stain.

"I don't suppose I can do *very* much damage, if all I do is listen," and the ghoul smiles a crooked smile for her and touches a claw to the bloody place where Madam Terpsichore nicked the base of his right ear with her sharp incisors.

"Thank you, Barnaby," she says and draws a thoughtless half circle on the dirt floor with the scuffed toe of one shoe. "It isn't a very long dream. It won't take but a minute," and what she tells him, then, isn't the dream of Adrian Mobley and the Lovecraft tree, and it isn't the barn and the blizzard, the white thing waiting for her inside the barn. This is another dream, a moonless night at Swan Point, and someone's built a great, roaring bonfire near the river's edge. Dead Girl's watching the flames reflected in the water, the air heavy with wood smoke and the hungry sound of fire; and Bobby and Gable are lying on the rocky beach, laid out neat as an undertaker's work, their arms at their sides, pennies on their eyes. And they're both slit open from collarbones to crotch, stem to stern, ragged Y-incisions, and their innards glint wetly in the light of the bonfire.

"No, I don't think it was me," Dead Girl says, even though it isn't true, and she draws another half circle on the floor to keep the first one company. Barnaby has stopped scrubbing at the table and is watching her uneasily with his distrustful scavenger eyes.

"Their hearts are lying there together on a boulder," and she's speaking very quietly now, almost whispering as if she's afraid someone upstairs might be listening, too, and Barnaby perks up his ears and leans towards her. Their hearts on a stone, and their livers, too, and she burns the organs in a brass bowl until there's nothing left but a handful of greasy ashes.

"I think I eat them," Dead Girl says. "But there are blackbirds then, a whole flock of blackbirds, and all I can hear are their wings. Their wings bruise the sky."

And Barnaby shakes his head, makes a rumbling, anxious sound deep in his throat, and he starts scrubbing at the table again. "I should learn to quit while I'm only a little ways behind," he snorts. "I should learn what's none of my goddamn business."

"Why, Barnaby? What does it mean?" and at first he doesn't answer her, only grumbles to himself and the pigbristle brush flies back and forth across the surgical table even though there are no stains left to scrub, nothing but a few soap suds and the candlelight reflected in the scratched and dented silver surface.

"The Bailiff would have my balls in a bottle of brine if I told you that," he says. "Go away. Go back upstairs where you belong and leave me alone. I'm busy."

"But you do know, don't you? I heard a story, Barnaby, about another dead girl named Mercy Brown. They burned *her* heart—"

And the ghoul opens his jaws wide and roars like a caged lion, hurls his brush at Dead Girl, but it sails over her head and smashes into a shelf of Ball mason jars behind her. Broken glass and the sudden stink of vinegar and pickled kidneys, and she runs for the stairs.

"Go pester someone else, *corpse,*" Barnaby snarls at her back.

"Tell your blasphemous dreams to those effete cadavers upstairs. Ask one of *those* snotty fuckers to cross him," and then he throws something else, something shiny and sharp that whizzes past her face and sticks in the wall. Dead Girl takes the stairs two at a time, slams the basement door behind her and turns the lock. And if anyone's heard, if Miss Josephine or Signior Garzarek or anyone else even notices her reckless dash out the front doors and down the steps of the big old house on Benefit Street, they know better than Barnaby and keep it to themselves.

In the east, there's the thinnest bluewhite sliver of dawn to mark the horizon, the light a pearl would make, and Bobby hands Dead Girl another stone. "That should be enough," she says, and so he sits down in the grass at the edge of the narrow beach to watch as she stuffs this last rock inside the hole where Gable's heart used to be. Twelve big rocks shoved inside her now, granite-cobble viscera to carry the vampire's body straight to the bottom of the Seekonk, and this time that's where it will stay. Dead Girl has a fat roll of grey duct tape to seal the wound.

"Will they come after us?" Bobby asks, and the question takes her by surprise, not the sort of thing she would ever have expected from him. She stops wrapping Gable's abdomen with the duct tape and stares silently at him for a moment, but he doesn't look back at her, keeps his eyes on that distant, jagged rind of daylight.

"They might," she tells him. "I don't know for sure. Are you afraid, Bobby?"

"I'll miss Miss Josephine," he says. "I'll miss the way she read us stories," and Dead Girl nods her head, and "Yes," she says. "Me too. But I'll always read you stories," and he smiles when she says that.

When Dead Girl is finally finished, they push Gable's body out into the water and follow it all the way down, wedge it tight between the roots of the sunken willow tree below Henderson Bridge. And then Bobby nestles close to Dead Girl, and in a moment he's asleep, lost in his own dreams, and she closes her eyes and waits for the world to turn itself around again.

Afterword

"So Runs the World Away" was written in August 2000, not long after my first trip to Rhode Island. While in Providence, I was fortunate enough to spend a night on Benefit Street, just across from Lovecraft's "shunned house" (the Stephen Harris House at 135 Benefit). I'd been warned ahead of time that someone had painted it yellow, but, since I have long associated the color yellow with sickness and unease, it seemed oddly appropriate. Walking the streets of College Hill, encountering the Lovecraft Tree just behind HPL's modest plot in Swan Point Cememtery, hearing stories of vampirism and vampire hysteria in Rhode Island, all these things came together to inspire "So Runs the World Away." The "yellow house" with its ghouls and silver-eyed vampires would become an important element in all my stories with Providence connections, including "In the Garden of Poisonous Flowers," *Low Red Moon*, "The Dead and the Moonstruck," "The Daughter of the Four of Pentacles," and *Daughter of Hounds* (in progress). Indeed, I have often thought it likely that the silver-eyed girl who meets Deacon at the end of *Low Red Moon* may be Dead Girl (i.e., Mercy Brown).

Standing Water

MONDAY AFTERNOON and Elvin Sloss is having a cigarette behind the bookstore when he notices the mud puddle for the first time. The narrow alley that runs between Twenty-Second and Twenty-Third streets, alley of broken, rustbarred windows and dented trash cans, high walls of brick laid and mortar set when Birmingham was a steel town and the mills belched fire and sootblack fumes. Elvin takes a thoughtful, long drag off his Winston, holds the smoke in his lungs like a drowning man's last breath, and watches the mirrorsmooth surface of the puddle. Then he glances up at the sky, exhales, and a grey nicotine ghost hangs in the stale and scalding summer air trapped between the rear of Second Chance Books and the empty warehouse on the other side of the alley.

There isn't a cloud anywhere in the high whiteblue sky, the narrow slice of it he can see draped between the buildings. There haven't been any clouds for almost two weeks now. No clouds and not a single drop of rain, just ozone alerts and the mercury climbing above one hundred day after day, hardly dropping below ninety at night, but here's this mud puddle anyway.

Elvin takes another drag and flicks the butt of his cigarette at the oily looking water. There's a brief, faint hiss, and the Winston's filter bobs and floats on the surface, sending out concentric rings of tiny ripples to lap against the edges of the puddle, the crumbled asphalt and limestone gravel margins of the pothole. Here and there, the sticky yellowbrown clay beneath the blacktop is visible, like an old secret the city's trying to hide from itself.

Elvin chews at his lip and stares up at the sky again, the dogday sun only an hour past noon, and there's no end at all to that dry shade of blue.

The back door of the shop slams opens, then, releasing an unexpected draft of staler air that smells like dust and silverfish, old paperbacks and coffee grounds, bookscented air that's only slightly cooler than the summer day. Shanna sticks her head out and squints at him, her hair the color of a dead mouse and chopped off almost down to the scalp.

"Didn't we have a copy of *Bleak House?*" she asks and blinks. "Didn't someone bring one in just last week?"

"English lit," Elvin says, and when he looks back at the puddle, there's no sign of the cigarette butt, and the water is as smooth as melted plastic.

"Yeah, I already looked there. The only Dickens I can find is five copies of *David Copperfield* and one of *Great Expectations.*"

"Did you look in the B's? It might be there," he says; Shanna clicks her tongue loud against the roof of her mouth, a curt, annoyed sort of a sound, and "Why the hell would Dickens be stuck in the B's?" she asks.

But instead of an answer, he points at the mud puddle and asks another question.

"Was that there yesterday?"

"What? What are you pointing at, Elvin?"

And he almost tells her, but it is only a mud puddle. Only a mud puddle in the alley behind the bookstore, and Shanna sighs and clicks her tongue again. There are already little beads of sweat standing out on her forehead.

"Never mind. It's nothing," he says.

"You're gonna bake your brains if you don't come back inside," she grumbles in a voice that almost sounds like his mother, almost sounds like she might actually give a shit.

"You must'a read my mind, Ladybug," he says, smiles, and Elvin follows the girl out of the blinding August glare and back into the mustywarm shadows waiting on the other side of the door.

She got him the job in May, about three weeks before they split up, and this grudge match has been going on ever since, Elvin refusing to quit because he needs the job and Shanna refusing to quit because she was there first. And it's usually not that bad, except for the days when Mr. Culliver's arthritis is bothering him or his bowels are acting up, and he doesn't come in to the store, and so they both have to work. Days when they have to pass the awkward hours trying to stay out of each other's way, ten o'clock to four-thirty, and maybe it wouldn't be so difficult if there were a few more customers. But hardly anyone ever comes into Second Chance, and so they take turns sitting behind the antique cash register and pretending to sweep the floor or tidy up the rows and rows of books that are hardly ever out of order.

Sometimes Elvin gets a bunch of them out of order on purpose, ignores Mr. Culliver's obsessive categories and alphabetizing and sticks *Bleak House* under the B's or *Gravity's Rainbow* under New Age, just so they'll have something to do. Once, he hid all the Ayn Rand and Germaine Greer together under "Ichthyology," but it was almost two months before anyone even noticed.

Mostly, he does the work, or lack thereof, that Mr. Culliver pays him to do; better than flipping burgers so he ought to be grateful, even when it's a hundred and two in the shade and the old electric fans suspended from the ceiling of the shop do little more than rearrange the heat.

On Tuesday, Mr. Culliver is feeling better again, and Shanna has the day off. Elvin spends half the morning slowly unpacking boxes of encyclopedias from a flea market, three whole sets of *The World Book* from 1970 and not a single J-K volume in the bunch. And so maybe Mr. Culliver plays a few games of his own, maybe he doesn't actually *want* to sell any of these moldering, dog-eared books, or he's just really fucking curious to see how many people don't care whether or not their ten-dollar set of Nixon-era *World Books* has listings for "Jet Engines" or "Kuwait."

At noon, Elvin retrieves the brown paper Piggly Wiggly bag with his lunch from the little refrigerator in the stock room and opens the back door, steps out into the sundrenched alleyway, and the mud puddle is still there. If anything, it seems a little wider than the day before, never mind the heat or the drought or the trucks and cars that use the alley every now and then. He thought about the trucks and cars last night, lying in bed, thinking because it was too hot to sleep, and he thought how water would get splashed out of the puddle whenever anyone drove across it.

The water in the puddle is the color of chocolate milk, and there's a definite iridescent sheen to it.

Elvin sits down on the wooden steps and opens his brown paper sack, removes a Ziploc baggy containing a white-bread-and-egg-salad sandwich cut diagonally into two neat triangles, takes a big bite, and watches the puddle while he chews. The sandwich isn't very good, because he forgot the black pepper and didn't have any pickle relish, so it's just boiled eggs and mayonnaise mushed together. He thinks that there's a small tin of black pepper sitting on top of the refrigerator in the break room, but doesn't want to go back inside to look for it, doesn't want to take his eyes off the chocolate-colored puddle that long.

Elvin takes another bite of his sandwich, another gooey, bland yellowwhite mouthful, and the puddle shimmers and glints wet beneath the Alabama sun. *Yes,* he thinks, *it is wider than yesterday.* At least two feet across now, and the water's risen over the edges of the pothole. So maybe it's a leaky pipe under the alley, not actually busted, just a slow leak or there'd be a lot more water. He smiles, feeling stupid because he didn't think of that to start with.

Elvin finishes his sandwich, and there's still a Hershey bar at the bottom of the bag, but it's already started to melt in the heat, going soft inside its wrapper, and he decides to put it back in the fridge for a while, save it for later. He lights a cigarette instead, stares at the spray-paint graffiti on the other side of the alley and then at a stunted patch of dandelions and clover that's managed to push its way up through a crack in the asphalt. Keeping his eyes on anything except the mud puddle, that mystery solved, and tonight he'll only lie awake because of the heat. Tonight, he can toss and turn and only think about the things he could have said to Shanna, the things that might have kept her from walking out on him.

He glances at his watch and stubs his cigarette out against the bookstore wall, leaves an ashy, black smudge on the bricks, and then Elvin starts to flick the butt at the puddle. But there's a sudden ripple across it, like a gust of wind, when there isn't any wind, when there's nothing but the stagnant, broiling air. For a moment, the iridescent water seems to twitch, prism bands of oily color stretching out and winding quickly back upon themselves. And then the puddle's calm again, as if it had never been anything else. Elvin drops the butt of his Winston on the ground, grinds it back and forth with the toe of his right sneaker, and he reminds himself about the leaky pipe some-where under the alley and goes back inside the shop.

Wednesday, and that's almost always Shanna's day, so Elvin sleeps until nearly eleven o'clock. Up half the night until he took an icy-cold bath at three am and drank two bottles of Sterling with some allergy pills, and when he finally wakes up he only feels like shit. He lies naked in bed wondering if there's enough sugar left for coffee, and if he's ever going to get off his ass and find another air conditioner. There used to be a window unit in the bedroom, a huge, noisy contraption that rumbled and whirred and thumped like some ridiculous cartoon gizmo, but Shanna took that with her when she left. She'd paid for it, so Elvin didn't argue with her, but sometimes he wishes that he had.

After breakfast (four frosted blueberry Pop-Tarts and bitter coffee, because there wasn't any sugar after all), he goes back to bed and sits staring out the open window that used to hold the air conditioner. The sun is burning the city alive out there, roasting it up for some feast the sky has planned, the sky or the stars, and from here he can see all the way across the tracks, past the first row of buildings, and right there's the roof of Second Chance Books. Shanna's under that roof, so at least she's safe from the sun, safe inside the bunker with all the dustbunnies and Mr. Culliver's applestinking pipe smoke; safe until the sun stops fooling around, gets its act together, and there's finally nowhere left to hide. Elvin imagines the city wrapped in flames, the brick and glass skyline turning soft as a melted candy bar.

"Jesus," he whispers, laughs a very dry, dishonest laugh, and wipes at his face. Sweat that stings his eyes and dissolves in salty drops on his tongue. He wonders if the heat has ever driven anyone insane, is wondering if there's a word for that sort of insanity and if it's true that more people commit murder and suicide in the summer, when the phone begins to ring in the next room.

It'll stop soon, he thinks, no more than six or seven rings even if the caller is very determined, even if it's his mother or the landlord because he's two months behind on the rent. So Elvin sits staring at the sun and the city, counting the shrill telephone rings. Five, six, seven, and there, *that* ought to convince them that he's not at home or at least that he has no intention of picking up. But then it rings again, eight, and again, nine, and he frowns and spits out the window; Elvin gets up, and by the time he makes it all the way out to the coffee table with the old black rotary phone it's rung exactly thirteen times. He isn't superstitious, but he waits until it rings once more, just in case.

"Are you drunk or something?" Shanna asks, her voice small and tinny and seeming farther away than it should.

"No, I'm not drunk," he says, too relieved it isn't his mother or the landlord to be annoyed that it's Shanna. "I'm only medium rare. I won't be drunk for at least another hour and a half."

"Ha ha," she says and clicks her tongue against the roof of her mouth.

"What do you want, Shanna? I'm not coming in today, so don't even ask."

"I wasn't going to, asshole," and there's a pause then, familiar pause that he knows means she's working up to something, and maybe she's only going to ask if she can borrow twenty bucks or if he still knows someplace cheap to score a bag of weed. Maybe she wants to borrow twenty bucks to *buy* a bag of weed, he thinks, and reads the cover of an old issue of *Wired* while he waits for her to get it over with.

"I'm not getting any younger, Ladybug," he says, and she clicks her tongue at him again.

"Day before yesterday," Shanna says, "Monday afternoon, you were pointing at something out back of the store. Do you remember doing that?"

"Yeah," Elvin mumbles, "I remember," and that's the first time he's thought about the damned thing since leaving the store on Tuesday; he wishes Shanna were standing in the room with him so he could kick her in the ankle just for reminding him.

"It was just a mud hole, wasn't it?"

And there's a cold, empty feeling deep in his belly then, his guts full of ice water even if the weathermen will be frying eggs sunny side up on the hoods of cars on the six o'clock news.

"Elvin? It was, wasn't it?"

"So what," he says, trying too hard to sound like he really doesn't care. "I was pointing at a mud puddle behind the store."

"Do you even know the last time it rained?"

"I think Noah was building an ark," and oh, Christ, that was clever, he thinks, that was smoother than oyster shit on greased Teflon, and starts reading the magazine cover over again.

"Well, *I* know how long its been. I checked," Shanna says, and she's whispering now, like Mr. Culliver's walked up, or there's a customer at the register, someone she doesn't want to hear what she's saying.

"I left something on the stove," Elvin says, glancing towards the kitchenette, the dirty dishes heaped in the sink, the garbage can overflowing with fast-food bags and beer cans and Chinese take-out boxes.

There's another long pause from the other end of the line, and Shanna clicks her tongue twice. "Sure," she says, sounding nervous, almost sounding scared, but that might just be his sweltering imagination, might be nothing more than wishful thinking.

"Look, Shanna, I've *got* to go. Right now. A pot's about to boil over."

"August third," she whispers. "That's the last time it rained, Elvin. Seventeen days ago," and then Shanna hangs up before he can say anything else. And Elvin stands there holding the telephone receiver and feeling like an asshole, listening to the insistent dial tone and staring out the living room window at the endless fireball day.

Almost four o'clock on Thursday afternoon, and they're sitting together on the back steps of the bookstore, smoking and watching the puddle. Shanna's holding a black umbrella over both their heads, a stifling scalloped-edged shadow and the two of them huddled underneath. She came by after her Greek and Roman history class let out, rode the bus downtown instead of walking because the air's so bad, and it's better to give up a dollar and a quarter than risk a heat stroke.

The puddle's nearly half as wide as the alley now, five feet across, at least, and the muddy water's gone the mottled black-green of overripe avocado skin.

"Sewage would smell," she says, reluctantly dismissing his latest explanation. "I don't smell anything at all."

"Then maybe it's only water," Elvin says, and cigarette smoke leaks slow from his nostrils and chapped lips. "Maybe the rust or something from the broken pipes is making it turn that color. Doesn't copper make green rust?"

"I don't think they use copper for water pipes. I think it's poisonous."

And then neither of them says anything else for a minute or two, just sit watching the puddle and the sun glistening off the rotten avocado-colored water. The surface of the puddle is perfectly smooth, even though there's a hot wind blowing down the alley today, coughdry wind to send the pages of a discarded newspaper flapping noisily past and stir up clouds of grit and dust.

Shanna sighs, a long, exhausted sigh, and Elvin takes his eyes off the puddle and looks at her; she's staring down at the scuffed leather toes of her boots, and there's a fat bead of sweat dangling from the end of her nose.

"When I was a little girl, I had a Dr. Seuss book," she says and "Yeah, *Green Eggs and Ham*," Elvin says for no particular reason, just the first Dr. Seuss book that comes to mind, and she shakes her head. The drop of sweat falls off the tip of her nose and leaves a dark splotch on the knee of her blue jeans.

"No, Elvin, it wasn't *Green Eggs and Ham.* I never had a copy of *Green Eggs and Ham.* It was called *McElligot's Pool.*"

"I don't think I remember that one," he says.

"It was about this pool, and this kid that was trying to catch fish out of it, even though everyone kept telling him there was nothing in McElligot's Pool but old bottles and cans and shit."

"So, did he ever catch anything?"

"No, but that's not the point of the story. He kept saying how maybe the pool might be connected to an underground river that ran all the way to the sea, and there was no telling what was at the other end, what might come swimming up into McElligot's Pool if he sat there with his fishing pole and waited long enough."

Elvin turns back to the puddle, then, and it hasn't changed at all.

"That damned book used to scare the bejeesus out of me," Shanna says very quietly.

Elvin rubs at his chin, the stubble there like sandpaper to remind him how many days it's been since he's bothered to shave. A lot easier to forget without Shanna around to bitch about his beard scratching her face. "This is fucking bullshit," he says and puts out his cigarette on the side of the steps. There's a broken broom handle leaning against the wall of the bookstore, and Elvin reaches for it, ducks out of the sanctuary shade of the umbrella and walks quickly to the edge of the puddle.

"What are you doing?" she asks, but he doesn't answer her, his heart beating too fast now, adrenaline and the faintest silver taste at the back of his tongue like a new filling. Fucking ridiculous, scaring themselves like children telling spooky stories when it's just a goddamn mud hole, a busted pipe or something, and Elvin holds the broom handle right out over the puddle, as close to the middle as he can reach.

"Elvin, just come back and leave it alone, okay?" but he ignores her and lets go of the broom handle instead, and it sinks straight down into the dark puddle and disappears. Not even so much as a splash or a ripple, only those restless, iridescent greens and blues and reds writhing across the water. *Dragonfly colors,* he thinks, *June bug colors,* and he stands there, waiting for the broom handle to pop back up again, because it doesn't matter how *deep* the thing is, wood still fucking floats.

"Come on, Elvin. Let's go back inside now," Shanna says. "Mr. Culliver will be wanting to close up soon," and she's standing beside him, shielding him from the laughing sun with her big black umbrella. "It isn't ever coming back," she says and takes his hand, her sweatslicked palm against his, and when he's sure that she's right, Elvin steps away from the edge of the puddle and lets her lead him back inside.

"It's gone," she says again. "It's just *gone.*" Elvin is standing with Shanna on the sidewalk outside Second Chance, and the wind blowing down the street smells like rain and lightning. It's Friday afternoon, and the sky hangs low and furious above the sunblind city, the violetredyellowchartreuse sky like an old bruise, something beaten and battered and finally, *finally,* This is enough, it might have said, and the civil defense sirens have been wailing their tornado-warning cries for almost an hour.

"Just come and see for yourself," and she herds him roughly through the front door of the shop; the brass cowbell nailed above the door jangles loud, and now there's the musty, wordy smell of books instead of the smell of rain. Past a bargain bin of coverless paperback mysteries and romance novels, between the towering, overcrowded shelves of science and history, philosophy and more occult conceits, and she's squeezing his hand so hard it almost hurts. Shanna tugs and hurries him through the inkscarred, pagepressed belly of the shop and right back out its ass, and then they're standing on the steps and the air smells like rain again.

"See? It was still here this morning, Elvin, but now, now it's just fucking gone," and she sounds frightened and confused and disappointed all at the same time.

He stares up at the stormy sky and then back down at the alley, the very dry place where the mud puddle was the day before, and the day before that. But now there's only an empty pothole no bigger around than a hubcap, no deeper than any pothole has a right to be, and "Let go of my hand," he says, and she does.

"I heard something back here, and when I came to see, it was gone. Have you ever heard a rabbit screaming?"

"No," he tells her, because he hasn't and never wants to, and in a few more minutes the rain begins to fall, light at first, then in sheets, and they stand together behind the bookstore and watch as the hole fills up again with nothing but rainwater and the soggy bits of trash washing down the alley.

Afterword

"Standing Water" was written early in September 2000. There were two notable and fairly transparent sources of inspiration for this story, the first being Dr. Seuss' *McElligot's Pool* (actually mentioned) and the other being Kathe Koja's excellent first novel, *The Cipher*. In this story, I wanted to explore a "wrong thing," one that might be only the visible tip of something enormous, but do it on a small scale in a somewhat matter-of-fact way. The cosmic as seen through the lens of the mundane. And what could be more mundane than a mud puddle? The alley in the story was only a few blocks from the loft where I was living at the time, and I passed the pothole in question repeatedly that summer. Mercifully, it was always dry.

LA MER DES RÊVES

"**A**YE, THERE'S THE VERY reef what scuttled the *Asrai* back in '89," the fisherman says. "There's her bowsprit, poking up above the waves," and Emmie opens her eyes to see. Salt spray like icebitter needles against her face, the clammy, armored thing still wrapped up tight in her arms, and she blinks as the room undissolves, congeals around her. Four stark walls the color of nothing healthy and the door to the hall, long hall of closed and threatful doors and a stairway crouched at one end. The flat she shares with Caroline, their mattresses and brown paper grocery bags of filthy clothes, the candle stubs and windows all painted black so the winterpale Boston sun can't get in.

If it were only disappointment, falling from the old man's weathered, sailorvoice to this ugliness and the dank, infection-sour smells that seem to seep from the plaster walls—if it were *only* that, she might feel no more or less cheated than any other junky dragged back into the waking, conscious world. She might sit and stare vacantly at the door, shivering beneath her orange blanket, burntorange wool with leaping white rabbits, and no emotion but the sicksweat fear that Caroline may not come back this time, the anger that she hasn't come back already, and in a little while Emmie will start to hurt.

But it isn't only that.

"Mr. Gearty?" she whispers, her breath a handful of fog in the freezing air, and she pulls the blanket up around her ears. "Mr. Gearty, I think I've slipped away again."

The January-raw wind like hungry dogs slinking around the brick and mortar corners of the building, and she closes her eyes.

"I didn't mean to, I swear to god almighty I didn't mean to go," straining to sound as sincere as she can remember how to sound, and then she can hear the waves somewhere behind the wind and not so very far away after all. Thinnest drift-net membrane cast for her, flung across the wide gulf between *Here* and *There*, and all she has to do is listen, just shut up and pay attention to the rise and fall, rise and fall, rise and fall of the stormweary sea so the mackerel-tangled weave can snag her.

"You gotta keep an eye on that undertow, missy," the fisherman says. "Gets its hooks into you, it'll carry you all the way down to hell and Davy Jones."

And the little boat bobs and rolls on the water like a toy while the old man fusses with the sail, tattered lateen canvas and his hands cracked and bleeding from the ropes. Her and the huge seahorse huddled together in the bow and Mr. Gearty in his yellow southwester cap, Mr. Gearty like an ad for frozen fish sticks.

"The *Asrai* was just rounding the Cobb there," he shouts, shouts to be heard, and points a crooked finger towards the horizon, pointing straight into the silverblack heart of the storm, and Emmie squints but all she sees is the restless blur of rain and sea and sky.

"Lost her foresail and got turned round with the wind on her port side," and then the sea lifts the little boat high on the crest of a wave, and the old man curses to himself, wrestles with the backstay as they ride swiftly down into the next trough.

The seahorse struggles in her arms, rolls its dark and cowsad eyes, and Emmie wishes she could think of anything at all to say so it wouldn't be so afraid; one word of comfort, and "That's what done her in," the old man says. "Got dragged up on the rocks and had her belly ripped out."

The seahorse makes a sound like a small child whistling and curls its long tail around Emmie's bare ankle.

"Shhh," she whispers, her chapped lips pressed against the slippery place an ear should be, if fish had ears. "We're almost there. It's almost over now," but the seahorse doesn't hear her, or it doesn't understand, or it simply doesn't believe a word she's saying.

The wind rustling through canvas like the flutter of terrible wings, like the dark birds hanging low above the place where the sea batters itself against the shore, and Mr. Gearty chews at his pipe and shakes his head.

"She's expectin' us," he says.

"Maybe they haven't seen us yet," Emmie replies, even though she knows better. Knows that the terns and gulls and snake-necked cormorants, the kestrels and clockwork ravens are all the Duchess' willing, eager eyes.

"Eh? What's that?" and he spares her a quick, disapproving glance.

"We might be lucky," Emmie whispers, and the seahorse whistles again. "We might."

"If we drown 'fore she finds us, aye, that we might, missy. I wager the Lady's at the headlands by now. She'll have the black gulpers and the bristlemouths—"

A crackling roar from the sky, then, so she can't hear the rest, and the next wave tips the skiff perilously to starboard, tosses it, and the greedy sea is sloshing in; all the fisherman's junk in the bottom washing around and rattling about, an oar and an empty lobster pot, his tackle box and the pear-shaped Spanish mandolin.

"Easy!" he shouts. "Easy there now! Ye watch yourself back there!"

But Emmie slips anyway, and the seahorse lands on top of her, pricklesharp spines to jab and slice her flesh, to tear the clinging fabric of her soggy dress, and both of them floundering helpless for a long, long second or two while her mouth and nose fill up with brine and her eyes are burning from the salt. She coughs, spits out a mouthful of ocean, and the boat rolls violently to port before Mr. Gearty finds a patch of calmer water, a fleeting pocket of saner wind.

And the old woman opens her eyes in the hospital-white room and listens to the mechanical sounds of the machines that keep her alive, that breathe for her and piss for her and strain the poisons from her blood. Woman as old and brittle as the last day of November. Tears streaming from her amber-cloudy eyes and her mouth too dry to speak, her tongue an Arabian desert, but the dream so much more real than these antiseptic walls, the fluorescent ceiling, and *Find me quick*, she thinks. *Find me quick, Mr. Gearty.*

And the Duchess, then, the ebony and crimson-scaled Lady of Abyssal Plains, the Dowager Oneirodes muttering across the worlds, words to burst like fat and greasy bubbles inside Emmie's head—*Stay awake, old woman. Stay awake, or we'll make a basket from your ribs. We'll plant coral and anemones in your shriveled skull.*

We'll leave you here.

And the pretty, young woman in her white nurse's uniform and squeaky nurse shoes bending over Emmie, woman with round sand-dollar eyes and hair the greenbrown of a kelp forest. Her suctioncup fingertips at Emmie's thin wrist and something scribbled on a clipboard; she smiles a lipless barracuda smile, and "Are we feeling better this morning, Miss Carmichael?" she asks. "Are we having bad dreams again?"

"*There!*" Mr. Gearty shouts, the storm snatching at his voice, and Emmie sees it; past the tall and jagged stacks like Neptune's rotting teeth, the towering sea arch where shale and sandstone have been carved away by a hundred thousand merciless years of wind and rain, frost and waves. The high rock span and the current driving them towards it, as if it knows, as if that one thing in all the wide and godforsaken sea has taken their side. The birds wheel above the little boat, screeching their shrill warnings and alarms for the Lady's blackguard, and the old man curses at them and gives the backstay more slack.

You don't have to die with him, the Duchess whispers, her voice laced between the freezing drops of rain. *We can forgive everything. We can send you home.*

"Hurry, Mr. Gearty," she says, and the seahorse shudders in her arms. "She's found me. She's found us all."

He coughs, wipes water from his eyes, and nods to show that yes, he's heard her; the lunatic sea beneath them heaves and roils like the draining edge of a flat planet, last cataract before the endless plunge through stars and the gaseous skeletons of stars. Final nightmare that would be kinder than whatever's waiting for them, and Emmie hugs the seahorse and whispers a half-remembered prayer.

A hundred ships gone down in this narrow cove, a hundred barques and brigs and sleekhulled schooners, brigantines and whaling boats, so what's this tiny bucket of kindling and pitch against those odds? What's one old fisherman against the lost souls of captains and admirals and pirate kings?

Open your eyes, my dear. We'll look the other way.

And the ocean parts for them, then, splits itself wide like Moses raising his arms and God on his side; Mr. Gearty turns and shouts something that Emmie can't understand as the boat tilts forward and slips suddenly down the steep and frothing face of the water, racing itself down towards the bottom of the sea.

Emmie makes a grab for the tiller, desperate, clumsy lunge and losing her grip on the seahorse, anyway, the terrified, whistling animal sliding helpless from her arms, and she only succeeds in knocking a pencil off the edge of her desk. It clatters to the floor and rolls a few feet, just out of reach, and she looks up to see if Dr. Farish has noticed.

"So, it then becomes a question of precisely what the image of the siren, the nymph, and the mermaid meant to all these *fin de siècle* painters," he says. "And to poets like Silvestre and Swinburne, as well."

Emmie leaves the fallen pencil where it is and stares out the third-floor classroom window at Washington Square, instead, the Manhattan late afternoon sun turning the weathered white marble of the Arch the softest shades of gold. Trying to remember something that seemed so important only a moment ago, something forgotten but its aftertaste lingering on the tip of her tongue, and "Duplicity and seduction," Dr. Farish says, "and the essentially cold-blooded, predatory nature of women, unrealized by the naive fisherboys."

A small bird at the window then, a wren or a sparrow, and Emmie wouldn't know the difference, ornithology never one of her strong points, and it hops about on the sill and pecks once or twice at the smudgy glass.

See, child? You can have this life, if you want it. You can have any life you ask for. Any life at all.

A moment's panic for such a strange thought, strange and ravenous voice speaking without words from somewhere behind her eyes, or the bird is talking, and she opens her mouth to scream and vomits saltwater. Hot bile and a cold bellyful of the Atlantic gushing past her lips, her throat on fire, and then she lies down on her side in the stinking mud and seafloor slime and waits for the roaring, whirling walls of the maelstrom to collapse. Waits for the bewitched water to fall in a final, crushing curtain, and then she can finally be dead, and no one can ever say she didn't try.

She can see the shattered keel of the little boat half-buried in the mud, the greygreen slurry of silt and living ooze, dying fish and the wriggling bodies of spider crabs and trilobites, squid and moray eels all snarled in the stranded, sargassum tangle. And the fisherman, too, on his knees and one of the anchor's iron flukes driven through his chest, his head flung back as if one last view of forfeited Heaven might redeem them all. Dark blood trickles from his mouth and into his beard, and his eyes are wide and empty as the sky far, far above them. But there's no sign of the seahorse anywhere, her charge shepherded halfway around the globe, so maybe it escaped, she thinks. Maybe they haven't failed, after all, and even now the Duchess is fleeing back into the depths, dragging her demons and blackguard with her.

No worse than any other lie that Emmie's told herself, and she doesn't shut her eyes or look away as the Lady rises from behind the ruined skiff, spreads her stickling angelfins and lifts the severed head of the seahorse in one webbed and phosphorescent hand.

"We would have kept our promises to you, dear," she says, her voice the sound of continents tearing themselves apart to drift and air bubbling from the lungs of drowning men. "A billion worlds, a hundred billion lives merely for the asking. We didn't want to see you come to this."

Mr. Gearty makes a rheumy, strangling noise that might have been words or only his last, hemorrhaging breath, raises his left hand, and Emmie sees the big boning knife clutched in his fist a second before the Duchess reaches down and tears the old fisherman in half. She steps over the body, bluepink intestine loops and wet white bone, and kneels in the mud beside Emmie.

"Did you think we were lying to you, child?" the witch asks her, something like regret pooled in her sharkflat eyes, and "No," Emmie says. "No, Lady. But I had to be sure. I had to make the right choice. And I had to find my own way."

And, in the end, the trick so much easier than she ever would have dared imagine. The gauzy smell of thunder and pain like chitinous fingers pinching at her heart, pinching at her soul; the Duchess' long jaws swing open, slackjawed understanding come too late, and it's over before she can scream, before she even begins to believe what's happening, and Emmie stands with the seahorse's severed head, staring down at herself writhing broken in the mud.

"You can have *this* life," she says, "if you want it," and the Duchess looks back up at her from Emmie's own discarded eyes. Blue eyes filled to overflowing with simple, mortal horror as the whirlpool spins around once more, one last, clockwise revolution as the magic frays, and the sea finds gravity again and crashes down upon them.

Afterword

"La Mer des Rêves" was written in December 2000 and completed on Decmber 29th. It was originally intended for an anthology of short fiction inspired by the work of William Hope Hodgson. When that project was shelved, the story was published in John Pelan's *A Walk on the Darkside: Visions of Horror* (2004). In truth, though, the inspiration for this piece lies more with a Christmas card I'd recieved that year from Rick Lieder and Kathe Koja than in the maritime tales of Hodgson. The card, which features Rick's art and which, unfortunately, I seem to have misplaced, bears a black-and-white illustration of a boat on a stormy sea, and inside the boat is an old fisherman, a young girl, and a very large seahorse. The image was the germ for this story. In some ways which are likely obvious, *"La Mer des Rêves"* prefigures some of what I'd do a couple of years later in *Murder of Angels*. This may be my shortest work of fiction.

THE ROAD OF PINS

May

WITHOUT A DOUBT, Mr. Perrault's paintings are some of the most hideous things that Alex has ever seen, and if her head didn't hurt so much, if it hadn't been hurting all day long, she might have kept her opinions to herself, might have made it all the way through the evening without pissing Margot off again. The first Thursday of the month so another opening night at Artifice, another long evening of forced smiles for the aesthete zombies, the shaking of hands and digging about for dusty scraps of congeniality when all she wants is to be home soaking in a hot, soapy bath or lying facedown on the cool hardwood floor of their bedroom while Margot massages her neck. Maybe something quiet playing on the stereo, something soothing, and the volume so low there's almost no sound at all, Nina Simone or Billie Holiday, and then her headache would slowly begin to pull its steelburr fingers out of the soft places behind her eyes, and she could breathe again.

"You shouldn't have even come tonight," Margot whispers, sips cheap white wine from a plastic cup and stares glumly at the floor. "If you were going to be like this, I wish you'd gone home, instead."

"You and me both, baby," and Alex frowns and looks past her lover at the smartly dressed crowd milling about the little gallery like a wary flock of pigeons.

"So why don't you leave? I can get a taxi home, or Paul will be happy to give me a ride," and now Alex thinks that Margot's starting to sound even more impatient with her than usual, probably afraid that someone might have overheard the things she said about the paintings.

"I'm here now," Alex says. "I suppose I might as well stick it out," and she rubs roughly at the aching space between her eyebrows, squints across the room at the high white walls decorated with Perrault's canvases, the tracklights to fix each murky scene in its own warm incandescent pool.

"Then will you please try to stop sulking. Talk to someone. I have to get back to work."

Alex shrugs noncommittally, and Margot turns and walks away, threading herself effortlessly into the murmuring crowd. Almost at once, a man in a banana-yellow turtleneck sweater and tight black jeans stops her, and he points at one of the paintings. Margot nods her head and smiles for him, already wearing her Pleasant Face again, annoyance tucked safe behind the mask, and the man smiles back at her and nods his head, too.

Five minutes later, and Alex has made her way across the gallery, another cup of the dry, slightly bitter Chardonnay in her hand, her fourth in half an hour, but it hasn't helped her head at all, and she wishes she had a gin and tonic, instead. She's been eavesdropping, listening in on an elderly German couple even though she doesn't speak a word of German. The man and woman are standing close together before one of the larger paintings; the same sooty blur of oils as all the rest, at least a thousand shades of grey, faint rumors of green and alabaster, and a single crimson smudge floating near the center. The small printed card on the wall beside the canvas reads

84

Fecunda ratis, no date, no price, and Alex wonders if the old man and woman understand Latin any better than she understands German.

The man takes a sudden, deep breath then, hitching breath almost like the space between sobs, and holds one hand out, as if he intends to touch the canvas, to press his thick fingertips to the whirling chaos of charcoal brush strokes. But the woman stops him, her nervous hand at his elbow, hushed words passed between them, and in a moment they've wandered away, and Alex is left standing alone in front of the painting.

She takes a swallow of wine, grimacing at the taste, and tries to concentrate on the painting, tries to *see* whatever all the others seem to see; the red smudge for a still point, nexus or fulcrum, and she thinks maybe it's supposed to be a cap or a hat, crimson wool cap stuck on the head of the nude girl down on her hands and knees, head bowed so that her face is hidden, only a wild snarl of hair and the cruel, incongruent red cap. There are dark, hulking forms surrounding the girl, and at first glance Alex thought they were only stones, some crude, megalithic ring, standing stones, but now she sees that they're meant to be beasts of some sort. Great, shaggy things squatting on their haunches, watching the girl, protective or imprisoning captors, and perhaps this is the final, lingering moment before the kill.

"Amazing, isn't it?" and Alex hadn't realized that the girl was standing there beside her until she spoke. Pretty black girl with four silver rings in each earlobe, and she has blue eyes.

"No, actually," Alex says. "I think it's horrible," never mind what Margot would *want* her to say; her head hurts too much to lie, and she doesn't like the way the painting is making her feel. Her stomach is sour from the migraine and the bitter Chardonnay.

"Yes, it is, isn't it," the black girl says, undaunted, and she leans closer to the canvas. "We saw this one in San Francisco last year. Sometimes, I dream about it. I've written two poems about this piece."

"No kidding," Alex replies, not trying very hard to hide her sarcasm, and she scans the room but there's no sign of Margot anywhere. She catches a glimpse of the artist, though—tall, scarecrow-thin and rumpled man in a shiny black suit that looks too big for him. He's talking with the German couple. Or he's only listening to them talk to him, or pretending to, standing with his long arms crossed and no particular expression on his sallow face. Then the crowd shifts, and she can't see him anymore.

"You're Alex Marlowe, aren't you? Margot's girlfriend?" the black girl asks, and "Yeah," Alex says. "That's me," and the girl smiles and laughs a musical, calculated sort of a laugh.

"I liked your novel a lot," she says. "Aren't you ever going to write another one?"

"Well, my agent doesn't think so," and maybe the girl can see how much Alex would rather talk about almost anything else in the world, and she laughs again.

"I'm Jude Sinclair. I'm writing a review of the show for *Artforum*. You don't care very much for Perrault's work, I take it."

"I'm pretty sure I'm not supposed to have opinions about painting, Jude. That's strictly Margot's department—"

"But you *don't* like it, do you?" Jude says, pressing the point and her voice lower now, and there's something almost conspiratorial in the tone. A wry edge to her smile, and she glances back at *Fecunda ratis*.

"No," Alex says. "I'm sorry. I don't."

"I'm not sure I did either, not at first. But he gets in your head. The first time I saw a Perrault, I thought it was contrived, too self-consciously retro. I thought, this guy wants to be Edvard Munch and Van Gogh and Albert Pinkham Ryder all rolled into one. I thought he was way too hung up on Romanticism."

"So are those things supposed to be bears?" Alex asks, pointing at one of the looming objects that isn't a megalith, and Jude Sinclair shakes her head. "No," she says. "They're wolves."

"Well, they don't look like wolves to me," and then Jude takes her hand and leads Alex to the next painting, this one barely half the size of the last. A sky the sickly color of sage and olives, ocher and cheese draped above a withered landscape, a few stunted trees in the foreground and their bare and crooked branches claw vainly at an irrevocable Heaven. Between their trunks the figure of a woman is visible in the middle distance, lean and twisted as the blighted limbs of the trees, and she's looking apprehensively over her shoulder at something the artist has only hinted at, shadows of shadows crouched menacingly at the lower edges of the canvas. The card on the wall next to the painting is blank except for a date—1893. Jude points out a yellowed strip of paper pasted an inch or so above the woman's head, narrow strip not much larger than a fortune-cookie prognostication.

"Read it," she says, and Alex has to bend close because the words are very small, and she isn't wearing her glasses.

"No. Read it out loud."

Alex sighs, quickly growing very tired of this, but "'A woman in a field,'" she says. "'Something grabbed her,'" and then she reads it over again to herself, just in case she missed the sense of it the first time. "What the hell is that supposed to mean?"

"It's from a book by a man named Charles Hoy Fort. Have you ever heard of him?"

"No," Alex says, "I haven't." She looks back down at the woman standing in the wide and barren field beyond the trees, and the longer she stares, the more frightened the woman seems to be. Not merely apprehensive, no, genuinely terrified, and she would run, Alex thinks, she would run away as fast as she could, but she's too afraid to even move. Too afraid of whatever she sees waiting there in the shadows beneath the trees, and the painter has trapped her in this moment forever.

"I hadn't either, before Perrault. There are passages from Fort in most of these paintings. Sometimes they're hard to find."

Alex takes a step back from the wall, her mouth gone dry as dust and wishing she had more of the wine, wishing she had a cigarette, wondering if Judith Sinclair smokes.

"His genius—Perrault's, I mean—lies in what he *suggests*," the black girl says, and her blue eyes sparkle like gems. "What he doesn't have to *show* us. He understands that our worst fears come from the pictures that we make in our heads, not from anything he could ever paint."

"I'm sorry," Alex says, not exactly sure what she's apologizing for this time, but it's the only thing she can think to say, her head suddenly too full of the frightened woman and the writhing, threatful trees, the pain behind her eyes swelling, and she only knows for certain that she doesn't want to look at any more of these ridiculous paintings. That they make her feel unclean, almost as if by simply seeing them she's played some unwitting part in their creation.

"There's nothing to be sorry for," Jude says. "It's pretty heady stuff. My boyfriend can't stand Perrault, won't even let me *talk* about him."

And Alex says something polite then, nice to meet you, good luck with the review, see you around, something she doesn't mean and won't remember later, and she leaves the girl still gazing at the painting labeled *1893*. On the far side of the gallery, Margot is busy smiling for the scarecrow in his baggy black suit, and Alex slips unnoticed through the crowd, past another dozen of Albert Perrault's carefully hung grotesques, the ones she hasn't examined and doesn't ever want to; she keeps her eyes straight ahead until she's made it through the front door and is finally standing alone on the sidewalk outside Artifice, breathing in the safe and stagnant city smells of the warm Atlanta night.

June

The stuffy little screening room on Peachtree Street reeks of ancient cigarette smoke and the sticky, fermenting ghosts of candy and spilled sodas, stale popcorn and the fainter, musky scent of human sweat. Probably worse things, too, this place a porn theater for more than a decade before new management and the unprofitable transition from skin flicks to art-house cinema. Alex sits alone in the back row, and there are only eleven or twelve other people in the theater, pitiful Saturday night turnout for a Bergman double-feature. She's stopped wondering if Margot's ever going to show, stopped wondering that halfway through the third reel of *Wild Strawberries*, and she knows that if she goes to the pay phone outside the lobby, if she stands in the rain and calls their apartment, she'll only get the answering machine.

Later, of course, Margot will apologize for standing her up, will explain how she couldn't get away from the gallery because the carpenters tore out a wall when they were only supposed to mark studs, or the security system is on the fritz again and she had to wait two hours for a service tech to show. Nothing that could possibly be helped, but she's sorry anyway, and these things wouldn't happen, she'll say, if Alex would carry a cell phone or a least a pager.

Wild Strawberries has ended, and after a ten- or fifteen-minute intermission, the house lights have gone down again, a long moment of darkness marred only by the bottle-green glow of an exit sign before the screen is washed in a flood of light so brilliant that it hurts Alex's eyes. She blinks at the countdown leader, five, four, three, the staccato beep at two, one, and then the grainy black-and-white picture. No front titles—a man carrying a wooden staff walks slowly across a scrubby, rock-strewn pasture, and a dog trails close behind him. The man is dressed in peasant clothes, at least the way that European peasants dress in old Hollywood movies, and when he reaches the crest of a hill, he stops and looks down at something out of frame, something hidden from the audience. His lips part, and his eyes grow wide, an expression that is anger and surprise, disgust and horror all at the same time. There's no sound but his dog barking and the wind.

"Hey, what is *this* shit?" someone shouts near the front of the theater, a fat man, and he stands and glares up at the projection booth. Some of the others have started mumbling, confused or annoyed whispers, and Alex has no idea what the film is, only that it isn't *The Seventh Seal*. On-screen, the camera cuts away from the peasant, and now there's a close-up of a dead animal, instead, a ragged, woolly mass streaked with gore the color of molasses; it takes her a second or two to realize that it's a sheep. Its throat has been ripped out, and its tongue lolls from its mouth. The camera pulls back as the man kneels beside the dead animal, then cuts to a close-up of the dog. It's stopped barking and licks at its lips.

"Jesus fucking *Christ*," the fat man growls, and then he storms up the aisle, past Alex and out the swinging doors to the lobby. No one else leaves their seat, though a few heads have turned to watch the fat man's exit. Someone laughs nervously, and on-screen the peasant has lifted the dead sheep in his arms, is walking quickly away from the camera, and his dog follows close behind. The camera lingers as the man grows smaller and smaller in the distance, and the ground where the sheep lay glistens wetly.

A woman sitting a couple of seats in front of Alex turns around, and "Do *you* have any idea at all what this is?" she asks.

"No," Alex replies. "No, I don't."

The woman frowns and sighs loudly. "The projectionist must have made a mistake," she says and turns back towards the screen before Alex can say anything else.

When the man and the dog have shrunk to bobbing specks,

the camera finally cuts away, trades the stony pasture, the blood-soaked patch of grass, for a close-up of a church steeple and the cacophony of tolling bells spills out through tinny stereo speakers and fills the theater.

"Well, this isn't what I paid six dollars to see," the woman two seats in front of Alex grumbles.

The fat man doesn't come back, and if the projectionist *has* made a mistake, no one seems to be in much of a hurry to correct it. The audience has grown quiet again, apparently more curious than perturbed, and the film moves from scene to scene, flickering progression of images and story, dialogue pared to little more than whispers and occasional, furtive glances between the actors. A mountain village and a wolf killing sheep somewhere that might be France or Italy, but impossible to tell because everyone speaks with British accents. The peasant man from the opening scene (if that truly *was* the opening scene) has a blind daughter who spends her days inside their little house gazing out a window, as though she could see the mountains in the distance.

"Ingmar Bergman didn't make this film," the woman sitting in front of Alex says conclusively. "I don't know who made this film," and then someone turns and asks her to stop talking, please.

Finally, a young boy is found dead, and a frantic hunt for the wolf ensues, night and wrathful villagers with torches, hounds and antique rifles wandering through a mist-shrouded forest. It's obvious that this scene was shot on a soundstage, the contorted, nightmare trees too bizarre to possibly be real, nothing but plywood and chicken wire and papier-mâché. Some of the trunks, the tortuous limbs, are undoubtedly meant to suggest random scraps of human anatomy—the arch of a spine, a pair of arms ending in gnarled roots, a female torso sprouting half-formed from the bole of an oak.

And Alex thinks that maybe there's something big skulking

along through the gloom just beyond the wavering light of the torches, insinuation of spiderlong legs, and sometimes it seems to move a little ahead of the hunters, other times it trails behind.

The woman seated two rows in front of Alex makes a disgusted, exasperated sound and stands up, her silhouette momentarily eclipsing the screen. "This is absurd," she says. "I'm asking for my money back right now," speaking to no one or to everyone who might be listening. She leaves the theater, and someone down front laughs, and "Good fucking riddance," a husky male voice whispers.

On-screen, a shout, the bonewet snap of living wood, and one of the villagers raises his gun, extreme close-up of his finger around the trigger before the boom and flash of gunpowder. The tinny speakers blare rifle fire and the furious barking of dogs, so loud that Alex puts her hands over her ears. A man screams and the scene dissolves, then, fades away to daylight and a high-angle view of a dirt road winding across the fields towards the village. The camera zooms slowly in on a small gathering of peasant women waiting at the end of the road; silent despair in their weathered faces, loss, resignation, fear, and one by one they turn and walk back towards their homes.

Alex squints down at her watch, leans forward in her seat and angles her wrist towards the screen, the greysilver light off the scratched crystal so she can read the black hour and minute hands. Only half an hour since the film began, though it seems like it's been much longer, and she wonders if Margot is home yet. She thinks again about the pay phone outside the theater, about the gallery and the answering machine.

She glances back at the screen, and now there's a close-up of a skull, a sheep's, perhaps, but Alex isn't sure; bone bleached dry and stark as chalk, a leathery patch of hide still clinging to its muzzle, the empty sockets for eyes that have rotted away or been eaten by insects and crows. The lonely sound of the wind, and the film cuts to the peasant's blind daughter, a music box playing the theme from *Swan Lake* softly in the background, and she stares out the window of her dead father's house. She's neither smiling nor does she look unhappy, her hands folded neatly in her lap, and then a man is speaking from somewhere behind her. The cold, guttural voice so entirely unexpected that Alex jumps, startled, and she misses the first part of it, whatever was said before the girl turns her head towards the unseen speaker, raises a hand and places one index finger to the center of her forehead.

"I saw the light again last night," she says, the milky, colorless cataracts to prove that she's a liar or insane, and then the girl's hand returns to her lap. "Floating across the meadow," she adds.

The music box stops abruptly, and now there's the small, hard sound of a dog barking far, far away.

"Who are you? Your hand is cold—"

"Which road will you take?" the guttural voice asks, interrupting her. "That of the needles or that of the pins?"

She turns to the window again, imperfect, transparent mirror for her plain face, and for an instant there seems to be another reflection there, a lean and hungry shadow crouched close behind the blind girl's chair. And then there's a popping, fluttering racket from the projection booth as the world is swallowed in pure white light, and Alex knows that the film hasn't ended, it's merely *stopped* as inexplicably as it began.

The house lights come up, and she keeps her seat, sits waiting for her eyes to adjust as the handful of people remaining in the theater stands and begins to drift towards the lobby doors, confused and thoughtful faces, overheard bits of conjecture and undisguised bewilderment.

"It could've been Robert Florey," a man who looks like a college professor says to a blonde girl in a KMFDM T-shirt, slender girl young enough to be his daughter, and "Do you know, Florey, dear?" he asks. "I've always heard there was a lost Florey out there somewhere."

"Well, they might have told us they didn't have *The Seventh Seal*," another man complains. "They could have said *something.*"

And when they've all gone, and Alex is alone with the matte-black walls and the sugar-and-vinegar theater smells, she sits and stares at the blank screen for another minute, trying to be cetain what she saw, or didn't see, at the end.

July

Margot away for the entire week, a lecture series in Montreal—"Formalism, Expressionism, and the Post-Modernist Denial," according to the flier stuck to the refrigerator with a magnet shaped like an apple core—and Alex left alone in the Midtown condo paid for with the advance money from *The Boats of Morning.* Four days now since she's gone any farther than the row of mailboxes in the building's lobby. Too hot to go out if she doesn't absolutely have to, eggs frying on sidewalks out there, so she stays half-drunk on Absolut and grapefruit juice, smokes too much and watches black-and-white movies on television. Whatever it takes not to think about the typewriter in her office down the hall from their bedroom, the desk drawer full of blank paper. Margot called on Wednesday night, and they talked for twenty minutes about nothing in particular, which is almost all they ever talk about these days.

"You'd like it here," Margot said. "You'd like the sky here. It's very big and blue."

Late Thursday afternoon, and Alex comes back upstairs with the day's mail, the usual assortment of bills and glossy catalogs, a new *Rolling Stone,* an offer for a platinum Visa card at twenty-one and one-half percent interest. And a large padded envelope the color of a grocery bag. Her name and address are printed neatly on the front in tall, blocky letters—MS. ALEX MARLOWE—and there's no return address, only the initials J. S. written very small in the upper left-hand corner. She leaves everything else on the dining table, a small mountain of unopened mail accumulated there already, debts and distractions for Margot to deal with when she gets home. Alex pours herself a drink, takes the big brown envelope to the sofa in front of the television and opens it with the pull tab on the back. Inside, there's a videocassette, along with a couple of pages of lavender stationary and some newspaper and magazine clippings held together with a lavender paper clip.

Alex sips her drink, the vodka too strong, so she stirs it absently with an index finger and looks down at the top sheet of stationary. It takes her a moment to place the name there— Jude Sinclair—a moment before she remembers the pretty girl from the gallery, dark-skinned, blue-eyed girl who'd tried ardently to explain Albert Perrault's work to her. Alex leans back against the sofa cushions, glancing at the TV screen (an old gangster film she doesn't recognize), and takes another sip from her glass. "Dear Alex," the letter begins, and she notices that it was typed on a typewriter that drops its "t"s.

Dear Alex,

I'm sure that you won't remember me. We talked briefly at the gallery in May. I was the chick with a serious hard-on for M. Perrault. I think I told you that I'd written poems about the "Fecunda ratis," do you remember that? I suspect you may have thought I was a flake. Did you know about P.'s accident?? Terrible. I was at the funeral in Paris. I thought you might want to read one of the poems (I have burned the other one). Hope you are well. My love to Margot.

Jude S.

Alex pulls the pages free of the lavender paper clip, places the first page on the bottom, and the second is the poem, the one Jude Sinclair didn't burn; Alex looks at the black videocassette, considers stuffing it all back into the envelope and tossing the whole mess into the garbage can in the kitchen. Perrault one of the last things she's in the mood to think about right now; she'd almost managed to forget him and his paintings, although Margot talked about him for weeks after the show. They heard about the accident, of course, a motorcycle wreck somewhere in France, and finally, that seemed to close the subject.

Alex takes a long swallow of her drink and scans the first few lines of the short poem, a copy obviously produced on the same typewriter as the letter, the same telltale dropped "t"s and a few inky smudges and fingerprints on the lavender stationary.

"Jesus, who the hell still uses carbon paper," she wonders aloud, setting her drink down on the coffee table, and Alex starts over and reads the poem through from the beginning. "The Night We Found Red Cap" and then a forced and clumsy attempt at Italian sonnet form, eight-line stanza, six-line stanza, to relay Jude Sinclair's slightly stilted, perfectly unremarkable impressions of the painting.

Alex glances quickly through the clippings, then: the *Artforum* review of the show at Artifice, a review of another Perrault exhibit last summer in Manhattan, *Le Monde*'s account of his motorcycle accident, and a short French obituary. And at the bottom of the stack, a photocopy of a very old lithograph; she sets the rest aside and stares at it, a pastoral scene centered around some strange animal that resembles a huge wolf more than anything else she can think of, though it's reared up on its hind limbs and its long, sinuous tail makes her think of a big cat, a lion or a panther, maybe. The creature is attacking a young woman and there are other mutilated bodies scattered about on the ground. In the distance are men wearing tricorne hats on horseback, and the creature has raised its head, is gazing fearlessly over one shoulder towards them. Beneath the scene is the legend, "La Bête du Gévaudan." On the back, someone, presumably Jude Sinclair, has scribbled a date in pencil—1767.

Alex lays the small bundle of paper down on the coffee table and picks up her drink. The glass has left a ring of condensation on the dark wood, the finish already beginning to turn pale and opaque underneath. An heirloom from Margot's grandmother or a great aunt or some such, and she'll have a cow when she sees it, so Alex wipes the water away with the hem of her T-shirt. But the ring stays put, defiant, accusing, condemning tattoo, and she sighs, sits back, and takes another swallow of the vodka and grapefruit juice.

"What are you supposed to be, anyway?" she asks the videotape; no label of any sort on it for an answer, but almost certainly more Perraultiana, an interview, possibly, or maybe something a bit more exotic, more morbid, a news report of his accident taped off TF1 or even footage shot during the funeral. Alex wouldn't be surprised, has seen and heard of worse things being done by art groupies like Jude Sinclair. She decides to save the video for later, a few moments' diversion before bed, leaves it on the couch, and she goes to fix herself a fresh drink.

Something from the freezer for dinner, prepackaged Chinese that came out of the microwave looking nothing at all like the photograph on the cardboard box, Kung Pao pencil erasers and a bottle of beer, and Alex sits on the living room floor, watching *Scooby Doo* on the Cartoon Network. The end of another day that might as well not have happened, more of yesterday and the day before that, the weeks and months since she's finished anything at all piling up so fast that soon it'll have been a year. Today, she stood in the doorway to her office for fifteen minutes and stared uselessly at her typewriter, the vintage Royal she inherited from her father, and she's never been able to write on anything else, the rough clack-clack-clack of steel keys, all the mechanical clicks and clatters and pings to mark her progress down a page, through a scene, the inharmonious chapter to chapter symphony towards conclusion and THE END.

When the beer's gone and she's swallowed enough of the stuff from the freezer to be convinced that she's better off not finishing it, Alex slides her plate beneath the coffee table and retrieves Jude Sinclair's videocassette from the couch. She puts it into the VCR, hits the play button, and in a moment Scooby and Shaggy are replaced by a loud flurry of static. Alex starts to turn down the volume, but the snow and white noise have already been replaced by a silent black screen. She sits watching it, half-curious, impatient, waiting for whatever it is to begin, whatever the blue-eyed girl from the gallery wants her to see.

In the kitchen, the phone rings, and Alex looks away from the television screen, not particularly interested in talking to anyone, and so she thinks she'll let the machine pick up. Third ring, and she turns back to the TV, but it's still just as dark as before, and she checks to be sure that she doesn't have it on pause by mistake. The soft, green glow of digital letters, play and a flashing arrow to let her know that she doesn't, that either the tape's blank or the recording hasn't begun yet. Or maybe Jude Sinclair's filmed a perfectly dark room as a tribute or eulogy to Perrault.

"This is bullshit," Alex mutters, and she presses fast forward. Now the blackness flickers past as the counter tallies all the minutes of nothing stored on the tape. In the kitchen, the telephone rings once more and then the answering machine switches on, Margot's voice reciting their number, politely informing the caller that no one can come to the phone right now, but if you'll please leave your name and number, the date and time, someone will get back to you as soon as possible.

And then Margot answers herself, her voice sounding small and distant, sounding upset, and "Alex?" she says. "Alex, if you're there please pick up, okay? I need to talk to you."

Alex sighs and rubs at her temples. A bright burst of pain behind her left eye, maybe the beginnings of a migraine, and she's really not up to one of Margot's long-distance crises, the two of them yelling at each other with half a continent in between. She glances back to the television screen, presses play and the nothing stops flickering.

"Hello? Alex? Come *on*. I know you're at home. Pick up the damned phone, *please.*"

It really is blank, she thinks. *The crazy bitch sent me a fucking blank videotape.*

"Alex! I'm not kidding, okay? Please answer the goddamn telephone!"

"Alright! Jesus, I'm *coming!*" she shouts at the kitchen, gets up too fast and one foot knocks over the empty beer bottle; it rolls noisily away towards a bookshelf, leaves behind a glistening, semi-circular trickle of liquid as it goes. By the time Alex lifts the receiver, Margot has started crying.

"*What?* What's wrong?"

"Christ, Alex. Why can't you just answer the fucking phone? Why do I have to get fucking hysterical to get you to answer the phone?"

And for a second Alex considers the simple efficacy of a lie, the harmless convenience of *I was on the toilet,* or *I just walked in the front door.* Any plausible excuse to cover her ass.

"I'm sorry," she says, instead. "I've been in a funk all day long. I'm getting a headache. I just didn't want to talk to anyone."

"For fuck's sake, Alex," and then she coughs, and Alex can tell that Margot's trying to stop crying.

"Margot, what's wrong," Alex asks again. "Has something happened?" She wants a cigarette, but she left them in the living room, left her lighter, too, and she settles for chewing on a ragged thumbnail.

"I saw something today," Margot says, speaking very quietly. Alex hears her draw a deep breath, the pause as she holds it in a moment, then the long uneven exhalation, and "I saw something terrible today," she says.

"So what was it? What did you see?"

"A dog attack," and she's almost whispering now. "I saw a little girl attacked by a dog."

For a moment, neither of them says anything, and Alex stares out the window above the kitchen sink at the final indigo and violet dregs of sunset beyond the Atlanta skyline. The pain behind her left eye is back, more persistent than before, keeping time with her heartbeat. She has no idea what to say next, is about to tell Margot that she's sorry, default sentiment better than nothing, better than standing here as the pain in her head gets bigger, listening to the faint electric buzz and crackle coming through the telephone line.

"I was walking in the park," Margot says. "Lafontaine, it's not far from my hotel. This poor little girl, she couldn't have been more than five, and she must have wandered away from her mother—"

And now Alex realizes that she can hear the faint metallic notes of a music box playing from the next room, something on the video after all, and she turns and looks through the doorway at the television screen.

"—she was dead before anyone could get it off her."

Grainy blacks and whites, light and shadow, and at first Alex isn't sure what she's seeing, unable to force all those shades of grey into a coherent whole. Movement, chiaroscuro, the swarm of pixels pulled from a magnetized strip of plastic, and then the picture resolves and a young woman's face stares back at Alex from the screen. Pupiless eyes like the whites of hard-boiled eggs, a strand of hair across her cheek, and the music box stops playing. A dog barks.

"Who are you? Your hand is cold—"

"I never saw anything so horrible in my life," Margot says. "The damned thing was *eating* her, Alex."

"Which road will you take?" a guttural voice from the video-tape asks the young woman. "That of the needles or that of the pins?"

The pain in Alex's head suddenly doubling, trebling, and she shuts her eyes tight, grips the edge of the counter and waits for the dizziness and nausea to pass, the disorientation that has nothing whatsoever to do with the migraine. The entire world tilting drunkenly around her, and "I have to go," she says. "I'm sorry, Margot. I'll call you back, but I have to go right now."

"Alex, no. *Wait*, please—"

"I promise. I'll call you back as soon as I can," and she opens her eyes, hanging up the phone quickly so that she doesn't have to hear the confusion in Margot's voice, the anger, and the young woman on the television gazes at her blind reflection in the window of her father's house. Her reflection and the less certain reflection of the hunched, dark figure crouched close behind her.

"The road of pins," she says. "Isn't it much easier to fasten things with pins, than to have to sew them together with needles?"

Then the film cuts to a shot of the door of the house—unpainted, weathered boards, the bent and rusted heads of nails, a cross painted on the wood with something white; slow pan left, and now the window is in frame, the clean glint of morning sunlight off glass and the round face of the peasant's daughter, the indistinct shape bending over her, and the camera zooms out until the house is very small, a lonely, run-down speck in a desolate, windswept valley.

Alex hits the stop button, and the VCR whirs and thunks and is silent, the screen filled with nothing now but shoddy, Saturday-morning animation, four hippie teenagers and a great dane bouncing along a swampy back road in their psychedelic van, the cartoon sliver moon hung high in the painted sky, and she sits down on the floor in front of the television.

When she presses eject, the tape slides smoothly, obediently out of the cassette compartment, and Alex reaches for it, holds it in trembling, sweatslick hands while her heart races and the pain behind her eyes fades to a dull, bearable ache.

A few minutes more and the phone begins to ring again, and this time she doesn't wait for the answering machine.

> *Incommensurable, impalpable,*
> *Yet latent in it are forms;*
> *Impalpable, incommensurable,*
> *Yet within it are entities.*
> *Shadowy it is and dim.*
> Lao-tzu, *Tao Teh Ching*

Afterword

"The Road of Pins," which was written April of 2001, was originally intended as part of *Wrong Things*, though I eventually decided that "Onion" was better suited to that collection. The spring of 2001 was an extremely difficult time for me artistically. I was exhausted and miserable from my years of work on *The Dreaming*, had just abandoned work on a stalled-out sequel to *Silk* (that manuscript would eventually be salvaged and grow into *Murder of Angels*), and I'd resolved to quit writing and go back to school to pursue paleontology. I think the resolve lasted all of two short weeks, and then I sat down and wrote "The Road of Pins." This was the first time that I would try to write of the mysterious *La Bête de Gévaudan*, which has fascinated me since childhood; I was surprised, pleased, and a little unnerved at the release of Christophe Gans' *Le Pacte des loups* only two months later. I should note that the work of the enigmatic painter Albert Perrault turns up again briefly in *"La Peau Verte."*

ONION

FRANK WAS SEVEN years old when he found the fields of red grass growing behind the basement wall. The building on St. Mark's where his parents lived after his father took a job in Manhattan and moved them from the New Jersey suburbs across the wide grey Hudson. And of course he'd been told to stay out of the basement, no place for a child to play because there were rats down there, his mother said, and rats could give you tetanus and rabies. Rats might even be carrying plague, she said, but the sooty blackness at the foot of the stairs was too much temptation for any seven-year-old, the long, long hallway past the door to the super's apartment, and sometimes a single naked bulb burned way down at the end of that hall. Dirty whiteyellow stain that only seemed to emphasize the gloom, drawing attention to just how very dark dark could be, and after school Frank would stand at the bottom of the stairs for an hour at a time, peering into the hall that led down to the basement.

"Does your mama know you're always hanging around down here?" Mr. Sweeney would ask whenever he came out and found Frank lurking in the shadows. Frank would squint at the flood of light from Mr. Sweeney's open door, would shrug or mumble the most noncommittal response he could come up with.

"I bet you she don't," Mr. Sweeney would say. "I bet she *don't* know."

"Are there really rats down there?" Frank might ask, and Mr. Sweeney would nod his head, point towards the long hall and say "You better *believe* there's rats. Boy, there's rats under this dump big as German shepherd puppies. They got eyes like acetylene blow torches and teeth like carving knives. Can chew straight through concrete, these rats we got."

"Then why don't you get a cat?" Frank asked once, and Mr. Sweeney laughed, phlegmy old man laugh, and "Oh, we had some cats, boy," he said. "We had whole goddamn cat *armies*, but when these rats get done, ain't never anything left but some gnawed-up bones and whiskers."

"I don't believe that," Frank said. "Rats don't get that big. Rats don't eat cats."

"You better get your skinny rump back upstairs, or they're gonna eat you, too," and then Mr. Sweeney laughed again and slammed his door, left Frank alone in the dark, his heart thumping loud and his head filled with visions of the voracious, giant rats that tunneled through masonry and dined on any cat unlucky enough to get in their way.

And that's the way it went, week after week, month after month, until one snowblind February afternoon, too cold and wet to go outside, and his mother didn't notice when he slipped quietly downstairs with the flashlight she kept in a kitchen drawer. Mr. Sweeney was busy with a busted radiator on the third floor, so nobody around this time to tell him scary stories and chase him home again, and Frank walked right on past the super's door, stood shivering in the chilly, mildewstinking air of the hallway. The unsteady beam of his flashlight to show narrow walls that might have been blue or green a long time ago, little black-and-white, six-sided ceramic tiles on the floor, but half of them missing, and he could see the rotting boards underneath. There were doors along the length of the hall, some of them boarded up, nailed shut, one door frame without any door at all, and he stepped very fast past that one.

Indiana Jones wouldn't be afraid, he thought, counting his footsteps in case that might be important later on, listening to the winter wind yowling raw along the street as it swept past the building on its way to Tompkins Square Park and the East River.

Twenty steps, twenty-five, thirty-three, and then he was standing below the dangling bulb, and for the first time Frank stopped and looked back the way he'd come. And maybe he'd counted wrong, because it seemed a lot farther than only thirty-three steps back to the dim and postage-stamp-sized splotch of day at the other end of the hall.

Only ten steps more down to the basement door, heavy grey steel door with a rusted hasp and a Yale padlock, but standing wide open like it was waiting for him, and maybe Mr. Sweeney only forgot to lock it the last time he came down to check the furnace or wrap the pipes. And later, Frank wouldn't remember much about crossing the threshold into the deeper night of the basement, the soupthick stench and taste of dust and rot and mushrooms, picking his way through the maze of sagging shelves and wooden crates, decaying heaps of rags and newspapers, past the ancient furnace crouched in one corner like a cast-iron octopus. Angry, orangered glow from the furnace grate like the eyes of the super's cat-eating rats—he *would* remember that— and then Frank heard the dry, rustling sound coming from one corner of the basement.

Years later, through high school and college and the slow purgatory of his twenties, *this* is where the bad dreams would always begin, the moment that he lifted the flashlight and saw the wide and jagged crack in the concrete wall. A faint draft from that corner that smelled of cinnamon and ammonia, and he *knew* better than to look, knew he should turn and run all the way back because it wasn't ever really rats that he was supposed to be afraid of. The rats just a silly, grown-up lie to keep him safe, a smaller, kinder nightmare for his own good, and *Run, boy*, Mr Sweeney whispered inside his head. *Run fast while you still can, while you still don't know.*

But Frank didn't run away, and when he pressed his face to the crack in the wall, he could see that the fields stretched away for miles and miles, crimson meadows beneath a sky the yellowgreen of an old bruise. The white trees that writhed and rustled in the choking, spicy breeze, and far, far away, the black thing striding slowly through the grass on bandy, stilt-long legs.

Frank and Willa share the tiny apartment on Mott Street, roachy Chinatown hovel one floor above an apothecary so the place always stinks of ginseng and jasmine and the powdered husks of dried sea creatures. Four walls, a gas range, an ancient Frigidaire that only works when it feels like it, but together they can afford the rent, most of the time, and the month or two they've come up short Mrs. Wu has let them slide. His job at a copy shop and hers waiting tables, and sometimes they talk about moving out of the city, packing up their raggedy-ass belongings and riding a Greyhound all the way to Florida, all the way to the Keys, and then it'll be summer all year long. But not this sticky, sweltering New York summer, no, it would be clean ocean air and rum drinks, sunwarm sand and the lullaby roll and crash of waves at night.

Frank is still in bed when Willa comes out of the closet that passes as their bathroom, naked and dripping from the shower, her hair wrapped up in a towel that used to be white, and he stops staring at the tattered Cézanne print thumbtacked over the television and stares at her instead. Willa is tall and her skin so pale he thought she might be sick the first time they met, so skinny that he can see intimations of her skeleton beneath that

skin like milk and pearls. Can trace the bluegreen network of
veins and capillaries in her throat, between her small breasts,
winding like hesitant watercolor brush strokes down her arms.
He's pretty sure that one day Willa will finally figure out she
can do a hell of lot better than him and move on, but he tries
not to let that ruin whatever it is they have now.

"It's all yours," she says, his turn even though the water won't
be hot again for at least half an hour, and Willa sits down in a
chair near the foot of the bed. She leans forward and rubs vig-
orously at her hair trapped inside the dingy towel.

"We could both play hooky," Frank says hopefully, watching
her, imagining how much better sex would be than the chug-
ging headache drone of Xerox machines, the endless dissatis-
faction of clients. "You could come back to bed, and we could
lie here all day. We could just lie here and sweat and watch
television."

"Jesus, Frank, how am I supposed to resist an offer like *that?*"

"Okay, so we could screw and sweat and watch television."

She stops drying her hair and glares at him, shakes her head
and frowns, but the sort of frown that says, *I wish I could* more
than it says anything else.

"That new girl isn't working out," she says.

"The fat chick from Kazakhstan?" Frank asks, and he rolls
over onto his back, easier to forget the fantasies of a lazy day
alone with Willa if he isn't looking at her sitting there naked.

"Fucking *Kazakhstan.* I mean, what the hell were Ted and
Daniel thinking? She can't even speak enough English to tell
someone where the toilet is, much less take an order."

"Maybe they felt sorry for her," Frank says unhelpfully, and
now he's staring up at his favorite crack on the waterstained
ceiling, the one that always makes him think of a Viking orbiter
photo of the Valles Marineris from one of his old astronomy
books. "I've heard that people do that sometimes, feel sorry for
people."

"Well, they'd probably lose less money if they just sent the bitch to college, the way she's been pissing off customers."

"Maybe you should suggest that today," and a moment later Willa's wet towel smacks him in the face, steamydamp terry cloth that smells like her black hair dye and the cheap baby shampoo she uses. It covers his eyes, obscuring his view of the Martian rift valley overhead, but Frank doesn't move the towel immediately, better to lie there a moment longer, breathing her in.

"Is it still supposed to rain today?" Willa asks, and he mumbles through the wet towel that he doesn't know.

"They keep promising it's going to rain, and it keeps not raining."

Frank sits up, and the towel slides off his face and into his lap, lies there as the dampness begins to soak through his boxers.

"I don't know," he says again; Willa has her back turned to him, and she doesn't reply or make any sign to show that she's heard. She's pulling a bright yellow T-shirt on over her head, the Curious George shirt he gave her for Christmas, has put on a pair of yellow panties, too.

"I'm sorry," she says. "It's the heat. The heat's driving me crazy."

Frank glances towards the window, the sash up but the chintzy curtains hanging limp and lifeless in the stagnant July air; he'd have to get out of bed, walk all the way across the room, lean over the sill and peer up past the walls and rooftops to see if there are any clouds. "It might rain today," he says, instead.

"I don't think it's ever going to rain again as long as I live," Willa says and steps into her jeans. "I think we've broken this goddamn planet, and it's never going to rain anywhere ever again."

Frank rubs his fingers through his stiff, dirty hair and looks back at the Cézanne still life above the television—a tabletop, the absinthe bottle and a carafe of water, an empty glass, the fruit that might be peaches.

"You'll be at the meeting tonight?" he asks, and Frank keeps his eyes on the print because he doesn't like the sullen, secretive expression Willa gets whenever they have to talk about the meetings.

"Yeah," she says, sighs, and then there's the clothmetal sound of her zipper. "Of course I'll be at the meeting. Where the hell else would I be?"

And then she goes back into the bathroom and shuts the door behind her, leaves Frank alone with Cézanne and the exotic reek of the apothecary downstairs, Valles Marineris and the bright day spilling uninvited through the window above Mott Street.

Half past two and Frank sits on a plastic milk crate in the stockroom of Gotham Kwick Kopy, trying to decide whether or not to eat the peanut butter and honey sandwich he brought for lunch. The air conditioning's on the blink again, and he thinks it might actually be hotter inside the shop than out on the street; a few merciful degrees cooler in the stockroom, though, shadowy refuge stacked high with cardboard boxes of copy paper in a dozen shades of white and all the colors of the rainbow. He peels back the top of his sandwich, the doughy Millbrook bread that Willa likes, and frowns at the mess underneath. So hot out front that the peanut butter has melted, oily mess to leak straight through wax paper and the brown bag, and he's trying to remember if peanut butter and honey can spoil.

Both the stockroom doors swing open, and Frank looks up, blinks and squints at the sunframed silhouette, Joe Manske letting in the heat and "Hey, don't do that," Frank says as Joe switches on the lights. The florescents buzz and flicker uncertainly, chasing away the shadows, drenching the stockroom in their bland, indifferent glare.

"Dude, why are you sitting back here in the dark?" Joe asks, and for a moment Frank considers throwing the sandwich at him.

"Why aren't you working on that Mac?" Frank asks right back, and "It's fixed, good as new, " Joe says, grins his big, stupid grin and sits down on a box of laser-print paper near the door.

"That fucker won't *ever* be good as new again."

"Well, at least it's stopped making that sound. That's good enough for me," and Joe takes out a pack of Camels, offers one to Frank, and Frank shakes his head no. A month now since his last cigarette, quitting because Willa's stepmother is dying of lung cancer, quitting because cigarettes cost too goddamn much, anyhow, and "Thanks, though," he says.

"Whatever," Joe Manske mumbles around the filter of his Camel, thumb on the strike wheel of his silver lighter, and in a moment the air is filled with the pungent aroma of burning tobacco. Frank gives up on the dubious sandwich, drops it back into the brown bag and crumples the bag into a greasy ball.

"I fuckin' hate this fuckin' job," Joe says, disgusted, smoky cloud of words about his head, and he points at the stockroom doors with his cigarette. "You just missed a real piece of work, man."

"Yeah?" and Frank tosses the sandwich ball towards the big plastic garbage can sitting a few feet away, misses, and it rolls behind the busted Canon 2400 color copier that's been sitting in the same spot since he started this job a year ago.

"Yeah," Joe says. "I was trying to finish that pet store job, and this dude comes in, little bitty old man looks like he just got off the boat from Poland or Armenia or some Balkan shit—"

"My grandfather was Polish," Frank says, and Joe sighs loudly, long impatient sigh, and he flicks ash onto the cement floor. "You *know* what I mean."

"So what'd he want, anyway?" Frank asks, not because he cares, but the shortest way through any conversation with Joe Manske is usually right down the middle, just be quiet and listen, and sooner or later he'll probably come to the end and shut up.

"He had this *old* book with him. The damned thing must have been even older than him, and it was falling apart. I don't think you could so much as look at it without the pages crumbling. Had it tied together with some string, right, and he kept askin' me all these questions, real technical shit about the machines, you know."

"Yeah? Like what?"

"Dude, I don't know. I can't remember half of it, techie shit, like I was friggin' Mr. Wizard or somethin'. I finally just told him we couldn't be responsible if the copiers messed up his old book, but he still kept on askin' these questions. Lucky for me, one of the self-service machines jammed, and I told him I had to go fix it. By the time I was finished, he was gone."

"You live to serve," Frank says, wondering if Willa would be able to tell if he had just one cigarette. "The customer is always right."

"Fuck that shit," Joe Manske says. "I don't get paid enough to have to listen to some senile old fart jabberin' at me all day."

"Yes sir, helpful is your middle name."

"Fuck you."

Frank laughs and gets up, pushes the milk crate towards the wall with the toe of one shoe so no one's going to come along later and trip over it, break their neck and have him to blame. "I better get back to work," he says, and "You do that," Joe grumbles and puffs his Camel.

Through the stockroom doors and back out into the stifling, noisy clutter of the shop, and it must be at least ten degrees warmer out here, he thinks. There's a line at the register, and the phone's ringing, no one out front but Maggie, and she glowers at him across the chaos.

"I'm on it," Frank says; she shakes her head doubtfully and turns to help a woman wearing a dark purple dress and matching beret. Frank's reaching across the counter for the telephone receiver when he notices the business card lying near a display of Liquid Paper. Black sans-serif print on an expensive white-cotton card stock and what appears to be an infinity symbol in the lower left-hand corner. FOUND: LOST WORLDS centered at the top, Terrae Novum et Terrae Indeterminata on the next line down in smaller letters. Then a name and an address—Dr. Solomon Monalisa, Ph. D., 43 W. 61st St., Manhattan—but no number or e-mail, and Frank picks up the card, holds it so Maggie can see.

"Where'd this come from?" he asks, but she only shrugs, annoyed but still smiling her strained and weary smile for the woman in the purple beret. "Beats me. Ask Joe, if he ever comes back. Now, will you *please* answer the phone?"

He apologizes, lifts the receiver, "Gotham Kwick Kopy, Frank speaking. How may I help you?" and slips the white card into his back pocket.

The group meets in the basement of a synagogue on Eldridge Street. Once a month, eight o'clock until everyone who wants to talk has taken his or her turn, coffee and stale doughnuts before and afterwards. Metal folding chairs and a lectern down front, a microphone and crackly PA system even though the room isn't really large enough to need one. Never more than fourteen or fifteen people, occasionally as few as six or seven, and Frank and Willa always sit at the very back, near the door. Sometimes Willa doesn't make it all the way through a meeting, and she says she hates the way they all watch her if she gets up to leave early, like she's done something wrong, she says, like this is all her fault, somehow. So they sit by the door, which is fine with Frank; he'd rather not have everyone staring at the back of his head, anyway.

He's sipping at a styrofoam cup of the bitter black coffee, three sugars and it's still bitter, watching the others, all their familiar telltale quirks and peculiarities, their equivocal glances, when Willa comes in. First the sound of her clunky motorcycle boots on the concrete steps, and then she stands in the doorway a moment, that expression like it's always the first time for her and it can never be any other way.

"Hey," Frank says quietly. "Yeah, I made it," she replies and sits down beside him. There's a stain on the front of her Curious George T-shirt that looks like chocolate sauce.

"How was your day?" he asks her, talking so she doesn't lock up before things even get started.

"Same as ever. It sucked. They didn't fire Miss Kazakhstan."

"That's good, dear. Would you like a martini?" and he jabs a thumb towards the free-coffee-and-stale-doughnut table. "I think I'll pass," Willa says humorlessly, rubs her hands together and stares at the floor between her feet. "I think my stomach hurts enough already."

"Would you rather just go home? We can miss one night. I sure as hell don't care—"

"*No,*" she says, answering too fast, too emphatic, so he knows she means yes. "That would be silly. I'll be fine when things get started."

And then Mr. Zaroba stands, stocky man with skin like tea-stained muslin, salt-and-pepper hair and beard and his bushy grey eyebrows. Kindly blue grandfather eyes, and he raises one hand to get everyone's attention, as if they aren't all looking at him already, as if they haven't all been waiting for him to open his mouth and break the tense, uncertain silence.

"Good evening, everyone," he says, and Willa sits up a little straighter in her chair, expectant arch of her back as though she's getting ready to run.

"Before we begin," Mr. Zaroba continues, "there's something I wanted to share. I came across this last week," and he takes a piece of paper from his shirt pocket, unfolds it, and begins to read. An item from the *New York Tribune*, February 17th, 1901; reports by an Indian tribe in Alaska of a city in the sky that was seen sometimes, and a prospector named Willoughby who claimed to have witnessed the thing himself in 1897, claimed to have tried to photograph it on several occasions and succeeded, finally.

"And now this," Zaroba says, and he pulls a second folded sheet of paper from his shirt pocket, presto, bottomless bag of tricks, that pocket, and this time he reads from a book, *Alaska* by Miner Bruce, page 107, he says. Someone else who saw the city suspended in the arctic sky, a Mr. C. W. Thornton of Seattle, and "'It required no effort of the imagination to liken it to a city,'" Mr. Zaroba reads, "'but was so distinct that it required, instead, faith to believe that it was not in reality a city.'"

People shift nervously in their seats, scuff their feet, and someone whispers too loudly.

"I have the prospector's photograph," Zaroba says. "It's only a xerox from the book, of course. It isn't very clear, but I thought some of you might like to see it," and he hands one of the sheets of paper to the person sitting nearest him.

"Damn, I need a cigarette," Willa whispers, and "You and me both," Frank whispers back. It takes almost five minutes for the sheet of paper to make its way to the rear of the room, passed along from hand to hand to hand while Zaroba stands patiently at the front, his head bowed solemn as if leading a prayer. Some hold onto it as long as they dare and others hardly seem to want to touch it. A man three rows in front of them gets up and brings it back to Willa.

"I don't see nothing but clouds," he says, sounding disappointed.

And neither does Frank, fuzzy photograph of a mirage, deceit of sunlight in the collision of warm and freezing air high above a glacier, but Willa must see more. She holds the paper tight and chews at her lower lip, traces the distorted peaks and cumulonimbus towers with the tip of an index finger.

"My god," she whispers.

In a moment, Zaroba comes up the aisle and takes the picture away, leaves Willa staring at her empty hands, her eyes wet like she might start crying. Frank puts an arm around her bony shoulders, but she immediately wiggles free and scoots her chair a few inches farther away.

"So, who wants to get us started tonight?" Mr. Zaroba asks when he gets back to the lectern. At first no one moves or speaks or raises a hand, each looking at the others or trying hard to look nowhere at all. And then a young woman stands up, younger than Willa, filthy clothes and bruisedark circles under her eyes, hair that hasn't been combed or washed in ages. Her name is Janice, and Frank thinks that she's a junky, probably a heroin addict because she always wears long sleeves.

"Janice? Very good, then," and Mr. Zaroba returns to his seat in the first row. Everyone watches Janice as she walks slowly to the front of the room, or they pretend not to watch her. There's a small hole in the seat of her dirty threadbare jeans, and Frank can see that she isn't wearing underwear. She stands behind the lectern, coughs once, twice, and brushes her shaggy bangs out of her face. She looks anxiously at Mr. Zaroba, and "It's all right, Janice," he says. "Take all the time you need. No one's going to rush you."

"Bullshit," Willa mutters, loud enough that the man sitting three rows in front of them turns and scowls. "What the hell are you staring at?" she growls, and he turns back towards the lectern.

"It's okay, baby," Frank says and takes her hand, squeezes hard enough that she can't shake him loose this time. "We can leave anytime you want."

Janice coughs again, and there's a faint feedback whine from the mike. She wipes her nose with the back of her hand, and "I was only fourteen years old," she begins. "I still lived with my foster parents in Trenton, and there was this old cemetery near our house, Riverview Cemetery. Me and my sister, my foster sister, we used to go there to smoke and talk, you know, just to get away from the house."

Janice looks at the basement ceiling while she speaks, or down at the lectern, but never at the others. She pauses and wipes her nose again.

"We went there all the time. Wasn't anything out there to be afraid of, not like at home. Just dead people, and me and Nadine weren't afraid of dead people. Dead people don't hurt anyone, right? We could sit there under the trees in the summer, and it was like things weren't so bad. Nadine was almost a year older than me."

Willa tries to pull her hand free, digs her nails into Frank's palm, but he doesn't let go. They both know where this is going, have both heard Janice's story so many times they could recite it backwards, same tired old horror story, and "It's okay," he says out loud, to Willa or to himself.

"Mostly it was just regular headstones, but there were a few big crypts set way back near the water. I didn't like being around them. I told her that, over and over, but Nadine said they were like little castles, like something out of fairy tales.

"One day one of them was open, like maybe someone had busted into it, and Nadine had to see if there were still bones inside. I begged her not to, said whoever broke it open might still be hanging around somewhere, and we ought to go home and come back later. But she wouldn't listen to me.

"I didn't want to look inside. I swear to God, I didn't."

"Liar," Willa whispers, so low now that the man three rows in front of them doesn't hear, but Frank does. Her nails are digging deeper into his palm, and his eyes are beginning to water

from the pain. *"You* wanted to see," she says. "Just like the rest of us, you wanted to see."

"I said, 'What if someone's still in there?' but she wouldn't listen. She wasn't ever afraid of anything. She used to lay down on train tracks just to piss me off."

"What did you see in the crypt, Janice, when you and Nadine looked inside?" Mr. Zaroba asks, but no hint of impatience in his voice, not hurrying her or prompting, only helping her find a path across the words as though they were slippery rocks in a cold stream. "Can you tell us?"

Janice takes a very deep breath, swallows, and "Stairs," she says. "Stairs going down into the ground. There was a light way down at the bottom, a blue light, like a cop-car light. Only it wasn't flashing. And we could hear something moving around down there, and something else that sounded like a dog panting. I tried to get Nadine to come back to the house with me then, but she wouldn't. She said 'Those stairs might go *anywhere,* Jan. Don't you want to *see?* Don't you want to *know?'"*

Another pause, and "I couldn't stop her," Janice says.

Willa mutters something Frank doesn't understand, then, something vicious, and he lets go of her hand, rubs at the four crescent-shaped wounds her nails leave behind. Blood drawn, crimson tattoos to mark the wild and irreparable tear in her soul by marking him, and he presses his palm to his black work pants, no matter if it stains, no one will ever notice.

"I waited at the top of the stairs until dark," Janice says. "I kept on calling her. I called her until my throat hurt. When the sun started going down, the blue light at the bottom got brighter, and once or twice I thought I could see someone moving around down there, someone standing between me and the light. Finally, I yelled I was going to get the goddamn cops if she didn't come back ... " and Janice trails off, hugs herself like she's cold and gazes straight ahead, but Frank knows she doesn't see any of them sitting there, watching her, waiting for the next word, waiting for *their* turns at the lectern.

"You don't have to say any more tonight," Zaroba says. "You know we'll all understand if you can't."

"No," Janice says. "I *can*…I really *need* to," and she squeezes her eyes shut tight. Mr. Zaroba stands, takes one reassuring step towards the lectern.

"We're all right here," he says, and "We're *listening*," Willa mumbles mockingly. "We're listening," Zaroba says a second later.

"I didn't go get the police. I didn't tell anyone anything until the next day. My foster parents, they just thought she'd run away again. No one would believe me when I told them about the crypt, when I told them where Nadine had really gone. Finally, they made me show them, though, the cops did, so I took them out to Riverview."

"Why do we always have to fucking start with her?" Willa whispers. "I can't remember a single time she didn't go first."

Someone sneezes, and "It was sealed up again," Janice says, her small and brittle voice made big and brittle by the PA speakers. "But they opened it. The cemetery people didn't want them to, but they did anyway. I swore I'd kill myself if they didn't open it and get Nadine out of there."

"Can *you* remember a time she didn't go first?" Willa asks, and Frank looks at her, but he doesn't answer.

"All they found inside was a coffin. The cops even pulled up part of the marble floor, but there wasn't anything under it, just dirt."

A few more minutes, a few more details, and Janice is done. Mr. Zaroba hugs her, and she goes back to her seat. "Who wants to be next?" he asks them, and it's the man who calls himself Charlie Jones, though they all know that's not his real name. Every month he apologizes because he can't use his real name at the meetings, too afraid someone at work might find out, and then he tells them about the time he opened a bedroom door in his house in Hartford, and there was nothing on the other side but stars. When he's done, Zaroba shakes his hand, pats him on the back, and now it's time for the woman who got lost once on the subway, two hours just to get from South Ferry to the Houston Street station, alone in an empty train that rushed along through a darkness filled with the sound of children crying. Then a timid Colombian woman named Juanita Lazarte, the night she watched two moons cross the sky above Peekskill, the morning the sun rose in the south.

And all the others, each in his or her turn, as the big wall clock behind the lectern ticks and the night fills up with the weight and absurdity of their stories, glimpses of impossible geographies, entire worlds hidden in plain view if you're unlucky enough to see them. "If you're damned," Juanita Lazarte once said and quickly crossed herself. Mr. Zaroba there whenever anyone locks up, his blue eyes and gentle ministrations, Zaroba who was once an atmospheric scientist and pilot for the Navy. He's seen something, too, of course, the summer of 1969, flying supplies in a Hercules C-130 from Christchurch, New Zealand to McMurdo Station. A freak storm, whiteout conditions and instrument malfunction, and when they finally found a break in the clouds somewhere over the Transantarctic Mountains, the entire crew saw the ruins of a vast city, glittering obsidian towers and shattered crystal spires, crumbling walls carved from the mountains themselves. At least that's what Zaroba says. He also says the Navy pressured the other men into signing papers agreeing never to talk about the flight, and when he refused, he was pronounced mentally unsound by a military psychiatrist and discharged.

When Willa's turn comes, she glances at Frank, not a word but all the terrible things right there in her eyes for him to see, unspoken resignation, surrender, and then she goes down the aisle and stands behind the lectern.

Frank wakes up from a dream of rain and thunder, and Willa's sitting crosslegged at the foot of their bed, nothing on but her pajama bottoms, watching television with the sound off and smoking a cigarette. "Where the hell'd you get that?" he asks, blinks sleepily and points at the cigarette.

"I bought a pack on my break today," she replies, not taking her eyes off the screen. She takes a long drag, and the smoke leaks slowly from her nostrils.

"I though we had an agreement."

"I'm sorry," but she doesn't sound sorry at all, and Frank sits up and blinks at the TV screen, rubs his eyes, and now he can see it's Jimmy Stewart and Katharine Hepburn, *The Philadelphia Story.*

"You can turn the sound up, if you want to," he says. "It won't bother me."

"No, that's okay. I know it by heart, anyway."

And then neither of them says anything else for a few minutes, sit watching the television, and when Willa has smoked the cigarette down to the filter she stubs it out in a saucer.

"I don't think I want to go to the meetings anymore," she says. "I think they're only making it worse for me."

Frank waits a moment before he replies, waiting to be sure that she's finished, and then, "That's your decision, Willa. If that's what you want."

"Of course it's my decision."

"You know what I meant."

"I can't keep reciting it over and over like the rest of you. There's no fucking point. I could talk about it from now till doomsday, and it still wouldn't make sense, and I'd still be afraid. Nothing Zaroba and that bunch of freaks has to say is going to change that, Frank."

Willa picks up the pack of Camels off the bed, lights another cigarette with a disposable lighter that looks pink by the flickering, grainy light from the TV screen.

"I'm sorry," Frank says.

"Does it help you?" she asks, and now there's an angrysharp edge in her voice, Willa's switchblade mood swings, sullen to pissed in the space between heartbeats. "Has it *ever* helped you at all?"

Frank doesn't want to fight with her tonight, wants to close his eyes and slip back down to sleep, back to his raincool dreams. Too hot for an argument, and "I don't know," he says, and that's almost not a lie.

"Yeah, well, whatever," Willa mumbles and takes another drag off her cigarette.

"We'll talk about it in the morning if you want," Frank says, and he lies back down, turns to face the open window and the noise of Mott Street at two am, the blinking orange neon from a noodle shop across the street.

"I'm not going to change my mind, if that's what you mean," Willa says.

"You can turn the sound up," Frank tells her again and concentrates on the soothing rhythm of the noodle-shop sign, orange pulse like campfire light, much, much better than counting imaginary sheep. In a moment he's almost asleep again, scant inches from sleep, and "Did you ever see *Return to Oz?*" Willa asks him.

"What?"

"*Return to Oz*, the one where Fairuza Balk plays Dorothy and Piper Laurie plays Auntie Em."

"No," Frank replies. "I never did," and he rolls over onto his back and stares at the ceiling instead of the neon sign. In the dark and the grey light from the television, his favorite crack looks even more like the Valles Marineris.

"It wasn't anything like *The Wizard of Oz*. I was just a little kid, but I remember it. It scared the hell out of me."

"Your mother let you see scary movies when you were a little kid?"

Willa ignores the question, her eyes still fixed on *The Philadelphia Story* if they're fixed anywhere, and she exhales a cloud of smoke that swirls and drifts about above the bed.

"When the film begins, Auntie Em and Uncle Henry think Dorothy's sick," she says. "They think she's crazy, because she talks about Oz all the time, because she won't believe it was only a nightmare. They finally send her off to a sanitarium for electric shock treatment—"

"Jesus," Frank says, not entirely sure that Willa isn't making all this up. "That's horrible."

"Yeah, but it's true, isn't it? It's what really happens to little girls who see places that aren't supposed to be there. People aren't ever so glad you didn't die in a twister that they want to listen to crazy shit about talking scarecrows and emerald cities."

And Frank doesn't answer because he knows he isn't supposed to, knows that she would rather he didn't even try, so he sweats and stares at his surrogate, plaster Mars instead, at the shadow play from the television screen; she doesn't say anything else, and in a little while more, he's asleep.

In this dream there is still thunder, no rain from the ocher sky but the crack and rumble of thunder so loud that the air shimmers and could splinter like ice. The tall red grass almost as high as his waist, rippling gently in the wind, and Frank wishes that Willa wouldn't get so close to the fleshy white trees. She thinks they might have fruit, peaches, and she's never eaten a white peach before, she said. Giants fighting in the sky, and Willa picking up windfall fruit from the rocky ground beneath the trees; Frank looks over his shoulder, back towards the fissure in the basement wall, back the way they came, but it's vanished.

I should be sacred, he thinks. *No, I should be* scared.

And now Willa is coming back towards him through the crimson waves of grass, her skirt for a linen basket to hold all the pale fruit she's gathered. She's smiling, and he tries to remember the last time he saw her smile, *really* smile, not just a smirk or a sneer. She smiles and steps through the murmuring grass that seems to part to let her pass, her bare arms and legs safe from the blades grown sharp as straight razors.

"They *are* peaches," she beams.

But the fruit is the color of school-room chalk, its skin smooth and slick and glistening with tiny pinhead beads of nectar seeping out through minute pores. "Take one," she says, but his stomach lurches and rolls at the thought, loathe to even touch one of the things, and then she sighs and dumps them all into the grass at his feet.

"I used to know a story about peaches," Willa says. "It was a Japanese story, I think. Or maybe it was Chinese."

"I'm pretty sure those *aren't* peaches," Frank says, and he takes a step backwards, away from the pile of sweating albino fruit.

"I heard the pits are poisonous," she says. "Arsenic, or maybe it's cyanide."

A brilliant flash of chartreuse lightning, then, and the sky sizzles and smells like charred meat. Willa bends and retrieves a piece of the fruit, takes a bite before he can stop her; the sound of her teeth sinking through its skin, tearing through the colorless pulp inside, is louder than the thunder, and milky juice rolls down her chin and stains her Curious George T-shirt. Something wriggles from between her lips, falls to the grass, and when Willa opens her jaws wide to take another bite Frank can see that her mouth is filled with wriggling things.

"They have to be careful you don't swallow your tongue," she says, mumbling around the white peach. "If you swallow your tongue, you'll choke to death."

Frank snatches the fruit away from her, grabs it quick before she puts any more of it in her belly, and she frowns and wipes the juice staining her hands off onto her skirt. The half-eaten thing feels warm, and he tosses it away.

"Jesus, that was fucking silly, Frank. The harm's already done, *you* know that. The harm was done the day you looked through that hole in the wall."

And then the sky booms its symphony of gangrene and sepsis, and lightning stabs down at the world with electric claws, thunder then lightning but that's only the wrong way round if he pretends Willa isn't right, if he pretends that he's seven again, and this time he doesn't take the flashlight from the kitchen drawer. This time he does what his mother says and doesn't go sneaking off the minute she turns her back.

Frank stands alone beneath the restless trees, his aching, dizzy head too full of all the time that can't be redeemed, now or then or ever, and he watches as Willa walks alone across the red fields towards the endless deserts of scrap iron and bone, towards the bloated scarletpurple sun. The black things have noticed her and creep along close behind, stalking silent on ebony mantis legs.

This time, he wakes up before they catch her.

The long weekend, then, hotter and drier, the sky more white than blue, and the air on Mott Street and everywhere else that Frank has any reason to go has grown so ripe, so redolent, that sometimes he pulls the collars of his T-shirts up over his mouth and nose, breathes through the cotton like a surgeon or a wild-west bandit, but the smell always gets through anyway. On the news, there are people dying of heat stroke and dehydration, people dying in the streets and ERs, but fresh-faced weather-men still promise that it will rain very soon. He's stopped believing them, and maybe that means that Willa's right, and it never will rain again.

Frank hasn't shown the white card—FOUND: LOST WORLDS—to Willa, keeps it hidden in his wallet, only taking it out when he's alone and no one will see, no one to ask where or what or who. He's read it over and over again, has each line committed to memory, and Monday morning he almost calls Mr. Zaroba about it. The half hour between Willa leaving for the cafe and the time that he has to leave for the copy shop if he isn't going to be late, and he holds the telephone receiver and stares at Dr. Solomon Monalisa's card lying there on the table in front of him. The sound of his heart, the dial-tone drone, and the traffic down on Mott Street, the spice-and-dried-fish odor of the apothecary leaking up through the floorboards, and a fat drop of sweat slides down his forehead and spreads itself painfully across his left eyeball. By the time he's finished rubbing at his eye, calling Zaroba no longer seems like such a good idea after all, and Frank puts the white card back into his wallet, slips it in safe between his driver's license and a dog-eared, expired MetroCard.

Instead he calls in sick, gets Maggie, and she doesn't believe for one moment that there's anything at all wrong with him.

"I fucking swear, I can't even get up off the toilet long enough to make a phone call. I'm calling *you* from the head," only half an effort at sounding sincere because they both know this is only going through the motions.

"As we speak—" he starts, but Maggie cuts him off.

"That's enough, Frank. But I'm telling you, man, if you wanna keep this job, you better get your slacker ass down here tomorrow morning."

"Right," Frank says. "I hear you," and she hangs up first.

And then Frank stares at the open window, the sun beating down like the Voice of God out there, and it takes him almost five minutes to remember where to find the next number he has to call.

Sidney McAvoy stopped coming to the meetings at the synagogue on Eldridge Street almost a year ago, not long after
Frank's first time. Small, hawk-nosed man with nervous, ferrety
eyes, and he's always reminded Frank a little of Dustin Hoffman
in *Papillon*. Some sort of tension or wound between Sidney and
Mr. Zaroba that Frank never fully understood, but he saw it
from the start, the way their eyes never met, and Sidney never
took his turn at the lectern, sat silent, brooding, chewing the
stem of a cheap, unlit pipe. And then an argument after one of
the meetings, the same night that Zaroba told Janice that she
shouldn't ever go back to the cemetery in Trenton, that she
should never try to find the staircase and the blue light again.
Both men speaking in urgent, angry whispers, Zaroba looking
up occasionally to smile a sheepish, embarrassed, apologetic
smile. Everyone pretending not to see or hear, talking among
themselves, occupied with their stale doughnuts and tiny pack-
ets of non-dairy creamer, and then Sidney McAvoy left and
never came back.

Frank would've forgotten all about him, almost had forgotten, and then one night he and Willa were coming home late
from a bar where they drink sometimes, whenever they're feeling irresponsible enough to spend money on booze. Cheap
vodka or cheaper beer, a few hours wasted just trying to feel
like everyone else, the way they imagined other, normal people
might feel, and they ran into Sidney McAvoy a few blocks from
their apartment. He was wearing a ratty green raincoat, even
though it wasn't raining, and chewing on one of his pipes, carrying a large box wrapped in white butcher's paper, tied up
tight and neat with twine.

"Shit," Willa whispered. "Make like you don't see him," but
Sidney had already noticed them, and he was busy clumsily
trying to hide the big package behind his back.

"I *know* you two," he declared, talking loudly, a suspicious, accusatory glint to his quavering voice. "You're both with Zaroba, aren't you? You still go to his *meetings.*" That last word a sneer, and he pointed a short, grubby finger at the center of Frank's chest.

"That's really none of your goddamn business, is it?" Willa growled and Frank stepped quickly between them; she mumbled and spit curses behind his back, and Sidney McAvoy glared up at Frank with his beadydark eyes. A whole lifetime's worth of bitterness and distrust trapped inside those eyes, eyes that have seen far too much or far too little, and "How have you been, Mr. McAvoy," Frank said, straining to sound friendly, and he managed the sickly ghost of a smile.

Sidney grunted and almost dropped his carefully-wrapped package.

"If you *care* about that girl there," he said, speaking around the stem of the pipe clenched between his yellowed teeth, "you'll keep her away from Zaroba. And you'll both stop *telling* him things, if you know what's good for you. There are more useful answers in a road atlas than you're ever going to get out of that old phony."

"What makes you say that?" Frank asked. "What were you guys fighting about?" but Sidney was already scuttling away down Canal Street, his white package hugged close to his chest. He turned a corner without looking back and was gone.

"Fucking nut job," Willa mumbled. "What the hell's his problem, anyway?"

"Maybe the less we know about him the better," Frank said, and he put an arm around Willa's small waist, holding her close to him, trying hard not to think about what could have been in the box but unable to think of anything else.

And two weeks later, dim and snowy last day before Thanksgiving, Frank found Sidney McAvoy's number in the phone book and called him.

A wet comb through his hair, cleaner shirt and socks, and Frank goes out into the sizzling day; across Columbus Park to the Canal Street Station, and he takes the M to Grand Street, rides the B line all the way to the subway stop beneath the Museum of Natural History. Rumbling along through the honeycombed earth, the diesel and dust and garbage-scented darkness and him swaddled inside steel and unsteady fluorescent light. Time to think that he'd rather not have, unwelcome luxury of second thoughts, and when the train finally reaches the museum, he's almost ready to turn right around and head back downtown. Almost, but Dr. Solomon Monalisa's card is in his wallet to keep him moving, get him off the train and up the concrete steps to the museum entrance. Ten dollars he can't spare to get inside, but Sidney McAvoy will never agree to meet him anywhere outside, too paranoid for a walk in Central Park or a quiet booth in a deli or a coffee shop somewhere.

"People are always listening," he says, whenever Frank has suggested or asked that they meet somewhere without an entrance fee. "You never know what they might overhear."

So sometimes it's the long marble bench in front of the *Apatosaurus,* or the abyssal blueblack gloom of the Hall of Fishes, seats beneath a planetarium constellation sky, whichever spot happens to strike Sidney's fancy that particular day. His fancy or his cabalistic fantasies, if there's any difference, and today Frank finds him in the Hall of Asiatic Mammals, short and rumpled man in a worn-out tweed jacket and red tennis shoes standing alone before the Indian leopard diorama, gazing intently in at the pocket of counterfeit jungle and the taxidermied cats. Frank waits behind him for a minute or two, waiting to be noticed, and when Sidney looks up and speaks, he speaks to Frank's reflection.

"I'm very busy today," he says, brusque, impatient. "I hope this isn't going to take long."

And no, Frank says, it won't take long at all, I promise, but Sidney's doubtful expression to show just how much he believes that. He sighs and looks back to the stuffed leopards, papier-mâché trees and wax leaves, a painted flock of peafowl rising to hang forever beneath a painted forest canopy. Snapshot moment of another world and the walls of the dimly-lit hall lined with a dozen or more such scenes.

"You want to know about Monalisa," Sidney says. "That's why you came here, because you think I can tell you who he is."

"Yeah," Frank admits and reaches into his pocket for his wallet. "He came into the place where I work last week and left this." He takes out the card, and Sidney turns around only long enough to take it from him.

"So, you talked to him?"

"No, I didn't. I was eating my lunch in the stockroom. I didn't actually see him for myself."

Sidney stares at the card, seems to read it carefully three or four times, and then he returns it to Frank and goes back to staring at the leopards.

"Why didn't you show this to Zaroba?" he asks sarcastically, taunting, but Frank answers him anyway, not in the mood today for Sidney's grudges and intrigues.

"Because I didn't think he'd tell me anything. You know he's more interested in the mysteries than ever finding answers." And Frank pauses, silent for a moment, and Sidney's silent, too, both men watching the big cats now—glass eyes, freeze-frame talons, and taut, speckled haunches—as though the leopards might suddenly spring towards them, all this stillness just a clever ruse for the tourists and the kiddies; maybe dead leopards know the nervous, wary faces of men who have seen things that they never should have seen.

"He knows the truth would swallow him whole," Sidney says.

The leopards don't pounce and he adds, "He knows he's a coward."

"So who is Dr. Monalisa?"

"A bit of something the truth already swallowed and spat back up," and Sidney chuckles sourly to himself and produces one of his pipes from a pocket of the tweed jacket. "He's a navigator, a pilot, a cartographer..."

Frank notices that one of the two leopards has captured a stuffed peacock, holds it fast between velvet, razored paws, and he can't remember if it was that way only a moment before.

"He draws maps," Sidney says. "He catalogs doors and windows and culverts."

"That's bullshit," Frank whispers, his voice low now so the old woman staring in at the giant panda exhibit won't hear him. "You're trying to tell me he can *find* places?"

"He isn't a sane man, Frank," Sidney says, and now he holds up his left hand and presses his palm firmly against the glass, as if he's testing the invisible barrier, gauging its integrity. "He has answers, but he has prices, too. You think *this* is Hell, you see how it feels to be in debt to Dr. Solomon Monalisa."

"It isn't me. It's Willa. I think she's starting to lose it."

"We all lost 'it' a long time ago, Frank."

"I'm afraid she's going to do something. I'm afraid she'll hurt herself."

And Sidney turns his back on the leopards then, takes the pipe from his mouth, and glares up at Frank. But some of the anger, some of the bitterness, has gone from his eyes, and "He *might* keep her alive," he says, "but you wouldn't want her back when he was done. If she'd even *come* back. No, Frank. You two stay away from Monalisa. Look for your own answers. You don't think you found that card by accident, do you? You don't really think there are such things as coincidences? That's not even his real address—"

"She can't sleep anymore," Frank says, but now Sidney McAvoy isn't listening, glances back over his shoulder at the Indian rain forest, incandescent daylight, illusory distances, and "I have to go now," he says. "I'm very busy today."

"I think she's fucking *dying*, man," Franks says as Sidney straightens his tie and puts the pipe back into his pocket; the old woman looks up from the panda in its unreal bamboo thicket and frowns at them both.

"I'm very busy today, Frank. Call me next week. I think I can meet you at the Guggenheim next week."

And he walks quickly away towards the Roosevelt Rotunda, past the Siberian tiger and the Sumatran rhinoceros, leaving Frank alone with the frowning woman. When Sidney has vanished into the shadows behind a small herd of Indian elephants, Frank turns back to the leopards and the smudgy hand print Sidney McAvoy has left on their glass.

Hours and hours later, past sunset to the other side of the wasted day, the night that seems even hotter than the scorching afternoon, and Frank is dreaming that the crack in the basement wall on St. Mark's Place is much too narrow for him to squeeze through. Maybe the way it really happened after all, and then he hears a small, anguished sound from somewhere close behind him, something hurting or lost, and when he turns to see, Frank opens his eyes, and there's only the tangerine glow of the noodle-shop sign outside the apartment window. He blinks once, twice, but this stubborn world doesn't go away, doesn't break apart into random kaleidoscopic shards to become some other place entirely. So he sits up, head full of the familiar disappointment, this incontestable solidity, and it takes him a moment to realize that Willa isn't in bed. Faint outline of her body left in the wrinkled sheets, and the bathroom light is burning, the door open, so she's probably just taking a piss.

"You okay in there?" he asks, but no reply. The soft drip, drip, drip of the kitchenette faucet, tick of the wind-up alarm clock on the table next to Willa's side of the bed, street noise, but no answer. "Did you fall in or something?" he shouts. "Did you drown?"

And still no response, but his senses are waking up, picking out more than the ordinary, everynight sounds, a trilling whine pitched so high he feels it more than hears it, and now he notices the way that the air in the apartment smells.

Go back to sleep, he thinks, but both legs already over the edge of the bed, both feet already on the dusty floor. *When you wake up again, it'll be over.*

The trill worming its way beneath his skin, soaking in, pricking gently at the hairs on his arms and the back of his neck, and all the silver fillings in his teeth have begun to hum along sympathetically. Where he's standing, Frank can see into the bathroom, just barely, a narrow slice of linoleum, slice of porcelain toilet tank, a mildew and polyurethane fold of shower curtain. And he thinks that the air has started to shimmer, an almost imperceptible warping of the light escaping from the open door, but that might only be his imagination. He takes one small step towards the foot of the bed, and there's Willa, standing naked before the tiny mirror above the bathroom sink. The jut of her shoulder blades and hip bones, the anorexic swell of her rib cage, all the minute details of her painful thinness seem even more pronounced in the harsh and curving light.

"Hey. Is something wrong? Are you sick" and she turns her head slowly to look at him, or maybe only looking towards him because there's nothing much like recognition on her face. Her wide, unblinking eyes, blind woman's stare, and "Can't you hear me, Willa?" he asks as she turns slowly back to the mirror. Her lips move, shaping rough, inaudible words.

The trilling grows infinitesimally louder, climbs another half-octave, and there's a warm, wet trickle across Frank's lips, and he realizes that his nose is bleeding.

Behind Willa the bathroom wall, the shower, the low ceiling—everything—ripples and dissolves, and there's a sudden, staccato *pop* as the bulb above the sink blows. And after an instant of perfect darkness, perfect nothing, dull and yellow-green shafts of light from somewhere far above, flickering light from an alien sun shining down through the waters of an alien sea; dim, translucent shapes dart and flash through those depths, bodies more insubstantial than jellyfish, more sinuous than eels, and Willa rises to meet them, arms outstretched, her hair drifting about her face like a halo of seaweed and algae. In the ocean-filtered light, Willa's pale skin seems sleek and smooth as dolphinflesh. Air rushes from her lips, her nostrils, and flows eagerly away in a glassy swirl of bubbles.

The trilling has filled Frank's head so full, and his aching skull, his brain, seem only an instant from merciful implosion, fragile, eggshell bone collapsed by the terrible, lonely sound and the weight of all that water stacked above him. He staggers, takes a step backwards, and now Willa's face is turned up to meet the sunlight streaming down, and she's more beautiful than anyone or anything he's ever seen or dreamt.

Down on Mott Street, the screech of tires, the angry blat of a car horn, and someone begins shouting very loudly in Mandarin.

And now the bathroom is only a bathroom again, and Willa lies in a limp, strangling heap on the floor, her wet hair and skin glistening in the light from the bulb above the sink. The water rolls off her back, her thighs, spreads across the floor in a widening puddle, and Frank realizes that the trilling has finally stopped, only the memory of it left in his ringing ears and bleeding nose. When the dizziness has passed, he goes to her, sits down on the wet floor and holds her while she coughs and pukes up gouts of saltwater and snotty strands of something the color of verdigris. Her skin so cold it hurts to touch, cold coming off her like a fever, and something small and chitinous slips from her hair and scuttles away behind the toilet on long and jointed legs.

"Did you *see?*" she asks him, desperate, rheumy words gurgling out with all the water that she's swallowed. "Did you, Frank? Did you *see* it?"

"Yes," he tells her, just like every time before. "Yes, baby. I did. I saw it all," and Willa smiles, closes her eyes, and in a little while she's asleep. He carries her, dripping, back to their bed and holds her until the sun rises, and she's warm again.

The next day neither of them goes to work, and some small, niggling part of Frank manages to worry about what will happen to them if he loses the shit job at Gotham Kwick Kopy, if Willa gets fired from the cafe, obstinate shred of himself still capable of caring about such things. How the rent will be paid, how they'll eat, everything that hasn't really seemed to matter in more years than he wants to count. Half the morning in bed, and his nosebleed keeps coming back, a roll of toilet paper and then one of their towels stained all the shades of dried and drying blood; Willa wearing her winter coat despite the heat, and she keeps trying to get him to go to a doctor, but no, he says. That might lead to questions, and besides, it'll stop sooner or later. It's always stopped before.

By twelve o'clock, Willa's traded the coat for her pink cardigan, feels good enough that she makes them peanut-butter-and-grape-jelly sandwiches, black coffee and stale potato chips, and after he eats Frank begins to feel better, too. But going to the park is Willa's idea, because the apartment still smells faintly of silt and dead fish, muddy, low-tide stink that'll take hours more to disappear completely. He knows the odor makes her nervous, so he agrees, even though he'd rather spend the afternoon sleeping off his headache. Maybe a cold shower, another cup of Willa's bitterstrong coffee, and if he's lucky he could doze for hours without dreaming.

They take the subway up to Fifth, follow the eastern edge of the park north, past the zoo and East Green all the way to Pilgrim Hill and the Conservatory Pond. It's not so very hot that there aren't a few model sailing ships on the pond, just enough breeze to keep their miniature Bermuda sails standing tall and taut as shark fins. Frank and Willa sit in the shade near the Alice in Wonderland statue, her favorite spot in all of Central Park, rocky place near the tea party, granite and rustling leaves, the clean laughter of children climbing about on the huge bronze mushrooms. A little girl with frizzy black hair and red and white peppermint-striped tights is petting the kitten in Alice's lap, stroking its metal fur and meowling loudly, and "I can't ever remember her name," Willa says.

"What?" Franks asks. "Whose name?" not sure if she means the little girl or the kitten or something else entirely.

"Alice's kitten. I know it had a name, but I never can remember it."

Frank watches the little girl for a moment, and "Dinah," he says. "I think the kitten's name was Dinah."

"Oh, yeah, Dinah. That's it," and he knows that she's just thinking out loud, whatever comes to mind so that she won't have to talk about last night, so the conversation won't accidentally find its own way back to those few drowning moments of chartreuse light and eel shadows. Trying so hard to pretend, and he almost decides they're both better off if he plays along and doesn't show her Dr. Solomon Monalisa's white calling card.

"That's a good name for a cat," she says. "If we ever get a kitten, I think I'll name it Dinah."

"Mrs. Wu doesn't like cats."

"Well, we're not going to spend the rest of our lives in that dump. Next time, we'll get an apartment that allows cats."

Frank takes the card out and lays his wallet on the grass, but Willa hasn't even noticed, too busy watching the children clambering about on Alice, too busy dreaming about kittens. The card is creased and smudged from a week riding around in his back pocket and all the handling it's suffered, the edges beginning to fray, and he gives it to her without any explanation.

"What's this?" she asks, and he tells her to read it first, just read it, so she does. Reads it two or three times, and then Willa returns the card, goes back to watching the children. But her expression has changed, the labored, make-believe smile gone, and now she just looks like herself again, plain old Willa, the distance in her eyes, the hard angles at the corners of her mouth that aren't quite a frown.

"Sidney says he's for real," half the truth, at best, and Frank glances down at the card, reading it again for the hundredth or two-hundredth time.

"Sidney McAvoy's a fucking lunatic."

"He says this guy has maps—"

"Christ, Frank. What do you want me to say? You want me to give you *permission* to go talk to some crackpot? You don't need my permission."

"I was hoping you'd come with me," he says so softly that he's almost whispering, and he puts the card back into his wallet where neither of them will have to look at it, stuffs the wallet back into his jeans pocket.

"Well, I won't. I go to your goddamn meetings. I already have to listen to that asshole Zaroba. That's enough for me, thank you very much. That's more than enough."

The little girl petting Dinah slips, loses her footing and almost slides backwards off the edge of the sculpture, but her mother catches her and sets her safely on the ground.

"I see what it's doing to you," Frank says. "I have to watch. How much longer do you think you can go on like this?"

She doesn't answer him, opens her purse and takes out a pack of cigarettes, only one left, and she crumples the empty package and tosses it over her shoulder into the bushes.

"What if this guy really can help you? What if he can make it *stop?*"

Willa is digging noisily around in her purse, trying to find her lighter or a book of matches, and she turns and stares at Frank, the cigarette hanging unlit from her lips. Her eyes shining bright as broken gemstones, shattered crystal eyes, furious, resentful, and he knows then that she could hate him, that she could leave him here and never look back. She takes the cigarette from her mouth, licks her upper lip, and for a long moment Willa holds the tip of her tongue trapped tight between her teeth.

"What the hell makes you think I want it to stop?"

And silence as what she's said sinks in, and he begins to understand that he's never understood her at all. "It's killing you," he says, finally, the only thing he can think to say, and Willa's eyes seem to flash and grow brighter, more broken, more eager to slice.

"No, Frank, it's the only thing keeping me *alive*. Knowing that it's out there, that I'll see it again, and someday maybe it won't make me come back *here*."

And then she gets up and walks quickly away towards the pond, brisk, determined steps to put more distance between them. She stops long enough to bum a light from an old black man with a dachshund, then ducks around the corner of the boathouse, and he can't see her anymore. Frank doesn't follow, sits watching the tiny sailboats and yachts gliding gracefully across the mossdark surface of the water, their silent choreography of wakes and ripples. He decides maybe it's better not to worry about Willa for now, plenty enough time for that later, and he wonders what he'll say to Monalisa when he finds him.

We shall be less apt to admire what this World calls great, shall nobly despise those Trifles the generality of Men set their Affections on, when we know that there are a multitude of such Earths inhabited and adorn'd as well as our own.
                                    —Christiaan Huygens (c. 1690)

Afterword

"Onion" is another story written shortly after a trip to New York City. In May 2001, I was once again in Manhattan examining the mosasurs in the collection of the American Museum of Natural History. We spent a couple of nights at Peter Straub's house and had our van towed by the crew of *Mr. Deeds*. I had lunch with my agent and did a reading at KGB Bar on East Fourth Street. I'd been struggling all spring with a severe case of "writer's block," which had finally led to my shelving the first draft of what would eventually become *Murder of Angels*. But when I got back to Birmingham, I discovered that I had the idea for a new short story, which I started out calling "Found: Lost Worlds." Originally written for *Wrong Things*, my collaboration with Poppy Z. Brite, "Onion" received the 2001 International Horror Guild Award for Best Short Fiction and was subsequently reprinted in *The Year's Best Fantasy and Horror, Fifteenth Annual Collection*.

APOKATASTASIS

"**W**ELL, IT WAS THERE," Terry says, pointing, pointing again in case he wasn't paying attention before, and Aaron sighs and makes a show of looking at the alarm clock. He tells her what time it is, 3:38 am, like she might care, like that makes any difference at all. She's sitting at the foot of their bed, watching the dark hallway beyond the open door; third night in a row, and she knows better than to hope that maybe this time he'll believe her, maybe this time it'll come back, and he'll have to see it, too.

"Well, was it a dog or not?"

"I don't *know*," she says again, sounding more annoyed than the first time he asked. "It was like a dog."

"I don't know what that's supposed to mean."

"It was an animal," Terry says, not taking her eyes off the hall, the night driven back a few grudging feet by the glow from her reading lamp. "It was an animal like a dog."

"It was a dream," he says. "Now go back to sleep," and lies down again, turning his back to her and the lamp and the bedroom door. Terry looks away from the hall long enough to glance at him over her shoulder.

"I know the difference," she says, trying not to sound angry or irrational, trying to sound calm and not at all afraid, her

143

heart still beating just a little too fast and her mouth gone dry as dust, but he doesn't have to know that. "I wasn't asleep."

"Then where the hell is it now? And how's it getting in and out of the apartment?" He's talking to her without opening his eyes, without even turning over to look at her. "Jesus, Terry. Go back to sleep, please."

So she watches the hallway alone, the straight white walls, plaster washed the delicate color of eggshells, and an oil painting in a walnut frame that her grandmother did when she was only seventeen. A field with wildflowers and a line of trees in the distance, but the shadows hide everything, and the canvas is only an indistinct outline in the gloom.

"I know the difference," she says again, even though Aaron's probably already asleep, and she's talking to no one but herself. Maybe if she hadn't been so frightened when it woke her, the eager, snuffling sounds it made nosing about in the hall, maybe if she'd awakened Aaron immediately he would have seen it, too, and somehow it would have been something that was easier for two people to understand. The answer not half so strange, not so difficult, if *two* people have to think about it together. But instead she lay perfectly still, waiting for it to see her, waiting for it not be there anymore, until, finally, the thing raised its head and fixed her with those eyes like pearls and mercury, quicksilver fire, and then she couldn't have moved for all the angels in Heaven. It might have smiled, she thinks, but it was only an animal, and dogs don't smile.

"Go to sleep, Terry," Aaron says. "We'll talk about it in the morning."

"I don't want to sleep anymore," she tells him, and he doesn't reply. A few minutes more, and Aaron's snoring softly, gentle-rough sound that she's always found so comforting, and now it's nothing but a reminder that he doesn't believe her, that whatever waits for her between this moment and the next and dawn is there for her and her alone. Terry thinks about her legs dangling carelessly over the edge of the bed, her bare feet and the blackness between the floor and the box springs, blackness that might hide more than old photo albums and lost socks. She pulls her legs up, feet tucked safely beneath her thighs, protective lotus, and she watches the hallway and waits for morning.

Meeting Cyn for lunch at the little coffee shop and deli down the street from the shoe store where she works, expensive hipster shoes for hipster yuppies and suburban punker kids, Doc Martens and Birkenstocks, London Underground and Fluevogs, and they sit at one of the outside tables despite the August heat because there's no smoking allowed inside. A faded green-and-white canvas umbrella for shade and hardly any breeze at all; Cyn orders the curried chicken salad plate, and Terry only orders iced coffee, black, and sips it while Cyn picks indifferently at slices of tomato and avocado.

"Have you thought about trying to take a picture of it?" Cyn asks, brushing her lavender bangs from her eyes. "If it worked and you had a photograph, well, he'd have to believe you then, wouldn't he?" She stabs a slice of tomato with her fork and then shakes it loose again.

Terry shrugs and takes another sip of coffee, not wanting to admit that she's afraid what might happen if she did try to take a picture of the animal. Maybe it wouldn't much like having its picture taken. Or maybe it isn't anything that can be photographed, and where would she be then? No proof one way or another, and "There's something wrong with our camera," she lies. "It's been acting up, and I haven't had time to have it fixed."

"I could loan you mine," Cyn offers unhelpfully, pushing, cornering her, and Terry knows better than to think this means that Cyn believes she's really seeing anything at all.

"I don't even believe in ghosts," Terry says and shakes her

head, hoping Cyn will shut up about the camera. "If it wasn't happening to me, if it was happening to you instead, and you were trying to convince me, I wouldn't believe you."

"Gee, thanks, kiddo."

"I just don't believe in ghosts, that's all. I don't even think I believe in souls, so how can I believe in ghosts? And if I did, I don't think I'd believe that animals have them."

"Souls or ghosts?"

"What?"

Cyn frowns at her and chews a forkful of avocado and chicken, washes it down with ginger ale before she answers. "*Which* wouldn't you believe that animals have, souls or ghosts?"

"Well, either. If I don't believe animals have souls, I can't very well believe they have ghosts."

"I thought you were Catholic?"

"My mother was Catholic. I'm not anything."

"Hell, I always thought being Catholic was practically genetic. I didn't know you had a choice."

Cyn stares at her plate for a moment, then pushes it away and takes a pack of cigarettes from her purse. She lights one, and the smoke hangs in the stagnant air above the table.

"I fucking hate dogs," she says. "When I was five, I was bitten by a dog. I still have a scar on my ass from where the damned thing took a plug out of me. I thought sure it was gonna eat me, just like the wolf in 'Little Red Riding Hood.'"

"It might not be a dog. I only said it looked like a dog."

Cyn takes another drag off her cigarette, glancing up at the simmering Wedgwood sky while smoke leaks slow from her nostrils. "Scared the holy shit out of me. I had to have eight fucking stitches," she says. "Jesus, if I woke up and there was a big, black dog in my bedroom, I'd probably have a heart attack."

"It wasn't in the bedroom. It was in the hall."

"Pete keeps saying he wants a Doberman, and I told him no fucking way, mister, not if he wants me around."

Terry sips her bitter, icy coffee, watches Cyn and her purple hair, and she wishes that she hadn't stopped smoking, wishes she'd taken her lunch break alone today. "I'm not afraid of dogs," she says when Cyn finally stops talking. "But I'm not sure this is a dog."

Cyn looks at her watch and sighs, stubs her cigarette out in her plate. "Damn. I gotta get back to work, kiddo. Listen, if you change your mind about the camera, give me a ring."

"Thanks."

"Hey, anytime at all. That's what I'm here for," and she leaves a ten-dollar bill on the table, leaves Terry alone in the heat and the summer sun as bright as the eyes of God.

Home an hour before Aaron, almost always home before Aaron, and she stands in the hall, the bathroom at her back, bedroom to her left, dining room to her right. Listening and hearing only the traffic sounds from the street, the windy whup-whup-whup of the ceiling fan from the living room, all the small and inconsequential daytime noises that the building makes. Faint smell of garbage from the kitchen because she forgot to take it down before work, coffee grounds and last night's spaghetti, soap and potpourri from the bathroom—everything in its place, nothing that shouldn't be there.

"Here doggy," she whispers. "Here boy."

No reply but a car alarm going off somewhere, and Terry feels more foolish than she can remember ever having felt before. What if someone heard her? What if Mr. Dugan next door heard her? He might think she and Aaron had gotten a dog, and all pets are strictly forbidden by their lease. No dogs, no cats, no birds, not even fish because someone on the second floor once had a huge saltwater aquarium that broke and soaked straight through the floor.

Terry chews at a thumbnail and stares at her grandmother's oil painting: the field, the careful dabs of orange and blue and red, a thousand shades of green beneath a wide and perfect sky. No signature, but there's a date—1931—in the lower right-hand corner, and for a moment, she's only thinking about how long it's been since she's taken flowers to the old woman's grave, instead of thinking about the black animal watching her while she slept. A whole house full of antiques when her grandmother died, but her sisters claiming most of them and Terry not really wanting anything but the painting, anyway. A long ago day in June, maybe, a June afternoon seventy years ago, and Terry leans closer, examining the trees at the far edge of the field; never really daylight beneath those trees, between those crooked trunks, the sagging limbs, and then Terry notices the tiny figure standing where the trees begin. Her whole life and all the time spent staring at this painting, and that's something she somehow hasn't seen before.

"Who are you?" Terry asks the canvas, touching it gently with her ring finger, wedding-ring finger, and she squints because she isn't wearing her reading glasses; trying to make out the features, the cherub-round face, golden hair, dress the color of butter, and she realizes that the canvas feels cold, damp, and pulls her hand quickly away. She curses under her breath and takes a step back from the wall, and now she can clearly see the damp spot, no larger than a dime, but completely surrounding, enclosing, the girl in the yellow dress standing at the edge of the forest. She lifts the painting off its hook, and there's a slightly larger stain hiding on the wall behind it. Something that glistens like a slug trail, and Terry sets the canvas down on the floor.

"Goddamn it," she mutters and thinks it's probably the plumbing, the ancient pipes that should have been replaced decades ago, and just the other day Aaron was complaining about the way they clank and wheeze, the way water sometimes comes out of the tap brown after a particularly heavy rain. Terry imagines the leak behind the wall, corroding iron or copper, the patient trickle to seep through the plaster and ruin her grandmother's painting. She touches the wall, and it feels slick, sticky, colder than the spot on the canvas. When she sniffs her fingertip the smell isn't anything that she'd expected, not the moldy, dank scent of wet rot, but something meaty, more like a piece of steak that's gone over or a dead animal at the side of a road.

A dead dog, she thinks, wiping her fingers on her pants leg, and there's a sound behind her, then, the sharp, staccato click of long nails against the hardwood floor. *Don't look, don't see it, just wait for it to go away again,* but she's already turning, worse not to know, worse to have to lay awake wondering and wishing she'd had the nerve . . .

And there's only the empty hallway, a shaft of late afternoon sunlight spilling through the bathroom window, dust motes drifting from shadow into light and back into shadow again. Terry stands very still for a minute, five minutes, and then she goes to the sink to wash the rotting-meat smell off her hand.

"You've just never noticed it, that's all," he said, not looking at her, reading his novel in bed and only half listening while she talked about the girl in the painting, the blonde girl in the yellow dress who hadn't ever been there before, the sticky spot behind the stained canvas. She'd shown him both as soon as he'd come home, and Aaron had only shrugged his shoulders, shaken his head, and "Maybe it's a mouse," he suggested. "Maybe a mouse died back there somewhere," and then he'd asked if she thought they should order Thai or Chinese take-out for dinner.

"It wasn't there before," she said, and he turned a page, scowling at the book instead of scowling at her.

"Of course it's always been there. Don't be silly."

"But Aaron, the wall—"

"I'll call Mrs. White to get a plumber up here to look at the wall," he said. "I'll call her first thing tomorrow."

And now, hours and hours later, she lies wide awake, alone with the night and the contented sound of his snoring, all the restless, old building noises, the muffled murmur of the city outside that never quite goes to sleep, never completely. Like me, she thinks, wishing now that she'd shut the bedroom door so she couldn't see the hallway or her grandmother's painting propped there against the wall beneath the stain. But Aaron doesn't like to sleep with the door shut, so she left it standing open. Terry forces herself to close her eyes.

Of course it's always been there, he said. *Don't be silly,* but she knows better, because she has a photograph, a Polaroid of herself sitting beneath the painting when it was still hanging in the dining room, before Aaron asked her to move it to the hall to make room for a Rothko print he'd ordered from a catalog. The Polaroid is very clear, and there's no girl standing where the trees meet the edge of the field. She showed it to him after dinner, but he only frowned and told her that the girl was too small to see, that there wasn't enough detail in the picture to make her out.

Click, click, click, click, claws on wood, and when she opens her eyes it's standing in the hall, sniffing at the painting.

Wake him up. Wake him up now, but then it turns its head, sleek skull, skin stretched too tight, those shining silver eyes, and she doesn't say a word, doesn't move a muscle. Would stop breathing, would stop her heart from beating if she knew how, and the black thing sits back on velvet haunches and watches her from the doorway. It holds its head cocked to one side, curious-dog expression on its not-quite-dog face, and the dim light through the bedroom window plays tricks in its eyes.

Like rain, the sudden, soft patter of something falling against the roof, and *Let me shut my eyes,* she thinks. *Please God let me shut my eyes.* In the doorway, ebony lips pull back to show teeth like antique ivory, and there's that smile for her again, that smile for her fear, her silent prayers, and now the rain against the roof is so much louder, the loudest raindrops she's ever heard, and how the hell could Aaron sleep through that?

The animal opens its jaws wide, and its howl is the thunder waiting behind the rain, the brittle crackling of the sky, and Terry thinks that there are words in there, too. A small voice sewn up taut, held fast in the rumbling cacophony, lost little girl at the edge of a wood that runs on and on forever.

Let me not see, not hear, please not ever again if I won't have to see this, ready to give up eternity for an instant, begging to a god she doesn't believe in as the black thing steps, finally, across the threshold into the room, stands at the foot of the bed, and the air smells like wildflowers and oil paints, turpentine and warm sunshine on grass.

And then the rain stops falling (if it was rain), and the summer and brush-stroke smells are gone (if they were ever there at all), and where the black thing stood there's only a view of the hallway and the stained wall and the painting leaned against it.

Sleepwalking though the sun-drowned morning, waking disoriented and more exhausted than when she went to bed. Terry called the shoe store and told them she was sick and wouldn't be in today, not so sure it was a lie, nausea and the dull beginnings of a headache, sweating even though the air conditioning was turned down to sixty-five. Not bothering to get dressed, no point if she wasn't going to work, just the gaudy Six Flags T-shirt she'd slept in, panties, bare legs, bare feet. "You don't look so good," Aaron said on his way out the door, and then she was alone. Another cup of coffee, too much milk and not enough sugar, and she's watching sparrows at the bird feeder outside the kitchen window, tiny, nervous beaks snatching greedy mouthfuls of millet and canaryseed until a big blue jay comes along to frighten them away.

A heavy, tumbling sound from the hall, like falling books or rocks, and then surprise that it doesn't startle either her or the hungry bird at the windowsill. She turns to see, the perfect, unobstructed view through the dining room to show her nothing at all, and Terry sets her coffee cup down on the table. The jay watches cautiously as she gets up, slides her chair back, and goes to the drawer where Aaron keeps the few tools they own; she takes out the hammer, a pair of needle-nosed pliers, a sharp linoleum knife, and carries them with her to the hall.

There are no fallen books, or anything else, but she's sure the stain is much larger than it was the day before, that it's grown in the night, almost as big as a grapefruit now. The smell's much stronger, too, and Terry lays the tools on the floor, presses the fingertips of her right hand against the damp place and discovers that it's grown soft, as well. It gives a little when she pushes and then slowly springs back again when she takes her hand away. She wipes her sticky fingers on the front of her shirt and moves the painting into the bedroom, leans it carefully against the foot of the bed. The girl in the yellow dress is still waiting at the edge of the forest, though Terry thinks that maybe the sky isn't quite as bright as it was, grey-blue hint of storm clouds that she doesn't recall, and then the phone rings.

She sits on Aaron's side of the bed and talks to Cyn, but doesn't look away from the wall.

"I was worried, kiddo. You never get sick."

"It's probably something I picked up from a customer. I hate having to handle money. It's probably just a virus."

"Lots of clear fluids and vitamin C," Cyn says.

"Right."

"So, how's the ghost dog? Have you seen it again?"

"No," she says, answering too quickly and wishing she were a better liar. "No, I haven't. I think Aaron was right. I think it was only a bad dream."

A moment's silence from Cyn's end, and Terry doesn't have to see her to know her expression, that practiced skepticism, the doubtful frown, and "No kidding," Cyn says. "That's really too bad. I was starting to look forward to the séance."

"I was being silly. But I never said it was a ghost, did I?"

"No, you didn't. You never said it was a dog, either."

"It might have been a dog," Terry says, staring at the wall, the soft, wet spot, and trying hard to think of a way to end the conversation without making Cyn more suspicious. "It might have been a dream about a dog."

"You know what, kiddo? I get off at two-thirty today. Maybe I should stop by on my way home, just to see how you're doing. See if you need some chicken soup or anything—"

"But I'm not even on your way home, Cyn. I'll be fine, really. I'm feeling much better already. Listen, I left the kettle on the stove. I was making tea when you called."

"I'll call you later," Cyn says, sounding confused, sounding almost angry, and she makes Terry promise to call her if she needs anything before then, if she needs anything at all.

"Sure thing," Terry tells her, and they say good-bye, Cyn drawing it out as long as she can. *Like she's afraid she's never going to talk to me again, like she's afraid I'll disappear the second she hangs up.*

"Just take it easy, you hear me? I mean it," and then there's only the dial-tone drone and the work that's waiting for her in the hall.

— ✧ —

Maybe I won't need the hammer after all, she thinks, picking up the linoleum knife instead, and that's when Terry notices the single dark drop of blood on the floor at her feet. And she stands there, wondering what it means, this new wrinkle, how it fits or doesn't fit, until she finds the smear running down the inside of her left thigh, the red bloom at her crotch. Only that, nothing ghostly, nothing strange, and the relief makes her smile; she briefly considers going to the bathroom to deal with it, but that would take time, and the damage is already done, the stain on her panties, so she sets the curved blade against the wall and drives it in all the way to the wooden handle. It requires hardly any effort at all, the plaster gone soft as cheese, and a stream of something clear leaks from the wound she's made.

"You think it's ever as simple as that?" the black dog (if it is a dog, which she doubts) asks from somewhere directly behind her. "Having cut it out, you can cut it right back in again?"

"I never cut anything," Terry says, no longer smiling, and she draws the blade down the length of the soft spot. The edges of the slit fold back like the petals of a flower, sticky, sweating orchid flesh, and now she can see that the wall isn't white inside.

The black dog laughs, and its claws click, click, click like rosary beads. "Of course you didn't," it chuckles. "Are you sure you have the stomach for this?"

"Go away," Terry growls. "I'm done with you now. I don't have to look at you, anymore."

"He'll see this, you know," it says. "When he comes home, he'll see this and know what you've done."

"Go away!" and she yanks the blade free of the wall and turns quickly around, slashing the empty air where the taunting black dog might have been standing an instant before. Stringy droplets fly from the tip of the linoleum knife and spatter the walls.

"I'm not hiding *anything* from him," she says. "I've *never* tried to hide anything from him," and Terry thinks that she can still hear it laughing at her from somewhere very, very far away. Laughter like bad memories and wasted time, laughter black as its skin, and she turns back to the hole she's made in the wall. At least twice as big as only the moment before, tearing itself wider as she watches, and the linoleum knife slips from her fingers and clatters to the floor.

The laughter fades like thunder, rumbling, rolling away.

When she reaches into the wall, it's warm and soft and Terry breathes in the clinging odor that is as much being born as it is dying, as much conception as decay. She removes the small, hard thing from the quivering center and holds it cupped in one palm, the tiny porcelain doll grown so old the glaze has cracked and some of the paint has flaked away to show bone white underneath.

"You did the right thing," she whispers to the doll. "Never go into those woods alone," and Terry sits down on the floor, dabs the porcelain clean with the hem of her shirt. In a few more minutes, the hole in the wall has closed completely, and there's no sign that it was ever there at all. She glances through the doorway to the bedroom, and the canvas is still leaning against the footboard, paint dried seventy years ago, whole long lifetimes ago, and now there's no one standing at the shadowy place where the wildflowers end and the dark trees start.

Afterword

Originally, and only briefly, titled "The View from the Field," "Apokatastasis" is a peculiar and difficult story, even by own own peculiar and difficult standards. Though written for Ellen Datlow's *The Dark: New Ghost Stories*, it first appeared as part the March 2002 number of the now-defunct webzine, *The Spook* (this was the last time I permitted my fiction to be "published" online, and the webzine's editor, Anthony Sapienza, has *yet* to pay me for use of this story). Though my stories often take a direction I'd not intented when I began, never before or since has one proved as willful as "Apokatastasis." I sometimes feel my conscious mind had only a very small role in writing this story. It was written in August of 2001. Also, it's notable as the *only* thing I was able to complete while living at 60 Delmont Drive in Atlanta (for an account of this particular and memorable disaster, see my blog entry for Thursday, 28 March, 2002). The Changs still owe me money, too.

La Peau Verte

1

IN A DUSTY, antique-littered back room of the loft on St. Mark's Place, room with walls the color of ripe cranberries, Hannah stands naked in front of the towering, mahogany-framed mirror and stares at herself. No—not *her* self any longer, but the new thing that the man and woman have made of her. Three long hours busy with their airbrushes and latex prosthetics, grease paints and powders and spirit gum, their four hands moving as one, roaming excitedly and certainly across her body, hands sure of their purpose. She doesn't remember their names, if, in fact, they ever told their names to her. Maybe they did, and the two glasses of brandy have set the names somewhere just beyond recall. Him tall and thin, her thin but not so very tall, and now they've both gone, leaving her alone. Perhaps their part in this finished; perhaps the man and woman are being paid, and she'll never see either of them again, and she feels a sudden, unexpected pang at the thought, never one for casual intimacies, and they have been both casual and intimate with her body.

The door opens, and the music from the party grows suddenly louder. Nothing she would ever recognize, probably nothing that has a name, even; wild impromptu of drumming hands and flutes, violins and cellos, an incongruent music that is both primitive and drawing-room practiced. The old woman with the mask of peacock feathers and gown of iridescent satin stands in the doorway, watching Hannah. After a moment, she smiles and nods her head slowly, appreciatively.

"Very pretty," she says. "How does it feel?"

"A little strange," Hannah replies and looks at the mirror again. "I've never done anything like this before."

"Haven't you?" the old woman asks her, and Hannah remembers her name, then—Jackie, Jackie something that sounds like Shady or Sadie but isn't either. A sculptor from England, someone said. When she was very young, she knew Picasso, and someone said that, too.

"No," Hannah replies. "I haven't. Are they ready for me now?"

"Fifteen more minutes, give or take. I'll be back to bring you in. Relax. Would you like another brandy?"

Would I? Hannah thinks and glances down at the crystal snifter sitting atop an old secretary next to the mirror. It's almost empty now, maybe one last warm amber sip standing between it and empty. She wants another drink, something to burn away the last, lingering dregs of her inhibition and self-doubt, but "No," she tells the woman. "I'm fine."

"Then chill, and I'll see you in fifteen," Jackie Whomever says, smiles again, her disarming, inviting smile of perfect white teeth, and she closes the door, leaving Hannah alone with the green thing watching her from the mirror.

The old Tiffany lamps scattered around the room shed candy puddles of stained-glass light, light as warm as the brandy, warm as the dark chocolate tones of the intricately carved frame holding the tall mirror. She takes one tentative step nearer the glass, and the green thing takes an equally tentative step nearer her. *I'm in there somewhere,* she thinks. *Aren't I?*

Her skin painted too many competing, complementary

shades of green to possibly count, one shade bleeding into the next, an infinity of greens that seem to roil and flow around her bare legs, her flat, hard stomach, her breasts. No patch of skin left uncovered, her flesh become a rain-forest canopy, waves on the deepest sea, the shells of beetles and leaves from a thousand gardens, moss and emeralds, jade statues and the brilliant scales of poisonous tropical serpents. Her nails polished a green so deep it might almost be black, instead. The uncomfortable scleral contacts to turn her eyes into the blaze of twin chartreuse stars, and Hannah leans a little closer to the mirror, blinking at those eyes, *with* those eyes, the windows to a soul she doesn't have. A soul of everything vegetable and living, everything growing, soul of sage and pond scum, malachite and verdigris. The fragile translucent wings sprouting from her shoulder blades—at least another thousand greens to consider in those wings alone—and all the many places where they've been painstakingly attached to her skin are hidden so expertly she's no longer sure where the wings end and she begins.

The one, and the other.

"I definitely should have asked for another brandy," Hannah says out loud, spilling the words nervously from her ocher, olive, turquoise lips.

Her hair—not *her* hair, but the wig *hiding* her hair—like something parasitic, something growing from the bark of a rotting tree, epiphyte curls across her painted shoulders, spilling down her back between and around the base of the wings. The long tips the man and woman added to her ears so dark that they almost match her nails, and her nipples airbrushed the same lightless, bottomless green, as well. She smiles, and even her teeth have been tinted a matte pea green.

There is a single teardrop of green glass glued firmly between her lichen eyebrows.

I could get lost in here, she thinks and immediately wishes she'd thought something else instead.

Perhaps I already am.

And then Hannah forces herself to look away from the mirror, reaches for the brandy snifter and the last swallow of her drink. Too much of the night still ahead of her to get freaked out over a costume, too much left to do and way too much money for her to risk getting cold feet now. She finishes the brandy, and the new warmth spreading through her belly is reassuring.

Hannah sets the empty glass back down on the secretary and then looks at herself again. And this time it *is* her self, after all, the familiar lines of her face still visible just beneath the make-up. But it's a damn good illusion. *Whoever the hell's paying for this is certainly getting his money's worth,* she thinks.

Beyond the back room, the music seems to be rising, swelling quickly towards crescendo, the strings racing the flutes, the drums hammering along underneath. The old woman named Jackie will be back for her soon. Hannah takes a deep breath, filling her lungs with air that smells and tastes like dust and old furniture, like the paint on her skin, more faintly of the summer rain falling on the roof of the building. She exhales slowly and stares longingly at the empty snifter.

"Better to keep a clear head," she reminds herself.

Is that what I have here? and she laughs, but something about the room or her reflection in the tall mirror turns the sound into little more than a cheerless cough.

And then Hannah stares at the beautiful, impossible green woman staring back at her and waits.

2

"Anything forbidden becomes mysterious," Peter says and picks up his remaining bishop, then sets it back down on the board without making a move. "And mysterious things always become attractive to us, sooner or later. Usually sooner."

"What is that? Some sort of unwritten social law?" Hannah

asks him, distracted by the Beethoven that he always insists on whenever they play chess. *Die Geschöpfe des Prometheus* at the moment, and she's pretty sure he only does it to break her concentration.

"No, dear. Just a statement of the fucking obvious."

Peter picks up the black bishop again, and this time he almost uses it to take one of her rooks, then thinks better of it. More than thirty years her senior and the first friend she made after coming to Manhattan, his salt-and-pepper beard and mustache that's mostly salt, his eyes as grey as a winter sky.

"Oh," she says, wishing he'd just take the damn rook and be done with it. Two moves from checkmate, barring an act of divine intervention, and that's another of his games, Delaying the Inevitable. She thinks he probably has a couple of trophies for it stashed away somewhere in his cluttered apartment, chintzy *faux* golden loving cups for his Skill and Excellence in Procrastination.

"Taboo breeds desire. Gluttony breeds disinterest."

"Jesus, I ought to write these things down," she says, and he smirks at her, dangling the bishop teasingly only an inch or so above the chessboard.

"Yes, you really should. My agent could probably sell them to someone or another. *Peter Mulligan's Big Book of Tiresome Truths.* I'm sure it would be more popular than my last novel. It certainly couldn't be *less*—"

"Will you stop it and *move* already? Take the damned rook, and get it over with."

"But it *might* be a mistake," he says and leans back in his chair, mock suspicion on his face, one eyebrow cocked, and he points towards her queen. "It could be a trap. You might be one of those predators that fakes out its quarry by playing dead."

"You have no idea what you're talking about."

"Yes, I do. You know what I mean. Those animals, the ones that only *pretend* to be dead. You might be one of those."

"I *might* just get tired of this and go the hell home," she sighs, because he knows that she won't, so she can say whatever she wants.

"Anyway," he says, "it's work, if you want it. It's just a party. Sounds like an easy gig to me."

"I have that thing on Tuesday morning though, and I don't want to be up all night."

"Another shoot with Kellerman?" asks Peter, and he frowns at her, taking his eyes off the board, tapping at his chin with the bishop's mitre.

"Is there something wrong with that?"

"You hear things, that's all. Well, *I* hear things. I don't think you ever hear anything at all."

"I need the work, Pete. The last time I sold a piece, I think Lincoln was still President. I'll never make as much money painting as I do posing for *other* people's art."

"Poor Hannah," Peter says. He sets the bishop back down beside his king and lights a cigarette. She almost asks him for one, but he thinks she quit three months ago, and it's nice having at least that one thing to lord over him; sometimes it's even useful. "At least you *have* a fallback," he mutters and exhales; the smoke lingers above the board like fog on a battlefield.

"Do you even know who these people are?" she asks and looks impatiently at the clock above his kitchen sink.

"Not firsthand, no. But then they're not exactly my sort. Entirely too, well . . . " and Peter pauses, searching for a word that never comes, so he continues without it. "But the Frenchman who owns the place on St. Mark's, Mr. Ordinaire—excuse me, *Monsieur* Ordinaire—I heard he used to be some sort of anthropologist. I think he might have written a book once."

"Maybe Kellerman would reschedule for the afternoon," Hannah says, talking half to herself.

"You've actually never tasted it?" he asks, picking up the

bishop again and waving it ominously towards her side of the board.

"No," she replies, too busy now wondering if the photographer will rearrange his Tuesday schedule on her behalf to be annoyed at Peter's cat and mouse with her rook.

"Dreadful stuff," he says and makes a face like a kid tasting brussels sprouts or Pepto-Bismol for the first time. "Might as well have a big glass of black jelly beans and cheap vodka, if you ask me. *La Fée Verte* my fat ass."

"Your ass isn't fat, you skinny old queen," Hannah scowls playfully, reaching quickly across the table and snatching the bishop from Peter's hand. He doesn't resist. This isn't the first time she's grown too tired of waiting for him to move to wait any longer. She takes her white rook off the board and sets the black bishop in its place.

"That's suicide, dear," Peter says, shaking his head and frowning. "You know that, don't you?"

"You know those animals that *bore* their prey into submission?"

"No, I don't believe I've ever heard of them before."

"Then maybe you should get out more often."

"Maybe I should," he replies, setting the captured rook down with all the other prisoners he's taken. "So, are you going to do the party? It's a quick grand, you ask me."

"That's easy for you say. You're not the one who'll be getting naked for a bunch of drunken strangers."

"A fact for which we should *all* be forevermore and eternally grateful."

"You have his number?" she asks, giving in, because that's almost a whole month's rent in one night and, after her last show, beggars can't be choosers.

"There's a smart girl," Peter says and takes another drag off his cigarette. "The number's on my desk somewhere. Remind me again before you leave. Your move."

3

"How old were you when that happened, when your sister died?" the psychologist asks, Dr. Edith Valloton and her smartly-cut hair so black it always makes Hannah think of fresh tar, or old tar gone deadly soft again beneath a summer sun to lay a trap for unwary, crawling things. Someone she sees when the nightmares get bad, which is whenever the painting isn't going well or the modeling jobs aren't coming in or both. Someone she can tell her secrets to who has to *keep* them secret, someone who listens as long as she pays by the hour, the place to turn when faith runs out and priests are just another bad memory to be confessed.

"Almost twelve," Hannah tells her and watches while Edith Valloton scribbles a note on her yellow legal pad.

"Do you remember if you'd begun menstruating yet?"

"Yeah. My periods started right after my eleventh birthday."

"And these dreams, and the stones, this is something you've never told anyone?"

"I tried to tell my mother once."

"She didn't believe you?"

Hannah coughs into her hand and tries not to smile, that bitter, wry smile to give away things she didn't come here to show.

"She didn't even *hear* me," she says.

"Did you try more than once to tell her about the fairies?"

"I don't think so. Mom was always pretty good at letting us know whenever she didn't want to hear what was being said. You learned not to waste your breath."

"Your sister's death, you've said before that it's something she was never able to come to terms with."

"She never tried. Whenever my father tried, or I tried, she treated us like traitors. Like we were the ones who put Judith in her grave. Or like we were the ones *keeping* her there."

"If she couldn't face it, Hannah, then I'm sure it did seem that way to her."

"So, no," Hannah says, annoyed that she's actually paying someone to sympathize with her mother. "No. I guess never really told anyone about it."

"But you think you want to tell me now?" the psychologist asks and sips her bottled water, never taking her eyes off Hannah.

"You said to talk about all the nightmares, all the things I think are nightmares. It's the only one that I'm not sure about."

"Not sure if it's a nightmare, or not sure if it's even a dream?"

"Well, I always thought I was awake. For years, it never once occurred to me I might have only been dreaming."

Edith Valloton watches her silently for a moment, her cat-calm, cat-smirk face, unreadable, too well-trained to let whatever's behind those dark eyes slip and show. Too detached to be smug, too concerned to be indifferent. Sometimes, Hannah thinks she might be a dyke, but maybe that's only because the friend who recommended her is a lesbian.

"Do you still have the stones?" the psychologist asks, finally, and Hannah shrugs out of habit.

"Somewhere, probably. I never throw anything away. They might be up at Dad's place, for all I know. A bunch of my shit's still up there, stuff from when I was a kid."

"But you haven't tried to find them?"

"I'm not sure I *want* to."

"When is the last time you saw them, the last time you can remember having seen them?"

And Hannah has to stop and think, chews intently at a thumbnail and watches the clock on the psychologist's desk, the second hand traveling round and round and round. Seconds gone for pennies, nickels, dimes, and *Hannah, this is the sort of thing you really ought to try to get straight ahead of time,* she thinks in a voice that sounds more like Dr. Valloton's than her own thought-voice. *A waste of money, a waste of time...*

"You can't remember?" the psychologist asks and leans a little closer to Hannah.

"I kept them all in an old cigar box. I think my grandfather gave me the box. No, he didn't. No, he gave it to Judith, and then I took it after the accident. I didn't think she'd mind."

"I'd like to see them someday, if you ever come across them again. Wouldn't that help you to know whether it was a dream or not, if the stones are real?"

"Maybe," Hannah mumbles around her thumb. "And may- be not."

"Why do you say that?"

"A thing like that, words scratched onto a handful of stones, it'd be easy for a kid to fake. I might have made them all myself. Or someone else might have made them, someone playing a trick on me. Anyone could have left them there."

"Did people do that often? Play tricks on you?"

"Not that I can recall. No more than usual."

Edith Valloton writes something else on her yellow pad and then checks the clock.

"You said that there were always stones after the dreams. Never before?"

"No, never before. Always after. They were always there the next day, always in the same place."

"At the old well," the psychologist says, like Hannah might have forgotten and needs reminding.

"Yeah, at the old well. Dad was always talking about doing something about it, before the accident, you know. Something besides a couple of sheets of tin to hide the hole. Afterwards, of course, the county ordered him to have the damned thing filled in."

"Did your mother blame him for the accident, because he never did anything about the well?"

"My mother blamed *everyone*. She blamed him. She blamed me. She blamed whoever had dug that hole in the first goddamn place. She blamed God for putting water underground so people would dig wells to get at it. Believe me, Mom had blame down to an art."

And again, the long pause, the psychologist's measured consideration, quiet moments she plants like seeds to grow ever deeper revelations.

"Hannah, I want you to try to remember the word that was on the first stone you found. Can you do that?"

"That's easy. It was 'follow'."

"And do you also know what was written on the last one, the very last one that you found?"

And this time she has to think, but only for a moment.

"'Fall'," she says. "The last one said 'fall'."

4

Half a bottle of Mari Mayans borrowed from a friend of Peter's, a goth chick who djs at a club that Hannah's never been to because Hannah doesn't go to clubs. Doesn't dance and has always been more or less indifferent to both music and fashion. The goth chick works days at Trash And Vaudeville on St. Mark's, selling Doc Martens and blue hair dye only a couple of blocks from the address on the card that Peter gave her. The place where the party will be. *La Fête de la Fée Verte*, according to the small white card, the card with the phone number. She's already made the call, has already agreed to be there, seven sharp, seven on the dot, and everything that's expected of her has been explained in detail, twice.

Hannah's sitting on the floor beside her bed, a couple of vanilla-scented candles burning because she feels obligated to make at least half a half-hearted effort at atmosphere. Obligatory show of respect for mystique that doesn't interest her, but she's gone to the trouble to borrow the bottle of liqueur; the bottle passed to her in a brown paper bag at the boutique, anything but inconspicuous, and the girl glared out at her, cautious from beneath lids so heavy with shades of black and purple that Hannah was amazed the girl could open her eyes.

"You're a friend of Peter's?" the girl asked suspiciously.

"Yeah," Hannah replied, accepting the package, feeling vaguely, almost pleasurably illicit. "We're chess buddies."

"A painter," the girl said.

"Most of the time."

"Peter's a cool old guy. He made bail for my boyfriend once, couple of years back."

"Really? Yeah, he's wonderful," and Hannah glanced nervously at the customers browsing the racks of leather handbags and corsets, then at the door and the bright daylight outside.

"You don't have to be so jumpy. It's not illegal to have absinthe. It's not even illegal to drink it. It's only illegal to import it, which you didn't do. So don't sweat it."

Hannah nodded, wondering if the girl was telling the truth, if she knew what she was talking about. "What do I owe you?" she asked.

"Oh, nothing," the girl replied. "You're a friend of Peter's, and, besides, I get it cheap from someone over in Jersey. Just bring back whatever you don't drink."

And now Hannah twists the cap off the bottle, and the smell of anise is so strong, so immediate, she can smell it before she even raises the bottle to her nose. *Black jelly beans,* she thinks, just like Peter said, and that's something else she never cared for. As a little girl, she'd set the black ones aide, and the pink ones, too, saving them for her sister. Her sister had liked the black ones.

She has a wine glass, one from an incomplete set she bought last Christmas, secondhand, and a box of sugar cubes, a decanter filled with filtered tap water, a spoon from her mother's mismatched antique silverware. She pours the absinthe, letting it drip slowly from the bottle until the fluorescent yellow-green liquid has filled the bottom of the glass. Then Hannah balances the spoon over the mouth of the goblet and places one of the sugar cubes in the tarnished bowl of the spoon. She remembers watching Gary Oldman and Winona Ryder doing this in *Dracula*, remembers seeing the movie with a boyfriend who eventually left her for another man, and the memory and all its associations are enough to make her stop and sit staring at the glass for a moment.

"This is so fucking silly," she says, but part of her, the part that feels guilty for taking jobs that pay the bills but have nothing to do with painting, the part that's always busy rationalizing and justifying the way she spends her time, assures her it's a sort of research. A new experience, horizon-broadening something to expand her mind's eye, and, for all she knows, it might lead her art somewhere it needs to go.

"Bullshit," she whispers, frowning down at the entirely uninviting glass of Spanish absinthe. She's been reading, *Absinthe: History in a Bottle* and *Artists and Absinthe,* accounts of Van Gogh and Rimbaud, Oscar Wilde and Paul Marie Verlaine and their various relationships with this foul-smelling liqueur. She's never had much respect for artists who use this or that drug as a crutch and then call it their muse; heroin, cocaine, pot, booze, what-the-hell-ever, all the same shit as far as she's concerned. An excuse, an inability in the artist to hold himself accountable for his *own* art, a lazy cop-out, as useless as the idea of the muse itself. And *this* drug, this drug in particular, so tied up with art and inspiration there's even a Renoir painting decorating the Mari Mayans label, or at least it's something that's supposed to *look* like a Renoir.

But you've gone to all this trouble, hell, you may as well taste it, at least. Just a taste, to satisfy curiosity, to see what all the fuss is about.

Hannah sets the bottle down and picks up the decanter, pouring water over the spoon, over the sugar cube, and the absinthe louches quickly to an opalescent, milky white-green.

Then she puts the decanter back on the floor and stirs the half-dissolved sugar into the glass, sets the spoon aside on a china saucer.

"Enjoy the ride," the goth girl said as Hannah walked out of the shop. "She's a blast."

Hannah raises the glass to her lips, sniffs at it, wrinkling her nose, and the first, hesitant sip is even sweeter and more piquant than she expected, sugar-soft fire when she swallows, a seventy-proof flower blooming warm in her belly. But the taste not nearly as disagreeable as she thought it would be, the sudden licorice and alcohol sting, a faint bitterness underneath that she guesses might be the wormwood. The second sip is less of a shock, especially since her tongue seems to have gone slightly numb.

She opens *Absinthe: History in a Bottle* again, opening the book at random, and there's a full-page reproduction of Albert Maignan's *The Green Muse*. Blonde woman with marble skin, golden hair, wrapped in diaphanous folds of olive, her feet hovering weightless above bare floorboards, her hands caressing the forehead of an intoxicated poet. The man is gaunt and seems lost in some ecstasy or revelry or simple delirium, his right hand clawing at his face, the other hand open in what might have been meant as a feeble attempt to ward off the attentions of his unearthly companion. *Or,* Hannah thinks, *perhaps he's reaching for something.* There's a shattered green bottle on the floor at his feet, a full glass of absinthe on his writing desk.

She takes another sip and turns the page.

A photograph, Verlaine drinking absinthe in the Café Procope.

Another, bolder swallow, and the taste is becoming familiar now, almost, *almost* pleasant.

Another page. Jean Béraud's *Le Boulevard, La Nuit.*

When the glass is empty and the buzz in her head and eyes

so gentle, buzz like a stinging insect wrapped in spider silk and honey, Hannah takes another sugar cube from the box and pours another glass.

5

"Fairies.

'Fairy crosses.'

Harper's Weekly, 50-715:

That, near the point where the Blue Ridge and the Allegheny Mountains unite, north of Patrick County, Virginia, many little stone crosses have been found.

A race of tiny beings.

They crucified cockroaches.

Exquisite beings—but the cruelty of the exquisite. In their diminutive way they were human beings. They crucified.

The 'fairy crosses,' we are told in *Harper's Weekly,* range in weight from one-quarter of an ounce to an ounce: but it is said, in the *Scientific American,* 79-395, that some of them are no larger than the head of a pin.

They have been found in two other states, but all in Virginia are strictly localized on and along Bull Mountain...

... I suppose they fell there."

Charles Fort, *The Book of the Damned* (1919)

6

In the dream, which is never the same thing twice, not precisely, Hannah is twelve years old and standing at her bedroom window watching the backyard. It's almost dark, the last rays of twilight, and there are chartreuse fireflies dappling the shadows, already a few stars twinkling in the high indigo sky, the call of a whippoorwill from the woods nearby.

Another whippoorwill replies.

And the grass is moving. The grass grown so tall because her father never bothers to mow it anymore. It could be wind, only there is no wind; the leaves in the trees are all perfectly, silently still, and no limb swaying, no twig, no leaves rustling in even the stingiest breeze. Only the grass, and *It's probably just a cat,* she thinks, *a cat or a skunk or a raccoon.*

The bedroom has grown very dark, and she wants to turn on a lamp, afraid of the restless grass even though she knows it's only some small animal, awake for the night and hunting, taking a short cut across their backyard. She looks over her shoulder, meaning to ask Judith to please turn on a lamp, but there's only the dark room, Judith's empty bunk, and she remembers it all again. It's always like the very first time she heard, the surprise and disbelief and pain always that fresh, the numbness that follows that absolute.

"Have you seen your sister?" her mother asks from the open bedroom door. There's so much night pooled there that she can't make out anything but her mother's softly glowing eyes the soothing color of amber beads, two cat-slit pupils swollen wide against the gloom.

"No, Mom," Hannah tells her, and there's a smell in the room then like burning leaves.

"She shouldn't be out so late on a school night."

"No, Mom, she shouldn't," and the eleven-year-old Hannah is amazed at the thirty-five-year-old's voice coming from her mouth; the thirty-five-year-old Hannah remembers how clear, how unburdened by time and sorrow, the eleven-year-old Hannah's voice could be.

"You should look for her," her mother says.

"I always do. That comes later."

"Hannah, have you seen your sister?"

Outside, the grass has begun to swirl, rippling round and round upon itself, and there's the faintest green glow dancing a few inches above the ground.

The fireflies, she thinks, though she knows it's not the fireflies, the way she knows it's not a cat, or a skunk, or a raccoon making the grass move.

"Your father should have seen to that damned well," her mother mutters, and the burning-leaves smell grows a little stronger. "He should have done something about that years ago."

"Yes, Mom, he should have. You should have made him."

"No," her mother replies angrily. "This is not my fault. None of it's my fault."

"No, of course it's not."

"When we bought this place, I told him to see to that well. I *told* him it was dangerous."

"You were right," Hannah says, watching the grass, the softly pulsing cloud of green light hanging above it. The light is still only about as big as a basketball. Later, it'll get a lot bigger. She can hear the music now, pipes and drums and fiddles, like a song from one of her father's albums of folk music.

"Hannah, have you seen your sister?"

Hannah turns and stares defiantly back at her mother's glowing, accusing eyes.

"That makes three, Mom. Now you have to leave. Sorry, but them's the rules," and her mother does leave, obedient phantom fading slowly away with a sigh, a flicker, a half-second when the darkness seems to bend back upon itself, and she takes the burning-leaves smell with her.

The light floating above the backyard grows brighter, reflecting dully off the windowpane, off Hannah's skin and the room's white walls. The music rises to meet its challenge.

Peter's standing beside her now, and she wants to hold his hand, but doesn't, because she's never quite sure if he's supposed to be in this dream.

"I am the Green Fairy," he says, sounding tired and older than he is, sounding sad. "My robe is the color of despair."

"No," she says. "You're only Peter Mulligan. You write books about places you've never been and people who will never be born."

"You shouldn't keep coming here," he whispers, the light from the backyard shining in his grey eyes, tinting them to moss and ivy.

"Nobody else does. Nobody else ever could."

"That doesn't mean—"

But he stops and stares speechlessly at the backyard.

"I should try to find Judith," Hannah says. "She shouldn't be out so late on a school night."

"That painting you did last winter," Peter mumbles, mumbling like he's drunk or only half awake. "The pigeons on your windowsill, looking in."

"That wasn't me. You're thinking of someone else."

"I hated that damned painting. I was glad when you sold it."

"So was I," Hannah says. "I should try to find her now, Peter. It's almost time for dinner."

"I am ruin and sorrow," he whispers.

And now the green light is spinning very fast, throwing off gleaming flecks of itself to take up the dance, to swirl about their mother star, little worlds newborn, universes, and she could hold them all in the palm of her right hand.

"What I need," Peter says, "is blood, red and hot, the palpitating flesh of my victims."

"Jesus, Peter, that's purple even for you," and Hannah reaches out and lets her fingers brush the glass. It's warm, like the spring evening, like her mother's glowing eyes.

"I didn't write it," he says.

"And I never painted pigeons."

She presses her fingers against the glass and isn't surprised when it shatters, explodes, and the sparkling diamond blast is blown inward, tearing her apart, shredding the dream until it's only unconscious, fitful sleep.

"I wasn't in the mood for this," Hannah says and sets the paper saucer with three greasy, uneaten cubes of orange cheese and a couple of Ritz crackers down on one corner of a convenient table. The table is crowded with fliers about other shows, other openings at other galleries. She glances at Peter and then at the long white room and the canvases on the walls.

"I thought it would do you good to get out. You never go anywhere anymore."

"I come to see you."

"My point exactly, dear."

Hannah sips at her plastic cup of warm merlot, wishing she had a beer, instead.

"And you said that you liked Perrault's work."

"Yeah," she says. "I'm just not sure I'm up for it tonight. I've been feeling pretty morbid lately, all on my own."

"That's generally what happens to people who swear off sex."

"Peter, I didn't *swear off* anything."

And she follows him on their first slow circuit around the room, small talk with people that she hardly knows or doesn't want to know at all, people who know Peter better than they know her, people whose opinions matter and people whom she wishes she'd never met. She smiles and nods her head, sips her wine, and tries not to look too long at any of the huge, dark canvases spaced out like oil and acrylic windows on a train.

"He's trying to bring us down, down to the very core of those old stories," a woman named Rose tells Peter. She owns a gallery somewhere uptown, the sort of place where Hannah's paintings will never hang. "'Little Red Riding Hood,' 'Snow White,' 'Hansel and Gretel,' all those old fairy tales," Rose says. "It's a very post-Freudian approach."

"Indeed," Peter says. *As if he agrees,* Hannah thinks, *as if he even cares,* when she knows damn well he doesn't.

"How's the new novel coming along?" Rose asks him.

"Like a mouthful of salted thumbtacks," he replies, and she laughs.

Hannah turns and looks at the nearest painting, because it's easier than listening to the woman and Peter pretend to enjoy one another's company. A somber storm of blacks and reds and greys, dappled chaos struggling to resolve itself into images, images stalled at the very edge of perception; she thinks she remembers having seen a photo of this canvas in *Artforum*.

A small beige card on the wall to the right of the painting identifies it as *Night in the Forest*. There isn't a price because none of Perrault's paintings are ever for sale. She's heard rumors that he's turned down millions, tens of millions, but suspects that's all exaggeration and PR. Urban legends for modern artists, and from the other things that she's heard, he doesn't need the money, anyway.

Rose says something about the exploration of possibility and fairy tales and children using them to avoid any *real* danger, something that Hannah's pretty sure she's lifted directly from Bruno Bettelheim.

"Me, I was always rooting for the wolf," Peter says, "or the wicked witch or the three bears or whatever. I never much saw the point in rooting for silly girls too thick not to go wandering about alone in the woods."

Hannah laughs softly, laughing to herself, and takes a step back from the painting, squinting at it. A moonless sky pressing cruelly down upon a tangled, writhing forest, a path and something waiting in the shadows, stooped shoulders, ribsy, a calculated smudge of scarlet that could be its eyes. There's no one on the path, but the implication is clear—there will be, soon enough, and the thing crouched beneath the trees is patient.

"Have you seen the stones yet?" Rose asks and no, Peter replies, no we haven't.

"They're a new direction for him," she says. "This is only the second time they've been exhibited."

If I could paint like that, Hannah thinks, *I could tell Dr. Valloton to kiss my ass. If I could paint like that, it would be an exorcism.*

And then Rose leads them both to a poorly-lit corner of the gallery, to a series of rusted wire cages, and inside each one is a single stone. Large pebbles or small cobbles, stream-worn slate and granite, and each stone has been crudely engraved with a single word.

The first one reads "follow."

"Peter, I need to go now," Hannah says, unable to look away from the yellow-brown stone, the word tattooed on it, and she doesn't dare let her eyes wander ahead to the next one.

"Are you sick?"

"I need to go, that's all. I need to go *now.*"

"If you're not feeling well," the woman named Rose says, trying too hard to be helpful, "there's a restroom in the back."

"No, I'm fine. Really. I just need some air."

And Peter puts an arm protectively around her, reciting his hurried, polite good-byes to Rose. But Hannah still can't look away from the stone, sitting there behind the wire like a small and vicious animal at the zoo.

"Good luck with the book," Rose says and smiles, and Hannah's beginning to think she *is* going to be sick, that she will have to make a dash for the toilet, after all. A taste like foil in her mouth and her heart like a mallet on dead and frozen beef, adrenaline, the first eager tug of vertigo.

"It was good to meet you, Hannah," the woman says, and Hannah manages to smile, manages to nod her head.

And then Peter leads her quickly back through the crowded gallery, out onto the sidewalk and the warm night spread out along Mercer Street.

8

"Would you like to talk about that day at the well?" Dr. Valloton asks, and Hannah bites at her chapped lower lip.

"No. Not now," she says. "Not again."

"Are you sure?"

"I've already told you everything I can remember."

"If they'd found her body," the psychologist says, "perhaps you and your mother and father would have been able to move on. There could have at least been some sort of closure. There wouldn't have been that lingering hope that maybe someone would find her, that maybe she was alive."

Hannah sighs loudly, looking at the clock for release, but there's still almost half an hour to go.

"Judith fell down the well and drowned," she says.

"But they never found the body."

"No, but they found enough, enough to be sure. She fell down the well. She drowned. It was very deep."

"You said you heard her calling you—"

"I'm not sure," Hannah says, interrupting the psychologist before she can say the things she was going to say next, before she can use Hannah's own words against her. "I've never been absolutely sure. I told you that."

"I'm sorry if it seems like I'm pushing," Dr. Valloton says.

"I just don't see any reason to talk about it again."

"Then let's talk about the dream, Hannah. Let's talk about the day you saw the fairies."

9

The dreams, or the day from which the dreams would arise and, half-forgotten, seek always to return. The dreams or the day itself, the one or the other, it makes very little difference. The mind exists only in a moment, always, a single flickering moment, remembered or actual, dreaming or awake or something between the two, the precious, treacherous illusion of Present floundering in the crack between Past and Future.

The dream of the day—or the day—and the sun is high and small and white, a dazzling July sun coming down in shafts through the tall trees in the woods behind Hannah's house. She's running to catch up with Judith, her sister two years older and her legs grown longer, always leaving Hannah behind. *You can't catch me, slowpoke. You can't even keep up.* Hannah almost trips in a tangle of creeper vines and has to stop long enough to free her left foot.

"Wait up!" she shouts, and Judith doesn't answer. "I want to see. Wait for me!"

The vines try to pull one of Hannah's tennis shoes off and leave bright beads of blood on her ankle. But she's loose again in only a moment, running down the narrow path to catch up, running through the summer sun and the oak-leaf shadows.

"I found something," Judith said to her that morning after breakfast. The two of them sitting on the back porch steps, and "Down in the clearing by the old well," she said.

"What? What did you find?"

"Oh, I don't think I should tell you. No, I *definitely* shouldn't tell you. You might go and tell Mom and Dad. You might spoil everything."

"No, I wouldn't. I wouldn't tell them anything. I wouldn't tell anyone."

"Yes, you would, big mouth."

And, finally, she gave Hannah half her allowance to tell, half to show whatever there was to see. Her sister dug deep down into the pockets of her jeans, and her hand came back up with a shiny black pebble.

"I just gave you a whole dollar to show me a *rock?*"

"No, stupid. *Look* at it," and Hannah held out her hand.

The letters scratched deep into the stone—JVDTH—five

crooked letters that almost spelled her sister's name, and Hannah didn't have to pretend not to be impressed.

"Wait for me!" she shouts again, angry now, her voice echoing around the trunks of the old trees and dead leaves crunching beneath her shoes. Starting to guess that the whole thing was a trick after all, just one of Judith's stunts, and her sister's probably watching her from a hiding place right this very second, snickering quietly to herself. Hannah stops running and stands in the center of the path, listening to the murmuring forest sounds around her.

And something faint and lilting that might be music.

"That's not all," Judith said. "But you have to *swear* you won't tell Mom and Dad."

"I swear."

"If you do tell, well, I *promise* I'll make you wish you hadn't."

"I won't tell anyone *anything.*"

"Give it back," Judith said, and Hannah immediately handed the black stone back to her. "If you *do* tell—"

"I already said I won't. How many times do I have to say I won't tell?"

"Well then," Judith said and led her around to the back of the little tool shed where their father kept his hedge clippers and bags of fertilizer and the old lawnmowers he liked to take apart and try to put back together again.

"This better be *worth* a dollar," Hannah said.

She stands very, very still and listens to the music, growing louder; she thinks it's coming from the clearing up ahead.

"I'm going back home, Judith!" she shouts, not a bluff because suddenly she doesn't care whether or not the thing in the jar was real, and the sun doesn't seem as warm as it did only a moment ago.

And the music keeps getting louder.

And louder.

And Judith took an empty mayonnaise jar out of the empty

rabbit hutch behind the tool shed. She held it up to the sun, smiling at whatever was inside.

"Let me see," Hannah said.

"Maybe I should make you give me another dollar first," her sister replied, smirking, not looking away from the jar.

"No way," Hannah said indignantly. "Not a snowball's chance in hell," and she grabbed for the jar, then, but Judith was faster, and her hand closed around nothing at all.

In the woods, Hannah turns and looks back towards home, then turns back towards the clearing again, waiting for her just beyond the trees.

"Judith! This isn't funny! I'm going home right this second!"

Her heart is almost as loud as the music now. Almost. Not quite, but close enough.

Pipes and fiddles, drums and a jingle like tambourines.

And Hannah takes another step towards the clearing, because it's nothing at all but her sister trying to scare her, stupid because it's broad daylight, and Hannah knows these woods like the back of her hand.

Judith unscrewed the lid of the mayonnaise jar and held it out so Hannah could see the small, dry thing curled in a lump at the bottom. Tiny mummy husk of a thing, grey and crumbling in the morning light.

"It's just a damn dead mouse," Hannah said disgustedly. "I gave you a whole dollar to see a rock and a dead mouse in a jar?"

"It's *not* a mouse, stupid. Look closer."

And so she did, bending close enough that she could see the perfect dragonfly wings on its back, transparent, iridescent wings to glimmer faintly in the sun. Hannah squinted and realized that she could see its face, realized that it *had* a face.

"Oh," she said, looking quickly up at her sister, who was grinning triumphantly. "Oh, Judith. Oh my god. What is it?"

"Don't you know?" Judith asked her. "Do I have to tell you everything?"

Hannah picks her way over the deadfall just before the clearing, the place where the path through the woods disappears beneath a jumble of fallen, rotting logs. There was a house back here, her father said, a long, long time ago. Nothing left but a big pile of rocks where the chimney once stood and the well covered over with sheets of rusted corrugated tin. There was a fire, her father said, and everyone in the house died.

On the other side of the deadfall, Hannah takes a deep breath and steps out into the daylight, leaving the tree shadows behind, forfeiting her last chance not to see.

"Isn't it cool," Judith said. "Isn't it the coolest thing you ever seen?"

Someone's pushed aside the sheets of tin, and the well is so dark that even the sun won't go there. And then Hannah sees the wide ring of mushrooms, the perfect circle of toadstools and red caps and spongy brown morels growing round the well. The heat shimmers off the tin, dancing mirage shimmer like the air here is turning to water, and the music is very loud now.

"I found it," Judith whispered, screwing the top back onto the jar as tightly as she could. "I found it, and I'm going to keep it. And you'll keep your mouth shut about it, or I'll never, *ever* show you anything else again."

Hannah looks up from the mushrooms, from the open well, and there are a thousand eyes watching her from the edges of the clearing. Eyes like indigo berries and rubies and drops of honey, gold and silver coins, eyes like fire and ice, eyes like seething dabs of midnight. Eyes filled with hunger beyond imagining, neither good nor evil, neither real nor impossible.

Something the size of a bear, squatting in the shade of a poplar tree, raises its shaggy charcoal head and smiles.

"That's another pretty one," it growls.

And Hannah turns and runs.

10

"But you *know*, in your soul, what you must have really seen that day," Dr. Valloton says and taps the eraser end of her pencil lightly against her front teeth. There's something almost obscenely earnest in her expression, Hannah thinks, in the steady *tap tap tap* of the pencil against her perfectly spaced, perfectly white incisors. "You saw your sister fall into the well, or you realized that she just had. You may have heard her calling out for help."

"Maybe I pushed her in," Hannah whispers.

"Is that what you *think* happened?"

"No," Hannah says and rubs at her temples, trying to massage away the first dim throb of an approaching headache. "But, most of the time, I'd rather believe that's what happened."

"Because you *think* it would be easier than what you remember."

"Isn't it? Isn't easier to believe she pissed me off that day, and so I shoved her in? That I made up these crazy stories so I'd never have to feel guilty for what I'd done? Maybe that's what the nightmares are, my conscience trying to fucking force me to come clean."

"And what are the stones, then?"

"Maybe I put them all there myself. Maybe I scratched those words on them myself and hid them there for me to find, because I knew that would make it easier for me to believe. If there was something that real, that tangible, something solid to remind me of the story, that the story is supposed to be the truth."

A long moment of something that's almost silence, just the clock on the desk ticking and the pencil tapping against the psychologist's teeth. Hannah rubs harder at her temples, the real pain almost within sight now, waiting for her just a little ways past this moment or the next, vast and absolute, deep purple shot through with veins of red and black. Finally, Dr. Valloton lays her pencil down and takes a deep breath.

"Is this a confession, Hannah?" she asks, and the obscene earnestness is dissolving into something that may be eager anticipation or simple clinical curiosity or only dread. "Did you kill your sister?"

And Hannah shakes her head and shuts her eyes tight.

"Judith fell into the well," she says calmly. "She moved the tin and got too close to the edge. The sheriff showed my parents where a little bit of the ground had collapsed under her weight. She fell into the well, and she drowned."

"Who are you trying so hard to convince? Me or yourself?"

"Do you really think it matters?" Hannah replies, matching a question with a question, tit for tat, and "Yes," Dr. Valloton says. "Yes, I do. You need to know the truth."

"Which one?" Hannah asks, smiling against the pain swelling behind her eyes, and this time the psychologist doesn't bother answering, lets her sit silently with her eyes shut until the clock decides her hour's up.

11

Peter Mulligan picks up a black pawn and moves it ahead two squares; Hannah removes it from the board with a white knight. He isn't even trying today, and that always annoys her.

Peter pretends to be surprised that's he's lost another piece, then pretends to frown and think about his next move while he talks.

"In Russian," he says, "'chernobyl' is the word for wormwood. Did Kellerman give you a hard time?"

"No," Hannah says. "No, he didn't. In fact, he said he'd actually rather do the shoot in the afternoon. So everything's jake, I guess."

"Small miracles," Peter sighs, picking up a rook and setting it back down again. "So you're doing the anthropologist's party?"

"Yeah," she replies. "I'm doing the anthropologist's party."

"*Monsieur* Ordinaire. You think he was born with that name?"

"I think I couldn't give a damn, as long as his check doesn't bounce. A thousand dollars to play dress-up for a few hours. I'd be a fool not to do the damned party."

Peter picks the rook up again and dangles it in the air above the board, teasing her. "Oh, his book," he says. "I remembered the title the other day. But then I forgot it all over again. Anyway, it was something on shamanism and shape-shifters, werewolves and masks, that sort of thing. It sold a lot of copies in '68, then vanished from the face of the earth. You could probably find out something about it online."

Peter sets the rook down and starts to take his hand away.

"Don't," she says. "That'll be checkmate."

"You could at least let me *lose* on my own, dear," he scowls, pretending to be insulted.

"Yeah, well, I'm not ready to go home yet." Hannah replies, and Peter Mulligan goes back to dithering over the chessboard and talking about Monsieur Ordinaire's forgotten book. In a little while, she gets up to refill both their coffee cups, and there's a single black and grey pigeon perched on the kitchen windowsill, staring in at her with its beady piss-yellow eyes. It almost reminds her of something she doesn't want to be reminded of, and so she raps on the glass with her knuckles and frightens it away.

12

The old woman named Jackie never comes for her. There's a young boy, instead, fourteen or fifteen, sixteen at the most, his nails polished poppy red to match his rouged lips, and he's

dressed in peacock feathers and silk. He opens the door and
stands there, very still, watching her, waiting wordlessly. Something like awe on his smooth face, and for the first time Hannah
doesn't just feel nude, she feels *naked*.

"Are they ready for me now?" she asks him, trying to sound
no more than half as nervous as she is, and then turns her head
to steal a last glance at the green fairy in the tall mahogany
mirror. But the mirror is empty. There's no one there at all, neither her nor the green woman, nothing but the dusty back
room full of antiques, the pretty hard-candy lamps, the peeling
cranberry wallpaper.

"My Lady," the boy says in a voice like broken crystal shards,
and then he curtsies. "The Court is waiting to receive you, at
your ready." He steps to one side, to let her pass, and the music
from the party grows suddenly very loud, changing tempo, the
rhythm assuming a furious speed as a thousand notes and
drumbeats tumble and boom and chase one another's tails.

"The mirror," Hannah whispers, pointing at it, at the place
where her reflection should be, and when she turns back to the
boy there's a young girl standing there, instead, dressed in his
feathers and make-up. She could be his twin.

"It's a small thing, My Lady," she says with the boy's sparkling,
shattered tongue.

"What's happening?"

"The Court is assembled," the girl child says. "They are all
waiting. Don't be afraid, My lady. I will show you the way."

The path, the path through the woods to the well, the path down
the well . . .

"Do you have a name?" Hannah asks, surprised at the calm
in her voice; all the embarrassment and unease at standing
naked before this child, and the one before, the fear at what
she didn't see gazing back at her in the looking glass, all of that
gone now.

"My name? I'm not such a fool as that, My Lady."

"No, of course not," Hannah replies. "I'm sorry."

"I will show you the way," the child says again. "Never harm, nor spell, nor charm, come our Lady nigh."

"That's very kind of you," Hannah replies. "I was beginning to think that I was lost. But I'm not lost, am I?"

"No, My Lady. You are here."

"Yes. Yes, I *am* here, aren't I?" and the child smiles for her, showing off its sharp crystal teeth. Hannah smiles back, and then she leaves the dusty back room and the mahogany mirror, following the child down a short hallway; the music has filled in all the vacant corners of her skull, the music and the heavy living-dying smells of wildflowers and fallen leaves, rotting stumps and fresh-turned earth. A riotous hothouse cacophony of odors—spring to fall, summer to winter—and she's never tasted air so violently sweet.

. . . the path down the well, and the still black water at the bottom. Hannah, can you hear me? Hannah?

It's so cold down here. I can't see . . .

At the end of the hall, just past the stairs leading back down to St. Mark's, there's a green door, and the girl opens it.

And all the things in the wide, wide room—the unlikely room that stretches so far away in every direction that it could never be contained in any building, not in a thousand buildings—the scampering, hopping, dancing, spinning, flying, skulking things, each and every one of them stops and stares at her. And Hannah knows that they should frighten her, that she should turn and run from this place. But it's really nothing she hasn't seen before, a long time ago, and she steps past the child (who is a boy again) as the wings on her back begin to thrum like the frantic, iridescent wings of bumblebees and hummingbirds, red wasps and hungry dragonflies. Her mouth tastes of anise and wormwood, sugar and hyssop and melissa, and sticky verdant light spills from her skin and pools in the grass and moss at her bare feet.

Sink or swim, and so easy to imagine the icy black well water clos-ing thickly over her sister's face, filling her mouth, slipping up her nostrils, flooding her belly, as clawed hands dragged her down.

And down.

And down.

And sometimes, Dr. Valloton says, sometimes we spend our entire lives just trying to answer one simple question.

The music is a hurricane, swallowing her.

My Lady. Lady of the Bottle. *Artemisia absinthium,* Chernobyl, *absinthion,* Lady of Waking Dreaming, Green Lady of Elation and Melancholy.

I am ruin and sorrow.

My robe is the color of despair.

They bow, *all* of them, and Hannah finally sees the thing wait-ing for her on its prickling throne of woven branches and bird's nests, the hulking antlered thing with blazing eyes, wolf-jawed hart, the man and the stag, and she bows, in her turn.

Afterword

I consider *"La Peau Verte"* my single most accomplished short story to date. Of course, that probably won't last for long. My favorites never seem to get to stay my favorites for more than a couple of years. This is a piece where everything just seems to come together for me, exactly the way I'd intended it to come together. Perhaps I can attribute this to the fact that it was written under the influence of Mari Mayans absinthe. Perhaps the Green Fairy herself made sure I got this one right. Regardless, *"La Peau Verte"* stands as proof that I can write an entire story while intoxicated. In truth, there are several sources of inspiration here: absinthe, various books on fairies, my work with make-up artist Andre P. Freitas, the illustrations of Brian Froud, Charles Vess, Arthur Rackham, and Richard Kirk, and the writings of Charles Fort (again) and Algernon Blackwood. It was written in January and February of 2003 and is published here for the first time.

The Dead and the Moonstruck

BENEATH PROVIDENCE, below the ancient yellow house on Benefit Street where silver-eyed vampires sleep away the days and pass their dusty waxwork evenings with Spanish absinthe and stale memories; this house that once belonged to witches, long ago, this house with as many ghosts and secrets and curses as it has spiders and silverfish—beneath the yellow house, at half past midnight on a bitter February night, Mesdames Terpsichore and Mnemosyne are finishing a lecture with corporeal demonstrations. Lessons for ghoul pups and for the children of the Cuckoo—the changeling brats stolen as babies and raised in the warrens—and for an hour the two old hounds have droned on and on and on about the most efficacious methods for purging a corpse of embalming fluid and other funereal preservatives before it can be safely prepared in the kitchens. The skinny, mouse-haired girl named Starling Jane nodded off twice during the lecture, earning a snarl from Madam Mnemosyne and a mean glare from Madam Terpsichore's blazing yellow eyes.

"That's all for tonight," Madam Terpsichore growls, folding shut the leather satchel that holds her scalpels and syringes, her needles and knives. "But every one of you'd best know *all* the purgatives and detoxicants by the morrow. And you, young lady," and now the *ghul* points a long and crooked finger at Starling Jane, one ebony claw aimed straight at her heart. "*You* need to learn that the day, not the classroom, is the proper place for sleeping."

"Yes, ma'am," Starling Jane whispers and keeps her eyes on the dirt floor of the basement, on her bare feet and an ivory scrap of bone protruding from the earth. "It won't happen again."

There's a hushed titter of laughter and guttural yapping from the rest of the class, and Jane pretends that she's only a beetle or a small red worm, something unimportant that can scurry or slither quickly away, something that can tuck itself out of sight in an unnoticed cranny or crevice, and she'll never have to sit through another dissection lecture or be scolded for dozing off again. Madam Mnemosyne silences the muttering class with a glance, but Jane can still feel their eyes on her, and "I'm sorry," she says.

"I should think that you are," Madam Terpsichore barks. "You're plenty old enough to know better, child," and then, to the other students sitting cross-legged on the basement floor, "Mistress Jane's Third Confirmation is scheduled for the full Hunger Moon, four nights hence. But perhaps she isn't ready, hmmmm? Perhaps she'll be found wanting, and the razor jaws will close tight about her hands. Then maybe we'll have *her* meat on the slab before much longer."

"And no nasty embalming fluid to contend with," Madam Mnemosyne adds.

"Ah, she would be sweet," Madam Terpsichore agrees.

"I'm sorry," Jane says again. "But I'll be ready on the moon."

Madam Terpsichore flares her wide black nostrils, sniffs at the musty cellar air, and her eyes glitter in the candlelight. "See that you are, child," she says. "It would be a shame to lose another sprout so very soon after young Master Lockheart's unfortunate rejection," and then she dismisses the class, and Jane follows all the others from the basement into the old tunnels winding like empty veins beneath the city.

— ◇ —

Later, after Elementary Thaumaturgy and Intermediate Necromancy and a rambling, unscheduled address on the history of the upper nightlands by Master Tantalus, visiting Providence from the Boston warrens. After dinner and the predawn free hour, after all the time lying awake in her narrow bunk, wishing she were asleep but afraid to close her eyes, Starling Jane finally drifts out and down, slipping through the familiar dormitory smells of wet masonry and mildew and millipedes, past the snores and grunts and gentle breathing noises of those who aren't afraid of their dreams. A hundred feet beneath the day-washed pavement of Angell Street, and she spirals easily through velvet folds of consciousness and unconsciousness. Countless bits of senseless, inconsequential remembrance and fancy—simple dreams—leading and misleading her step by step, moment by moment, to the nightmare place she's visited almost every morning or afternoon for two months.

That place where there is a wide blue sky and the sun hanging inconceivably bright directly overhead. Where there is grass and the scent of flowers, and she stands at the top of a hill looking down on a sparkling sea.

"You should have stayed with me," her mother says from somewhere close behind her, and Jane doesn't turn around, because she doesn't want to see. "If you'd have stayed with me, I'd have loved you, and you'd have grown up to be a beautiful woman."

The salt-warm wind off the sea makes waves in the tall grass and whistles past Starling Jane's ears.

"I would have stayed," she says, just like she always says. "If they'd have let me. I would have stayed, if I'd had a choice."

"I knew I'd lose you," her mother replies. "Before you were even born, I knew the monsters would come and steal you away from me. I knew they'd hide you from me and make you forget my face."

"How could you have known all that?" Jane asks. Down on the beach, there are children playing with a big yellow-brown dog. They throw pieces of driftwood, and the dog runs after them, and sometimes it brings them back again.

"Oh, I knew, all right," her mother says. "Trust me, I *knew* what was coming. I heard them in the night, outside my bedroom window, scratching at the glass, wanting in."

"I have to pass one more test, Mother. I just have to pass one more test, and they'll let me live."

"You would have been such a beautiful girl. Just look at what they've made of you, instead."

On the beach, the children chase the yellow-brown dog through the surf, laughing and splashing so loudly that Starling Jane can hear them all the way up at the top of the hill.

"They'll make you a monster, too," her mother says.

"I wish they could," Jane mutters to herself, because she knows it doesn't matter whether or not her mother hears the things she's saying. "I wish to all the dark gods that they could make me like them. But that's not what happens. That's not what happens at all."

"You could come home. Every night, I sit up, waiting for you to come back, for them to bring you back to me."

"You shouldn't do that," Jane whispers, and the hill rumbles softly beneath her. Down on the beach, the children stop playing and turn towards her. She waves to them, but they don't seem to see her.

Or they're afraid of me, she thinks.

"If you fail the test, they might bring you back to me," her mother says hopefully.

"If I fail, they'll kill me," Jane replies. "They'll kill me and eat me. No one ever goes back, once they're chosen by the Cuckoo. No one."

"But you would have been such a beautiful girl," her mother says again. "I would have given you everything."

"It's the last test," Jane whispers.

Beneath her, the hill rumbles again, and the sea has turned to blood, and there are wriggling white things falling from the sky. On the beach, the children and the yellow-brown dog have vanished.

"I'll be waiting," her mother says.

And Jane opens her eyes, tumbling breathlessly back into flesh and bone, and she lies awake until sunset, listening to her heart and the sounds the sleepers make and the faraway din of traffic up on Angell Street.

"You're scared," the ghoul pup named Sorrow says, not asking her but telling her, and then he scratches determinedly at his left ear.

"I'm not scared," Starling Jane tells him, and shakes her head, but she knows it's a lie and, worse still, knows, too, that *he* knows it's a lie.

"Sure, and neither was Lockheart."

"Lockheart wasn't ready. Everyone knew he wasn't ready."

They're sitting on stools near one of the tall kitchen hearths, scrubbing tin plates clean with wire-bristle brushes, sudsy water up to their elbows and puddled on the cobbles at their feet. The washtub between them smells like soap and grease.

"Would *you* eat me?" she asks Sorrow. And he grunts and drops the plate he was scrubbing back into the washtub, then tugs thoughtfully at the coarse, straw-colored tuft of hair sprouting from the underside of his muzzle.

"That's not a fair question. You know underlings never get delicacies like that. Not a scrap. You'd be served to Master Danaüs and the—"

"I was speaking hypothetically," Jane says and adds another

plate to the stack drying in front of the fire. "If they made an exception and you had the opportunity, would you eat me?"

Sorrow stares at her for a long moment, furrows his brow uncertainly and blinks his yellow eyes, and "Wouldn't you *want* me to?" he asks her, finally.

"It wouldn't bother you, eating your best friend?"

Sorrow pulls another plate from the washtub and frowns, looking down at the dishwater now instead of Starling Jane. He scrubs halfheartedly at the bits of meat and gravy and potatoes clinging to the dented tin and then drops the plate back into the tub.

"That wasn't clean, and you know it."

"It's just not a fair question, Jane. Of *course*, I'd eat you. I mean, speaking hypothetically and all. I'm not saying I wouldn't *miss* you, but—"

"You'd eat me, anyway."

"It'd be awful. I'd probably cry the whole time."

"I'm sure you would," Starling Jane says with a sigh, pulling the plate Sorrow didn't wash out of the tub again. There's a piece of burnt potato skin big as her thumb stuck to it. "I hope I'd give you indigestion. You'd have it coming."

"You really are scared," Sorrow scowls and spits into the washtub.

"You're a disgusting pig, you know that?"

"Oink," Sorrow oinks and wrinkles his nostrils.

"I'm *not* scared," Jane says again, because she needs to hear the words. "There's no reason for me to be scared. I've made it past the Harvest Moon and the full Frost Moon. I know my lessons—"

"Book lessons don't get you past the moons. You know that, Jane. Nobody's ever been confirmed because they got good marks."

"It doesn't hurt."

"It doesn't help, either."

"But it doesn't *hurt*," Jane snarls at him and flings her wire-bristle brush at his head. Sorrow ducks, and it hits the wall behind him and clatters to the floor.

"You're crazy," Sorrow says, and then he hops off his stool, knocking it over in the process. "I might be a pig, but you're crazy."

"You *want* me to fail. You want me to fail so you can go through all my things and take whatever you want."

"You don't *have* anything I want," Sorrow barks defensively and takes a quick step backwards, putting more distance between himself and Starling Jane.

"Yes, I do. That owl skull the Bailiff brought me from Salem. You want that. You've *told* me more than once that you wish he'd given it to you instead of me."

"I just said I liked it, that's all."

"And that Narragansett Indian arrowhead I found in the tunnels last summer, you want that, too, don't you?"

"Jane, stop and listen to yourself," Sorrow pleads and takes another step or two away from the hearth. "I do not want you to fail your Confirmation and die, just so I can have your things. That's crazy. You're my *friend*. And I don't have a lot of friends."

"Friends don't eat each other!"

"Someone's gonna *hear* you," Sorrow hisses, and holds a long finger up to his thin black lips. "If old Melpomene finds out you're making such a racket, we'll both be scrubbing pots and plates from now till Judgement Day," and he glances nervously over a shoulder into the shadows waiting just beyond the firelight's reach.

"So maybe I don't care anymore!" Jane shouts at him, and then she reaches into the washtub and yanks out a particularly filthy plate. "I'd rather spend the rest of my life washing dishes for that old bat than wind up in her stew pot or roasting on her spit with a turnip stuffed in my mouth!"

"You're *not* going to fail," Sorrow says, glancing over his left shoulder again. "You're not going to fail, and no one's going to eat you."

"You don't know that."

"Sure I do."

"Go away. Leave me alone," Jane says, letting the filthy plate slip from her fingers. Soapy, lukewarm dishwater splashes out onto her patchwork apron. "That's all I want, Sorrow. I want to be alone. I think I'm going to cry, and I don't want anyone to see. I especially don't want you to see."

"You sure?" Sorrow asks. "Maybe I should stay," and he sits down on the floor as if she's just agreed with him when she hasn't. "I don't mind if you cry."

"Lockheart wasn't ready," she whispers. "That's the difference. He wasn't ready, and I am."

"You bet. I've never seen anyone so ready for anything in my whole life."

"Liar," Jane says and glares at him. In the hearth, one of the logs cracks and shifts and, for a moment, the fire flares so brightly that Sorrow has to squint until it settles down again.

"I wouldn't eat you," he tells her. "Not even if they stewed both your kidneys in crab apples and carrots and parsnips and served them to me with mint jelly, I wouldn't eat you. I swear."

"Thank you," Jane replies, and she tries to smile, but it comes out more of a grimace than a smile. "I wouldn't eat you, either."

"Are you going to throw anything else at me?"

"No," she says. "I'm not going to throw anything else at you. Not ever," and she gets up and retrieves her brush from the floor behind Sorrow's stool.

In a life filled past bursting with mysteries—a life where the mysterious and the arcane, the cryptic and the magical, are the rule, not the exception—if anyone were to ever ask Starling

Jane what one thing she found the *most* mysterious, she would probably say the Bailiff. If he has a name, she's never heard it, this very large, good-natured man with his shiny, bald head and full grey beard, his pudgy link-sausage fingers and rusty iron loop of keys always jangling on his wide belt. Not a vampire nor a ghoul nor any of the other night races, just a man, and Jane's heard rumors that he's a child of the Cuckoo, too, a changeling but also something more than a changeling. And there are other rumors—that he's an exiled demon, or a wizard who's forgotten most of his sorcery, or an ancient, immortal thing no one's ever made up a word for—but to Starling Jane, he's just the Bailiff. A link between the yellow house on Benefit Street and other dark houses in other cities, courier for the most precious packages and urgent messages that can be trusted to no one else.

On the last night before her final rite of Confirmation, the ceremony on the night of the full Hunger Moon, the Bailiff returns from a trip to New Orleans, and after his business with the dead people upstairs and his business with the hounds downstairs, he takes his dinner in the long candlelit dining room where the changeling children and the ghoul pups are fed.

"You'll do fine," he assures Starling Jane, nibbling the last bit of meat from a finger bone. "Everyone gets the shakes before their third moon. It's natural as mold and molars, and don't let no one tell you any different."

Sorrow stops picking his teeth with a thumb claw, and "You heard about Lockheart?" he asks the Bailiff.

"Everyone's heard about Lockheart," a she-pup named Melancholy says and rolls her yellow eyes. "Of course he's heard about Lockheart, you slubberdegullion."

Sorrow snorts and bares his eyeteeth at Melancholy. "What the heck's a slubberdegullion?" he demands.

"If you weren't one, you'd know," she replies brusquely, and

Sorrow growls and tackles her. A moment later, and they're rolling about on the floor between the dinner tables, a blur of fur and insults and dust, and someone starts shouting, "Fight! Fight!" so everyone else comes scrambling to see.

Jane keeps her seat and picks indifferently at the green-white mound of boiled cabbage on her plate. "You have heard about Lockheart?" she asks the Bailiff.

"As it so happens, and with all due respect paid to the sesquipedalian Miss Melancholy down there," and he glances at the commotion on the dining-room floor, "no, my dear, I haven't."

"Oh," Starling says and jabs her cabbage with the bent tines of her fork. "He failed his second."

"Ah, I see. Well, now, I'd have to say that's certainly a bloody shame, of one sort or another."

"He was scared. He froze up right at the start, didn't even make it past the sword bridge. They had to bring him down in a burlap sack."

The Bailiff belches and excuses himself. "Was he a friend of yours?" he asks her.

"No," Jane says. "I always thought he was a disgusting little toad."

"But now you're thinking him failing has something to do with you, is that it?"

"Maybe," Jane replies. "Or maybe I was scared to start with, and that only made it worse."

On the floor, Melancholy pokes Sorrow in his left eye, and he yelps and punches her in the belly.

"Don't seem fair, sometimes, does it?" the Bailiff asks, and then he takes a bite of her cabbage.

"What doesn't seem fair?"

"All these trials for them that never asked to be taken away from their rightful mommas and brought down here to the dark, all these tribulations, while *others*—not naming names, mind you," but Starling Jane knows from the way he raised his voice when he said "others" that he means Sorrow and Melancholy and all the *ghul* pups in general. "All they have to do is be born, then watch their p's and q's, keep their snouts clean, and not a deadly deed in sight."

"Madam Terpsichore says nothing's fair, and it's only asking for misery, expecting things to turn out that way."

"Does she now?"

"All the time."

"Well, you listen to your teachers, child, but, on the other hand, Madam Terpsichore never had to face what's waiting down in that pit during the full Hunger Moon, now did she?"

"No," Jane says, pushing her plate over to the Bailiff's side of the table. "Of course not."

"See, that's what really draws the line between you and her, Miss Starling Jane. Not a lot of words written in some old book by gods no one even remembers but the hounds, not the color of your eyes or how sharp your teeth might be. What matters..." and he pauses to finish her cabbage and start on her slice of rhubarb-and-liver pie. Jane pushes Sorrow's plate across the table to the Bailff, as well.

"Thank you," he says with his mouth full. "I do hate to see good food go to waste. Now, as I was saying, what matters, Miss Jane, what you need to understand come tomorrow night..." and then he stops again to swallow.

"You really shouldn't talk with your mouth full," Jane says. "You'll choke."

The Bailiff takes a drink from his cup and nods his bald head. Now there are a few beads of red wine clinging to his whiskers. "My manners ain't what they used to be," he says.

"You were saying, what I need to understand..."

The Bailiff stops eating, puts his fork down and looks at her, his moss-green eyes like polished gems from the bottom of a deep stream. "You're a brave girl," he says, and smiles, "and one day soon you'll be a fine, brave woman. *That's* the difference, and that's what you need to understand. Madam Terpsichore won't ever have to prove herself the way you already have. What makes us brave isn't lacking the good sense to be afraid, it's looking back at what we've lived through and seeing if we faced it well. The ghouls are your masters, and don't you ever forget that, but they'll never have your courage, because no one's ever gonna make them walk the plank, so to speak."

And then he reaches into a pocket of his baggy coat and pulls out a small gold coin with a square hole punched in the center. The metal glimmers faintly in the candlelight as he holds it up for Jane to see.

"I want you to have this," he says. "But not to keep, mind you. No, when you offer your hands up to old Nidhogg's mouth tomorrow night, I want you to leave this on his tongue. I can't say why, but it's important. Now, do you think you can do that for me?"

Starling nods her head and takes the coin from his hand. "It's very pretty," she says.

"Don't you get scared and forget, now. I want you to put that right there on that old serpent's tongue."

"I won't forget. I promise. Put it on his tongue."

The Bailiff smiles again and goes back to eating, and Jane holds the coin tight and watches Sorrow and Melancholy tumbling about on the floor, nipping at each other's ears, until Madam Melpomene comes to break up the fight.

In the dream, she watches the children on the beach with their dog, and the crimson thunderheads piling up higher and higher above the darkening sea. Her mother has stopped talking, and, because this has never been part of the dream before, Starling Jane turns to see why. But there's no one standing behind her now, only the tall grass and the wind whispering furtively through it and the world running on that way forever.

And then there are no more nights left between Starling Jane and the full Hunger Moon, no more anxious days or hours or minutes, because all moons are inevitable, and no amount of fear or desire can forestall their coming. This is the year of her Third Confirmation, her time for the Trial of the Serpent, because she's survived the first two rites, the Trial of Fire and the Trial of Blades. There are no lessons or chores on the day of a trial, for Jane or any other changeling child, and by the appointed hour the warrens have emptied into the amphitheater carved from solid stone one hundred and fifty feet beneath Federal Hill.

Jane wears the long silver robes of passage and waits alone with blind, decrepit Master Solace in a tiny curtained alcove on the northern rim of the pit. The air stinks of wet stone and rot and the myrrh smoldering in a small brass pot on the floor. Her face is a mask of soot and drying blood, the red and black runes drawn on her skin by Madam Hippodamia, that she might make the descent with all the most generous blessings of the dark gods. From the alcove she can hear the murmuring crowd and knows that Sorrow's out there somewhere, crouched nervously on one of the stone benches, and she wishes she were sitting beside him, and it were someone else's turn to stand before the dragon.

"It's almost time, child," Master Solace barks and blinks at her, his pale, cataract-shrouded eyes the color of butter. "If you are ready, there's nothing to fear."

If I'm ready, she thinks and shuts her eyes tight.

And then the horn, and the ship's bell, and the steady *thump-thump-thump* of the drums begins.

"Walk true," Master Solace says and blinks at her again.

Jane opens her eyes, and the tattered curtain has been pulled back so she can see the torchlight and shadows filling the amphitheater and the pit.

"Walk this path with no doubt in your heart," Master Solace says, and then he ushers Starling Jane out of the alcove to stand on a narrow wooden platform jutting out over the abyss. Above and all around her, the murmuring rises to an excited, expectant crescendo, and *ghul* drum-wraiths hammer at their skins so loudly she wonders that the cavern doesn't collapse from the noise and bury them all alive. *That would be preferable*, she thinks. *That would be easier than dying alone.*

The drumming stops as abruptly as it began, and gradually the murmuring follows suit, and for a moment or two there's no sound from the great chamber but Jane's heartbeat and Master Solace sucking the dull stubs of his teeth. And then one note rings out from the ship's bell, and "All stand," Madam Terpsichore says, shouting to the assembled through her bullhorn.

"Tonight, we have come down to this sacred place of truth and choice to witness the deserved confirmation or the just rejection of Mistress Starling Jane of the Providence warrens. It has been eight years since she was delivered to us by the grace of the Cuckoo, and on this night of the full Hunger Moon we shall all know, once and for all, whether she will serve us until the end of her days."

"Watch your step, girl," Master Solace whispers. "It's a long way down," and then Jane hears the curtain drawn shut again, and she knows that he's left her alone on the wooden platform.

"Go down, Starling Jane," Madam Terpsichore growls. "Go down into the dark and find the hungry jaws of Nidhogg, the dragon that gnaws the very roots of the world tree, drawing ever closer the final days. Find him, changeling, and ask him if you are worthy."

And then the ghoul bows once before she pulls the mahogany lever on her right, and far overhead secret machineries begin to grind, the hesitant turning of iron wheels, the interlocking teeth of ancient, rusted gears, and somewhere on the surface a trapdoor opens and moonlight pours into this hollow place inside the earth.

"Walk true, Starling Jane," Madam Terpsichore says, and then passes the bullhorn to an underling before she sits down again.

The moonlight forms a single, brilliant shaft reaching from the vaulted ceiling of the amphitheater to the very bottom of the black pit, argent lunar rays held together by some clever trick of photomancy Jane knows she'll probably never learn, even if the dragon doesn't take her hands. The crowd makes no sound whatsoever as she turns right and begins her descent along the steep and rickety catwalk set into the walls of the pit. And the drum-wraiths begin drumming again, marking her every footstep with their mallets of bone and ivory.

Starling Jane keeps to the right side of the catwalk, because she's afraid of falling, because she's afraid she might look over the edge and lose her balance. She places one foot after the next, and the next, and the next after that, walking as slowly as she dares, spiraling around the pit, and each circuit is smaller than the last so that the distance to the moonbeam shrinks until she could reach out and brush it with her fingertips. The old planks creak and pop beneath her bare feet, and she tries not to imagine how many decades, how many centuries, it's been since they were anchored to the rock face.

And then, at last, she's standing at the bottom, only one final moment remaining to carry her from the darkness into the blazing white shaft; Jane hesitates a second, half a second, takes a deep breath and lets it out again, and then she steps into the light of the full Hunger Moon.

It's stolen my eyes, she thinks. *It's stolen away my eyes and left me as blind as Master Solace.* This pure and perfect light distilled and concentrated, focused on the dingy reflecting mirror of her soul. It spills over her, dripping from the silver robe, burning away anything less immaculate than itself. She realizes that she's crying, crying at the simple beauty of it. When she wipes her cheeks, the light dances in furious motes across the back of her hand, and she sees that she hasn't gone blind after all. So she kneels on the stone, and the dragon rumbles beneath her like an empty belly waiting to be filled.

Above her, the drum-wraiths fall silent.

"It's okay," she whispers. "It's all okay," and death's not such a terrible thing now that she's seen that light, felt it burrowing its way into her, washing her clean. On the ground in front of her there are two holes, each no more than a few inches across and ringed with hammered gold and platinum.

And she remembers the Bailiff's coin, gold for gold, and reaches into the deep pocket in the robe where she tucked it safely away before Madam Hippodamia led her down to wait in the tiny myrrh-scented alcove with Master Solace. Gold for gold, and the hole at the center of the coin is not so very different from the twin mouths of the dragon.

"Just get it over with," she says and leans forward, plunging both arms into the holes, the Bailiff's coin clutched tightly in her right hand.

Inside, the holes are warm, and the stone has become flesh, flesh and slime and dagger teeth that eagerly caress her fingers and prick her wrists. Nidhogg's poisonous breath rises from the holes—sulfur and brimstone, ash and acid steam—and Jane opens her hand and presses the coin against the thorny tongue of the dragon. The earth rumbles violently again, and Starling Jane waits for the jaws to snap shut.

But then the pit sighs, making a sound like the world rolling over in its sleep, and there's only cold, hard stone encircling her arms. She gasps, pulls her hands quickly from the holes and stares at them in disbelief, all ten fingers right there in front of her, and only a few scratches, a few drops of dark blood, to prove that there was ever any danger at all.

High above, the amphitheater erupts in a thunderous clamor, a joyful, relieved pandemonium of barks and shouts and clapping hands, howls and laughter and someone ringing the ship's bell again and again.

Jane sits back on her heels and stares up into the moonlight, letting it pour down into her, drinking its impossible radiance through her strangling pinpoint pupils and every pore of her body, letting it fill her against all the endless nights to come, all the uncountable darknesses that lie ahead. And when she cannot hold another drop, Starling Jane stands up again, bows once, and only once, to Nidhogg Rootnibbler, exactly the way that Madam Terpsichore said she should, and then the changeling starts the long walk back up the catwalk to the alcove. With the applause raining down around her and the moonlight in her eyes, it doesn't seem to take any time at all.

Afterword

"The Dead and the Moonstruck" takes its title from H. P. Lovecraft's celebrated essay, "Supernatural Horror in Literature" (1925-27), a line that also served as the title for Chapter Five of my novel, *Threshold*. Written in July 2003 for Candlewick Press' "young-adult" anthology, *Gothic! Ten Original Dark Tales*, it's the first time that I wrote a story aimed specifically at a younger readership. Approaching this anthology, I was very skeptical of my ability to write for the YA market, and after months had passed without one suitable idea coming to fruition, I very nearly pulled out of the project. Then, almost at the last minute, Kathryn suggested I might write a story about Starling Jane, the changeling girl who'd been an important supporting character in *Low Red Moon*. I loved the idea immediately. In the novel, she'd been a teenager, but here I had the opportunity to go back and revisit her as a child and to flesh out the formative years of the Children of the Cuckoo. In many ways, it was also a practice run for my next novel, *Daughter of Hounds*. I'm pleased with the result.

The Dandridge Cycle

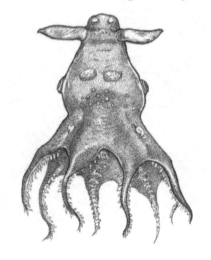

A Redress for Andromeda

WHERE THE LAND ENDS and the unsleeping, omnivorous Pacific has chewed the edge of the continent ragged, the old house sits alone in the tall grass, waiting for Tara. She parks the rental car at the edge of the sandy dirt road and gets out, stares towards the house and the sea, breathing the salt and the night, the moonlight and all the wine- and applecrisp October smells. The wind whips the grass, whips it into tall waves and fleeting troughs the way it whips the sea, and Tara watches the house as the house watches her. Mutual curiosity or wary misgiving, one or the other or both, and she decides to leave the car here and walk the rest of the way.

There are a few other cars, parked much closer to the house, though not as many as she expected, and the porch is burning down in a mad conflagration of jack-o'-lanterns, a hundred candle-glowing eyes and mouths and nostrils, or at least that's how it looks to her. Walking along the sandy road as it curves towards the ocean and the tall gabled house with its turrets and lightning rods, that's how it looks; the house besieged by all those carved and flaming pumpkins, and she takes her time, walks slow, listening to the wind and the sea slamming itself against the headland. The wind colder than she expected, and all she's wearing is a white dress, one of her simple shirt-waist dresses fashionable forty or forty-five years ago, a dress her mother might have worn when she was a girl; the white dress with its sensible cuffs and collars, and black espadrilles on her feet, shoes as simple as the dress because that's what Darren said. *It isn't a masquerade, nothing like that at all. Just be yourself.* But she wishes she'd remembered her coat. It's lying on the passenger seat of the rental car, and she thinks about going back for it, and then decides she can stand the chill as far as the front door.

She knows a little about this house, but only because Darren told her about it; never much of a geek for architecture herself, even old houses with stories like this one has. The Dandridge House, because the man who built it in 1890 was named Dandridge, and back in the sixties it was one of those places that hippies and occultists liked to haunt, someplace remote enough and out of sight and nobody to notice if you sacrificed a farm animal now and then. Darren told her ghost stories, too, because a house like this has to have ghost stories, but she took two Xanax on the drive up from Monterey, and they've all run together in her head.

Not much farther before a sandy walkway turns off the sandy road, a rusted mailbox on a post that's fallen over and no one's bothered to set it right again, and Tara follows the path towards the wide, pumpkincrowded porch that seems to wrap itself all the way around the house. Her shoes are already full of sand, sand getting in between her toes, and she stops and looks back towards her car, all by itself at the edge of the road, and now it seems a long way back.

There's a black-haired woman sitting on the porch steps, smoking a cigarette and watching her, and when Tara smiles the woman smiles back at her. "You must be Tara," the woman says and holds out her hand. "Darren said that you would be late. I thought someone should wait out here for you, a friendly face in the wilderness, you know."

Tara says thank you and shakes the woman's hand, and this close the jack-o'-lanterns seem very, very bright; they hurt her eyes after the night, and she squints at them and nods for the woman on the steps of the house.

"You didn't have any trouble finding us?" the woman asks, and "No," Tara says. "No trouble at all. Darren gives good directions."

"Well, it's not as if there's much of anything else out here," and she releases Tara's hand and glances past all the jack-o'-lanterns towards the cliffs and the sea. "Just keep going until there's nowhere left to go."

"Who carved all these things? There must be a hundred of them," Tara says, pointing at one of the jack-o-lanterns, and the woman on the steps smiles again and takes another drag off her brown cigarette, exhales smoke that smells like cloves and cinnamon.

"One hundred and eleven, actually," she says. "They're like birthday candles. One for every year since the house was built. We've been carving them for a week."

"Oh," Tara says because she doesn't know what else to say. "I see."

"You should go on inside, Tara," the woman says. "I expect they'll be waiting. It's getting late," and Tara says nice to meet you, we'll talk some more later, something polite and obligatory like that, and then she steps past the woman towards the front door, past and between the grinning and grimacing and frowning pumpkin faces.

"Yes, she's the one that I was telling you about last week," Darren is saying to them all, "The marine biologist," and he laughs, and Tara shakes someone else's hand, all these pale people in their impeccable black clothes, and she feels like a pigeon dropped down among the crows. Not a masquerade, not a costume party, but she could have at least had the good sense to wear black. A tall, painfully thin woman with a thick French accent touches the back of her hand, her nails the redbrown color of seaweed, and she smiles as gently as the woman out on the porch.

"It's always so nice to see a new face," the French woman says. "Especially when it's such a fine and splendid face." The woman kisses the back of Tara's hand, and then Darren's introducing her to a short, fat man wearing an ascot the color of a stormy summer sky.

"Ah," he says, and shakes Tara's hand so forcefully it hurts. "A scientist. That's grand. We've had so few scientists, you know." She isn't sure if his accent is Scots or Irish, but it's heavy, like his face. Jowls and wide, thin lips, and the man looks more than just a little like a frog, she thinks.

"We've had doctors, yes, lots and lots of doctors. Once we had a neurologist, even. But I've never thought doctors were quite the same thing. As scientists, I mean. Doctors aren't really much more than glorified mechanics, are they?"

"I never thought of it that way," Tara says, which isn't true, and she manages to slip free of the fat man's endless, crushing handshake without seeming rude, glances at Darren, hoping that he can read the discomfort, the unease, in her eyes.

"If you'll all please excuse us for a moment," Darren says, so she knows that he has seen, that he understands, and he puts one of his long arms around her shoulders. "I need to steal her away for just a few minutes," and there's a splash of soft, knowing laughter from the little crowd of people.

He leads her from the front parlor towards what might once have been a dining room, and Tara's beginning to realize how very empty the house is. The way it looked from the outside, she expected the place to be full of antiques, perhaps neglected antiques gone just a bit shabby, a threadbare and discrepant mix of Edwardian and Victorian, but still, she thought that it would be furnished. These rooms are almost empty, not even carpets on the floors or drapes on the tall windows; the velvet wallpaper is faded and torn in places, hanging down in strips here and there like a reptile shedding its skin. And no electricity, as far as she can tell, just candles and old-fashioned gaslight fixtures on the walls, warm and flickering light held inside frosted crystal flowers.

"They can be somewhat intimidating at first, I know that," Darren says. "It's a pretty close-knit group. I should have warned you," and she shakes her head, smiles and no, it's fine, she says, it's not a problem.

"They were probably as anxious about your being here," he says and rubs his hands together in a nervous way, glances back towards the crows milling about in the parlor, whispering among themselves. *Are they talking about me?* she wonders. *Are they asking each other questions about me?* and then Darren's talking again.

"I trust you didn't have any trouble finding the house? We had someone get lost once," he says, and "No," she says. "Finding the house was easy. With all those jack-o'-lanterns, it's almost like a lighthouse," and she thinks that's probably exactly what it would look like to a ship passing in the night, fishermen or a tanker passing on their way north or south, an unblinking lighthouse perched high on the craggy shore.

"That's one of the traditions," Darren says, brushes his long black bangs away from his face. Not exactly a handsome face, something more honest than handsome, something more secretive, and the reason she finds him attractive buried somewhere inside that contradiction.

"One of the traditions? Are there many others?"

"A few," he says. "I hope all this isn't freaking you out."

"No, it isn't," and she turns her head towards a window, the moonlight shining clean through the glass, shining white off the sea. "Not at all. It's all very dignified, I think. Not like Halloween in the city. All the noisy drunks and drag queens, those gaudy parades. I like this much better than that. I wish you'd told me to wear black, though," and he laughs at her then.

"Well, I don't think it's funny," she says, frowning slightly, still watching the moon riding on the waves, and he puts a hand on her arm. "I must stick out like a sore thumb."

"A bit of contrast isn't a bad thing," Darren says, and she turns away from the window, turns back towards him, his high cheekbones and high forehead, his long aquiline nose and eyes that are neither blue nor green.

"I think you need a drink," he says, and Tara nods and smiles for him.

"I think maybe I need two or three."

"That can be arranged," and now he's leading her back towards the crows. A few of them turn their heads to see, dark eyes watching her, and she half expects them to spread wide black wings and fly away.

"They'll ask you questions," and now Darren's almost whispering, hushed words meant for her and no one else. "But don't ever feel like you have to tell them anything you don't want to tell them. They don't mean to be pushy, Tara. They're just impatient, that's all." And she starts to ask what he means by that exactly, impatient, but then she and Darren are already in the parlor again; the small and murmuring crowd opens momentarily, parts long enough to take them in, and then it closes eagerly around them.

An hour later, after a string quartet, Bach and Chopin and only one piece that she didn't recognize, and now the musicians are carefully returning their sleek instruments to black violin and viola and cello cases, cases lined in aubergine and lavender velvet.

"It really isn't very fair of you, Mr. Quince," someone says, and Tara turns around and sees that it's the dapper fat man with the bluegrey ascot, the man who's either Irish or Scottish. "The way you're keeping her all to yourself like this," and he glances past her to Darren, then, coy glance, and the man smiles and rubs at his short salt-and-pepper beard.

"I'm sorry. I wasn't aware," Darren says, and he looks at Tara, checking to be sure it's okay before leaving her in the man's company; but he seems harmless enough, as eccentric as the rest, certainly, but nothing threatening in that eccentricity. He has a walking stick topped with a silver dolphin, and she thinks that he's probably gay.

"Oh, I think we'll be fine," she says, and Darren nods once and disappears into the crowd.

"I am Peterson," the man says, "Ahmed Peterson," and then he kisses the back of her hand the same way that the tall French woman did earlier. The same peculiar formality about him, about all of them, manners that ought to come across as affected but don't somehow.

"Quince tells us that you're a marine biologist," he says, releases her hand and stands very straight, but he's still a few inches shorter than Tara.

"An ichthyologist, actually," she says. "I do some work at the aquarium in Monterey and teach at Cal State. That's where I met Darren."

"Marvelous," Peterson beams. "You know, my dear, I once came across an oarfish, a great, long, spiny thing, stranded on the shingle at Lyme Regis. The fellow I was with thought sure we'd found ourselves a sea serpent."

"I saw an oarfish alive off the coast of Oregon about ten years ago, when I was still a graduate student," she tells him, happy to be swapping fish stories with the fat man, starting to relax, feeling less like an outsider. "We estimated it at almost twenty feet."

"Ah, well, mine was smaller," he says, sounding a little disappointed, perhaps, and then there's a jolting, reverberating noise, and Tara turns to see that one of the women is holding up a small brass gong.

"Oh my," the fat man says. "Is it really that late already? I lost track," and then Darren's standing next to her again.

"What's happening?" she asks, and "You'll see," he replies, takes her hand and slips something cold and metallic into her palm, a coin or a token.

"What's this?" and "Just hang onto it," he replies. "Don't lose it. You'll need it later." So, *It's a game,* she thinks. *Yes, it must be some sort of party game.*

And now everyone is starting to leave the parlor. She lets Darren lead her, and they follow the others, file down a narrow hallway to a locked door near the very back of the house; behind the door are stairs winding down and down and down, stone steps that seem to have been cut directly from the native rock, damp stone walls, and some of the guests have candles or oil lanterns. She slips once, and Darren catches her, leans close and whispers in her ear, and his breath is very faintly sour.

"Watch your step," he says, "It's not much farther, but you wouldn't want to fall," and there are cool gusts of salty air rising up from below, not the sort of air she'd expect from a cellar at all; cool air against her skin, but air tainted by an oily, fishy odor, low-tide sort of a smell, kelp and dying starfish trapped in stagnant tidal pools.

"Where the hell are we going?" she asks him, not bothering to whisper, and a woman with a conch shell tattooed on her forehead turns around and looks at her with a guarded hint of disapproval, and then she turns away again.

"You'll see," Darren whispers, and she realizes that there's something besides the salty darkness and the light from the candles and lanterns, a softer yellowgreen glow coming from somewhere below; chartreuse light that gets a little brighter with every step towards the bottom of the stairway.

And now, if Darren were to ask again whether or not she was getting freaked out, now she might say yes, now she might even tell him she really should be going, that it was late and she needed to get back to the city. Papers to grade or a test to write for her oceanography class, anything that sounded plausible enough to get her out of the house and onto the pumpkinlittered porch, back down the path to her rented car. The stars overhead instead of stone, but he doesn't ask again, and the chartreuse light grows brighter and brighter, and in a few more minutes they've come to the bottom.

"No one ever understands at first," Darren says. He has one hand gripped just a little too tightly around her left wrist, and she's about to tell him that it hurts, about to ask him to let go, when Tara sees the pool and forgets about everything else.

There's a sort of a boardwalk at the bottom of the stairs, short path of warped planks and rails and pilings gone driftwood soft from the alwaysdamp air, from the spray and seawater lapping restless at the wood. The strange light is coming from the water, from the wide pool that entirely fills the cavern at the foot of the stairs, light that rises in dancing fairy shafts to play across the uneven ceiling of the chamber. Tara's stopped moving, and people are having to step around her, all the impatient crows grown quiet and beginning to take their places on the board-walk, no sound now but the hollow clock, clock, clock of their shoes on the planks and the waves splashing against the pier and the limestone walls of the sea cave.

Like they've all done this thing a hundred, hundred times before, and she looks to Darren for an explanation, for a wink or a smile to tell her this really *is* just some odd Halloween game, but his bluegreen eyes are fixed on the far end of the boardwalk, and he doesn't seem to notice.

"Take me back now," she says, "I don't want to see this," but if he's heard her it doesn't show on his face, his long, angular face reflecting the light from the pool, and he has the awed and joyous expression of someone witnessing a miracle. The sort of expression that Hollywood always gives a Joan of Arc or a Bernadette, the eyes of someone who's seen God, she thinks, and then Tara looks towards the end of the boardwalk again. And the crowd parts on cue, steps aside so she can see the rocks jutting up from the middle of the pool, from whatever depths there are beneath her feet, stones stacked one upon the other as precarious as jackstraws. The rocks and the thing that's chained there, and in a moment she knows that it's seen her, as well.

"When I was five," she says, "When I was five I found a sea turtle dead on the beach near Santa Cruz," and she opens her hand again to stare at the coin that Darren gave her upstairs.

"No, dear," Ahmed Peterson says. "It was an oarfish. Don't you remember?" and she shakes her head, because it wasn't an oarfish that time. That time it was a turtle, and the maggots and the gulls had eaten away its eyes.

"You must be mistaken," the fat man says again, and her coin glints and glimmers in the yellowgreen light, glints purest moonlight silver in her palm. She doesn't want to give it away, the way all the others have already done. Maybe the only thing that's left, and she doesn't want to drop it into the water and watch as it spirals down to nowhere, see-saw spiral descent towards the blazing deep, and she quickly closes her hand again. Makes a tight fist, and the fat man huffs and grumbles, and she looks up at the moon instead of the pool.

"You may not have lived much under the sea," he says, and "No, I haven't," Tara confesses, "I haven't."

"Perhaps you were never even introduced to a lobster," he says.

She thinks about that for a moment, about brown claws boiled orange, jointed crustacean legs on china plates, and "I once tasted—" but then she stops herself, because it's something she isn't supposed to say, she's almost certain.

"No, never," Tara whispers.

And the sea slams itself against the cliffs below the house, the angry sea, the cheated sea that wants to drown the world again. Darren is lying in the tall grass, and Tara can hear a train far away in the night, its steamthroat whistle and steelrazor wheels, rolling from there to there, and she traces a line in the dark with the tip of one index finger, horizon to horizon, sea to sky, stitching with her finger.

"She keeps the balance," Darren says, and Tara knows he's talking about the woman on the rocks in the cave below the house. The thing that was a woman once. "She stands between the worlds," he says. "She watches all the gates."

"Did she have a choice?" Tara asks him, and now he's pulling her down into the grass, the sea of grass washed beneath the harvest moon. He smells like fresh hay and pumpkin flesh, nutmeg and candy corn.

"Do saints ever have choices?"

And Tara's trying to remember, if they ever have, when Ahmed and the woman with the conch-shell tattoo lean close and whisper the names of deep-sea things in her ears, rushed and bathypelagic litany of fish and jellies, squid and the translucent larvae of shrimp and crabs.

Saccopharynx, Stylephorus, Pelagothuria, Asteronyx.

"Not so *fast*," she says. "Not so fast, *please.*"

"You can really have no notion, how delightful it will be," sings Ahmed Peterson, and then the tattooed woman finishes for him, "When they take us up and throw us, with the lobsters, out to sea."

It's easier to shut her eyes and lie in Darren's arms, hidden by the merciful, undulating grass; "The jack-o'-lanterns?" he says again, because she asked him why all the jack-o'-lanterns, and "You said it yourself, Tara. Remember? A lighthouse. One night a year, they rise, and we want them to know we're watching."

"Beneath the waters of the sea, Are lobsters thick as thick can be— They love to dance with you and me. My own and gentle Salmon."

"It hurts her," Tara says, watching the woman on the rocks, the lady of spines and scales and the squirming podia sprouting from her distended belly.

"Drop the coin, Tara," Darren murmurs, and his voice is urgent but not unkind. "Drop the coin into the pool. It helps her hold the line."

Drop the coin, the coin, the candy in a plastic pumpkin grinning basket.

"The reason is," says the Gryphon, who was a moment before the woman with the conch on her forehead, "that they *would* go with the lobsters to the dance. So they got thrown out to sea. So they had to fall a long, long way."

Trick or treat.

And the Mock Turtle, who was previously Ahmed Peterson, glares at the Gryphon; "I never went to him," he huffs. "He taught Laughing and Grief, they used to say."

"Someone got lost," Darren whispers. "We had to have another. The number is fixed," and the blacksalt breeze blows unseen through the concealing grass; she can't hear the train any longer. And the moon stares down at them with its single, swollen, jaundiced eye, searching and dragging the oceans against the rocks.

It will find me soon, and what then?

"Drop the coin, Tara. There's not much time left. It's almost midnight," and the woman on the rocks strains against her shackles, the rusted chains that hold her there, and cold corroded iron bites into her pulpy cheesewhite skin. The crimson tentacles between her alabaster thighs, the barnacles that have encrusted her legs, and her lips move without making a sound.

"They're rising, Tara," Darren says, and now he sounds scared, and stares down into the glowing water, the abyss below the boardwalk that's so much deeper than any ocean has ever been. And there *is* movement down there, she can see that, the coils and lashing fins, and the woman on the rock makes a sound like a dying whale.

"There is another shore, you know, upon the other side."

"Now, goddamn it," Darren says, and the coin slips so easily through her fingers.

"Will you, won't you, will you, won't you, will you join the dance . . ."

She watches it sink, taking a living part of her down with it, drowning some speck of her soul. Because it isn't only the woman on the rock that holds back the sea; it's all of them, the crows, and now she's burned as black as the rest, scorched feathers and strangled hearts, falling from the sun into the greedy maelstrom.

And the moon can see her now.

"I told them you were strong," Darren whispers, proud of her, and he wipes the tears from her face; the crows are dancing on the boardwalk, circling them, clomp clomp clomp, while the woman on the rock slips silently away into a stinging anemone-choked crevice on her island.

"Will you, won't you, will you, won't you, won't you join the dance?"

Tara wakes up shivering, lying beneath the wide grey sky spitting cold raindrops down at her. Lying in the grass, the wind and the roar of the breakers in her ears, and she lies there for a few more minutes, remembering what she can. No recollection of making her way back up the stairs from the sea cave, from the phosphorescent pool below the house. No memory of leaving the house, either, but here she is, staring up at the leaden sky and the faint glow where the sun is hiding itself safe behind the clouds.

Someone's left her purse nearby, Darren or some other thoughtful crow, and she reaches for it, sits up in the wet grass and stares back towards the house. Those walls and shuttered windows, the spires and gables, no less severe for this wounded daylight; more so, perhaps. The bitter face of anything that has to keep such secrets in its bowels, that has to hide the world's shame beneath its floors. The house is dark, all the other cars have gone, and there's no sign of the one hundred and eleven jack-o'-lanterns.

She stands and looks out to sea for a moment, watches a handful of white birds buffeted by the gales, whitecaps, and *Next year,* she thinks, next year she'll be here a week before Halloween to help carve the lighthouse faces, and next year she'll know to dress in black. She'll know to drop the silver coin quickly and turn quickly away.

One of the gulls dives suddenly and pulls something dark and wriggling from the seething, stormtossed ocean; Tara looks away, wipes the rain from her eyes, rain that could be tears, and wet bits of grass from her skirt, and then she begins the walk that will carry her past the house and down the sandy road to her car.

Afterword

"A Redress for Andromeda" was written late in June 2000, and is the first of the stories that would eventually comprise the Dandridge House trilogy. At the time, I didn't suspect that I'd eventually write so much more about the old house by the sea. I'm pretty sure this story also marks the beginning of my apparent obsession with Lewis Carroll's "Lobster Quadrille," which has since been quoted in the other two Dandridge House pieces, as well as in *Low Red Moon*, *Murder of Angels*, and several other of my recent short stories. The full poem may be found in Chapter X of *Alice's Adventure's in Wonderland* and was inspired by Mary Howitt's "The Spider and the Fly" and a "minstrel song" Carroll had heard the Liddell sisters singing. As best I can recall, I began work on "A Redress for Andromeda" with only two images in mind—the one hundred and eleven jack-o'-lanterns burning on the porch and the girl chained to the rocks beneath the house (though I didn't yet know her name was Meredith). Also, Judy Collins' "Albatross" should be acknowledged as a source of inspiration. The story was originally titled "Flotsam."

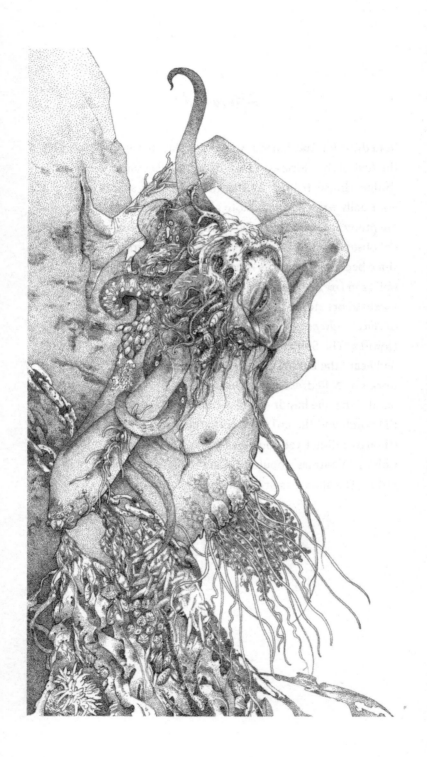

Nor the Demons
Down Under the Sea

1957

THE LATE SUMMER MORNING like a shattering bluewhite gem, crashing, liquid seams of fluorite and topaz thrown against the jagged-rough shale and sandstone breakers, roiling calcite foam beneath the cloudless sky specked with gulls and ravens. And Julia behind the wheel of the big green Bel Air, chasing the coast road north, the top down so the Pacific wind roars wild through her hair. Salt smell to fill her head, intoxicating and delicious scent to drown her city-dulled senses and Anna's alone in the backseat, ignoring her again, silent, reading one of her textbooks or monographs on malacology. Hardly a word from her since they left the motel in Anchor Bay more than an hour ago, hardly a word at breakfast, for that matter, and her silence is starting to annoy Julia.

"It was a bad dream, that's all," Anna said, the two of them alone in the diner next door to the motel, sitting across from one another in a naugahyde booth with a view of the bay, Haven's Anchorage dotted with the bobbing hulls of fishing boats. "You know that I don't like to talk about my dreams," and then she pushed her uneaten grapefruit aside and lit a cigarette. "God knows I've told you enough times."

"We don't have to go on to the house," Julia said hopefully. "We could always see it another time, and we could go back to the city today, instead."

Anna only shrugged her shoulders and stared through the glass at the water, took another drag off her cigarette and exhaled smoke the color of the horizon.

"If you're afraid to go to the house, you should just say so."

Julia steals a glance at her in the rearview mirror, wind-rumpled girl with shiny sunburned cheeks, cheeks like ripening plums and her short blonde hair twisted into a bun and tied up in a scarf. And Julia's own reflection stares back at her from the glass, reproachful, desperate, almost fifteen years older than Anna, so close to thirty-five now that it frightens her; her drab hazel eyes hidden safely behind dark sunglasses that also conceal nascent crow's feet, and the wind whips unhindered through her own hair, hair that would be mouse brown if she didn't use peroxide. The first, tentative wrinkles beginning to show at the corners of her mouth, and she notices that her lipstick is smudged, then, licks the tip of one index finger and wipes the candy-pink stain off her skin.

"You really should come up for air," Julia shouts, shouting just to be heard above the wind, and Anna looks slowly up from her book. She squints and blinks at the back of Julia's head, an irritated, uncomprehending sort of expression and a frown that draws creases across her forehead.

"You're missing all the scenery, dear."

Anna sits up, sighs loud and stares out at a narrow, deserted stretch of beach rushing past, the ocean beyond, and "Scenery's for the tourists," she says. "I'm not a tourist." And she slumps down into the seat again, turns a page and goes back to reading.

"You could at least tell me what I've done," Julia says, trying hard not to sound angry or impatient, sounding only a little bit confused, instead, but this time Anna doesn't reply, pretending not to hear or maybe just choosing to ignore her altogether.

"Well, then, whenever you're ready to talk about it," Julia says, but that isn't what she *wants* to say; she wants to tell Anna she's getting sick of her pouting about like a high-school girl, sick of these long, brooding silences and more than sick of always feeling guilty because she doesn't ever know what to say to make things better. Always feeling like it's her fault, somehow, and if she weren't a coward, she would never have become involved with a girl like Anna Foley in the first place.

But you are a coward, Julia reminds herself, the father-cruel voice crouched somewhere behind her sunglasses, behind her eyes. *Don't ever forget that, not even for a second,* and she almost misses her exit, the turnoff that would carry them east to Boonville if she stayed on the main road. Julia takes the exit, following the crude map Anna drew for her on a paper napkin; the road dips and curves sharply away from the shoreline, and the ocean is suddenly lost behind a dense wall of redwoods and blooming rhododendrons, the morning sun traded for the rapid flicker of forest shadows. Only a few hundred yards from the highway there's another, unpaved, road, unnamed road leading deeper into the trees, and she slows down, and the Chevrolet bounces off the blacktop onto the rutted, pock-marked logging trail.

The drive up the coast from San Francisco to Anchor Bay was Anna's idea, even though they both knew it was a poor choice for summertime shelling. But still a chance to get out of the laboratory, she said, to get away from the city, from the heat and all the people, and Julia knew what she really meant. A chance to be alone, away from suspicious, disapproving eyes, and besides, there had been an interesting limpet collected very near there a decade or so ago, a single, unusually large shell cataloged and tucked away in the vast Berkeley collections and then all but forgotten. The new species, *Diodora thespesius*, was described by one of Julia Winter's male predecessors in the department, and a second specimen would surely be a small feather in her cap.

So, the last two days spent picking their way meticulously over the boulders, kelp- and algae-slick rocks and shallow tide pools constantly buried and unburied by the shifting sand flats; hardly an ideal place for limpets or much of anything else to take hold. Thick-soled rubber boots and aluminum pails, sun hats and gloves, knives to pry mollusks from the rocks, and nothing much for their troubles but scallops and mussels. A few nice sea urchins and sand dollars, *Strongylocentrotus purpuratus* and *Dendraster excentricus*, and the second afternoon Anna had spotted a baby octopus, but it had gotten away from them.

"If we only had more time," Anna said. "I'm sure we would have found it if we had more time." She was sitting on a boulder smoking, her dungarees soaked through to the thighs, staring north and west towards the headland and the dark silhouette of Fish Rocks jutting up from the sea like the scabby backs of twin leviathans.

"Well, it hasn't been a total loss, has it?" Julia asked and smiled, remembering the long night before, Anna in her arms, Anna whispering things that had kept Julia awake until almost dawn. "It wasn't a *complete* waste."

And Anna Foley turned and watched her from her seat on the boulder, sloe-eyed girl, slate-grey irises to hide more than they would ever give away; *She's taunting me,* Julia thought, feeling ashamed of herself for thinking such a thing, but thinking it anyway. *It's all some kind of a game to her, playing naughty games with Dr. Winter. She's sitting there watching me squirm.*

"You want to see a haunted house?" Anna said, finally, and whatever Julia had expected her to say, it certainly wasn't that.

"Excuse me?"

"A haunted house. A *real* haunted house," and Anna raised an arm and pointed northeast, inland, past the shoreline. "It isn't very far from here. We could drive up tomorrow morning."

This is a challenge, Julia thought, *She's trying to challenge me, some new convolution in the game meant to throw me off balance.*

"I'm sorry, Anna. That doesn't really sound like my cup of tea," she said, tired and just wanting to climb back up the bluff to the motel for a hot shower and an early dinner.

"No, really. I'm serious. I read about this place last month in *Argosy*. It was built in 1890 by a man named Machen Dandridge who supposedly worshipped Poseidon and—"

"Since when do you read *Argosy?*"

"I read everything, Julia," Anna said. "It's what I do," and she turned her head to watch a ragged flock of sea gulls flying by, ash and charcoal wings skimming just above the surface of the water.

"And an article in *Argosy* magazine said that this house was *really* haunted?" Julia asked skeptically, watching Anna watch the gulls as they rose and wheeled high over the Anchorage.

"Yes, it did. It was written by Dr. Johnathan Montague, an anthropologist, I think. He studies haunted houses."

"Anthropologists aren't generally in the business of ghosthunting, dear," Julia said, smiling, and Anna glared at her from her rock, her stormcloud eyes narrowing the slightest bit.

"Well, this one seems to be, *dear.*"

And then neither of them said anything for a few minutes, no sound but the wind and the surf and the raucous gulls, all the soothing, lonely ocean noises. Finally the incongruent, mechanical rumble of a truck up on the highway to break the spell, the taut, wordless space between them.

"I think we should be heading back now," Julia said finally. "The tide will be coming in soon."

"You go on ahead," Anna whispered and chewed at her lower lip. "I'll catch up."

Julia hesitated, glanced down at the cold saltwater lapping against the boulders, each breaking and withdrawing wave tumbling the cobbles imperceptibly smoother. Waves to wash the greenbrown mats of seaweed one inch forward and one inch back; *Like the hair of drowned women,* she thought and then pushed the thought away.

"I'll wait for you at the top, then," she said. "In case you need help."

"Sure, Dr. Winter. You do that," and Anna turned away again and flicked the butt of her cigarette at the sea.

Almost an hour of hairpin curves and this road getting narrower and narrower still, strangling dirt road with no place to turn around, before Julia finally comes to the edge of the forest and the fern thickets and giant redwoods release her to rolling, open fields. Tall yellowbrown pampas grass that sways gentle in the breeze, air that smells like sun and salt again, and she takes a deep breath. A relief to breathe air like this after the stifling closeness of the forest, all those old trees with their shaggy, shrouding limbs, and this clear blue sky is better, she thinks.

"There," Anna says, and Julia gazes past the dazzling green hood of the Chevy, across the restless grass, and there's something dark and far away silhouetted against the western sky.

"That's it," Anna says. "Yeah, that *must* be it," and now she's sounding like a kid on Christmas morning, little girl at an amusement park excitement; she climbs over the seat and sits down close to Julia.

I could always turn back now, Julia thinks, her hands so tight around the steering wheel that her knuckles have gone a waxy white. *I could turn this car right around and go back to the highway. We could be home in a few hours. We could be home before dark.*

"What are you *waiting* for?" Anna asks anxiously, and she points at the squat rectangular smudge in the distance. "That's it. We've found it."

"I'm beginning to think this is what you wanted all along," Julia says, speaking low, and she can hardly hear herself over the Bel Air's idling engine. "Anchor Bay, spending time together, that was all just a trick to get me to bring you out here, wasn't it?"

Anna looks reluctantly away from the house. "No," she says. "That's not true. I only remembered the house later, when we were on the beach."

Julia looks towards the distant house again, if it *is* a house. It might be almost anything, sitting out there in the tall grass, waiting. It might be almost anything at all.

"You're the one that's always telling me to get my nose out of books," and Anna's starting to sound angry, cultivated indignation gathering itself protectively about her like a caul, and she slides away from Julia, slides across the vinyl car seat until she's pressed against the passenger door.

"I don't think this was what I had in mind."

Anna begins kicking lightly at the floorboard, then, the toe of a sneaker tapping out the rhythm of her impatience like a Morse code signal, and "Jesus," she says, "It's only an old house. What the hell are you so afraid of, anyway?"

"I never said I was afraid, Anna. I never said anything of the sort."

"You're *acting* like it, though. You're acting like you're scared to death."

"Well, I'm not going to sit here and argue with you," Julia says and tells herself that just this once it doesn't matter if she sounds more like Anna's mother than her lover. "It's my car, and we never should have driven all the way out here alone. I would have turned around half an hour ago, if there'd been enough room on that road." And then she puts the Bel Air into reverse and backs off the dirt road, raising an alarmed and fluttering cloud of grasshoppers, frantic insect wings beating all about them as she shifts into drive and cuts the wheel sharply in the direction of the trees.

"I thought you'd understand," Anna says. "I thought you were different," and she's out of the car before Julia can try to stop her, slams her door shut and walks quickly away, following the path that leads between the high and whispering grass towards the house.

Julia sits in the Chevy and watches her go, watches helplessly as Anna seems to grows smaller with every step, the grass and the brilliant day swallowing her alive, wrapping her up tight in golden stalks and sunbeam teeth. And she imagines driving away alone, simply taking her foot off the brake pedal and retracing that twisting, treeshadowed path to the safety of paved roads. How *easy* that would be, how perfectly *satisfying,* and then Julia watches Anna for a few more minutes before she turns the car to face the house and tries to pretend that she never had any choice at all.

The house like a grim and untimely joke, like something better off in a Charles Addams cartoon than perched on the high, sheer cliffs at the end of the road. This ramshackle grotesquerie of boards gone the silvergrey of old oyster shells, the splinter-skin walls with their broken windows and crooked shutters, steep gables and turrets missing half their slate shingles, and there are places where the roof beams and struts show straight through the house's weathered hide. One black lightning rod still standing guard against the sky, a rusting garland of wrought iron filigree along the eaves, and the uppermost part of the chimney has collapsed in a redgreen scatter of bricks gnawed back to soft clay by moss and the corrosive sea air. Thick weeds where there might once have been a yard and flower beds, and the way the entire structure has begun to list perceptibly leaves Julia with the disconcerting impression that the house is cringing, or that it has actually begun to pull itself free of the earth and is preparing to crawl, inch by crumbling inch, away from the ocean.

"Anna, wait," but she's already halfway up the steps to the wide front porch, and Julia's still sitting behind the wheel of the Chevy. She closes her eyes for a moment, better to sit listening to the wind and the waves crashing against the cliffs and the smaller, hollow sound of Anna's feet on the porch, than to let the house think that she *can't* look away. Some dim instinct to tell her that's how this works, the sight of it to leave you dumbstruck and vulnerable.

My god, she thinks. *It's only an ugly, old house. An ugly, old house that no one wants anymore,* and then she laughs out loud, like it can hear.

After she caught up with Anna and made her get back into the car, and after Julia agreed to drive her the rest of the way out to the house, Anna Foley started talking about Dr. Montague's article in *Argosy* again, talked as though there'd never been an argument. The tension between them forgotten or discarded in a flood of words, words that came faster and faster as they neared the house, almost piling atop each other towards the end.

"There were stories that Dandridge murdered his daughter as a sacrifice, sometime after his wife died in 1914. But no one ever actually found her body. No, she just vanished one day, and no one ever saw her again. The daughter, I mean. The daughter vanished, not the wife. His wife is buried behind the house, though I'm not sure ... "

Only an ugly, old house sitting forgotten beside the sea.

"... to Poseidon, or maybe even Dagon, who was a sort of Mesopotamian corn king, half man and half fish. Dandridge traveled all over Iraq and Persia before he came back and settled in California. He had a fascination with Persian and Hindu antiquities."

Then open your eyes and get this over with, and she does open her eyes, then, staring back at the house, and Julia relaxes her grip on the steering wheel. Anna's standing on the porch now, standing on tip-toes and peering in through a small shattered window near the door.

"Anna, wait on me. I'm coming," and Anna turns and smiles, waving to her, then goes back to staring into the house through the broken window.

Julia leaves the keys dangling in the ignition and picks her way towards the house, past lupine and wild white roses and a patch of poppies the color of tangerines, three or four orange-and-black monarch butterflies flitting from blossom to blossom, and there's a line of stepping stones almost lost in the weeds. The stones lead straight to the house, though the weedy patch seems much wider than it did from the car.

I should be there by now, she thinks, looking over her shoulder at the convertible and then ahead, at Anna standing on the porch, standing at the door of the Dandridge house, wrestling with the knob. *No. I'm so anxious, it only seems that way,* but five, seven, ten more steps, and the porch seems almost as far away as it did when she got out of the car.

"Wait on me," she shouts at Anna, who doesn't seem to have heard. Julia stops and wipes the sweat from her forehead before it runs down into her eyes. She glances up at the sun, directly overhead and hot against her face and bare arms, and she realizes that the wind has died. The blustery day grown suddenly so still, and she can't hear the breakers anymore, either. Only the faint and oddly muted cries of the gulls and grasshoppers.

She turns towards the sea, and there's a brittle noise from the sky that makes her think of eggshells cracking against the edge of a china mixing bowl, and on the porch Anna's opening the door. And the shimmering, stickywet darkness that flows out and over and *through* Anna Foley makes another sound, and Julia shuts her eyes so she won't have to watch whatever comes next.

The angle of the light falling velvetsoft across the dusty floor, the angle and the honey color of the sun, so she knows that it's late afternoon, and somehow she's lost everything in between. That last moment in the yard before this place without even unconsciousness to bridge the gap, then and now, and she understands it's as simple as that. Her head aches and her stomach rolls when she tries to sit up to get a better look at the room, and Julia decides that maybe it's best to lie still a little while longer. Just lie here and stare out that window at the blue sky framed in glass-jagged mouths. There might have been someone there a moment ago, a scarecrow face looking in at her through the broken window, watching, waiting, and there might have been nothing but the partitioned swatches of the fading day.

She can hear the breakers again, now only slightly muffled by the walls, and the wind around the corners of the house; these sounds through air filled with the oily stench of rotting fish and the neglected smell of any very old and empty house. A barren, fishstinking room and a wall with one tall arched window just a few feet away from her, sunbleached and peeling wallpaper strips, and she knows that it must be a western wall, the sunlight through the broken window panes proof enough of that.

Unless it's morning light, she thinks. *Unless it's morning light, and this is another day entirely, and the sun is rising now instead of setting.* Julia wonders why she ever assumed it was afternoon, how she can ever again assume anything. And there's a sound, then, from somewhere behind her, inside the room with her or very close to it; the crisp sound of a ripe melon splitting open, scarlet flesh and black teardrop seeds, sweet red juice, and now the air smells even worse. Fish putrefying under a baking summer sun, beaches strewn with bloated fishsilver bodies as far as the eye can see, beaches littered with everything in the sea heaved up onto the shore, an inexplicable, abyssal vomit, and she closes her eyes again.

"Are you here, Anna?" she says. "Can you hear me?"

And something quivers at the edge of her vision, a fluttering darkness deeper than the long shadows in the room, and she ignores the pain and the nausea and rolls over onto her back to see it more clearly. But the thing on the ceiling sees her too and moves quickly towards the sanctuary of a corner; all feathery, trembling gills and swimmerets, and its jointed lobster carapace almost as pale as toadstools, chitin soft and pale, and it scuttles backwards on raw and bleeding human hands. It drips and leaves a spattered trail of itself on the floor as it goes.

She can see the door now, the absolute blackness waiting in the hall through the doorway, and there's laughter from that direction, a woman's high, hysterical laugh, but so faint that it can't possibly be coming from anywhere inside the house.

"Anna," she calls out again, and the laughter stops, and the thing on the ceiling clicks its needle teeth together.

"She's gone down, *that* one," it whispers. "She's gone all the way down to Mother Hydra and won't hear you in a hundred hundred million years."

And the laughing begins again, seeping slyly up through the floorboards, through every crack on these moldering plaster walls.

"'I saw a something in the Sky,'" the ceiling crawler whispers from its corner, "'No bigger than my fist.'"

And the room writhes and spins around her like a kaleidoscope, that tumbling gyre of colored shards, remaking the world, and it wouldn't matter if there was anything for her to hold onto. She would still fall; no way not to fall with this void devouring even the morning, or the afternoon, whichever, even the colors of the day sliding down that slick gullet.

"I can't *see* you," Anna says, definitely Anna's voice but Julia's never heard her sound this way before. So afraid, so insignificant. "I can't see you *anywhere*," and Julia reaches out (or down or up) into the furious storm that was the house, the maelstrom edges of a collapsing universe, and her arm sinks in up to the elbow. Sinks through into dead-star cold, the cold ooze of the deepest seafloor trench, and "Open your eyes," Anna says, and she's crying now. "Please, god, open your *eyes*, Julia."

But her eyes *are* open, and she's standing somewhere far below the house, standing before the woman on the rock, the thing that was a woman once, and part of it can still recall that lost humanity. The part that watches Julia with one eye, the pale green and desperate, hatefilled eye that hasn't been lost to the seething ivory crust of barnacles and sea lice that covers half its face. The woman on the great rock in the center of the phosphorescent pool, and then the sea rushes madly into the cavern, surges up and foams around the rusted chains and scales and all the squirming pinkwhite anemones sprouting from her thighs.

Alone, alone, all all alone,

And the woman on the rock raises an arm, her ruined and shellstudded arm, and reaches across the pool towards Julia.

Alone on the wide wide Sea

Her long fingers and the webbing grown between them, and Julia leans out across the frothing pool, ice water wrapping itself around her ankles, filling her shoes, and she strains to take the woman's hand. Straining to reach as the jealous sea rises and falls, rises and falls, threatening her with the bottomless voices of sperm whales and typhoons. But the distance between their fingertips doubles, triples, origami space unfolding itself, and the woman's lips move silently, yellow teeth and pleading, gillslit lips as mute as the cavern walls.

—*murdered his daughter, sacrificed her*—

Nothing from those lips but the small and startled creatures nesting in her mouth, not *words* but a sudden flow of surprised and scuttling legs, the claws and twitching antennae, and a scream that rises from somewhere deeper than the chained woman's throat, deeper than simple flesh, soulscream spilling out and swelling to fill the cave from wall to wall. This howl that is every moment that she's spent down here, every damned and saltraw hour made aural, and Julia feels it in her bones, in the silver amalgam fillings of her teeth.

Will you, won't you, will you, won't you, will you join the dance?

And the little girl sits by the fire in a rocking chair, alone in the front parlor of her father's big house by the sea, and she reads fairy tales to herself while her father rages somewhere overhead, in the sky or only upstairs but it makes no difference, in the end. Father of black rags and sour, scowling faces, and she tries not to hear the chanting or the sounds her mother is making again, tries to think of nothing but the Mock Turtle and Alice, the Lobster Quadrille by unsteady lantern light. *Don't look at the windows,* she thinks, or Julia tries to warn her. Don't look at the windows ever again.

Well, there was mystery. Mystery, ancient and modern, with Seaography: then Drawling—the Drawling-Master was an old conger-eel . . .

An old *conjure* eel—

Don't ever look at the windows even when the scarecrow fingers, the dry-grass bundled fingers, are tap-tap-tapping their song upon the glass. And she has seen the women dancing naked by the autumn moon, dancing in the tall moonwashed sheaves, bare feet where her father's scythe has fallen again and again, every reaping stroke to kill and call the ones that live at the bottom of the pool deep below the house. Calling them up and taunting them and then sending them hungrily back down to Hell again. Hell or the deep, fire or icedark water, and it makes no difference whatsoever in the end.

Would not, could not, would not, could not, would not join the dance.

Julia's still standing at the wavesmoothed edge of the absinthe pool, or she's only a whispering, insubstantial ghost afraid of parlor windows, smokegrey ghost muttering from nowhen, from hasn't-been or never-will-be, and the child turns slowly towards her voice as the hurting thing chained to the rock begins to tear and stretches itself across the widening gulf.

"Julia, *please.*"

"You will be their queen, in the cities beneath the sea," the old man says. "When I am not even a *memory*, child, you will hold them to the depths."

And they all dead did lie, And a million million slimy things Liv'd on—and so did I...

"Open your eyes," Anna says, and this time Julia does. All these sights and sounds flickering past like the last frames of a movie, and she's lying in Anna's arms, lying on her back in the weedy patch between the car and the brooding, spiteful house.

"I thought you were dead," Anna says, holding onto her so tightly she can hardly breathe, and Anna sounds relieved and frightened and angry all at once, the tears rolling down her sunburned face and dripping off her chin onto Julia's cheeks.

"You were so goddamn cold. I thought you were dead. I thought I was alone."

Alone, alone, all all alone...

"I smell flowers," Julia says, "I smell roses," because she does and she can think of nothing else to say, no mere words to ever make her forget, and she stares up past Anna, past the endless, sea-hued sky, at the summerwarm sun staring back down at her like the blind and blazing eye of Heaven.

Afterword

"Nor the Demons Down Under the Sea," which borrows its title from Edgar Allan Poe, was written in July and August of 2000. I'd been asked to contribute a story to an anthology of Lovecraftian mythos tales, *The Children of Cthulhu*, and though I'd intended to write a straightforward mythos piece, the story had ideas of its own. I found myself wanting to speak softly, as I'd done in "Spindleshanks (New Orleans, 1956)," trying to keep the mythos elements relatively quiet and indirect, essentially creating a ghost story which revolves around a difficult relationship between two women. This is one of those stories which takes very seriously my belief that dark fiction dealing with the inexplicable should, itself, present to the reader a certain inexplicability. It's not about resolution nor understanding, but that brief, disturbing contact which usually characterizes actual paranormal encounters. However, someone at Del Rey felt that "Nor the Demons Down Under the Sea" wasn't "Lovecraftian enough" for the anthology, and it was almost cut from the book. Fortunately, the books editors felt otherwise and insisted it stay put. "Nor the Demons Down Under the Sea" was selected for *The Mammoth Book of Best New Horror*, Volume Fourteen.

R. KIRK

Andromeda Among the Stones

"I cannot think of the deep sea without shuddering..."
—H. P. Lovecraft

1.

October 1914

"**I**S SHE REALLY AND TRULY DEAD, Father?" the girl asked, and Machen Dandridge, already an old man at fifty-one, looked up at the low buttermilk sky again and closed the black book clutched in his hands. He'd carved the tall headstone himself, the marker for his wife's grave there by the relentless Pacific, black-shale obelisk with its hasty death's head, and his daughter stepped gingerly around the raw earth and pressed her fingers against the monument.

"Why did you not give her to the sea?" she asked. "She always wanted to go down to the sea at the end. She often told me so."

"I've given her back to the earth, instead," Machen told her and rubbed at his eyes. The cold sunlight through thin clouds enough to make his head ache, his daughter's voice like thunder, and he shut his aching eyes for a moment. Just a little comfort in the almost blackness trapped behind his lids, parch-

ment skin too insubstantial to bring the balm of genuine darkness, void to match the shades of his soul, and Machen
whispered one of the prayers from the heavy black book and
then looked at the grave again.

"Well, that's what she always said," the girl said again, running her fingertips across the rough-hewn stone.

"Things changed at the end, child. The sea wouldn't have
taken her. I had to give her back to the earth."

"She said it was a sacrilege, planting people in the ground
like wheat, like kernels of corn."

"She did?" and he glanced anxiously over his left shoulder,
looking back across the waves the wind was making in the high
and yellow-brown grass, the narrow trail leading back down to
the tall and brooding house that he'd built for his wife twenty-
four years ago, back towards the cliffs and the place where the
sea and sky blurred seamlessly together.

"Yes, she did. She said only barbarians and heathens stick
their dead in the ground like turnips."

"I had no choice," Machen replied, wondering if that was
exactly the truth or only something he'd like to believe. "The
sea wouldn't take her, and I couldn't bring myself to burn her."

"Only heathens burn their dead," his daughter said disap-
provingly and leaned close to the obelisk, setting her ear
against the charcoal shale.

"Do you hear anything?"

"No, Father. Of course not. She's dead. You just said so."

"Yes," Machen whispered. "She is." And the wind whipping
across the hillside made a hungry, waiting sound that told him
it was time for them to head back to the house.

*This is where I stand, at the bottom gate, and I hold the key to the
abyss...*

"But it's better that way," the girl said, her ear still pressed
tight against the obelisk. "She couldn't stand the pain any
longer. It was cutting her up inside."

"She told you that?"

"She didn't have to tell me that. I saw it in her eyes."

The ebony key to the first day and the last, the key to the moment when the stars wink out, one by one, and the sea heaves its rotting belly at the empty, sagging sky.

"You're only a child," he said. "You shouldn't have had to see such things. Not yet."

"It can't very well be helped now," she answered and stepped away from her mother's grave, one hand cupping her ear like maybe it had begun to hurt. "You know that, old man."

"I do," and he almost said her name then, Meredith, his mother's name, but the wind was too close, the listening wind and the salt-and-semen stink of the breakers crashing against the cliffs. "But I can wish it were otherwise."

"If wishes were horses, beggars would ride."

And Machen watched silently as Meredith Dandridge knelt in the grass and placed her handful of wilting wildflowers on the freshly turned soil; if it were spring instead of autumn, he thought, there would be dandelions and poppies. If it were spring instead of autumn, the woman wrapped in a quilt and nailed up inside a pine-board casket would still be breathing. If it were spring, they would not be alone now, him and his daughter at the edge of the world. The wind teased the girl's long yellow hair, and the sun glittered dimly in her warm green eyes.

The key I have accepted full in the knowledge of its weight.

"Remember me," Meredith whispered, either to her dead mother or something else, and he didn't ask which.

"We should be heading back now," he said and glanced over his shoulder again.

"So soon? Is that all you're going to read from the book? Is that all of it?"

"Yes, that's all of it, for now," though there would be more, later, when the harvest moon swelled orange-red and bloated and hung itself in the wide California night. When the women came to dance, then there would be other words to say, to keep his wife in the ground and the gate shut for at least another year.

The weight that is the weight of all salvation, the weight that holds the line against the last, unending night.

"It's better this way," his daughter said again, standing up, brushing the dirt off her stockings, from the hem of her black dress. "There was so little left of her."

"Don't talk of that here," Machen replied, more sternly than he'd intended, but Meredith didn't seem to have noticed or, if she'd noticed, not to have minded the tone of her father's voice.

"I will remember her the way she was before, when she was still beautiful."

"That's what she would want," he said and took his daughter's hand. "That's the way I'll remember her, as well," but he knew that was a lie, as false as any lie any living man ever uttered. Knew that he would always see his wife as the writhing, twisted thing she'd become at the last, the way she was after the gates were almost thrown open, and she placed herself on the threshold.

The frozen weight of the sea, the burning weight of starlight and my final breath. I hold the line. I hold the ebony key against the last day of all.

And Machen Dandridge turned his back on his wife's grave and led his daughter down the dirt and gravel path, back to the house waiting for them like a curse.

2.

November 1914

Meredith Dandridge lay very still in her big bed, her big room with its high ceiling and no pictures hung on the walls, and she listened to the tireless sea slamming itself against the rocks. The sea to take the entire world apart one gritty speck at a time, the sea that was here first and would be here long after the continents had finally been weathered down to so much slime and sand. She knew this because her father had read to her from his heavy black book, the book that had no name, the book that she couldn't ever read for herself or the demons would come for her in the night. And she knew, too, because of the books he had *given* her, her books—*Atlantis: The Antediluvian World* and *The World Before the Deluge* and *Atlantis and Lost Lemuria.* Everything above the waves on borrowed time, her father had said again and again, waiting for the day when the sea rose once more and drowned the land beneath its smothering, salty bosom, and the highest mountains and deepest valleys will become a playground for sea serpents and octopi and schools of herring. Forests to become Poseidon's orchards, her father said, though she knew Poseidon wasn't the true name of the god-thing at the bottom of the ocean, just a name some man gave it thousands of years ago.

"Should I read you a story tonight, Merry?" her dead mother asked, sitting right there in the chair beside the bed. She smelled like fish and mud, even though they'd buried her in the dry ground at the top of the hill behind the house. Meredith didn't look at her, because she'd spent so much time already trying to remember her mother's face the way it was *before* and didn't want to see the ruined face the ghost was wearing like a mask. As bad as the face her brother now wore, worse than that, and Meredith shrugged and pushed the blankets back a little.

"If you can't sleep, it might help," her mother said with a voice like kelp stalks swaying slowly in deep water.

"It might," Meredith replied, staring at a place where the wallpaper had begun to peel free of one of the walls, wishing there were a candle in the room or an oil lamp so the ghost would leave her alone. "And it might not."

"I could read to you from Hans Christian Andersen, or one of Grimm's tales," her mother sighed. "'The Little Mermaid' or 'The Fisherman and his Wife'?"

"You could tell me what it's like in Hell," the girl replied.

"Dear, I don't have to tell you that," her ghost mother whispered, her voice gone suddenly regretful and sad. "I know I don't have to ever tell you that."

"There might be different hells," Meredith said. "This one, and the one father sent you away to, and the one Avery is lost inside. No one ever said there could only be one, did they? A hell for the dead German soldiers and another for the French, a hell for Christians and another for the Jews. And maybe another for all the pagans—"

"Your father didn't send me anywhere, child. I crossed the threshold of my own accord."

"So I would be alone in *this* hell."

The ghost clicked its sharp teeth together, and Meredith could hear the anemone tendrils between its iridescent fish eyes quickly withdrawing into the hollow places in her mother's decaying skull.

"I could read you a poem," her mother said hopefully. "I could sing you a song."

"It isn't all fire and brimstone, is it? Not the hell where you are? It's blacker than night and cold as ice, isn't it, mother?"

"Did he think it would save me to put me in the earth? Does the old fool think it will bring me back across, like Persephone?"

Too many questions, hers and her mother's, and for a moment Meredith Dandridge didn't answer the ghost, kept her eyes on the shadowy wallpaper strips, the pinstripe wall, wishing the sun would rise and pour warm and gold as honey through the drapes.

"I crossed the threshold of my *own* accord," the ghost said again, and Meredith wondered if it thought she didn't hear the first time. Or maybe it was something her mother needed to believe and might stop believing if she stopped repeating it. "Someone had to do it."

"It didn't have to be you."

The wind whistled wild and shrill around the eaves of the house, invisible lips pressed to a vast, invisible instrument, and Meredith shivered and pulled the covers up to her chin again.

"There was no one else. It wouldn't take your brother. The one who wields the key cannot be a man. You know that, Merry. Avery knew that, too."

"There are other women," Meredith said, speaking through gritted teeth, not wanting to start crying but the tears already hot in her eyes. "It could have been someone else. It didn't have to be my mother."

"Some other child's mother, then?" the ghost asked. "Some other mother's daughter?"

"Go back to your hell," Meredith said, still looking at the wall, spitting out the words like poison. "Go back to your hole in the ground, and tell your fairy tales to the worms. Tell them 'The Fisherman and his Wife.'"

"You have to be strong now, Merry. You have to listen to your father, and you have to be ready. I wasn't strong enough."

And finally she did turn to face her mother, what was left of her mother's face, the scuttling things nesting in her tangled hair, the silver scales and barnacles, the stinging anemone crown, and Meredith Dandridge didn't flinch or look away.

"One day," she said, "I'll take that damned black book of his, and I'll toss it into the stove. I'll take it, mother, and toss it into the hearth, and then they can come out of the sea and drag us both away—"

But then her mother cried out and came apart like a breaking wave against the shingle, water poured from the tin pail that had given it shape, her flesh gone suddenly as clear and shimmering as glass, before she drained away and leaked through the cracks between the floorboards. The girl reached out and dipped her fingers into the shallow pool left behind in the wicker seat of the chair. The water was cold and smelled unclean. And then she lay awake until dawn, listening to the ocean, to all the unthinking noises a house makes in the small hours of a night.

3.

May 1914

Avery Dandridge had his father's eyes, but someone else's soul to peer out through them, and to his sister he was hope that there might be a life somewhere beyond the rambling house beside the sea. Five years her senior, he'd gone away to school in San Francisco for a while, almost a year, because their mother wanted him to. But there had been an incident, and he was sent home again, transgressions only spoken of in whispers and nothing anyone ever bothered to explain to Meredith, but that was fine with her. She only cared that he was back, and she was that much less alone.

"Tell me about the earthquake," she said to him, one day not long after he'd returned, the two of them walking together along the narrow beach below the cliffs, sand the color of coal dust, noisy gulls and driftwood like bones washed in by the tide. "Tell me all about the fire."

"The earthquake? Merry, that was eight *years* ago. You were still just a baby, that was such long time ago," and then he picked up a shell and turned it over in his hand, brushing away some of the dark sand stuck to it. "People don't like to talk about the earthquake anymore. I never heard them say much about it."

"Oh," she said, not sure what to say next but still full of questions. "Father says it was a sign, a sign from—"

"Maybe you shouldn't believe everything he says, Merry. It was an earthquake." And she felt a thrill then, like a tiny jolt of electricity rising up her spine and spreading out across her scalp, that anyone, much less Avery, would question their father and suggest she do likewise.

"Have you stopped believing in the signs?" she asked, breathless. "Is *that* what you learned in school?"

"I didn't learn much of anything important in school," he replied and showed her the shell in his palm. Hardly as big around as a nickel, but peaked in the center like a Chinaman's hat, radial lines of chestnut brown. "It's pretty," she said as he placed it in her palm. "What's it called?"

"It's a limpet," he replied, because Avery knew all about shells and fish and the fossils in the cliffs, things he'd learned from their father's books and not from school. "It's a shield limpet. The jackmackerel carry them into battle when they fight the eels."

Meredith laughed out loud at that last part, and he laughed, too, then sat down on a rock at the edge of a wide tidepool. She stood there beside him, still inspecting the shell in her hand, turning it over and over again. The concave underside of the limpet was smoother than silk and would be white if not for the faintest iridescent hint of blue.

"That's not true," she said. "Everyone knows the jackmackerel and the eels are friends."

"Sure they are," Avery said. "Everyone knows that," but he was staring out to sea now and didn't turn to look at her. In a moment, she slipped the shell into a pocket of her sweater and sat down on the rock next to him.

"Do you see something out there?" she asked, and he nodded his head, but didn't speak. The wind rushed cold and damp across the beach and painted ripples on the surface of the pool at their feet; the wind and the waves seemed louder than usual, and Meredith wondered if that meant a storm was coming.

"Not a storm," Avery said, and that didn't surprise her because he often knew what she was thinking before she said it. "A war's coming, Merry."

"Oh yes, the jackmackerel and the eels," Merry laughed and squinted towards the horizon, trying to see whatever it was that had attracted her brother's attention. "The squid and the mussels."

"Don't be silly. Everyone knows that the squid and the mussels are great friends," and that made her laugh again. But Avery didn't laugh, looked away from the sea and stared down instead at the scuffed toes of his boots dangling a few inches above the water.

"There's never been a war like the one that's coming," he said after a while. "All the nations of the earth at each other's throats, Merry, and when we're done with all the killing, no one will be left to stand against the sea."

She took a very deep breath, the clean, salty air to clear her head, and began to pick at a barnacle on the rock.

"If that were true," she said, "Father would have told us. He would have shown us the signs."

"He doesn't see them. He doesn't dream the way I do."

"But you told him?"

"I tried. But he thinks it's something they put in my head at school. He thinks it's some kind of trick to make him look away."

Merry stopped picking at the barnacle because it was making her fingers sore, and they'd be bleeding soon if she kept it up. She decided it was better to watch the things trapped in the tidepool, the little garden stranded there until the sea came back to claim it. Periwinkle snails and hermit crabs wearing stolen shells, crimson starfish and starfish the shape and color of sunflowers.

"He thinks they're using me to make him look the other way, to catch him off his guard," Avery whispered, his voice almost lost in the rising wind. "He thinks I'm being set against him."

"Avery, I don't believe Father would say that about you."

"He didn't have to say it," and her brother's dark and shining eyes gazed out at the sea and sky again.

"We should be heading back soon, shouldn't we? The tide will be coming in before long," Meredith said, noticing how much higher up the beach the waves were reaching than the last time she'd looked. Another half hour and the insatiable ocean would be battering itself against the rough shale cliffs at their backs.

"'Wave after wave, each mightier than the last,'" Avery whispered, closing his eyes tight, and the words coming from his pale, thin lips sounded like someone else, someone old and tired that Meredith had never loved. "'Till last, a ninth one, gathering half the deep and full of voices, slowly rose and plunged roaring, and all the wave was in a flame—'"

"What's that?" she asked, interrupting because she didn't want to hear any more. "Is it from Father's book?"

"No, it's not," he replied, sounding more like himself again, more like her brother. He opened his eyes, and a tear rolled slowly down his wind-chapped cheek. "It's just something they taught me at school."

"How can a wave be in flame? Is it supposed to be a riddle?" she asked, and he shook his head.

"No," he said and wiped at his face with his hands. "It's nothing at all, just a silly bit of poetry they made us memorize. School is full of silly poetry."

"Is that why you came home?"

"We ought to start back," he said, glancing quickly over his shoulder at the high cliffs, the steep trail leading back up towards the house. "Can't have the tide catching us with our trousers down, now can we?"

"I don't even wear trousers," Merry said glumly, still busy thinking about that ninth wave, the fire and the water, and Avery put an arm around her and held her close to him for a moment while the advancing sea dragged itself eagerly back and forth across the moss-scabbed rocks.

4.

January 1915

Meredith sat alone on the floor in the hallway, the narrow hall connecting the foyer to the kitchen and a bathroom, and then farther along, all the way back at the very rear of the house, this tall door that was always locked. The tarnished brass key always hung on its ring upon her father's belt, and she pressed her ear against the wood and strained to hear anything at all. The wood was damp and very cold, and the smell of saltwater and mildew seeped freely through the space between the bottom of the door and the floor, between the door and the jamb. Once-solid redwood that had long since begun to rot from the continual moisture, the ocean's breath to rust the hinges so the door cried out like a stepped-on cat every time it was opened or closed. Even as a very small child, Meredith had feared this door, even in the days before she'd started to understand what lay in the deep place beneath her father's house.

Outside, the icy winter wind howled, and she shivered and pulled her grey wool shawl tighter about her shoulders; the very last thing her mother had made for her, that shawl. Almost as much hatred in Merry for the wind as for the sea, but at least it smothered the awful thumps and moans that came, day and night, from the attic room where her father had locked Avery away in June.

"There are breaches between the worlds, Merry," he had said, a few days before he picked the lock on the hallway door with the sharpened tip-end of a buttonhook and went down to the deep place by himself. "Rifts, fractures, ruptures. If they can't be

closed, they have to be guarded against the things on the other
side that don't belong here."

"Father says it's a portal," she'd replied, closing the book
she'd been reading, a dusty, dog-eared copy of Franz Unger's
Primitive World.

Her brother had laughed a dry, humourless laugh and shaken
his head, nervously watching the fading day through the parlour windows. "Portals are built on purpose, to be used. These
things are accidents, at best, casualties of happenstance, tears
in space when one world passes much too near another."

"Well, that's not what Father says."

"Read your book, Merry. One day you'll understand. One day
soon, when you're not a child anymore and he loses his hold on
you."

And she'd frowned, sighed, and opened her book again,
opening it at random to one of the strangely melancholy lith-
ographs—*The Period of the Muschelkalk [Middle Trias].* A violent
seascape and in the foreground a reef jutted above the waves,
crowded with algae-draped driftwood branches and the shells
of stranded mollusca and crinoidea, something like a crocodile
that the author called *Nothosaurus giganteus* clinging to the reef
so it wouldn't be swept back into the storm-tossed depths.
Overhead, the night sky was a turbulent mass of clouds with
the small white moon, full or near enough to full, peeking
through to illuminate the ancient scene.

"You mean planets?" she'd asked Avery. "You mean moons
and stars?"

"No, I mean *worlds.* Now, read your book, and don't ask so
many questions."

Meredith thought she heard creaking wood, her father's
heavy footsteps, the dry ruffling of cloth rubbing against cloth,
and she stood quickly, not wanting to be caught listening at
the door again, was busy straightening her rumpled dress when
she realized that he was standing there in the hall behind her,

instead. Her mistake, thinking he'd gone to the deep place, when he was somewhere else all along, in his library or the attic room with Avery or outside braving the cold to visit her mother's grave on the hill.

"What are you doing, child?" he asked her gruffly and tugged at his beard; there were streaks of silver-grey that weren't there only a couple of months before, scars from the night they lost her mother, his wife, the night the demons tried to squeeze in through the tear, and Ellen Dandridge had tried to block their way. His face grown years older in the space of weeks, dark crescents beneath his eyes like bruises, the deep creases in his forehead, and he brushed his daughter's blonde hair from her eyes.

"Would it have been different, if you'd believed Avery from the start?"

For a moment he didn't reply, and the silence, his face set as hard and perfectly unreadable as stone, made her want to strike him, made her wish she could kick open the rotting, sea-damp door and hurl him screaming down the stairs to whatever was waiting for them both in the deep place.

"I don't know, Meredith. But I had to trust the book, and I had to believe the signs in the heavens."

"You were too arrogant, old man. You almost gave away the whole wide world because you couldn't admit you might be wrong."

"You should be thankful that your mother can't hear you, young lady, using that tone of voice with your own father."

Meredith turned and looked at the tall door again, the symbols drawn on the wood in whitewash and blood.

"She can hear me," Meredith told him. "She talks to me almost every night. She hasn't gone as far away as you think."

"I'm still your father, and you're still a child who can't even begin to understand what's at stake, what's always pushing at the other side of—"

"—the gate?" she asked, finishing for him, and she put one hand flat against the door, the upper of its two big panels, and leaned all her weight against it. "What happens next time? Do you know that, Father? How much longer do we have left, or haven't the constellations gotten around to telling you that yet?"

"Don't mock me, Meredith."

"Why not?" and she stared back at him over her shoulder, without taking her hand off the door. "Will it damn me faster? Will it cause more men to die in the trenches? Will it cause Avery more pain than he's in now?"

"*I* was given the book," he growled at her, his stony face flashing to bitter anger, and at least that gave Meredith some mean scrap of satisfaction. "I was shown the way to this place. They entrusted the gate to me, child. The gods—"

"—must be even bigger fools than you, old man. Now shut up, and leave me alone."

Machen Dandridge raised his right hand to strike her, then, his big-knuckled hand like a hammer of flesh and bone, iron-meat hammer and anvil to beat her as thin and friable as the veil between Siamese universes.

"You'll need me," she said, not recoiling from the fire in his dark eyes, standing her ground. "You can't take my place. Even if you weren't a coward, you couldn't take my place."

"You've become a wicked child," he said, slowly lowering his hand until it hung useless at his side.

"Yes, Father, I have. I've become a *very* wicked child. You'd best pray that I've become wicked enough."

And he didn't reply, no words left in him, but walked quickly away down the long hall towards the foyer and his library, his footsteps loud as distant gunshots, loud as the beating of her heart, and Meredith removed her hand from the door. It burned very slightly, pain like a healing bee sting, and when she looked at her palm there was something new there, a fat and shiny swelling as black and round and smooth as the soulless eye of a shark.

5.

February 1915

In his dreams, Machen Dandridge stands at the edge of the sea and watches the firelight reflected in the roiling grey clouds above Russia and Austria and East Prussia, smells the coppery stink of Turkish and German blood, the life leaking from the bullet holes left in the Serbian Archduke and his wife. Machen would look away if he knew how, wouldn't see what he can only see too late to make any difference. One small man set adrift and then cast up on the shingle of the cosmos, filled to bursting with knowledge and knowing nothing at all. Canon fire and thunder, the breakers against the cliff side and the death rattle of soldiers beyond counting.

This is where I stand, at the bottom gate, and I hold the key to the abyss . . .

"A world war, father," Avery says. "Something without precedent. I can't even find words to describe the things I've seen."

"A world war, without precedent?" Machen replies skeptically and raises one eyebrow, then goes back to reading his star charts. "Napoleon just might disagree with you there, young man, and Alexander, as well."

"No, you don't understand what I'm—"

And the fire in the sky grows brighter, coalescing into a whip of red-gold scales and ebony spines, the dragon's tail to lash the damned, and *Every one of us is damned*, Machen thinks. *Every one of us, from the bloody start of time.*

"I have the texts, Avery, and the aegis of the seven, and all the old ways. I cannot very well set that all aside because you've been having nightmares, now can I?"

"I know these things, Father. I know them like I know my own heart, like I know the number of steps down to the deep place."

"There is a trouble brewing in Coma Berenices," his wife whispers, her eye pressed to the eyepiece of the big telescope in his library. "Something like a shadow—"

"She says that later," Avery tells him. "That hasn't happened yet, but it will. But you won't listen to her, either."

And Machen Dandridge turns his back on the sea and the dragon, on the battlefields and the burning cities, looking back towards the house he built twenty-five years ago; the air in the library seems suddenly very close, too warm, too thick. He loosens his paper collar and stares at his son sitting across the wide mahogany desk from him.

"I'm not sure I know what you mean, boy," he says, and Avery sighs loudly and runs his fingers through his brown hair.

"Mother isn't even at the window now. That's still two weeks from now," and it's true that no one's standing at the telescope. Machen rubs his eyes and reaches for his spectacles. "By then, it'll be too late. It may be too late already," Avery says.

"Listen to him, Father," Meredith begs with her mother's voice, and then she lays a small, wilted bouquet of autumn wildflowers on Ellen Dandridge's grave; the smell of the broken earth at the top of the hill is not so different from the smell of the trenches.

"I did listen to him, Merry."

"You let him talk. You know the difference."

"Did I ever tell you about the lights in the sky the night that you were born?"

"Yes, Father. A hundred times."

"There were no lights at your brother's birth."

Behind him, the sea makes a sound like a giant rolling over in its sleep, and Machen looks away from the house again, stares out across the surging black Pacific. There are the carcasses of whales and sea lions and a billion fish, bloated carcasses of things even he doesn't know the names for, floating in the surf, and scarlet-eyed night birds swoop down to eat their fill of carrion. The water is so thick with dead things and maggots and blood that soon there will be no water left at all.

"The gate chooses the key," his wife says sternly, sadly, standing at the open door leading down to the deep place beneath the house, the bottomless, phosphorescent pool at the foot of the rickety steps. The short pier and the rock rising up from those depths, the little island with its cave and shackles. "You can't change that part, no matter what the seven have given you."

"It wasn't me sent Avery down there, Ellen."

"It wasn't either one of us. But neither of us listened to him, so maybe it's the same as if we did."

The sea as thick as buttermilk, buttermilk and blood beneath a rotten moon, and the dragon's tail flicks through the stars.

"Writing the history of the end of the world," Meredith says, standing at the telescope, peering into the eyepiece, turning first this knob, then that one, trying to bring something in the night sky into sharper focus. "That's what he kept saying, anyway. 'I am writing the history of the end of the world. I'm writing the history of the future.' Father, did you know that there's trouble in Coma Berenices?"

"Was that you?" he asks her. "Was that you, or was that your mother?"

"Is there any difference? Do you know the difference?"

"Are these visions, Merry? Are these terrible visions that I may yet hope to affect?"

"Will you keep him locked in that room forever?" she asks, not answering his question, not even taking her eye from the telescope.

Before his wife leaves the hallway, before she steps onto the unsteady landing at the top of the stairs, she kisses Meredith on the top of her head and then glares at her husband, her eyes like judgment on the last day of all, the eyes of seraphim and burning swords. The diseased sea slams against the cliffs, dislodging chunks of shale, silt gone to stone when the great reptiles roamed the planet and the gods still had countless revolutions and upheavals to attend to before the beginning of the tragedy of mankind.

"Machen," his wife says. "If you had listened, had you allowed me to listen, everything might have been different. The war, what's been done to Avery, all of it. If you'd but *listened.*"

And the dream rolls on and on and on behind his eyes, down the stairs and to the glowing water, his wife alone in the tiny boat, rowing across the pool to the rocky island far beneath the house. The hemorrhaging, pus-colored sea throwing itself furiously against the walls of the cavern, wanting in, and it's always only a matter of time. Meredith standing on the pier behind him, chanting the prayers he's taught her, the prayers to keep the gate from opening before Ellen reaches that other shore.

The yellow-green light beneath the pool below the house wavers, then grows brighter by degrees.

The dragon's tail flicks at the suicidal world.

In his attic, Avery screams with the new mouth the gate gave him before it spit the boy, twisted and insane, back into this place, this time.

The oars dipping again and again into the brilliant, glowing water, the creak of the rusted oarlocks, old nails grown loose in decaying wood, and the shafts of light from the pool playing across the uneven walls of the cavern.

The dragon opens one blistered eye.

And Ellen Dandridge steps out of the boat onto the island, and she doesn't look back at her husband and daughter.

"Something like a shadow," Meredith says, taking her right eye from the telescope and looking across the room at her brother, who isn't sitting in the chair across from Machen.

"It's not a shadow," Avery doesn't tell her and goes back to the things he has to write down in his journals before there's no time left.

On the island, the gate tears itself open, the dragon's eye, angel eye and the unspeakable face of the titan sleeper in an unnamed, sunken city, tearing itself wide to see if she's the one it's called down or if it's some other. The summoned or the trespasser. The invited or the interloper. And Machen knows from the way the air has begun to shimmer and sing that the sleeper doesn't like what it sees.

"I stand at the gate and hold the key," she says. "You know my name, and I have come to hold the line. I have come only that you might not pass—"

"Don't look, Merry. Close your eyes," and he holds his daughter close to him as the air stops singing, as it begins to sizzle and pop and burn.

The waves against the shore.

The dragon's tail across the sky.

The empty boat pulled down into the shimmering pool.

Something glimpsed through a telescope.

The ribsy, omnivorous dogs of war.

And Machen woke in his bed, a storm lashing fiercely at the windows, the lightning exploding out there like mortar shells, and the distant *thump thump thump* of his lost son from the attic. He didn't close his eyes again, lay very still, sweating and listening to the rain and the thumping, until the sun rose somewhere behind the clouds to turn the black to cheerless, leaden grey.

6.

August 1889

After his travels, after Baghdad and the ruins of Ninevah and Babylon, after the hidden mosque in Reza'lyah and the peculiar artefacts he'd collected on the southernmost shore of Lake Urmia, Machen Dandridge went west to California. In the summer of 1889, he married Ellen Douglas-Winslow, black-sheep daughter of a fine old Boston family, and together they traveled by train, the smoking iron horses and steel rails that his own father had made his fortune from, all the way to the bustling squalor and Nob Hill sanctuaries of San Francisco. For a time they took up residence in a modest house on Russian Hill, while Machen taught his wife the things that he'd learned in the East—archaeology and astrology, Hebrew and Islamic mysticism, the Talmud and Quran, the secrets of the terrible black book that had been given to him by a blind and leprous mullah. Ellen had disgraced her family at an early age by claiming the abilities of a medium and then backing up her claims with extravagant séances and spectacular ectoplasmic displays, and Machen found in her an eager pupil.

"Why would he have given the book to you?" Ellen asked skeptically, the first time Machen had shown it to her, the first time he'd taken it from its iron and leather case in her presence. "If it's what you say it is, why would he have given it to anyone?"

"Because, my dear, I had a pistol pressed against his rotten skull," Machen had replied, unwrapping the book, slowly peeling back the layers of lambskin protecting it. "That, and knowledge he'd been searching for his entire life. It was a fair trade."

And just as the book had led him back from Asia to America and on to California, the brittle, parchment compass of its pages had shown him the way north along the coast to the high cliffs north of Anchor Bay. That first trip, he left Ellen behind, traveling with only the company of a Miwok Indian guide who claimed knowledge of "a hole in the world." But when they finally left the shelter of the redwood forest and stood at the edge of a vast and undulating sea of pampas grass stretching

away towards the Pacific, the Miwok had refused to go any farther. No amount of money or talk could persuade him to
approach the cliffs waiting beyond the grass, and so Machen
continued on alone.

Beneath the hot summer sun, the low, rolling hills seemed to
go on forever, and the gulls and a pair of red-tailed hawks
screamed at him like harpies warning him away, screeching
threats or alarum from the endless cornflower sky. But he found
it, finally, the "hole in the world," right where the Miwok guide
had said that he would, maybe fifty yards from the cliffs.

From what he'd taught himself of geology, Machen guessed
it to be the collapsed roof of a cavern, an opening no more than
five or six feet across, granting access to an almost vertical
chimney eroded through tilted beds of limestone and shale and
probably connecting to the sea somewhere in the darkness
below. He dropped a large pebble into the hole and listened
and counted as it fell, ticking off the seconds until it splashed
faintly, confirming his belief that the cavern must be connected
to the sea. A musty, briny smell wafted up from the hole,
uninviting, sickly, and though there was climbing equipment
in his pack, and he was competent with ropes and knots and
had, more than once, descended treacherous, crumbling shafts
into ancient tombs and wells, Machen Dandridge only stood
there at the entrance, dropping stones and listening to the
eventual splashes. He stared into the hole and, after a while,
could discern a faint but unmistakable light, not the fading
sunlight getting in from some cleft in the cliff face, but light
like a glass of absinthe, the sort of light he'd imagined abyssal
creatures that never saw the sun might make to shine their way
through the murk.

It wasn't what he'd expected, from what was written in the
black book, no towering gate of horn and ivory, no arch of gold
and silver guarded by angels or demons or beings men had
never fashioned names for, just this unassuming hole in the

ground. He sat in the grass, watching the sunset burning day to night, wondering if the Miwok had deserted him. Wondering if the quest had been a fool's errand from the very start, and he'd wasted so many years of his life and so much of his inheritance chasing connections and truths that only existed because he wished to see them. By dark, the light shone up through the hole like some unearthly torch, taunting or reassuring but beckoning him forward. Promising there was more to come.

"What is it you think you will find?" the old priest had asked after he'd handed over the book. "More to the point, what is it you think will find *you?*"

Not a question he could answer then and not one he could answer sitting there with the roar of the surf in his ears and the stars speckling the sky overhead. The question that Ellen had asked him again and again, and always he'd found some way to deflect her asking. But he *knew* the answer, sewn up somewhere deep within his soul, even if he'd never been able to find the words. Proof that the world did not end at his fingertips or with the unreliable data of his eyes and ears or the lies and half-truths men had written down in science and history books, that everything he'd ever seen was merely a tattered curtain waiting to be drawn back so that some more indisputable light might, at last, shine through.

"Is that what you were seeking, Mr. Dandridge?" and Machen had turned quickly, his heart pounding as he reached for the pistol at his hip, only to find the old Indian watching him from the tall, rustling grass a few feet away. "Is *that* the end of your journey?" and the guide pointed at the hole.

"I thought you were afraid to come here?" Machen asked, annoyed at the interruption, sitting back down beside the hole, looking again into the unsteady yellow-green light spilling out of the earth.

"I was," the Miwok replied. "But the ghost of my grandfather came to me and told me he was ashamed of me, that I was a coward for allowing you to come to this evil place alone. He has promised to protect me from the demons."

"The ghost of your grandfather?" Machen laughed and shook his head, then dropped another pebble into the hole.

"Yes. He is watching us both now, but he also wishes we would leave soon. I can show you the way back to the trail."

The key I have accepted full in the knowledge of its weight.

"You're a brave man," Machen said. "Or another lunatic."

"All brave men are lunatics," the Indian said and glanced nervously at the hole, the starry indigo sky, the cliff and the invisible ocean, each in its turn. "Sane men do not go looking for their deaths."

"Is that all I've found here? My death?"

A long moment of anxious silence from the guide, broken only by the ceaseless interwoven roar of the waves and the wind, and then he took a step back away from the hole, deeper into the sheltering pampas grass.

"I cannot say what you have found in this place, Mr. Dandridge. My grandfather says I should not speak its name."

"Is that so? Well, then," and he stood, rubbing his aching eyes and brushed the dust from his pants. "You show me the way back and forget you ever brought me out here. Tell your grandfather's poor ghost that I will not hold you responsible for whatever it is I'm meant to find at the bottom of that pit."

"My grandfather hears you," the Miwok said. "He says you are a brave man and a lunatic, and that I should kill you now, before you do the things you will do in the days to come. Before you set the world against itself."

Machen drew his Colt, cocked the hammer with his thumb, and stood staring into the gloom at the Indian.

"But I will not kill you," the Miwok said. "That is *my* choice, and I have chosen not to take your life. But I will pray it is not a decision I will regret later. We should go now."

"After you," Machen said, smiling through the quaver in his

voice that he hoped the guide couldn't hear, his heart racing
and cold sweat starting to drip from his face despite the night
air. And, without another word, the Indian turned and disappeared into the arms of the whispering grass and the August
night.

7.

July 1914

When she was very sure that her father had shut the double
doors to his study and that her mother was asleep, when the
only sounds were the sea and the wind, the inconstant, shifting
noises that all houses make after dark, the mice in the walls,
Meredith slipped out of bed and into her flannel dressing
gown. The floor was cool against her bare feet, cool but not
cold. She lit a candle and then eased the heavy bedroom door
shut behind her and went as quickly and quietly as she could
to the cramped stairwell leading from the second story to the
attic door. At the top, she sat down on the landing and held
her breath, listening, praying that no one had heard her, that
neither her father nor mother, nor the both of them together,
were already trying to find her.

There were no sounds at all from the other side of the narrow
attic door. She set the candlestick down and leaned close to it,
pressing her lips against the wood, feeling the rough grain
through the varnish against her flesh.

"Avery?" she whispered. "Avery, can you hear me?"

And at first there was no reply from the attic, and she took a
deep breath and waited a while, waiting for her parents' angry
or worried footsteps, waiting for one of them to begin shouting
her name from the house below.

But there were no footsteps, and no one called her name.

"*Avery?* Can you hear me? It's *me*, Merry."

That time there was a sudden thumping and a heavy dragging sort of a sound from the other side of the attic door. A body pulling itself roughly, painfully across the pine-board floor towards her, and she closed her eyes and waited for it. Finally, there was a loud thud against the door, and she opened her eyes again. Avery was trying to talk, trying to answer her, but there was nothing familiar or coherent in his ruined voice.

"Hold on," she whispered to him. "I brought a writing pad," and she took it out of a pocket of her gown, the pad and a pencil. "Don't try to talk any more. I'll pass this beneath the door to you, and you can write what you want to say. Knock once if you understand what I'm telling you, Avery."

Nothing for almost a full minute and then a single knock so violent that the door shivered on its hinges, so loud she was sure it would bring her parents running to investigate.

"Not so *loud,* Avery," she whispered. "They'll hear us," and now Meredith had begun to notice the odor on the landing, the odor leaking from the attic. Either she'd been much too nervous to notice it at first, or her brother had brought it with him when he'd crawled over to the door. Dead fish and boiling cabbage, soured milk and strawberry jam, the time she'd come across the carcass of a grey whale calf, half buried in the sand and rotting beneath the sun. She swallowed, took another deep breath, and tried not to think about the awful smell.

"I'm going to pass the pencil and a page from the pad to you now. I'm going to slide it under the door to you."

Avery made a wet, strangling sound, and she told him again not to try to talk, just write if he could, write the answers to her questions and anything else that he needed to say.

"Are you in pain? Is there any way I can help?" she asked, and in a moment the tip of the pencil began scritching loudly across the sheet of writing paper. "Not so hard, Avery. If the lead breaks, I'll have to try to find another."

He slid the piece of paper back to her, and it was damp and

something dark and sticky was smudged across the bottom. She held it close to her face, never mind the smell so strong it made her gag, made her want to vomit, so that she could read what he'd scrawled there. Nothing like Avery's careful hand, his tight, precise cursive she'd always admired and had tried to imitate, but sweeping, crooked letters, blocky print, and seeing that made her want to cry so badly that she almost forgot about the dead-whale-and-cabbages smell.

HURTSS ME MERY MORE THAN CAN NO
NO HELP NO HELLP ME

She laid down the sheet of paper and tore another from her pad, the pad she used for her afternoon lessons, spelling and arithmetic, and slid it beneath the door to Avery.

"Avery, you *knew* you couldn't bear the key. You knew it had to be me or mother, *didn't* you? That it had to be a woman?"

Again the scritching, and the paper came back to her even stickier than before.

HAD TO TRY MOTER WOULD NOT LISSEN SO
I HAD TOO TRIE

"Oh, Avery," Meredith said. "I'm sorry," speaking so quietly that she prayed he would not hear, and there were tears in her eyes, hot and bitter. A kind of anger and a kind of sorrow in her heart that she'd never known before, anger and sorrow blooming in her to be fused through some alchemy of the soul, and by that fusion be transformed into a pure and golden hate.

She tore another page from the pad and slipped it through the crack between the floor and the attic door.

"I need to know what to *do*, Avery. I'm reading the newspapers, but I don't understand it all. Everyone seems think war is coming soon, because of the assassination in Sarajevo, because of the Kaiser, but I don't *understand* it all."

It was a long time before the paper came back to her, smeared with slime and stinking of corruption, maybe five minutes of Avery's scritching and his silent pauses between the scritching. This time the page was covered from top to bottom with his clumsy scrawl.

TO LATE ~~IF~~ TO STOP WAR TOO LATE NOW
WAR IS COMING NOW CANT STP THAT MERRY
<u>ALL</u> SET IN MOTION NINTH WAVE REMEMBER?
BUT MERY YOU CAN DONT LISSEN TO FADER
YOU <u>CAN</u> HOLD ~~NINE~~ THEE LINE STILL TYME
YOU OR MOTHER KIN HOLD THEE LIN STILL
IT DOEZ NOT HALF TO BE THE <u>LADST</u> WAR

When she finished reading and then re-reading twice again everything Avery had written, Meredith lay the sheet of paper down on top of the other two and wiped her hand on the floor until it didn't feel quite so slimy anymore. By the yellow-white light of the candle, her hand shimmered as though she'd been carrying around one of the big banana slugs that lived in the forest. She quickly ripped another page from the writing pad and passed it under the door. This time she felt it snatched from her fingers, and the scritching began immediately. It came back to her only a few seconds later and the pencil with it, the tip ground away to nothing.

DUNT <u>EVER</u> COME BAK HERE AGIN MERRY
I LOVE YOU ALWAYTS AND WONT FERGET YOU
<u>PROMISS</u> ME YOU WILL KNOT COME BACK
<u>HOLD THEE LINE HOLD THE LINE</u>

"I can't promise you that, Avery," she replied, sobbing and leaning close to the door, despite the smell so strong that it had begun to burn her nose and the back of her throat. "You're my brother, and I can't ever promise you that."

Another violent thud against the door then, so hard that her father was sure to have heard, so sudden that it scared her, and Meredith jumped back and reached for the candlestick.

"I remember the ninth wave, Avery. I remember what you said—the ninth wave, greater than the last, all in flame. I *do* remember."

And because she thought that perhaps she heard footsteps from somewhere below, and because she couldn't stand to hear the frantic strangling sounds that Avery had begun making again, Meredith hastily gathered up the sticky, scribbled-on pages from the pad and then crept down the attic stairs and back to her bedroom. She fell asleep just before dawn and dreamt of flames among the breakers, an inferno crashing against the rocks.

8.

March 1915

"This is where it ends, Merry," her mother's ghost said. "But this is where it begins, as well. You need to understand that if you understand nothing else."

Meredith knew that this time she was not dreaming, no matter how much it might *feel* like a dream, this dazzling, tumbling nightmare wide-awake that began when she reached the foot of the rickety staircase leading her down into the deep place beneath the house. Following her mother's ghost, the dim glow of a spectre to be her Virgil, her Beatrice, her guiding lantern until the light from the pool was so bright it outshone Ellen Dandridge's flickering radiance. Meredith stood on the pier, holding her dead mother's barnacle- and algae-encrusted hand, and stared in fear and wonder towards the island in the pool.

"The infinite lines of causation," the ghost said. "What has brought you here. That is important as well."

"I'm here because my father is a fool," Meredith replied, unable to look away from the yellow-green light dancing across the stone, shining up from the depths beneath her bare feet.

"No, dear. He is only a man trying to do the work of gods. That never turns out well."

The black eye set deep into the flesh of Meredith's palm itched painfully and then rolled back to show its dead-white sclera. She knew exactly what it was seeing, because it always told her; she knew how close they were to the veil, how little time was left before the breach tore itself open once and for all.

"Try to forget your father, child. Concentrate on time and space, on the history that has brought you here. All the strands of the web."

Meredith squeezed the ghost's soft hand, and the dates and names and places spilled through her like the sea spilling across the shore, a flood of obvious and obscure connections, and she gritted her teeth and let them come.

On December 2, 1870, Bismark sends a letter to Wilhelm of Prussia urging him to become Kaiser. In 1874, all Jesuits are ordered to leave Italy, and on January 8th, 1877, Crazy Horse is defeated by the U.S. cavalry at Wolf Mountain in Montana. In June 1881, Austria signs a secret treaty with the Serbs, establishing an economic and political protectorate, and Milan is crowned King of Serbia—

"It hurts," she whispered; her mother frowned and nodded her head as the light from the pool began to pulse and spin, casting counterclockwise glare and shadow across the towering rock walls.

"It will always hurt, dear. It will be pain beyond imagining. You cannot be lied to about that. You cannot be led to bear this weight in ignorance of the pain that comes with the key."

Meredith took another hesitant step towards the end of the short pier, and then another, and the light swelled angrily and spun hurricane fury about her.

"They are rising, Merry. They have teeth and claws sharp as steel and will devour you if you don't hurry. You must go to the island now. The breach is opening—"

"I am afraid, mother. I'm so sorry, but I *am* afraid."

"Then the fear will lead you where I can't. Make the fear your shield. Make the fear your lance."

Standing at the very end of the pier, Meredith didn't dare look down into the shining pool, kept her eyes on the tiny island only fifteen or twenty feet away.

"They took the boat when you crossed over," she said to her mother's ghost. "How am I supposed to reach the gate when they've taken the boat away?"

"You're a strong swimmer, child. Avery taught you to swim."

A sound like lightning, and *No*, she thought. *I can't do that. I can do anything except step off this pier into that water with them. I can stand the pain, but—*

"If you know another way, Merry, then take it. But there isn't much time left. The lines are converging."

Merry took a deep breath, gulping the cavern's dank and foetid air, hyperventilating, bracing for the breathless cold to come, all the things that her brother had taught her about swimming in the sea. Together they'd swum out past the breakers, to the kelp forest in the deep water farther offshore, the undulating submarine weald where bat rays and harbor seals raced between the gigantic stalks of kelp, where she'd looked up and seen the lead-pale belly of an immense white shark passing silently overhead.

"Time, Merry. It is all in your hands now. See how you stand alone at the center of the web and the strands stretch away from you? See the intersections and interweaves?"

"I see them," she said. "I see them all," and she stepped off into the icy water.

October 30th, 1883, an Austro-German treaty with Roumania is signed, providing Roumania defence against the Russians. November 17th, 1885, the Serbs are defeated at the Battle of Slivnitza and then ultimately saved only by Austrian intervention. 1887, and the Mahdist War with Abyssinia begins. 1889, and a boy named Silas Desvernine sails up the Hudson River and first sees a mountain where a nameless being of moonlight and thunder is held inside a black stone. August 1889, and her father is led to the edge of the Pacific by a Miwok guide. August 27th, 1891, the Franco-Russian Entente—

The strands of the web, the ticking of a clock, the life and death of stars, each step towards Armageddon checked off in her aching head, and the water is liquid ice threatening to freeze her alive. Suddenly, the tiny island seemed miles and miles away.

1895 August, and Kaiser Wilhelm visits England for Queen Victoria's Golden Jubilee. 1896, Charles E. Callwell of the British Army publishes Small Wars—Their Principles and Practice. *February 4th, 1899, the year Aguinaldo leads a Philippine Insurrection against U.S. forces—*

All of these events, all of these men and their actions. Lies and blood and betrayals, links in the chain leading, finally, to this moment, to that ninth wave, mightier than the last, all in flame, and Meredith swallowed a mouthful of sea water and struggled to keep her head above the surface.

"Hurry, child!" her mother's ghost shouted from the pier. "They are rising," and Meredith Dandridge began to pray then that she would fail, would surrender in another moment or two and let the deep have her. Imagined sinking down and down for all eternity, pressure to crush her flat and numb, to crush her so small that nothing and no one would ever have any need to harm her again.

Something sharp as steel swiped across her ankle, slicing her skin, and her blood mingled with the sea.

And the next stroke drove her fingers into the mud and pebbles at the edge of the island, and she dragged herself quickly from the pool, from the water and the mire, and looked back the way she'd come. There were no demons in the water, and her mother's ghost wasn't watching from the pier. But her father was, Machen Dandridge and his terrible black book, his eyes upturned and arms outstretched to an indifferent Heaven;

she cursed him for the last time and ignored the blood oozing from the ugly gash in her right foot.

"This is where I stand," she said, getting to her feet and turning towards the small cave at the center of the island, her legs as weak and unsteady as a newborn foal's. "At the bottom gate, and I hold the key to the abyss."

The yellow-green light was almost blinding, and soon the pool would begin to boil.

"The ebony key to the first day and the last, the key to the moment when the stars wink out one by one and the sea heaves its rotting belly at the empty, sagging sky. The blazing key that even angels fear to keep."

For an instant, there was no cave, and no pool, and no cavern beneath a resentful, wicked house. Only the fire, pouring from the cave that was no longer there, to swallow her whole, only the voices of the void, and Meredith Dandridge made her fear a shield and a lance and held the line.

And in the days and weeks that followed, sometimes Machen Dandridge came down the stairs to stand on the pier and gaze across the pool to the place where the thing that had been his daughter nestled in the shadows, in the hollows between the stones. And every day the sea gave her more of its armour, gilding her frail human skin with the limey shells and stinging tentacles that other creatures had spent countless cycles of Creation refining from the rawest matter of life, the needle teeth, the scales and poisonous barbs. Where his wife and son had failed, his daughter crouched triumphant as any martyr, and sometimes, late at night, alone with the sound of the surf pounding against the edge of the continent, he sometimes thought of setting fire to the house and letting it burn down around him.

He read the newspapers.

He watched the stars for signs and portents.

When the moon was bright, the women still came to dance beside the sea, but he'd begun to believe they were only bad memories from some time before, and so he rarely paid them any heed.

When the weather was good, he climbed the hills behind the house and sat at the grave of his dead wife and whispered to her, telling her how proud he was of Meredith, reciting snatches of half-remembered poetry, telling her the world would come very close to the brink because of what he'd done, because of his blind pride, but, in the end, it would survive because of what their daughter had done and would do for ages yet.

On a long rainy afternoon in May, he opened the attic door and killed what he found there with an axe and his old Colt revolver. He buried it beside his wife, but left nothing to mark the grave.

He wrote long letters to men he'd once known in England and New York and Rio de Janeiro, but there were never any replies.

And time rolled on, neither malign nor beneficent, settling across the universe like the grey caul of dust settling thick upon the relics he'd brought back from India and Iran and the Sudan a quarter of a century before. The birth and death of stars, light reaching his aging eyes after a billion years racing across the vacuum, and sometimes he spent the days gathering fossils from the cliffs and arranging them in precise geometric patterns in the tall grass around the house. He left lines of salt and drew elaborate runes, the meanings of which he'd long since forgotten.

His daughter spoke to him only in his dreams, or hers, no way to ever be sure which was which, and her voice grew stronger and more terrible as the years rushed past. In the end, she was a maelstrom to swallow his withered soul, to rock him to sleep one last time, to show him the way across.

And the house by the sea, weathered and weary and insane, kept its secrets.

Afterword

"Andromeda Among the Stones" was written in October 2002 and was the last story that I wrote in Birmingham. It was commissioned for a Subterranean Press chapbook, *Embrace the Mutation,* to accompany a collection of short fiction (of the same name) based on images by J. K. Potter. I must admit that when I began work on the story, I was more concerned with finally telling the whole tale of Machen Dandridge's house than creating something to match the Potter illustration that was intended to serve as my inspiration (artwork which has also appeared in the CD booklet for Cradle of Filth's *Midian*). Ultimately, I managed to incorporate a few images from Potter, but I'd already had the broadstrokes of the story in my head long before I ever saw his illustration. In the end, "A Redress for Andromeda" and "Nor the Demons Down Under the Sea" seem to me little more than footnotes to this story, mere consequences of the events in this story. In its mention of Silas Desvernine, this is also the story that links *To Charles Fort, With Love* to the *Tales of Pain and Wonder* story cycle.

Afterword
A Certain Inexplicability

Ramsey Campbell

THE BEST ENIGMAS are more imaginatively stimulating than any solution could be. "It was just a colour out of space." We never know the nature of the invasion of "The Willows", nor can we be sure what Blackwood's Wendigo—accept no substitutes—does to its victims except to carry them through terror towards awe. Practically any of the supernatural tales of Robert Aickman or Walter de la Mare refuse to offer us the comfort of explication. That great film of unease, *L'Année Dernière à Marienbad*, is so enigmatic that it can be claimed for dark fantasy or, as Brian Aldiss does, for science fiction. *The Blair Witch Project*, the most Lovecraftian of all films, achieves its sense of supernatural dread purely through hints and glimpses and allusions. The utter horror of passages in various David Lynch films—*Lost Highway, Mulholland Drive* and pretty well the whole of *Eraserhead*—is intensified by the lack of explanation. I take all these to be examples of the art of disquiet at the top of its form, and the height is also occupied by the tales of Caitlín Kiernan. In less than a decade she has earned a thoro-ughly deserved reputation as one of the most accomplished contemporary writers in the field, and very possibly the most lyrical.

Trailing after such a feast of achievement with this afterword, I can only risk making observations that our readers have already enjoyed for themselves or that Caitlín has articulated more elegantly than I may manage. In her introduction, "Looking for Innsmouth", I'm especially unnerved by her and Kathryn's encounter on the beach, not just in itself but because of its resemblance to the image that forms the climax of "The Night Ocean", Lovecraft's final collaboration and subtlest tale: "a man or something like a man, which came towards the land from a dark ocean". Is it possible for one's influences to become manifest in some form that approaches the physical? Fort might have wondered too.

"Valentia" embodies many of its author's strengths, not least her recurrent elegiac feeling for palaeontology and her veneration of the aeons. Occasionally her prose contains the faintest echo of a predecessor-doesn't the first sight of Ireland here invoke the ghost of Joyce?—but it could never be called derivative. It quickly displays a favourite device of hers, the sentence that falls away to reveal it isn't one, having said all that it needs to say. In this book entire stories fall away to strand the reader with an experience that needs no explanation.

"Spindleshanks (New Orleans, 1956)" is another of several pieces here that touch on Lovecraft in precisely the allusive way he might have most appreciated. Its lack of resolution leaves its supernatural encounter to haunt us. "So Runs the World Away" treats Lovecraftian ghouls and other creatures with some of the affectionate humanisation that Ray Bradbury brought to the variously monstrous Elliott family, but Caitlín's psychological observations are all her own, not to mention the inspired touches of horror—"how or why to breathe"—and cadenzas of language. Has a creature that wasn't a ghost, despite the title of Peter Straub's novel, crept in here too? Adrian's name seems ominous.

"Standing Water" pretends to be just an excellent traditional horror story, with the gradual build-up the genre requires, but where the climax should be there's a pothole into the unknown, which is all the more effective. *"La Mer des Rêves"* isn't merely the shortest story in the book; its breathtaking terseness transforms the material into delirious poetry. It's a prose poem with considerably more plot than is usual for the form.

"The Road of Pins" extends a choice of enigmas to its protagonist and us. "Onion" saddles each of its characters with one. The sensuality of the glimpse of another place suggests one kind of compensation—the heightening of perception. The banality of those who meet to share their experiences of the inexplicable, much as alcoholics or any other addicts might, turns out not to be the point; the last page is, and it's a bleak yet visionary one. It sums up a central theme of the book, and perhaps it's as much a reassurance to the author as to anyone: after all, to dream a piece like "Apokatastasis" onto the page requires even more than the usual amount of trust in one's imaginative instincts that any good writer needs. I see that it also needed a protracted series of ghastly personal experiences as at least a background to its composition. I reflect that I wrote one of my better novels during the worst year of my life. In both cases I'd say that the story was worth it now that the disasters are past, but I can only speak for myself.

"La Peau Verte" was one of the tales that made my task of writing the introduction to an aborted absinthe anthology worth the time. Despite the nature of the commission and the state in which it was written, it is by no means just or even mainly an absinthe tale. Indeed, the poetic precision with which Caitlín describes the Mari Mayans high is, like the entire story, a triumph of artistic control. The remarkable compact-ness of the tale incorporates enough material for a novella if not a novel with no sense of strain or disproportion. It's even better second time around, believe me, but I think that can be said of all her work.

"The Dead and the Moonstruck" reacquaints us with the Children of the Cuckoo, and with Caitlín's apparently effortless ability to combine naturalistic observation of character, however inhuman, with delicately macabre humour or, just as deftly, with great poignancy. Like all her Lovecraftian fiction, it's remote from the slavish imitation too many fans of Lovecraft clamour for; it's a substantial contribution to his tradition—indeed, I think it and "So Runs the World Away" might very well have invented a new Lovecraftian form. It's certainly at least as magical as the old gent's gentler fantasies. Until I read Caitlín's afterword it hadn't occurred to me that the story had been aimed at young adults. It's worthy of them and of the rest of us too.

And so we come to the chronicles of the Dandridge clan, three tales that recede into the past, teasing us with hints of more of an explanation than we need. Who else but their author would have the audacity to concoct a potion of Lewis Carroll, Lovecraft and Greek myth? As much to the point, she has the panache to make it spellbinding. In "A Redress for Andromeda" both character and text undergo transformation, while "Nor the Demons down under the Sea" presents us with a classic haunted house only to render it more monstrous. "Andromeda among the Stones" manifests a wonderfully vivid spectre and revives the notion of the attic dweller in a strikingly personal way. The author's oceanic lyricism may seem inimical to Lovecraft's view of the sea, but just as Lovecraft built on the traditions of his field to create something of his own, so does Caitlín Kiernan incorporate his achievement to highly individual ends.

The trilogy of stories forms a splendid coda to a splendid volume. Caitlín Kiernan is one of the true visionaries and finest stylists in our field, and not just in contemporary terms. I'm delighted to be part of this book, even if my thoughts have fallen short of expressing all my enthusiasm. Let me finish by exhorting the reader to make sure of having all Caitlín's other books. If you've read them, they're better read again. They enrich the imagination and the literature of the dark at its most gorgeous and disturbing.

Ramsey Campbell
Wallasey, Merseyside
16 March 2005

Acknowledgments

I **AM GRATEFUL** to the following people, without whom this book would likely never have written, without whom it surely would not have taken the same shape: Poppy Z. Brite, Ramsey Campbell, Jennifer Caudle, Richard Chizmar, Ellen Datlow, Stephen Jones, Richard A. Kirk, Robert Morrish, Deborah Noyes, Ryan Obermeyer, John Pelan, Kathryn Pollnac, William Schafer, Peter Straub, and David Sutton, and my agent Merrilee Heifetz (Writers House).

Thank you all.